The Guys

David A. Weiss

"The Guys" by David A. Weiss, ISBN 978-1-63868-158-8.

Library of Congress Number on file with Publisher.

Published 2024 by Virtualbookworm.com Publishing Company Inc., P.O. Box 9949, College Station, TX 77842. Copyright 2024 by David A. Weiss.

Contents

ACNOWLEDGEMENTS

I gratefully acknowledge the following individuals who assisted me in the creation of this work: Linda Hoxie, a valued friend from my tennis group, and Adrienne Weiss, my sterling daughter-in-law, both of whom not only proofread this novel but also provided many excellent suggestions and insights; my wonderful daughter Lori Weiss who created the cover; and my dear and lovely wife Joyce, who is my sounding board and constant source of support.

I am fortunate to enjoy the assistance of four such exemplary individuals, each of whom affords me the benefit of their invaluable knowledge, skill, and encouragement, always with the utmost sensitivity.

PART ONE

PART ONE

Chapter I

The First Amendment to the United States Constitution lacks express verbiage furnishing freedom of association, but the Supreme Court has construed the provision as granting that right. People are entitled to pick and choose with whom they associate. Outside of protected areas, such as accommodations and employment, discrimination is permissible. That may be fine for one who is included; however, not so great, for those on the outside looking in. Now and then, everyone is included. That may be the best of all worlds. But it is hardly the norm.

Seated around a circular table in the clubhouse of Nick Stoner's Municipal Golf Course in the spring of 1969, our two teams awaited Larry Babbitt's calculation. Our food order, always the same, a pair of eighteen-inch pizzas, a pepperoni and a veggie, plus two pitchers of beer, had already been placed. For roughly fifteen years, throughout golf season, we had carried out the ritual most every Monday after work. We began in April when the course opened and continued until late September when thwarted by ever-earlier sunsets. For years we picked foursomes drawing numbers from a hat, but the preceding November, that had changed following our annual fall touch-football game. After a narrow defeat, our opponents, captained by Lefty Lucinski, refused to wait a year for revenge. They demanded an opportunity on the links once the golf season began. When April rolled around, first time out, they avenged their gridiron defeat. Our team insisted on a rematch the following week. A turnabout of fortunes occasioned a rubber match. An ensuing draw drew a unanimous vote to maintain the same teams indefinitely.

When we had first begun our golf matches, the rule was that losers buy the group's pizza and beer. Soon enough, it became apparent that the cost was incidental to higher stakes, bragging rights for a week. From then on, we simply split the check eight ways. Lest one assumes that the victors left emptyhanded, not so. They pocketed seven days of pleasure, busting on the vanquished. For the losers, paying at the pub was paltry next to the intolerable taste of their antagonists' taunts. And God forbid, a rainout occurred the ensuing Monday, a week's torture transmuted into two.

"The good guys," said Babbitt, referring to his team, "totaled 171 strokes."

Babbitt's teammates, Cooper, Lucinski and Longley, voiced a halfhearted cheer.

"The bad guys totaled (a sneer accompanied the hiatus in Babbitt's pronouncement) ...168."

Our team, Brady, Jackson, Porter, and I, raised our celebratory fists into the air and cheered.

"Let me see the scorecards." Whenever Cooper lost, he insisted on retotaling them. Only once had he unearthed a mistake. Rather than aiding his cause, the error inflated the amount by which his team lost.

"For the record," said Babbitt, "today's match produced no eagles. That brings our grand total for the season to a resounding zero."

"Well, I came close on the seventh," said Lucinski. "I got home in two and had an eagle putt."

"Yeah," said Babbitt. "And boy did you choke." Babbitt clutched his throat and gasped. "You yanked it so far left that it was below the hole from the get-go, not to mention that you left it five feet short."

"Look who's talking," said Lucinski. "The clod with the powder-puff swing. Even downwind when the fairways are rock-hard, your two best shots couldn't come near a par five. You couldn't..."

The trash talk, as always, had commenced. Though most was directed at one's opponents, intra-team jabs oozed as well. The inanity of the confab bore an inverse link to the beer remaining in the pitchers, its absurdity mounting as the pitchers emptied. Recounting the prattle would be as fatuous as the drivel itself. Accordingly, I will skip it and instead provide some background, including a bit about myself, after which I will introduce my seven friends, all of whom were classmates of mine years earlier at Grand Falls High School in central New York State.

I have long been the sole breadwinner for my middle-class family. Never wealthy, we were always comfortable. Recent events, however, altered the landscape. I received notice that my job as a high school history teacher could fall victim to the budget axe. Unexpected medical expenses, plus a lawsuit demanding damages far above the limits of our automobile insurance, have compounded our difficulties. And as luck would have it, these adverse events occurred shortly after our family had purchased our first new vehicle. Funds to make the car payments will be hard to find. Bottom line, our family's financial health has tanked. That is the short of it. Understanding the long of it, including its more intriguing and substantive aspects, demands that one traces back nearly three decades to the year 1942.

It was freshman year of high school, tenth grade. (In Grand Falls, junior high ran from 7th through 9th grade, while high school extended from 10th through 12th. High school included freshman, junior, and senior year. There was no sophomore year.) Back then, my hometown, Grand Falls, whose population was roughly 3,000, bore aspects of the yet-to-arrive seemingly idyllic 1950s. But Grand Falls also mirrored the Depression of the 1930s. Grand Falls was unique. But Grand Falls was a carbon copy of rural, small-town America. Grand Falls was a Norman Rockwell canvas with trees, streets, and structures bearing a fresh canopy of crystalline snow. But Grand Falls was the dour miens of the duo depicted in Grant Wood's renowned *American Gothic* painting. Grand Falls was the Sun. But Grand Falls was a black hole. Grand Falls was perspicuous simplicity. But Grand Falls was an enigma. Grand Falls was all the foregoing...but Grand Falls was none of it.

Even the name Grand Falls was an anomalous misnomer. While there were several small cascades in the area, there were no "grand" falls. That raises the obvious question: Why was town named Grand Falls? The answer: It was founded in the eighteenth century when a man named Grover Grand, a loner, built a house, more of a hovel, and began farming in what was then a heavily forested area. Whether it was owing to hubris or humor (I suspect it may have been both), Grover Grand named the place Grand Falls, erecting a sign on his property to that effect. Years later, when others settled nearby, they accepted the name he had given the place. And so, the curious moniker stuck.

Such is the early history, as well as the numerous contrasts, that defined Grand Falls when, with the nation in the throes of World War II, the jocks and cool guys in my homeroom decided to form a boys' club. Students of today, 1969, products of the first television generation, would likely scoff at our club. But times were different back in our youth. Around the country, especially in cities of size, high school fraternities and sororities remained widely popular, though not so in rural Grand Falls. Greek life was absent. Our response was to form a homeroom club. Some might deem it too juvenile for high school freshmen. Far be it from me to argue the point. That said, the continued camaraderie of eight of our thirteen founding members through the balance of World War II, the Korean War, and on into the era of the Vietnam War validates our endeavor.

At the time the group was formed, rumor had it that the "geeks," which included me, would be excluded. (We would have been labeled "nerds," except Dr. Seuss did not coin the term until the 1950s.) Needing to fend off the label of rejected outcasts, we squares talked up a club of our own. It had no plans or goals, apart from deflecting the gloom and shame of ostracism. Fortunately for us, Buster Brady, the football team's quarterback, intervened on our behalf. What prompted his magnanimity can be explained by events several years earlier. About the time we had started junior high, Buster's father, who theretofore had enjoyed a good supervisory job, joined the ranks of the unemployed. The chemical plant where he worked, about ten miles from Grand Falls, shuttered. With jobs in the area scarce, Buster's family was in dire straits. The father of Sam Porter – Sam, like me, was one of the geeks – rescued Buster's family. Mr. Porter hired Buster's father as Assistant

Manager of the Porter General Store. Thereafter, Buster was always protective of Sam. No way would he permit Sam's exclusion from the cool guys' club. In turn, Sam, my best friend, stuck up for me. And so, the pendulum, the push to exclude us, shifted, gathering sufficient momentum to crash through the wall, the cliquey classifications, that otherwise would have excluded us. By the time the dust settled, all thirteen boys in our homeroom were granted membership. Thus, the improbable bunch, what we called "The Guys," a remarkably egalitarian group in the exclusionary world of teenage elitism, launched. With a mishmash of backgrounds and personalities, that which connected us was nothing more than a common homeroom.

Following high school graduation in 1945, a number of us headed off to college, the military, and elsewhere. Some never returned to Grand Falls. But in 1951, with Larry Babbitt the prime mover, the eight of us who had settled in Grand Falls reconnected. No less disparate than before, we began meeting anew. Every two weeks we congregated at Orton's Ale House, a tavern-style restaurant serving bar food and brews. About three years after our first get-together, we began our ritual weekly golf competition at Nick Stoner's. In the off-season we continued to meet biweekly at Orton's. Over the years that followed we all changed, some more than others. On a micro basis, from week to week, and even year to year, our evolution was all but imperceptible. From a macro standpoint, looking at us in 1951 as compared to 1969, the differences were huge. But as much as we changed, America, the world around us, changed even more.

When we had graduated in 1945, V-E Day, the celebration of the Allies' World War II victory in Europe, had occurred six weeks earlier on May 8, 1945. And V-J Day, the celebration of victory over Japan, had followed on August 14th, less than two months after we had received our diplomas. Having defeated the Axis, a coalition of enemies that sought global conquest, America, virtually the only industrialized country still intact, sat atop the world. The troops returned home to a thankful nation. Across the country, unity, a byproduct of the war, abounded. A high-powered economy, rife with inflation, supplanted the monstrous unemployment and anemic climate that had prevailed prewar. The Depression of the 1930s had become a relic. An ever-expanding middle class, enamored with conspicuous consumption, flocked to what was to become the *Father Knows Best* and *Leave It to Beaver* suburbs.

However, by the time the summer of 1969 rolled around, escalating issues challenged those sublime neighborhoods. In cities everywhere, the turmoil was greater yet. Riots that had plagued Watts in 1965 and Detroit in 1967 spread. Washington D.C., Chicago, Baltimore, and Louisville erupted with violence following the April 4, 1968 assassination of Dr. Martin Luther King. What had been a small number of American advisors in Vietnam escalated amidst seemingly endless hostilities. Fought both in the jungles of Southeast Asia and on the nightly news of living-room televisions, the war cleaved the nation. By the advent of spring 1968, when President Lyndon Johnson announced that he would not run for another term, America's Vietnam troop authorization surpassed 500,000. The November 1968 election of Johnson's successor, Richard Nixon, did nothing to quell the mayhem in the cities and the protests against the Vietnam War. Little did the nation imagine that another dark cloud, Watergate, corruption at the highest levels of government, lay on the horizon. One notion was, nonetheless, apparent. The optimism and unity that had followed World War II had yielded to cynicism and dissention. Across the globe, America's image as the shining city on the hill had tarnished. The nation had strayed. Far from its post-World War II acme, it had devolved into a canyon, a divide so vast that those on either side could no longer hear one another. Even if they could, across the chasm, hermetically corked ears awaited.

In 1969, rural, conservative, and aging Grand Falls remained a reflection of prior days, only with a bit more rust and a gloomier future. When I was hit with the triple whammy, which included loss of my job, unexpected medical expenses, and a six-figure lawsuit for damages, 1945 appeared less distant in Grand Falls than in many other places across the nation. As I previously mentioned, to put my difficulties into proper perspective, familiarity with the other seven ongoing members of The Guys is necessary. Each bears a link to my current travails. Each has a story, anecdotal or otherwise, that connects to my misfortunes. Because these vignettes predate my problems, I will relate them first, beginning on the day our club was created in the autumn of 1942.

Minutes after the school day had ended, all thirteen of us boys from Homeroom 207 congregated beneath the giant cottonwood behind Grand Falls High School. We were young and naïve, but not so much so that we were oblivious to the events occurring around the world. Ever since that infamous day nine months earlier, December 7, 1941, when Japan had attacked Pearl Harbor and pulled America into the global conflict, ignoring the war had become impossible. Some of our parents, siblings, and other relatives were fighting for freedom in distant places. Yet day to day, we were still kids, and that was evident from the moment we gathered under the cottonwood. Someone asked what should have been the easiest of questions, an issue that should have preceded our club's formation: Why were we forming the group? What did we want to do? The questions drew a sea of foolish-looking high school males staring blankly at one another. The absurd became obvious. The club had no purpose, its mere creation the endgame. Temptation cajoled me to quip that our work was done, and we could disband. Were I one of the cool guys, rather than a geek, I would have made the wisecrack. Fearing its utterance might see me banished, I kept my mouth shut.

As bad as my sarcasm would have been, the staggering silence, the realization that we had no purpose, was worse. For the best part of a minute, no one spoke up. The mood devolved into a pall. Each passing second delivered another blow, dissembling what had been high expectations for a dynamic group.

Finally, Ronald Cooper said, "I have an idea, one that'll make us a tightknit bunch. Everyone should have a nickname, one blessed by the entire membership."

"What if someone gets a nickname he doesn't like?" said Pete Longley.

"Suppose we let everyone veto his own nickname?" said Cooper. "That way nobody gets stuck with a moniker he hates."

"Some of us, like Lefty and Buster, not to mention myself, already have nicknames we like," said Larry "George" Babbitt, his nickname an apropos reference to the character from the Sinclair Lewis novel that most of us had read in English class. "We oughta be able to use them."

"Any objections?" said Cooper.

Another time, under other circumstances, protestations might have been rampant. But less than a minute removed from ballooning ennui and disillusion, none was voiced. Any purpose, however contrived or vain, eclipsed nothing. And so, we, "The Guys," embarked on our first task. One hour later, after countless laughs and gibes, amidst growing camaraderie, each of us had a nickname. Over the course of this story, I will refer to some by their nicknames more than others, a reflection that some nicknames were universally used, while others were sporadically employed.

Complete with our sobriquets, below is a listing and introduction of the eight who remained members in 1969, over a quarter-century after our first meeting. (Also listed are the five others who were original members of The Guys but have long since ceased to live in Grand Falls.) Admittedly, eight characters are a lot to digest in one bite. Fear not. Their stories, which will appear more or less chronologically, will make them familiar. In advance of that, deem the listing and minimal introductions below a convenient reference point.

Larry (George) Babbitt: Nicknamed "George," owing to his resemblance, both physical and personality-wise, to the paunchy literary character from the Sinclair Lewis novel, Babbitt graduated Siena College, after which he opened an insurance agency in Grand Falls.

Robert (Buster) Brady: At 6'1" and handsome, Buster was the quarterback of the football team. His father worked as Assistant Manager for the Porter General Store. In 1969 Buster operated a successful home-building business.

Charles (Speedy) Jackson: Among our group Speedy was the sole Negro (the term commonly used to identify Black Americans in the 1940s). There were only two in the entire high school. Speedy was a wide receiver on the football team and ran the hundred-yard dash on the track team. Too small for college football, following high school graduation, he enlisted in the Army. He subsequently returned to Grand Falls where he later became the owner of the local hardware store.

Ronald (Coop) Cooper: A decent student, Cooper was active in student council, a starter on the basketball team, and third man on the golf team. After graduation from college, he returned to Grand Falls where he taught physical education at the junior high school. He rose to principal, and in 1967 was named superintendent of schools when the then superintendent resigned unexpectedly.

Peter (Shotgun) Longley: Except when at the wheel, Pete was quick to grab the front passenger seat. That earned him the nickname Shotgun. At six feet even, with wavy hair and blue eyes, he was popular with the girls. A good, though not exceptional student, he had plans for college. Unfortunate events at the end of junior year, which will be detailed later, derailed his plans.

Louis (Lefty) Lucinski: A lanky knuckleball pitcher on the baseball team, Lefty harbored dreams of a Major League career. Popular with the girls, he loved fast cars and flashy clothes.

Samuel (Doc) Porter: Valedictorian of our high school class and my best friend since elementary school, Doc was one of the geeks. The smartest in the class, his goal from a youthful age was a career in medicine. That earned him the nickname Doc. The moniker proved apropos. After graduating from high school, he went to Cornell University, subsequently getting his M.D. from Albany Medical College. A combination general practitioner and surgeon, he took over the practice of the village's lone physician, who delayed his age-78 retirement for a year until Doc completed his residency.

James (Geeko) Ward: Your narrator, I was one of the geeks. I received my B.A. and M.A. from Albany State Teachers' College (what subsequently became SUNY-Albany). Married with two children, I teach history at Grand Falls High School. I am 5'9", 158 pounds. Slow but steady youthful growth, lack of a surge, kept me small for my age for most of my school years. I liked sports but exceled at none. I made the high school golf team mainly because Grand Falls had few players. One might wonder why I failed to veto my nickname *Geeko*, a cross between Geek and Gecko. I had already vetoed two that were worse. One was vulgar and the other, nauseating. Resignation that Geeko was the best I could expect led me to accept the nickname.

The remaining five original members of The Guys: Don Baker, Vic Dolan, Pokey Paulsen, Shadow Sherwood, and Buddy Slack left Grand Falls after high school and never returned. They will appear in certain events from our high school years but not thereafter.

Chapter II:
Charles (Speedy) Jackson

Youthful years include occasions, perhaps one, few, or many, when judgment goes out the window, and curiosity, a yen for adventure, and/or downright recklessness supersede. Whether such antics beget fond memories, lessons, or dire consequences can be difficult to predict. Such secrets lie in the perspicacious realm of hindsight.

Charles Jackson, Speedy as we called him, the lone Negro in our homeroom, became my good friend owing to location as much as anything. Speedy lived on Elm Street. My family's small, framed house was situated on Maple Avenue two doors from Elm. To get to both Grand Falls Junior High, as well as the high school, I had to turn right onto Elm and walk about fifty yards before turning left onto Main Street. The walk took me directly past Speedy's home, a simple bungalow.

Back when we were in junior high, Speedy and I began walking to school together. Traveling the route to and from school, a mutually beneficial relationship developed. Bronze skinned, with curly hair, the sinewy Speedy was handsome. Agile and quick, whatever the athletic endeavor, he was good, at least by the standards of Grand Falls. But Speedy lacked the requisite talent to induce colleges to come calling with scholarships. His skills, coupled with his diminutive size, were insufficient to compete against top athletes from much larger high schools. At 5'6", 130 pounds, he was never destined to play football on a bigger stage. Though he was the fastest in our senior class, against the runners of other schools, he was an also ran. His future never held a track scholarship.

Around our neighborhood Speedy was a star. For me, a geek who loved sports but lacked talent, Speedy embodied what I yearned to be. I looked up to him. On the basketball court, flashy passes and slick dribbling complemented his hallmark, a deadeye set shot. An agile fielder, though never known for power, on the diamond he was a dependable hitter. Once on base, steals were inevitable. In neighborhood touch-football games, no way could I cover him. But reverse the roles, so I was the intended target and he, the defender, and too often the pigskin wound up in his hands. As a quarterback, Speedy threw tight spirals. I was renowned for wounded ducks, not that teammates tapped me to pilot the offense. Apart from golf, the pattern from hoop, baseball, and football held true whatever the sport. Speedy's prowess dwarfed mine. My ineptitude, as much as Speedy's proficiency, accounted for the gap.

In the classroom, our roles reversed, though the disparity was less than that which prevailed in sporting arenas. School came easily for me; harder for Speedy. It stemmed from the advantages I had enjoyed. Though my parents had limited schooling, they valued education, especially my mother who read voraciously. From the time I was small my parents inculcated the importance of learning. As early as elementary school, I understood that my primary responsibility was to study hard and earn good grades. With a head start, good work habits, and adequate ability, I did well. College was always a facet of my future.

Speedy's family came to Grand Falls when he was in seventh grade. Throughout elementary school his family had moved from state to state. The nomadic pattern compelled Speedy to repeatedly adjust to a new town, school, and friends. Acculturating transcended academics. When he arrived in Grand Falls, he was below his grade level in both reading and mathematics. He was playing catch-up. He needed help. I was happy to provide that help. It made me feel important. Being a mentor, especially to a multi-talented athlete, burnished my self-esteem. A symbiotic relationship developed. A willing learner, Speedy's grades improved. By high school Speedy was a good student, bordering the top third of the class.

Looking back, I suspect another factor may have led Speedy to cultivate me as a friend. As one of only two Negroes in our school, he confronted the intimidating task of fitting in, particularly when he first arrived in Grand Falls. Putting myself in his shoes, most any friend would have been welcome. One might argue that the foregoing demeans both Speedy and me; that it labels him "desperate" and me "better than nothing." I view it differently. Regardless, and more important than how our friendship began, it was grounded upon respect and was mutually beneficial. A more substantive beginning might have been nice, but how our relationship evolved, the loyalty and longevity it engendered, paramount. My time both as a student and teacher at Grand Falls High School has proved the point. All too often, I have watched friendships, however they started, deteriorate amidst evolving toxicity.

As with most friendships, the day arrived when ours was tested. It was the summer after tenth grade, a beautiful August day in 1943. In celebration of their eighteenth anniversary, Speedy's parents had taken a Greyhound bus excursion to Niagara Falls. They had left at seven o'clock in the morning and were due home around midnight. After eating dinner, I joined Speedy in the middle of Maple Avenue, where we played catch. As we were wont to do, we continued past dusk. With darkness descending, Speedy tossed the baseball my way. It was nearly on me before I spotted it. A desperate shift of my glove deflected the ball, saving my face. Catch it? I did not.

"This is nuts!" I yelled. "You can't see a damn thing!"

"Yeah, I guess you're right. Time to call it quits."

I glanced at my watch. "8:20. I've got forty minutes until I have to be inside." I thought for a moment. "I could go for an ice cream at Arctic Freeze."

"You'd never make it back on time. It's at least a 25-minute walk, one way. Tack on time to get ice cream, and you're certain to be late."

"We could make it if we drive." A spontaneous reaction, not a reasoned idea, triggered my suggestion.

"True," said Speedy. "And the same could be said if we flew...like pterodactyls."

I looked Speedy in the eye. "We can't fly...but we could drive."

"When you say we, who would be the driver...you or me?"

"Well, my father took our car to a meeting, so it can't be me." I was yet to get a learner's permit.

Speedy shot me a look. "You suggesting I should drive to Arctic Freeze? In case you've forgotten, I only have a permit. My driving is limited to daylight, and that's with a licensed adult driver in the car."

"Hey, it only takes five minutes to get there. And you could be super careful."

Speedy shook his head.

"They've got mint chocolate chip." My reference to the flavor, as well as my devilish tone, was calculated to seduce. "And I know you love that."

"Suppose someone at Arctic Freeze asks questions. Maybe it'll get back to my parents that I was there with the car. God, would that be a fiasco."

"We could park in the lot behind the old Sinclair gas station, the one that closed last year. From there we could walk the one hundred or so yards to Arctic Freeze. That way no one will know we drove." My own words, what had been bluster, inveigled me. The cleverness of my scheme cast an imprudent shadow over judgment. A vision of a flavorful ice cream cone popped into my teenage brain. Craving eclipsed discretion.

"Jeez. You've got all the answers."

"Nothing wrong with answers, is there?"

"A lot when they could get us into trouble."

"C'mon, you want that mint chocolate chip. You can taste it." I pretended to lick an imaginary cone.

Speedy pursed his lips.

"Think about it. The ride is a piece of cake. You've got a stop sign at Main and then straight down to Arctic Freeze. No big deal. And you're an excellent driver. I know because I rode with you and your dad all the way to Utica last month."

A sigh, almost a groan, emerged from Speedy's throat. "Ah...what the hell."

I could hardly believe I had talked him into the stunt. Even as I had cajoled him, I was unsure whether I was serious. Having made the sale, I could not back down, paint myself as all talk and no action. Regardless, my appetite for a cone refused to be spurned.

We headed to Speedy's house. I kept watch as he backed the car out of the unattached garage. The street was deserted. After closing the garage doors, I jumped into the passenger seat of the black 1936 Ford coupe, and we were off. Seconds later at the corner of Elm and Main, Speedy turned on the car's headlights as he drew to a stop. After checking and rechecking that no cars were coming, he turned left onto Main. With stores along the way already closed, the road through the sleepy village was quiet. Speedy crept along at twenty-five, well below the World War II "Victory Speed Limit" of thirty-five miles per hour. Congress had established it to preserve rubber and gas for the war effort. Four minutes after our departure, we reached the vacant gas station, where Speedy parked the car out back.

"Just to be sure that no one sees you, stay here. I'll get the ice cream. My treat." As I climbed out, I said, "Mint chocolate chip, both dips. Right?"

"Yup."

I pulled my Dodger baseball cap low over my forehead. I slinked to Arctic Freeze, much like a criminal casing surroundings in advance of a caper. The three cars in the lot were unfamiliar. Two were unoccupied. The third had a driver and a passenger, each with ice cream. I recognized neither. Three customers, none of whom I knew, stood at the Arctic Freeze window. The likelihood that anyone would recognize me was nil. Regardless, no harm done if someone did. From all appearances I had walked there. I stepped into line behind those being served. Once my turn came, I purchased a pair of double-dip cones, ten cents apiece, mint chocolate chip for Speedy and one scoop each of coffee and butter pecan for me. I hurried back to the car where I delivered Speedy's cone to him.

"Thanks." He took a few quick licks to stop an impending drip where the cone and ice cream met. "Everything go smoothly?"

Temptation lured me to give Speedy the business, to tell him that my neighbor was there and that he gave me a doubting look when, with me holding two cones, I claimed that I had walked there alone. But nervous as Speedy was about the outing, putting him though the ringer was unthinkable, especially after I had wheedled him into the caper. "It went like silk," I said. I licked my cone, which I had already brought under control with licks on the way back to the car.

"Anybody recognize you?"

I shook my head. "Relax. We're on easy street."

Speedy shrugged. "Maybe so, but I'll feel better once we're back home." He bit into his ice cream.

Conversation grew sparse as we savored our delectable indulgences. While I licked, Speedy chomped, devouring his ice cream with breakneck speed. I had barely finished one scoop when, with his cone polished off, Speedy started the car.

"Damn. That hit the spot!" he said. "Time to get back home before a happy-go-lucky lark turns into a dire disaster." Speedy pulled out onto Main and headed for home. He drove no faster than the trip the other way. Minutes later, he turned onto Elm and into his driveway. I hopped out and swung the two doors to the garage wide open. He pulled the car into the bay and climbed out of the vehicle.

"One hundred percent success," I said.

Speedy looked around. "Yeah...and I have to admit that cone was good, even better than usual." He gazed pensively into space. "Funny how a little intrigue can sweeten a treat."

I downed the last of my cone. "We'll have to do this again."

Speedy gave me a look and shook his head. "Stupidity has its limits, not to mention that sooner or later a gambler rolls snake-eyes." He jabbed his index finger into his chest. "This fool has no intention of pressing his luck. I'm quitting while I'm ahead."

"Well...another time, another place...we'll see." I slapped him on the back, and we headed to our respective homes. As I climbed our porch steps, a conscious smile draped my face. The trip to Arctic Freeze was bigger than a couple of ice cream cones. Speedy and I had demonstrated our growing independence. The escapade, not an act of defiance, evidenced that we were coming of age, approaching adulthood. Hubris, that which is inherent to youthful naivete, billowed. Gusto effervesced.

***

The adage posits, "Silence is golden." But the Bible counsels that not all things golden glitter. Indeed, some are abhorrent. In Exodus, a graven idol, the golden calf, drew the wrath of God. Synthesizing these sage lessons begets a guiding principle: Wear a muzzle...sometimes. Unfortunately, that begs the question: When?

It was the day following our ice-cream caper. I had just returned home from the park following an after-dinner, three-on-three basketball game in which my team, decided underdogs, had upset our more skilled opponents. The unexpected victory had me in a great mood. I headed into the kitchen where I got a Pepsi from the refrigerator. A moment later my father joined me.

"How'd your game go?"

"Benny and Ted Fuller, along with me, teamed up against three hotshots from the other side of town. Last week they whipped us 21-8 in a game to twenty-one. This time we turned the tables, nipping them 21-19."

"Good for you...Oh, before I forget, Mrs. Larsen from down the street called your mother a little while ago. She said that someone dumped her garbage can onto her lawn last evening. Left her with a mess. It happened around 8:45. She said she looked out her front window just as the culprit ran away. Mrs. Larsen thought she recognized you, though she acknowledged it was too dark to be sure. Mom told her you wouldn't do anything like that but promised to check with you."

"Mrs. Larsen is mistaken. I never touched her garbage can, and I have no idea who did."

"We knew you weren't involved. And just to satisfy Mrs. Larsen...to prove that you were elsewhere, what were you doing last evening between 8:30 and 9, before you came home?"

"I was – " I clipped my tongue. I could not tell my father that I was at Arctic Freeze. While the alibi would clear me of Mrs. Larsen's claim, it would prompt my father to seek details: who I was with; how we got there; and who saw us. I could not lie. Worse yet, I could not tell him that Speedy had driven. Speedy would be in deep doo-doo.

My father looked at me. "You didn't answer my question."

I looked away.

"Let me back track, just to be sure nothing got lost in translation. You had no part in the dumping of Mrs. Larsen's garbage can and you have no knowledge who did...Right?"

"Absolutely."

"Good. Now tell me what you were doing last evening around 8:45."

"I...I can't."

"What do you mean – you can't?"

I heaved a sigh. "Just what I said. I can't."

"That's not an answer, not one that'll fly." My father appeared to study me. "Your mother and I trust you. You know that. But when we ask a question, we expect an answer. Your silence gives us nothing to trust. On the contrary, it suggests that you don't trust us and worse yet, that you're concealing something. With that clear, I'll give you one more chance to answer my question."

"I can't." I bowed my head, knowing I faced repercussions.

"Fine!" My father's bark conveyed that he deemed my reaction anything but fine. "If that's your position, you leave me no alternative. You will be punished. For the next week, rather than spending days doing fun things with your friends, you'll do chores around the house. And you won't be allowed to listen to the radio." My father looked me in the eye. "Now that you know the consequences of silence, I'll give you one last chance to be forthcoming." He folded his arms and waited. Likely, he assumed I would alter my stance.

I stood mute...painfully mute.

My father pointed. "Go to your room. Now!"

***

Injustice, inherently painful, has been known to spawn anger. Anger can trigger consternation. Consternation can kindle guilt, all of which magnifies the pain of injustice. The foregoing can become a vicious cycle. But that assumes one's conscience comes to the fore, that one remains objective. Self-justification is a canny device to avoid a vexatious vicious cycle. As for anger, that is likely to persist.

The following morning, after my father had left for work, and with no one else around, I went to the living room, the site of our lone telephone, and dialed Speedy. I would have called the evening before, but not only was I consigned to my room, but in addition, privacy was imperative.

The telephone rang twice before Speedy's mother answered. Per my request, she put him on.

I whispered, "Are you alone enough that you can talk?"

"Sorta. What's up?"

I filled him in on my conversation with my father, beginning with Mrs. Larsen's allegation and concluding with my punishment.

"Gosh, I'm sorry," said Speedy.

I waited, hoping he would address the situation with something more substantive. The desired response failed to materialize. I said, "You've got to help me."

"What can I do?"

"You could come clean."

His voice lowered to a whisper. "Jeez, if I do that and my parents find out that I took the car, they'll go ballistic. They'll ground me...for God knows how long. I'll be out of high school before they let me drive again."

"You don't know that."

"Not for sure," said Speedy, "but guaranteed, my punishment will make yours seem like a day at the carnival."

His point had merit. Nonetheless, I was miffed. I said, "So, I'm here with chores and you're scot-free." I waited several seconds. "Aren't you going to say something?"

"I don't know what to say."

"Oh, that's terrific." My tone would have blown a sarcasm meter off its chart. "Well, at least I know where I stand. And on that lovely note, goodbye." I slammed the receiver. In the several years I had known Speedy, this was our first falling out, at least one that remained unresolved by the time we went our separate ways. Seething, I got a bottle of window cleaner and a rag and began cleaning the windows, a chore included in my punishment. The unappealing task did nothing to mitigate my anger. It did, however, allow me to weigh the facts. I had reason to be mad. I had remained silent to protect Speedy. He, on the other hand, rather than coming clean and proving my innocence, had chosen silence to protect himself. Phrased that way, the logic justifying my rage was impeccable. Further scrutiny suggested the matter was ambiguous. It grew harder to take my ire out on Speedy. Expecting him to disclose our jaunt to Arctic Freeze, when his punishment would be much worse than mine, was selfish. And the truth be known, the disclosure would do me more harm than good, especially when my parents learned that I had enticed him into the outing. A pang of guilt reared its odious head. A part of me considered calling Speedy and apologizing. With both anger and pride counteracting, the idea had little chance. I preferred denial. I viewed the matter from my perspective. I was being unfairly punished because some jerk had dumped Mrs. Larsen's garbage can. I refused to acknowledge that I too was being a jerk, that my own misconduct, coupled with my refusal to answer my father's questions, was the root of my difficulties. Rationalizations and misguided frustration, along with ego, prevented me from dialing Speedy's number. Instead, I seethed.

***

Injustice is difficult. But self-reflection can be enlightening. Intermingle them, and chaos is possible; but sometimes it all makes sense.

Three days had passed since I had spoken to Speedy. All the while that I had washed windows, painted the front porch, and cleaned the basement, I had stewed. But more and more, regrets fenced with anger. Ironically, both vexed me. Resentment ate me up. Remorse fostered guilt. Repeatedly rehashing the circumstances proved futile. It was late afternoon when the ring of the front doorbell drew me to the portal. Speedy stood on the front steps.

"Uh...hi," he said without conviction. A meek wave of his hand barely at shoulder height manifested discomfort. "Can we talk?"

"About what?" No sooner did the acerbity cross my lips than I regretted it. Shunning the apparent olive branch was not what I wanted. Pride, however, competed with judgment.

"I...I want to apologize," said Speedy. "I let you down...unfairly. Blame for overturning Mrs. Larsen's garbage was dumped on you. I knew you were innocent. I was your alibi. But I refused to come clean because it would incriminate me. You, on the other hand, remained silent, protecting me from my parents' wrath. It's unfair." Speedy took a deep breath. "Whatever the consequences, I'm ready to tell my parents that I took the car."

Speedy's contrition was disarming. It pressed me to confront my own regrets.

"Aren't you going to say something...even if it's to tell me to take a hike?"

I shook my head.

"I should go?"

I shook my head again. "It's not that at all." Speedy's comments had forced me to face the mirror. A revolting image confronted me. The time to halt my brooding and accept the facts was long past. I pointed at myself. "I'm the one who suggested that we go to Arctic Freeze, and I pushed you into taking your parent's car. The fault lies with me."

"Nope," said Speedy. "Years ago, my parents taught me that unless somebody sticks a gun to my head, I'm responsible for my conduct. I could have nixed your suggestion. Instead, I opted for mint chocolate chip."

His point had merit, not to mention that having someone to share my blame was welcome. "Yeah, I guess we both bear responsibility...Damn, the ice cream was good, not that it was worth the mess it manufactured."

Speedy chuckled...sardonically. "Well, as soon as I go back home, I'll tell my parents that I took the car, and then I'll tell your parents as well."

Once again, I shook my head.

"What does that mean?"

"Very simply, no."

Puzzlement showed on Speedy's face.

"Think about it. If you own up, you'll get a severe punishment, much worse than what I got."

"That's my tough luck."

"But it'll be my tough luck as well. When my parents learn that I talked you into sneaking your parent's car out of the garage, they'll be more upset than before. They'll ground me till I'm sixty."

"You're exaggerating."

"Yeah, but you get my point. The bottom line, we'll both be much worse off."

"So, you recommending silence?"

"You have a better suggestion?"

"Uh...I guess not." Speedy displayed an abashed expression.

"Why the look?"

"I came here to apologize and – "

"You did that."

"You didn't let me finish. And to make things right. I didn't do that."

"Hey, it's not your fault. And for that matter, you were willing to walk beneath Damocles' sword." My reference to Cicero's ancient parable, an anecdote told to us two days before in world history class, ripped at my conscience. Speedy had been a bigger man than I. Unlike me, whose sulking had threatened our friendship, he had come forward, willing to take responsibility and punishment. "Sorry," I said, extending my right hand.

A smiling Speedy shook it.

I would have joined him outside for a fun activity, but four more days of grounding and chores precluded me. That said, those four days were far better than their three predecessors. Anger, consternation, and guilt were absent. My punishment may have been for the wrong crime, garbage-can misconduct rather than joyriding, but my sentence was just. More important, I had reason to be thankful. Despite my intransigence, Speedy's courage had preserved our friendship.

Chapter III:
Robert (Buster) Brady

Many an innocent bystander has borne the consequences of guilt by association. Some have been victimized for even less.

A beautiful September day, barely two weeks into our junior year of high school, found Speedy and me arriving at school. Needing to return a book to the library, Speedy diverged down the first-floor hallway of the twenty-year-old, two-story, flat-façade, neoclassical cement structure. I climbed the stairs to our second-floor homeroom. Little did I imagine the mischief to which I was about to be linked. And before detailing that rascality, lest I create a false and unflattering impression that I was an incorrigible troublemaker, I'll proffer a few words of self-defense. Where the illicit jaunt in Speedy's parents' car, the most profligate stunt of my youth, constituted an indefensible act of stupidity, the Grand Falls High School misconduct I'm about to relate was neither of my doing, nor my suggestion. I was an unfortunate, innocent bystander.

That ill-fated morning, I was first to arrive in our homeroom. A minute later, the two top jocks in our class, Buster Brady, quarterback of the football team, and Lefty Lucinski, the baseball team's knuckleballing pitcher, entered. Before the recent formation of The Guys, neither would have given me the time of day. The group's creation had triggered a shift. Much as I had mixed feelings about each, especially Lefty, joining them in a club had afforded me elevated status, at least in the quirky world of teenage turbulence. Around the Grand Falls campus, there was no doubt: Buster and Lefty were cool. Both stood about an inch over six feet. The lithe Buster was more muscular than the lanky Lefty. Where Buster's hair was cropped, Lefty wore his slicked back and wavy. Measured by reactions of the females gracing the halls of Grand Falls High, both were hot. Some claimed Buster bore a resemblance to Burt Lancaster, while others compared Lefty to Jimmy Stewart.

As he came through the door, Buster, as he was wont to do, saluted me. "What's up, Geeko?"

"Not much," I said. The more I heard the derisive nickname, the more I regretted my failure to veto it. The consolation of knowing that alternatives would have been worse attenuated.

Buster hurried to a window of our second-floor homeroom that overlooked the parking lot. "Perfect," he said, nodding repeatedly with a devilish cast. "The green Ford is yet to occupy its usual spot. We've got a few minutes until Thompson joins us." Mr. Thompson was our homeroom teacher.

Buster turned away from the window, first eyeing Lefty and then me. "A little dull around here, don'tcha think?"

"I guess so," I said, only to be agreeable, not owing to an opinion.

"Whatcha got in mind?" said Lefty.

From his gym bag, Buster whipped out what looked like a large firecracker. The yellow and black cardboard tube, about six inches long, had a three-inch fuse protruding from the top.

"Is that a roman candle?" said Lefty.

"Nah," said Buster. "It's TNT...dynamite."

The response, much worse than I had imagined, knotted my stomach. I wanted no part of explosives. I headed for the door.

"Where ya goin'?" said Buster.

"I...uh...need to...uh...go to the Boys' Room before homeroom starts."

"Relax," said Buster. "I was only kidding. It ain't dynamite."

"What then?" said Lefty.

"A smoke bomb. Harmless, but guaranteed to produce excitement." Buster slipped the incendiary device into his pocket. He eased across the hall to the supply room. A minute later he returned. He whispered, "Take your seats. No tickets required. The show is about to begin."

Before heading to my assigned desk, I tried to steal a peek at the supply room. Its half-shut door impeded my view.

Lefty whispered, "Did you actually light the thing?"

"What do you think?" said Buster.

Lefty shrugged.

"Then I guess you'll just have to wait and see." Buster plopped down into his seat.

The instant I reached my desk, I opened a book, not that I read it. I wanted no part of what I feared was about to transpire.

Mary Wheeler, one of our classmates, came in and sat down. The better part of a minute ticked away. Nothing seemed amiss. I breathed a sigh of relief. Chances were, Buster had punked us. Maybe the cardboard tube was an empty nothing. Even if it was a smoke bomb, perhaps it was a dud. Or maybe Buster never lit it. Perhaps it remained in his pocket. A myriad of permutations raced through my brain. Even if all were inaccurate, time, its passage, reduced the probability that disaster would eventuate.

Buster turned to Lefty. "Problem six on last night's math homework – whad'ya get for an answer?"

Lefty shot Buster a look but then reached for his homework.

An instant later, a scream radiated from the hall. "Fire, fire…The supply room is on fire!"

Mary grabbed her things. We guys did as well. All of us raced to the door. Smoke had begun to fill the hallway. A fire alarm blared. Along with a crowd, we hurtled down the stairs and out of the building. Others climbed down the second-floor fire escape. All about the school, chaos reigned. Teachers and administrators directed us students to areas well removed from the structure. The roar of sirens filled the air as two fire engines pulled up. Firefighters, garbed in their protective helmets, coats, and boots, charged into the building.

Off to my left, I heard a girl say, "Did anyone see flames? There were none on the first floor. Just a little smoke."

Another girl, standing nearby, said, "Up on the second floor, coming from the supply room, there were tons of smoke...thick. But I didn't see any flames."

Buster motioned Lefty and me away from the throng.

"You really did it," whispered Lefty.

"Did what?" said Buster, jerking back theatrically.

"The smoke bomb," said Lefty, his voice even softer than before.

Buster winked.

"Aren't you worried that someone in the hall saw you?" said Lefty.

"Nah. When I crossed the hall from the supply room, the hall was nearly empty. The few there were going about their business. Nobody noticed me. Even if they did, by the time the fuse burned down and the smoke began spreading, another dozen or so must have gone up and down the hall. Apart from the three of us, no one has a clue as to the culprit. And you guys would never...never blab." Buster gave us each a telling look.

Even before he did, I knew he expected us to cover for him. Much as I wanted no part of his harebrained prank, the decision had been made for me. Buster had dragged me into his stunt.

***

The adage warns that life can be unfair. But a blind system of justice addresses the issue. Tell that to all the innocent people who have served time in prison.

Once the smoke had cleared and the building had been scoured for other incendiary devices, everyone went back inside. By that time, it was third period. Soon after, lunch followed and then fourth-period English class. We were silently reading Longfellow's narrative poem "Evangeline," when a boy entered our classroom and handed a note to our teacher, Miss Weidner. A moment later, she said, "Louis Lucinski and Jim Ward, please report to the office. Personnel there need to speak with you immediately."

I glanced at Lefty as I got out of my seat. He shrugged, just before we met near the door.

Once we reached the hallway, I whispered, "Why do you think they want to see us?"

"To give us an award, no doubt."

"C'mon, don't make jokes," I said. "Anyway, we did nothing wrong."

"That may be, but that doesn't mean we won't get blamed."

His point was well taken. Never had I been summoned to the office. No teacher had ever sent me there, except to pick up a folder or perform some such innocuous duty. On the other hand, Lefty's misconduct had earned him multiple command appearances in the imperial realm.

As we negotiated the terrazzo stairs to the first floor, Lefty said, "Don't know what's in store, but no way am I gonna take a fall for Buster." His voice, though soft, was emphatic.

"You can't throw him in. We agreed...sorta, not to rat on him, plus we're all members of The Guys."

Lefty pitched me an ambiguous look. He pressed a silencing finger to his lips as we approached the office doorway. A secretary gestured us in.

"Principal Armstrong wants to see you boys, one at a time." She motioned me through the door that led into the principal's inner sanctum. I followed her direction.

"Have a seat...right there." Principal Armstrong pointed to one of two chairs that fronted his big wooden desk. He closed the door and seated himself in his commodious high-back.

"James Ward...unless I'm mistaken, today marks your initial visit." His low-pitched, stentorian voice augmented his command of the scene.

"Uh...yes, Sir."

"You know why you received this invitation?"

"No, Sir," I said, though I had more than a suspicion.

"We had a very unfortunate incident this morning, one that disrupted the school and deprived our entire student population of the opportunity to learn. Two firetrucks, along with numerous firefighters, had to race here. For all we know, their service may have been needed at an emergency elsewhere. All this occurred at taxpayers' expense. Some may think a smoke bomb is funny, but it's no joke. Such stunts render us less prepared for a genuine emergency. False alarms breed complacency. Sadly, when a real fire occurs, folks fail to take it seriously. They delay. Some don't escape. Firefighters trying to save them become victims."

The more Principal Armstrong spoke, the graver the matter seemed, and the more worried I grew. I feared he was about to accuse me of detonating the smoke bomb.

"Let me come to the point. A student, name shall remain unmentioned, thought he saw Buster Brady exit the supply room a minute before the smoke bomb exploded. A classmate from your homeroom indicated that you, Lefty Lucinski, and Buster Brady were the only other persons in your homeroom when the smoke commenced."

Though Principal Armstrong provided no name, I assumed he was referring to Mary Wheeler when he mentioned a classmate from our homeroom. As to the person who had fingered Buster, I had no clue.

Principal Armstrong eyed me with a scrutinizing gaze. "I'm sure you understand the gravity of this matter. That said, perhaps you can shed light on it?"

I shook my head.

"Are you telling me that you have no information, even hearsay or comments from others, about the incident?"

Not wanting to lie, but unwilling to rat on Buster, I remained mute.

"Silence is unacceptable." With lips pursed and eyes steely, Principal Armstrong stared at me.

I sat frozen.

"Okay. We can tackle this the hard way." He pointed a menacing finger. "I'm giving you detention, one hour after school, for the next five days. And don't assume you've heard the last of this." With a scowl prominent, he said, "Go back to your class. But before you do, send Lucinski in."

I stepped out of Principal Armstrong's office into the clerical area. I said to the secretary, "Mr. Armstrong wants to see Lefty."

"He went to the Boys' Room. Perhaps you can fetch him, minimize any wait Mr. Armstrong will endure."

I hurried down the hall to the Boys' Room. Lefty was drying his hands.

"What happened?" he said.

I gestured at the stall doors and whispered, "We alone?"

Lefty nodded.

Nevertheless, I checked the two stalls, after which I gave Lefty a quick recap of Principal Armstrong's inquisition and my punishment.

"The hell with that!" said Lefty. "I'm not spendin' afternoons in detention, not when I did nothin' wrong."

"You can't throw Buster under the bus. Exploding a smoke bomb, creating an emergency that required the fire department and evacuation of the school...Armstrong might refer him to juvenile court. Buster could be suspended or expelled. Worse yet, they could ship him off to reform school."

"The ass brain should have thought about that before he lit his goddamn plaything."

"They're sure to kick him off the football team."

"That's Buster's problem."

"Maybe so. But it'll be yours when everyone finds out that the team lost its quarterback because you squealed on him." I could hardly believe I was defending Buster and challenging Lefty.

"Goddamn!" barked Lefty, banging a fist into the palm of his other hand. "You've twisted my arm. I'll cover for the bastard...or at least I'll keep my mouth shut...for now. But let me tell you, if Armstrong ups the ante, more than a week's detention, no way will I take the hit." Lefty stormed out of the bathroom toward the office.

I followed him out and headed back to class. Just before I arrived, the bell rang. Rather than going directly to Geometry, my next class, I hurried to the top of the stairs leading to the basement. I hoped to catch Buster coming up from wood shop. A minute later, I spotted him. I filled him in on the events: how Lefty and I had been yanked out of English, called down to the office, and what I had told Armstrong, as well as my punishment. I said, "Lefty is in there with Armstrong now."

32

"You think he'll throw me in?"

"I...I don't think so. At first, Lefty refused to back you. But when I pointed out that along with other punishments, you'd probably get booted off the football team and the entire student body would blame him for the loss of our quarterback, Lefty seemed to relent."

"Damn, he better not squeal."

Were I more sanguine, I would have offered reassuring words. Instead, I pointed at the clock. "We better get to class." I scurried to Geometry.

***

In the "Mikado," Englishmen Gilbert and Sullivan advised, "Let the punishment fit the crime." The instructive morsel makes no reference linking the offense to the perpetrator. Given that deterrence is sometimes said to be the primary goal of criminal laws, might such a link be superfluous, especially in an authoritarian universe in which order supersedes justice?

The school day ended. Where normally I waited for my pals, marching orders had me hurrying to my decreed destination, detention. A late entrance, even a few seconds, would tack additional time onto my sentence. I arrived at the "Gulag," the label we students had given the large room at the far end of the second floor used to house us inmates. I tiptoed to a seat in the morgue-like chamber, so quiet that a pencil falling from a desk to the floor would be tantamount to a cannon's blast. Up front sat the iron-fisted Harlamov, a massive man, 6'5" and at least 270 pounds. A persistent scowl draped over a protruding chin supplemented his cowing physicality with a visage of intimidation. We students referred to him as the Tsar, though only behind his back. Harlamov ran detention like a prison. Conversation between inmates, even a whispered phrase, increased the length of the speaker's punishment. Even a request to help another student with his/her work was verboten. Breathing was barely permissible.

A minute after I arrived, Lefty walked in. A moment later, Buster entered. That the former was there was expected; the latter, less certain. Exactly what facts had brought Buster there remained foggy. Had Lefty ratted? What did Armstrong know? Where did Buster stand? Might he be thrown off the football team, suspended, or expelled? Perhaps he would be charged with a crime. I was dying to know, but I had to wait.

Minute by minute, our hour of detention ticked away. I did my trigonometry homework. I read twenty pages from *Great Expectations*. Finally, the minute hand completed its 360-degree journey. Four o'clock arrived.

"You're excused," said Harlamov. "With the exception of Miss Cartright and Mr. Jenks, I'll see the rest of you reprobates back here at three o'clock tomorrow."

Buster, who was seated near the door, charged out and down the stairway. By the time I reached the bottom of the stairs, he was nowhere to be seen. I assumed he had made a break for the front door. I hurried to catch up to him. I stepped outside. No Buster. I went down the front walkway about forty yards and gazed up and down the street. No sight of him. A minute later, Lefty approached me.

"Why the big hurry?"

"I hoped to catch up with Buster. I wondered how he made out with Armstrong."

"Don't really know, except Jimmy Hack said Buster was hauled out of Biology, ordered to report to Armstrong's office. Other than that, plus his appearance at detention, no idea how he fared."

I glanced at the front entrance to the school building. That Buster was still inside was improbable. I said, "Now that I think about it, maybe he hurried to catch the rest of football practice. It must still be going on."

"Makes sense," said Lefty.

"How'd you do with Armstrong?" Lefty's circumstances came to me as an afterthought.

"Same as you. A week's detention."

"Did you rat on Buster?"

"No, but it pisses me off, gettin' a week with the Tsar, just 'cause I covered for the clod. And to make matters worse,

Armstrong said I may not have heard the last of it. Let me tell you, if Armstrong ups my punishment or if he calls my parents, it's Buster's ass, not mine. Just 'cause he quarterbacks the football team doesn't mean he can throw a pick-six and expect me, not even on the football team, to get sacked. If Buster wants the glory, Buster can take the pounding."

I shrugged. Lefty's point had too much merit to argue, not that I was so inclined. Like him, I was peeved about my unwarranted detention. It crossed my mind that if Armstrong contacted Lefty's parents, he would call mine as well. If so, a familiar predicament would ensnare me. My father would again be interrogating me. Remaining mute would ensure misery. The episode involving Mrs. Larsen's garbage can had proved the point. Another display of silence, especially in the face of a graver infraction, a smoke bomb necessitating evacuation of the school, would see my father go ballistic. My newest fate would make my previous punishment seem like a slap on the wrist. Like Lefty, when push came to shove, I might need to speak up. Justice demanded that the facts be laid bare. Unlike the joyride to Arctic Freeze where I had responsibility for the misconduct, I was innocent. Buster, the lone guilty party, deserved to suffer the consequences of the current misadventure. The logic was perfect, except it ignored reality. If I threw Buster in, I would be labeled a rat. If Buster was booted off the football team, blame would fall on me. Truth was wonderful, but if I voiced it, I would be the pariah of Grand Falls High. The proverbial rock, in this case, silence, and its formidable counterpart, a hard place, speaking the truth, confronted me. As for my innocence, it dissolved into irrelevance. I could only hope that detention, a week for Lefty and me, and whatever for Buster, would conclude the matter.

***

It is said that no news is good news. The bromide bears as much merit as one contending that no news is bad news...The truth be told, no news is no news.

I had finished dinner and was listening to the *Lone Ranger* on the radio. With bullets streaming, as varmints lurking in the rocks ambushed the masked champion of law and order, our telephone rang. I hurried to answer it. Like so many others around the country, especially in rural areas, we had a two-party line, one that we shared with another household. The pattern, two short rings, rather than a longer single one, indicated the call was for our house, not Mr. Thorton, the eighty-something curmudgeon who shared our party line. No more than a second after I picked up the receiver and said, "Hello," I heard Mr. Thorton, despite the two short rings, voice the same word. I had heard my neighbor's gravelly voice on the telephone numerous times and could recognize it easily. More than once when my parents were out and I was bored, I had picked up the receiver very delicately, discreetly listening in on Mr. Thorton's conversations. I was certain Mr. Thorton had done the same to our family. More than speculation had proved the point. Numerous times, after a call concluded, the click of an extra receiver as it was hung up furnished compelling evidence.

"Is that you, Geeko?" said the caller.

I recognized Buster's voice. "Yup...It's for me Mr. Thorton."

"I'll hang up," he said.

A moment later, I heard the click of his receiver. Whether he had hung up remained unknown. Everyone knew the trick. Push the receiver button down with a finger, so that those still on the line heard the click. Wait a bit, let the button up very slowly, and eavesdrop.

"It's just me on the line, I think," I said.

"Sorry that I cut out on you after our little...*meeting* this afternoon, but I had to get to football practice. Late was better than never, though Coach was none too happy when I told him my meetings would continue for an entire week."

Buster's odd way of communicating, his use of a euphemism for detention, might have confused me were it not common practice. With party lines widespread throughout Grand Falls, folks knew how to be circumspect lest their business become public knowledge. Teens, often engaged in mischief and other inappropriate behavior, knew to be particularly vigilant. I said, "Apart from the meetings, you think the matter is in the past?"

"Don't know, but I hope so. Anyway, I figured you deserved an update, and that's why I called. Also, to say thanks. We'll talk about it more in school tomorrow."

Buster and I exchanged goodbyes, and he hung up. I could be certain because I heard a dial tone, something that only ensued after the person who had originated the call hung up. I waited a minute to see if I heard another telephone click. If so, it would have to be Mr. Thorton's. It could not be one in our house because we had only a single telephone. Arguably, I was being paranoid, but one could never be too careful, especially when one had something to hide.

***

Sometimes life is ass backwards. Occasionally, ass backwards is good; for example, when the ridiculous becomes sublime, when Innocence + Punishment = Boon.

Nearly two weeks had passed since Buster's smoke bomb had emptied the school. Detention for Buster, Lefty, and me, afternoons in Harlamov's Gulag, was a week in the rear-view mirror. It was a Monday morning. Speedy and I were in homeroom just before the opening bell. We were debating the ongoing 1943 World Series. Speedy was rooting for the Yankees, while I was supporting the Cardinals. Affinity for the St. Louis team played no part in my favoritism. Loathing of the damn Yankees swayed me. They got all the press, while my team, the Brooklyn Dodgers, the Bums of Flatbush, constantly languished as the Big-Apple's also-rans.

"What's up?" said Buster, as he approached.

"Ward thinks the Cardinals have a shot to win the fall classic."

"They beat the Yankees last year," I said.

"Sure," said Buster. "It's like you at the bowling alley. Throw enough balls, and sooner or later, you get a strike. Same way with baseball. You have sixteen teams in two leagues. In

37

the past seven years, the Yankees have copped five World Series, while the other fifteen teams have a total of two. Yeah, the Cards have a shot, kinda like yours to roll a three-hundred game."

The bell rang. I started to my seat. Buster pulled me aside. He said, "Some longshots do come in."

I felt my brow furrow as I struggled to comprehend the perplexing message.

"I think the smoke is gone…if you get my drift."

I thought I did.

Buster whispered, "If Armstrong were still on my case, another shoe would have dropped. I would have heard something by now."

I nodded as I took a step in the direction of my seat.

Buster grabbed my shirt, stopping me in my tracks. "I appreciate what you did for me. Not just that you stayed mum, but more important, you helped keep Lefty's trap shut. You could have sat back while he squealed. That would have gotten you off the hook. As for me, my days as quarterback would have been history, not to mention that I probably would have been booted from school." Buster looked me in the eye. "You're definitely one of The Guys, a brother. I protect my brothers. If ever the tables are turned, I won't forget what you did."

I headed to my desk with a smile on my face. A dozen days earlier, one of my classmates, the quarterback of the football team, had pulled a harebrained stunt. Much as I had preferred to avoid its aftermath, I had found myself caught in the middle. To protect Buster, I had remained mute. At the time, common sense labeled it a foolish choice. Hindsight, 20-20, had proved otherwise. Admittedly, my silence had cost me a week, five hours in the Gulag. But that price paled compared to what I, a geek, had reaped. Rather than adding an enemy, and perhaps becoming a pariah among the many who cared about Grand Falls football, I had become tight with one of the coolest guys on campus. And when you were tight with a guy like Buster Brady, you were somebody. Wise guys, even bullies, knew better than to push you around.

Chapter IV:
Ronald (Coop) Cooper

In the 1930s, long before the coaching days of Vince Lombardi, UCLA football coach Henry Russell Sanders told his players, "Winning isn't everything; it's the only thing." Some would agree; others would not. Like beauty, it depends on the beholder.

Back in our high school days, Ronald Cooper was among those in the cool clique. Though never the star of the classroom, he got by respectably. Medium height, blond, and loaded with self-confidence, the girls took to him. A round face, decorated with a toothy smile and Roman nose, crowned his short neck. Athletic, he played on the basketball and golf teams. Racking up twelve points per game his senior year, he ranked second on the hoopsters' scoring list. On the links he displayed mediocre talents, but with golfers few, especially during the war, his nine-hole scoring average, just over forty-three, won him third spot on the five-man roster.

Following high school graduation, Cooper took courses at the extension program which Syracuse University had established in the 1930s in Utica, a city midway between Grand Falls and Syracuse. After one year in the program, he matriculated as a full-time student when Syracuse University formally launched Utica College in the city's downtown section. After graduating, Cooper began his professional career teaching physical education at Grand Falls Junior High. He earned a master's degree, taking courses over several summers at the New York State College for Teachers at Albany. In 1963, when the principal of the junior high retired, Cooper was tapped for the school's top job.

Three years later, Cooper was elevated to the school district's superintendency. Serendipity occasioned his appointment. He may not have been the right person for the job, but Cooper occupied the right place at the right time. In early June 1966, the then superintendent suddenly announced that he was taking a similar position in a larger district in Minnesota. The Grand Falls School Board found itself scrambling for a replacement. School board members acknowledged that had they enjoyed a year's notice, they would have opted for a widespread search. That said, Grand Falls, a rust-ridden town, whose best years lay in the past, would have struggled to lure an experienced superintendent from another district. Compensation rates at the low end of the school-district pay scale compounded the difficulty. Add to the circumstances that authoritarian high school principal Armstrong, the only local competition, enjoyed a reputation for standoffishness, and Cooper landed the superintendent's job almost by default. As a local, who had enjoyed a decent high school athletic career and had worked in the school system since college, he was well known throughout the community, enough so that he was an acceptable, though hardly celebrated, choice.

The mere fact that Cooper was superintendent in 1969 linked him to the circumstances that threatened my teaching job at that time. But to fully understand his connection, one must go back to the spring of 1944, the latter stages of our junior year in high school. Back then, golf was a spring sport. Many schools had no team. Golf courses were few. Most were private and exclusive. The ordinary folks of Grand Falls did not partake in the rich-man's sport. The Depression, followed by World War II, had arrested growth that the game had enjoyed in the 1920s. For that matter, the economic downturn had driven the game into deep decline. Those who played, whether they were righthanded or lefthanded, did so righthanded. A simple rationale shed light on the apparent anomaly. Lefthanded clubs were rarer than thundersnow.

At Grand Falls High School, good fortune enabled us to field a golf team. Nick Stoner's Golf Course at Caroga Lake, roughly fifteen miles away, availed their facility to our team.

Our season, a mere seven matches, ran from mid-April until early June. Weekly matches were nine holes. With one additional day of practice, we played just eighteen holes per week. Other than that, we practiced on a limited-availability field behind the school. Owing to the facility's size, use of real golf balls was confined to wedges and pitch shots. Shots with longer clubs required plastic practice balls.

It was the last Friday of May 1944. Our team had compiled a losing record, but a win would elevate us to .500. As sixth man, I only played when one of the starting five was unavailable. That had occurred just once, in late April, when the third man, having been caught with beer in the Boys' Room, earned a three-day suspension from school. A possible second opportunity came my way when the fourth man was out sick the day before an upcoming match. Though I wished him no ill, his absence the next day hardly disappointed me. My second chance to compete had arrived.

Being last man, I teed off first, along with my opponent. The fourth men from both our team and our competition, Dolgeville Central School, joined us in a foursome. With only a single win all season, Dolgeville should have been duck soup. But by the time our foursome had circled the links, progress toward a victory had not materialized. My teammate won his match, but I lost by a single stroke when my opponent canned a 15-foot birdie putt on Nick Stoner's 146-yard, par-three ninth hole. That left the team scores at 1-1.

Our foursome waited behind the ninth green to watch the other matches finish. The teams' second and third men followed directly behind us. As they approached the tee, their voices resounded. They appeared to be arguing. Discerning the nature of the dispute was impossible.

I turned to my Dolgeville opponent. "Looks like the foursome behind us abandoned civility."

My opponent heaved a sigh. "I'll bet it's Madsden. The jerk's a hothead. He got into it with his opponent the week before last."

Back at the tee, Cooper banged a club against the ground. He shouted, "Screw you, Jones, you goddamn asshole!"

My opponent turned to me. "Ain't nobody on our team named Jones."

I said, "Jones is our second man. Looks like the dispute involves two of our players." Bizarre though it seemed that my teammates would be quarreling, from all indications, Cooper was swearing at teammate Freddy Jones.

"Any idea why they'd be fighting...past bad blood, maybe?"

I shrugged.

The squabbling, which halted while the foursome teed off, resumed once they started down the fairway. As Cooper approached the green, he slammed his bag down adjacent to the putting surface. Storming toward his ball, he snarled inaudibly. The four finished the hole. Freddy Jones shook hands with his opponent. Cooper, still muttering, spun around and exhibiting the proficiency of a prodigious Olympic hammer thrower, hurled his putter, launching it thirty yards beyond his bag.

The two Dolgeville players, along with Freddy, came our way.

"How did you guys make out?" I said to Freddy.

"I won my match, but Coop lost."

"Given his antics, I assumed so," I said. "But what's his problem? We could hear him yelling at you all the way from the tee."

"First tell me how we stand," said Freddy. "Then I'll fill you in."

"Just like your foursome, we won one and lost one. So, it's 2-2. It all comes down to Jack's match." I looked back at the tee where Jack Lang, the number one player on our team, was arriving, along with his Dolgeville opponent. I said, "Any idea how Jack stands?"

Freddy shook his head. "No idea. They never caught up to us."

Back at the tee, Jack Lang addressed his ball.

"Jack has the honor," said Freddy. "That's a positive sign."

Jack swung. The shot was dead on line at the pin. The ball hit the green just three feet beyond the flag, spinning back a mere six inches from the hole.

"Man, what a time to almost make a hole-in-one," said Freddy.

Cooper approached. He gave Freddy the finger. "You goddamn son of a bitch!" He turned to me. "Our lovely teammate stole my match. But for him, we'd be up 3-1, not tied 2-2."

"How could he steal – " I clipped my tongue. With Dolgeville's first man on the tee and beginning his backswing, a more important matter grabbed my attention. From the moment he struck the ball, it was yanked left.

"That one is headed for bogey land," said Freddy. "Things are looking up."

"Big deal," said Cooper. "If you weren't such an asshole, the match would be in the bag. We'd be home free already."

"Go screw yourself!" said Freddy, as the final two players began their walk from tee to green.

Addressing myself to Cooper, I said, "What is going on? How could Freddy *steal* your match?"

"I was even heading to the eighth hole. The prick cost me two strokes. As a result, I came to nine, one down, not one up. And I lost one down."

"I didn't cost you two strokes," said Freddy.

"The hell you didn't, you lousy bastard! You called a two-stroke penalty on me after the hole was over."

I eyed Freddy. "Why would you call a penalty on Coop?"

"He hit his drive behind a bush in the left rough. My drive was down the left side of the fairway. The two Dolgeville players were a little shorter, but over on the right. While one of them was hitting, I saw Coop pull his ball clear of the bush with his clubhead. It gave him an open shot. He – "

"My match was none of your goddamn business!" said Cooper.

I gave him a look and refocused on Freddy. "What happened next?"

"To make a long story short, once the hole was over, Cooper said he had made a par to his opponent's bogey. I couldn't ignore his cheating. I told his opponent that he moved his ball, improved his lie, and thus, incurred a two-stroke penalty."

"I rest my case," said Cooper. "Tell me Freddy isn't a Benedict Arnold...a dick-faced asshole!"

Incredulous, I eyed Cooper. "Do you deny that you moved your ball?"

"That's not the point. Freddy shoulda kept his stinkin' mouth shut!"

I shook my head. "Cooper, you're right...There's an asshole here. But you're it. You cheated, and you got caught."

"Ward, you're an asshole too." Cooper kicked the ground.

"Enough for now," said Freddy. "We can still win. Let's focus on Jack's match."

He approached the green. He marked his ball, a mere six inches from the hole, and headed toward the edge of the putting surface. Just before laying his bag down, he called to us. "How do we stand?"

"Two all," said Freddy. "How you doing?"

Shoulders slumped, Jack shook his head. "I'm five shots down coming to the last hole."

The outcome became apparent. Even with his glorious shot, a guaranteed birdie, no way could Jack erase the huge deficit. Even a hole-in-one would not have saved him and our team. The inevitable went into the books when Jack's Dolgeville opponent, ten yards left of the green, played a superb pitch setting up an easy tap-in.

Cooper turned to me. "You still wanna defend Freddy. But for his big mouth, we'd have another notch in the win column. We'd be at .500, not two south of that figure." He turned to Freddy. "That's the last time I play in the same foursome as you...you damn dirtbag."

"Lay off him," I said.

Cooper's eyes were wide and fiery. "Don't tell me you're still taking his side."

"You're damn right, I am. We don't win by cheating."

"Jeez, give me a break. You'd think we were in Sunday school."

"What's that supposed to mean?" I said, to get Cooper on the record, spelling out his lunacy.

"This is sports...it's life."

"And?"

"Look at baseball. Runners on second base steal signs from catchers and relay them to the batters. And in football, offensive linemen hold all the time...whatever they can get away with."

"First off," I said, "those sports have umpires and referees who call illegal play. We don't. Regardless, we're talking about golf, a game where a player who commits an infraction is required to call it on himself."

"C'mon, you believe that most golfers penalize themselves?"

"Yeah, I do."

Cooper turned toward Freddy, whom he had been ignoring. "You gonna tell me you agree with Geeko. And before you answer, let me remind you that I've seen you pick up two-foot putts loads of times."

"Sure, when I'm out practicing, not keeping score. Or in a match, when my opponent gives me a putt. But never in a stroke play event against the field."

"You really believe our opponents don't cheat when they have the chance?" said Cooper. "If so, I've got loads of stars, billions of light-years away, that I'll sell you...real cheap."

Freddy shook his head. "No doubt, there are other creeps like you, but I'd bet that over ninety percent play it fair and square."

"You two are assholes." Cooper flashed a middle finger, first at Freddy, then at me.

I turned to Freddy. "You know what: I'm glad we lost. Dolgeville deserves the victory."

Cooper looked to the Heavens. "God, you're even dumber than I thought. I'd bet a dozen new Titleists against one lousy shag ball with two cuts that someone on the Dolgeville team cheated today."

"I suspect you would," I said. "A cheater like you naturally assumes dishonesty is par for the course. That's how you justify your conduct."

Cooper started to walk away but stopped. "Well, I have to admit that I learned one lesson from you two."

"What's that?" said Freddy.

"In the future, to be more discrete when bending the rules."

"Cooper," said Freddy, "you're a sad excuse for a human being."

Cooper laughed.

"You find that funny?" said Freddy.

"Well, let's just say ironic. Because the only thing sad around here is that come real life, the sharks of the world, the smart half of the population, will bleed you suckers dry. Goody-goodies get praised in church. On the streets, in the corporate world, and especially in politics, they finish last. Winners opt for the below-the-belt blows of boxing. Headbutts, rabbit punches, and even a knee to the groin, whatever you can get away with, are tools of the trade. That's not to say that sportsmanship and playing by the rules should be ignored. Such noble cliches make wonderful talking points. They promote the right image. But when the game is on, when the bucks are being bagged, only losers adhere to such pointless principles. As my grandfather, the former county chair of the Populist Party – may he rest in peace – used to say: 'It's not how you play the game, but whether you win or lose. Outcomes are determined by whom you know, not what.'…Oh, and one more thing. 'Nice guys play fair. That's why they're losers.'" Cooper looked at Freddy and then at me. "No doubt, you two are *nice* guys." Cooper grabbed his golf bag and marched away.

Freddy turned to me. "Coop just proved an interesting point."

"Really," I said, disbelieving that Freddy agreed with the snake.

"Not all losers are nice guys." He pointed at Cooper who was heading toward the clubhouse.

"Point well taken," I said.

***

Variety may be the spice of life, but sometimes it is the font of discrimination, particularly in the teenage years when peer acceptance is critical. As for discrimination, it comes in

*degrees. The blatant and hateful type screams its bigotry.
Subtle or disguised requires rigorous examination. Latent
demands even greater scrutiny. Harder yet to recognize is that
which is seemingly innocent, a blindness, not to color, but the
issues it raises.*

The first Friday of June 1944. We, The Guys, were still
juniors, but a premature case of senioritis was creeping in.
With the school year nearly over and summer close, we were
on the verge of donning the mantle as top dogs at Grand Falls
High School. The coming school year would be our time, at
least it was meant to be. But a huge question mark mined our
path. Where would America be one year hence when we
graduated? For roughly half of our male classmates,
irrespective of how they performed in the classroom,
graduation was far from guaranteed. Those who turned
eighteen in the first six months of the upcoming calendar year
would face the draft before earning their sheepskins. They
could apply for a temporary deferment, but with the ongoing
war and draft boards struggling to fill quotas, delay was an iffy
proposition. Now and then successes on both the European and
Pacific fronts stirred hope that World War II might end by the
time we completed our senior year. But scrutiny of the entire
picture counseled that such optimism was rooted in wishful
thinking, pie in the sky. Fierce battles in Europe and the Pacific
indicated the fighting was nowhere near its conclusion. Even if
the maniacal Hitler could be crushed, Japan appeared ready to
battle until the last man succumbed. Little did we realize that
the Manhattan Project was secretly developing the atomic
bomb, a weapon whose cloud of devastation would alter the
landscape both literally and figuratively.

Grand Falls High School males, like those across
America, realized that their senior year could be their last, not
just in school, but for all eternity. Many thousands had already
paid the ultimate price. Many more were sure to do so. Amidst
the uncertainty, The Guys, like our counterparts everywhere,
were determined to make the most of our senior year. Knowing
it could be our last hurrah, we refused to await its September
start.

That first Friday of June, during morning homeroom, Ronald Cooper called for The Guys to meet immediately after school under the big oak behind the west end of the building. No reason for the gathering was provided. Throughout the day, speculation abounded, but no one had what seemed a convincing guess, let alone the inside scoop. The rare intrigue, the curiosity it prompted, drew us to the designated spot. Apart from Pokey Paulsen, who had the mumps, the other twelve of us reached the oak within minutes after three.

Cooper stepped away from the stately tree and addressed us. "As you all know, class elections for the coming school year, rather than being held next September, have been shifted to the last week of school, to Wednesday, June 21st. I'm throwing my hat into the ring for president. With your support, I believe I can win. Unlike the other two candidates, Keith Carter and Helen Smith, I have a ready-made organization that will attract votes from all sectors of our senior class. Buster and Lefty can win over the jocks. They can lure the chicks as well. Doc and Geeko can make inroads with the eggheads, Helen Smith's base of support. Don and Shadow can bag the votes of the industrial-arts crowd. The rest of you can pull in votes from across the board, especially that forty-or-so percent that I call middle-of-the-roaders.

"These past two years, our group has enjoyed a great run. If I'm elected president, we'll climb higher yet, taking our place as lords of the campus. We'll turn senior year into an unforgettable wingding. But to do that, we gotta win the election. I need your support." Cooper ran his eyes over the group. "You with me?"

One or two voiced affirmative reactions. A couple nodded. Most displayed little. Taken as a whole, the response rated tepid. On the other hand, no overt dissents emerged. Bottom line, Cooper had managed an informal endorsement. The Guys would back him.

Sam Porter whispered to me, "What do you think?"

I shrugged.

Cooper said, "First thing Monday morning, I'll notify the office that I'm in it to win. And on that note, let the weekend commence."

Speedy joined Sam and me, and the three of us began our walk home.

"Didn't expect that," said Speedy.

"Doubt anyone did," said Sam. "But it could be good for The Guys."

"I suppose," I said, the dustup with Cooper following the Dolgeville golf match still coloring my views.

"He is a leader," said Sam.

I silently conceded the point, not that I was willing to voice it. Among The Guys I was probably the least enthusiastic about Cooper. Freddy Jones, the primary target of his outburst at Nick Stoner's, might have been more negative, but he was not in our homeroom and therefore, not a member of our club.

Shortly after we started down Main, Sam diverged toward his home on Pleasant. Speedy and I continued on our way. I said, "So, you're fine with Cooper's run?"

"Yeah, I guess." Speedy's phlegmatic tone all but contradicted his words.

"You don't sound thrilled."

"Hey, it's no skin off my back. If Cooper wants to be president, good for him. Do I think he'll do anything for The Guys? Not really. For that matter, I doubt he'll do much. But face it. School elections are popularity contests, an ego booster that dresses up a résumé."

Speedy had summed up the matter well. That said, it left a bad taste in my mouth. I said, "Fine that Cooper wants personal glory, but seems you've ignored a minor detail."

Speedy slowed his pace, giving me a look. "And what might that detail be?"

"He wants us to do the work needed for him to grab his glory." The idea of donating my time for a guy who had embarrassed our golf team and called me an asshole, among other names, peeved me.

Speedy shrugged. "Big deal. We'll make some signs and encourage classmates to vote for him. It's not as if we'll need to give up a weekend or skip a happening. And for that matter, I'd like to think that The Guys would do the same for any of us."

The point made sense; regardless, I disliked it, and my face apparently communicated that fact.

"Given your frown, appears someone is resentful...maybe even jealous."

"Of Cooper? You've gotta be kidding!"

"Well, something...and it isn't positive, is going on."

The comment forced me to scrutinize my feelings. Helping a member of The Guys win an office was fine. But helping Cooper annoyed me. I longed to tell Speedy what Cooper had done during the Dolgeville golf match. A mental tug of war exploded in my brain. After the match, the entire team, excluding Cooper, had agreed to bury the incident. We had made the decision immediately after the match, never telling Coach, who had been called away due to a personal matter. We promised one another that mum would be the word. First man, Jack Lang, was tasked with the unseemly job of reading Cooper the riot act, informing him that if he ever cheated again, we would permanently banish him from the team. I wanted to explain to Speedy why I resented assisting Cooper. I told myself that Speedy would maintain the confidence. Logic, as well as my conscience, balked. Expecting another to honor the very promise that I was breaking reeked of hypocrisy. Self-interest also kept me silent. In the past, others had shared information with me that they had promised not to disclose. Their breach had induced me to make a mental note to never share a confidence with them. If I failed to keep my mouth shut, I could earn that same reputation of unreliability. A final reason locked my lips. If I told Speedy and he told someone else, it might get back to my golfing teammates. If so, I could pay a price.

"Aren't you going to say something?" said Speedy.

"About what?" I said, my ruminations consuming me.

"My suggestion that – "

A car turning left from Main onto Hickory – we were crossing the latter in a crosswalk – cut us off, forcing us to jump back.

I shot a middle finger at the driver, not that he, having already passed, could see it. "Did you see that son of a bitch?"

"Yeah. The guy's a cretin." Speedy voiced the assessment matter-of-factly.

"That didn't piss you off?" I fired an incredulous look Speedy's way.

"Because some guy I don't know is a cretin, I should get aggravated?"

"No, but...but the guy could have run you over. You fine with that?"

"Of course not. But do I need to take it out on myself, especially after he's gone?" Speedy gestured at me. "Look at you. You're an over-stretched rubber band ready to snap."

Though the remark bore too much truth to debate, I refused to let Speedy off the hook. "You telling me you're not irked?"

"Sure, and I hope a cop gives him a ticket, and the louse loses his license. But aggravate me for more than an instant, he can't. I choose grace." His face pensive, Speedy halted. "I prefer peace."

Intrigued by his perspective, I stopped as well.

Speedy heaved a sigh. He peered off into space and mumbled, "Should I go there?...Oh, what the hell." He refocused on me and said, "As a Negro, especially in a community that's over 99% white, I have to exercise restraint. I need to turn the other cheek. If I get into a dispute with someone white, even if I'm right, I'm gonna lose. The system, supposedly color blind, is anything but."

I yearned to argue. I would have, except deep down, I knew Speedy was right. Though we had never discussed the issue of race, how it affected our lives, its undeniable influence torpedoed my inclination to rationalize. Race was the dinosaur that always walked between us, the skeletons of a nation that had countenanced slavery. Arguing that Jim Crow was ancient history disdained reality. A large portion of the country still banned persons of color from public schools, hotels, restaurants...even water fountains and bathrooms. That the United States Supreme Court had blessed segregation dispelled any doubt about the point.

Even within our homeroom, the subtle reverberations of racial discrimination lurked. Back when The Guys had been formed during freshman year, factions had debated whether the club should be a limited clique or include all males in our homeroom. From what I had later learned, Speedy, like me, had faced possible exclusion. The reason, however, differed from that which had threatened to bar me. Two individuals had demanded the club be white only. That issue was tabled until inclusion of the geeks could be determined. Resolution of the latter came fast when Buster stepped in. Any plan to exclude Sam after his father had saved Buster's dad from the breadline was a non-starter. As for me, as I mentioned before, I got in on Sam's coattails.

Speedy's inclusion was more complicated. Two, at least one of whom was a boldfaced bigot, voiced adamant opposition. Whether those who supported Speedy were equally strong has long been a matter of debate. A vote, predating my acceptance into the group, ensued. A majority backed Speedy. That he was a wide receiver on the football team and the fastest on the track squad influenced the outcome. Had he been a nobody, his ostracism would have slipped past without fanfare. Had our homeroom included another Negro or if anyone else had been excluded, Speedy probably would have gotten the axe. I could argue that his inclusion proved our group was egalitarian. A more honest assessment, however, reinforces Speedy's contention that the system was far from color blind. No one else in our homeroom was evaluated based upon his skin's pigment. Even among his peers, Speedy needed superior credentials to enjoy the benefits available to his white counterparts. I said, "I...I think I understand what you're saying...uh...about race."

"Sorry, I didn't mean to strike a tender nerve...make you uncomfortable."

"You have no reason to apologize." I gestured at myself. "My discomfort stems from the truth of your assessment. Our white community disadvantages people of color, like you." I realized my comment moments before, that I understood what he was saying, was grossly inaccurate. I had heard him. His words made sense. They struck a nerve. But I had at most the vaguest notion what it was like to walk in Speedy's shoes, to be misjudged and mistreated based upon my race. Acknowledging the inequity was one thing; enduring the prejudice day after day, in all manner of circumstances, eclipsed my comprehension. I said, "The difference in our skin color has never mattered to me...But sad to admit, I've never tried to understand the hurdles you face."

Speedy's gaze directed to his feet. "It's an issue I generally avoid, if only to survive."

The possibility I had put him in an awkward spot had me swallowing hard. "Sorry, I should have minded my own business."

"No apology needed. Difficult as it may be, I welcome this conversation. Better than having things said behind my back."

"You don't think I say things behind your back...because I swear (I raised my right hand), I don't."

"I know you don't, but others do. Eradicating the bias that fills their minds and hearts is a distant dream. It'll only happen if we pull up the rug and confront the dirt below. Conversations with people like yourself who are willing to listen can begin the cleansing process."

Having always viewed myself as open-minded, the remark, though it intended no malice, stung. I was part of the problem. Rather than confronting it, I had taken the easy route. I had turned a blind eye. I said, "I'm glad we're having this discussion."

"Me too." Speedy smiled.

We turned from Main onto Elm, moments away from Speedy's house. For several years we had been close friends. We knew each other well, but not so well as I had thought. Conversations about sports, school, television shows, and the like had been vast, but discussions which enabled us to delve deeply held feelings had been lacking. The exchange seconds before, a minuscule first step, was positive. The door to racial issues had been unlocked, though admittedly, it was barely ajar.

We reached Speedy's home. He said, "See you tomorrow."

"Uh...yeah, I'll...uh...see you then." Much as I longed to go further, to take our conversation to the next level, to engage in a meaningful discussion about race, I lacked the know-how. Addressing the subject, more delicate than the finest lace, demanded preparation. Self-conscious, I walked away, but with good intentions, confident I would revisit the matter soon. Did it happen? Only if one views the near future in the context of dinosaurs, the animals with which I earlier linked the subject. A quarter of a century passed before I seriously delved the matter with Speedy again. Juxtaposed against the millions of years that had elapsed since dinosaurs had roamed the Earth, twenty-five years was indeed, the near future. But judged by any reasonable standard, my procrastination constituted an abysmal excuse. One might ask *why*? That answer, unlike the involute issue of race, is simple. Avoiding a difficult subject is easy. And the longer one does, the easier it becomes.

***

Madison Avenue has mastered methods to foster results. Image is foremost. Quality counts less. The teenage world exhibits a striking similarity. Form prevails over substance. Style trumps merit.

The 6th of June 1944, the Allied Forces, under the command of Major General Dwight D. Eisenhower, began the liberation of France and the Western Front. Operation Overlord, the largest maritime invasion in history, saw 24,000 troops, confronted by mines, barbed wire, and German soldiers, storm the beaches of Normandy. Abetted by Operation Bodyguard, an artifice that helped disguise the time and place of the invasion, the landing troops faced ferocious gunfire from Germans stationed in protected positions above the beaches. Glorious as the goals of the undertaking may have been, huge risks loomed. Many would sacrifice themselves in the endeavor, one for which success was anything but assured.

Even as the invasion began, the world had failed to appreciate the magnitude of German atrocities. Like the brown crabs that burrowed in the sands of Normandy's beaches, people across the globe had buried their heads, denying that which was patent. As early as December 13, 1942, Edwin R.

54

Murrow, reporting on CBS radio, had declared: "What is happening is this. Millions of human beings, most of them Jews, are being gathered up with ruthless efficiency and murdered. The phrase 'concentration camps' is obsolete, as out of date as economic sanctions or non-recognition. It is now possible only to speak of extermination camps."

We students at Grand Falls High had little sense of the horrors that were occurring across the Atlantic. The newspapers and radio provided accounts of the battles and progress of the war. When it came to the invasion of Normandy, we, like Americans across the country, had no advance notice. But even in the days that followed, we failed to comprehend its scope and significance. One week after D-Day, following a shortened last period, our entire senior class was summoned to the auditorium. Principal Armstrong stepped to the podium.

"Tomorrow is the election of class officers, the most important of which is class president. In a few minutes, we will invite the three candidates for that highest office to step forward and detail the reasons they are running. Just before coming here, I drew their names from a hat, determining the order in which they will speak. Keith Carter will be first, followed by Ronald Cooper, and Helen Smith will go last. Yesterday afternoon all three were informed of this plan; so, each has had an opportunity to gather his or her thoughts. With that said, let us begin with Keith Carter's remarks.

Carter approached the lectern. He leaned against it, his shoulders rounding into a slouch. "The reason I'm running is because...several friends said I should. I...uh...guess you could say I was drafted." Carter's nervousness was apparent. His articulation, an amalgam of hesitations and rapidly uttered phrases, was difficult to hear. "I think I'd make a good president. I...uh...get along with people. I'm not afraid to give orders. I'd like to be your president. So...uh...I hope you'll give me your vote...and...uh...I guess that's about it."

As Carter left the lectern and Cooper headed to the stage, Sam Porter, who sat next to me said, "That was slightly worse than pathetic. Coop is bound to do better."

Cooper adjusted the microphone and began speaking. His voice was loud, and his tone, decisive. "Fellow classmates, as we look forward to our senior year, tomorrow marks our last opportunity to vote for class officers. The person chosen as president should be a leader. Without disparaging my opponents, I submit that of the three of us, I am the one with leadership qualities. People often say that high school elections are popularity contests. Whether or not that is true, knowing your classmates, not merely your own clique, is important. Not to brag, but I know as many people as anyone. Freshman year I served as your class vice-president. Accordingly, I have the background and experience to do the job. I hope you'll vote for me." Cooper headed back to his seat.

"Not bad," I said to Sam. "Good enough to beat Carter, not that the dunderhead ever had a chance."

"Agreed," said Sam. "And for that matter, I doubt Helen has much either."

His point was well taken. Like Sam and me, Helen Smith was a geek. Academically, she was second or third in the class. But a "plain Jane," who was quiet, she seemed ill-equipped to win a high school election. People who knew her liked her, but her circle of friends was small. Irrespective of whether she would make a good president, her odds of winning were long.

The diminutive Helen walked to the lectern. She adjusted the microphone down to her level. "My fellow soon-to-be seniors, I thank you for this opportunity to run for the highest office in our class. To the extent that this is a popularity contest, as one of my opponents, Ronald Cooper, has suggested, I am hard pressed to argue that I am the candidate of choice. But in selecting a president, should we not ask for more? Neither of my opponents provided compelling justifications for their candidacy. Indications of what they hope to accomplish, what they plan to do for our class, were conspicuously absent. So too, was evidence that they could achieve results. This past year I chaired a committee that won approval for second semester seniors to go to the library, art room, or gymnasium during study hall and to spend up to six hours per week for afternoon work release. I also helped establish Students for Seniors, a program in which our students visit and grocery-shop for homebound elderly citizens. If elected, I will push for a senior day spring picnic and an overnight trip to New York City. I will listen to your ideas and endeavor to bring them to fruition. I believe I can achieve real results. That is why I am running and why I would appreciate your vote tomorrow. Thank you."

Helen headed back to her seat to a smattering of applause, nothing overwhelming, but every bit as much as Carter or Cooper had enjoyed.

Sam turned to me. "I have to admit, she has more substance than the other two."

I nodded. I looked around to be sure none of The Guys were nearby. Knowing I could trust Sam, I put my hand to the side of my mouth and whispered, "Just between you and me, Cooper is not getting my vote. I'm casting it for Helen."

"You know," he whispered, "that makes two of us."

***

The polls are always right, except when wrong. As Yogi put it, "It ain't over till it's over."

In our homerooms, on the morning of the 14th, we cast our secret ballots. They were collected and delivered to the office for counting. Throughout the day, Cooper exuded confidence about the outcome. At lunch, with The Guys eating as a group, he announced that after school he was taking us all for ice cream cones at Arctic Freeze. At five cents apiece, thirteen treats, single dip, would set him back 65 cents. With his part-time job washing dishes at the diner paying 30 cents per hour, the national minimum wage, it would take him a bit over two hours to defray the cost.

At the end of the day, with all of us in our homerooms, the teachers announced the winning candidates. Our homeroom teacher, Mr. Thompson, began with class secretary, followed by treasurer, vice-president, and finally, president. As he reached the final contest, I peeked across the room at Cooper. His chest puffed out, he sat tall in his seat.

"And the winner of the senior-class presidency is…" Displaying a flare for the dramatic, akin to what game-show emcees exercised on the radio, Mr. Thomson said, "We need a drum roll." He grabbed two pens and did a rat-a-tat-tat on the blackboard.

The hammy delay heightened my conviction as to the outcome's inevitability. Cooper had scored a victory.

Mr. Thompson said, "The winner is…Helen Smith."

Cooper, who had been all but out of his seat, slumped. I was as shocked as he. But unlike him, I silently cheered the outcome. Comeuppance shattered the creep who had cheated during our Dolgeville golf match. The scoundrel who had cursed us for not defending his corruption was ingesting a humongous slice of humble pie. I asked myself – how did he lose? With hindsight, the answer became self-evident. Our senior class had voted for competence, not showmanship. They had chosen substance over style.

Mr. Thompson dismissed the class. As he loaded his briefcase, I recalled his drum roll, an apparent harbinger to the anointment of a member of our homeroom. It dawned on me that like someone else, Mr. Thompson may have been a closet supporter of Helen Smith. He taught science. His subjects encompassed advanced courses. Helen Smith starred in his classes. Seeing a member of his homeroom win the presidency would have been pleasing; the election of a highly qualified candidate whom he held in high esteem, much better. Unlike the students' vote, faculty preference for Helen Smith was predictable.

***

You win some and you lose some. That's how life goes. And sometimes when you win, your prize is less tasty than had you lost. Such is the illogical logic of life.

A somber mood prevailed as The Guys convened in the hallway outside our homeroom. Brief words of condolence such as "tough luck" greeted Cooper.

"Let's get out of here," he said, leading the way. "We can talk outdoors."

As I headed down the stairs and out of the building, I had mixed emotions. Admittedly, Cooper's defeat pleased me, but a tiny pang, owing to my disloyalty, demurred.

Once we were all outside, Cooper pulled us aside onto the grass, away from others who were exiting. He said, "You win some and you lose some...And much as I hate to admit it, Helen will probably make a better president. Unlike me, whose sole interest was adding a feather to my cap, she wants to do the job." He shrugged. "And from that standpoint, the outcome has a silver lining. Next year, when I plan to party, the bothersome responsibilities of office won't cramp my style."

Having anticipated that Cooper would rationalize his defeat, perhaps go into a rancor-ridden tirade, his grace confounded me. What followed shocked me more.

"These past ten days, as I campaigned, you guys have been great. I appreciate the posters, the support, and all you did to drum up votes. Just because I lost doesn't mean I shouldn't thank my buddies for their efforts. Ice cream cones at Arctic Freeze are still on me. Let's go!"

A spirited cheer rang out from the group. I joined in, but only to mask discomfiture. I glanced at Cooper. With no desire to make eye contact, I was thankful he was looking the other way. Out on Nick Stoner's golf course, Cooper had been a jerk, but back on the grounds of Grand Falls High School, he had displayed another side, proved that he could be a stand-up guy.

Five minutes later, after riding with seven in Lefty Lucinski's convertible and six in Cooper's jalopy, we arrived at Arctic Freeze. Where most went directly to the window, I stood back with Sam, who like me, had voted for Helen. Except for Cooper, we were the last to place our orders. As usual, I opted for my favorite, coffee. After thanking Cooper, Sam and I drifted off to the side where we licked our cones. Conversation between us remained sparse. That by itself was not unusual. Devoting full attention to our gastronomic delights, not allowing distractions such as chitchat to detract, squared with time-honored convention. However, expressions, non-verbal

David A. Weiss

communication, evidenced that a knottier reason spawned our silence. Guilt flavored our treats. And we both knew it.

Rather than slowly licking my cone, I bit off chunks, devouring it with record speed. Was the ice cream as good as ever? You bet! Did I enjoy it? No! For all I knew the vote was close. In a small class, with three candidates splitting the ballots, perhaps Sam's and my votes, two more for Helen and two less for Cooper, a swing of four, doomed Cooper's candidacy. Disloyalty disallowed delight. Compunctions trampled taste buds. Perfidy pillaged the palette. The tan of the ice cream may have been coffee, but the flavor was shame. Bad enough that I, a Brutus, had helped bring about my cohort's defeat. How could I be so disingenuous to accept his token of thanks? If Cooper knew of my duplicity, might he plunge the ice cream into my face, uttering, *"et tu,* Geeko." The unseemly image left me empty. I wished I had voted for Cooper. That way, I could have savored my ice cream with a clear conscience, and likely with what I preferred, Helen Smith as president.

60

Chapter V:
Peter (Shotgun) Longley

Challenges mine the highway of life. Sometimes we run. Sometimes we face them, only to fail. Other times we achieve success. And sometimes when all is said and done, we discover the challenges were minuscule nothings. Matters of greater gravity alter our perspective.

I met Pete Longley, Shotgun, our first day in kindergarten in 1932. Herbert Hoover was President, not that I remember anything about his time in office, apart from one event, his defeat by Franklin Delano Roosevelt in the November 1932 election. Whether I recall that election or my memories represent a product of subsequent information is debatable. As Pete and I progressed through elementary school, the country became mired in the quicksand of the Great Depression. Pete and I both lived in what were then traditional American families. We had breadwinning fathers and homemaking mothers. Unlike me, an only child, Pete had a sister, four years older. Our homes were free of the economic pain plaguing many in Grand Falls. Our fathers had steady blue-collar jobs paying a decent wage. My father was a repairman for the Utica Gas and Electric Company, which included a small hydroelectric plant in Little Falls. Pete's father worked as a line supervisor at a nearby hosiery manufacturing plant.

Pete was in my class all the way through ninth grade. During those years we were good friends, often playing together after school. We had been to each other's home numerous times. After Sam and Speedy, Pete was my next closest friend. A growth spurt in junior high school saw him tower over me. But by the time senior year of high school rolled around, that gap had narrowed. I had edged within three inches of his six-foot height. Physically, Pete was bigger than I, consistently outweighing me by twenty or thirty pounds. But fat, he was not. Pete was all muscle. A snub nose and large blue eyes decorated his oval face. In high school we shared the same homeroom but had few classes together. Where I was a geek, among those in the accelerated classes, Pete traveled in the middle realm. An above-average student, he outperformed his ability as measured by standardized tests. Hard work enabled him to maintain a B average.

As junior year arrived, we were both contemplating college. While I explored first-rate, four-year academic institutions, Pete aimed at the Syracuse University extension program in Utica, the one I mentioned earlier. It included an option allowing students to earn college credits while working part time. Unfortunately for Pete, a pair of unexpected events flipped his life upside down. Only one week before Christmas vacation, his father succumbed to a heart attack. His sister, who was married and lived with her husband and first child in Nebraska, had her own family and responsibilities. In a matter of heartbeats, in this case, the cessation thereof, Pete became the man of his household. Compounding his hardship, Pete's father had not only been the family's sole breadwinner but had also overseen its finances and major decisions. Pete's mother, a fine, hardworking homemaker, was ill-prepared to fill the roles her late husband had occupied. And so, the load fell onto Pete. Saddled with the new responsibilities, Pete was ready to quit school and enter the workforce full time. But with his mother's entreaty, the school's assistance, and the aid of Sam Porter's father, an arrangement evolved enabling Pete to graduate with our class by attending school and working, both part time. Sam's father hired Pete to work at the Porter General Store. Flexible hours, about thirty per week, including Saturdays, allowed Pete to spend enough time in school to earn sufficient credits for a timely graduation.

Sadly, the earthquake that shook Pete's life was amplified by an aftershock, nearly as devastating as the initial tumult. Only three weeks after Pete's father died, Vera Herman, a junior whom Pete had dated, informed him that she was pregnant with his baby. Herman's parents, devout Catholics, wanting nothing more to do with her or her yet to be born offspring, disowned her. Adhering to her deeply ingrained religious principles, Herman ruled out an abortion, which at the time would have been illegal and likely performed in an unseemly back room. Already a drug user, the pregnancy sent Herman off the deep end. She dropped out of school and got hooked on heroin, supporting her habit as a small-time seller. Herman's difficulties mounted when she was arrested and charged with a pair of drug-sale felonies. She copped a plea that earned her a prison sentence of four years. Responsibility for the unborn child fell upon Pete...and Pete's mother.

Two days before our junior year concluded, Pete's daughter, Laura Longley, was born. Three days later, while the rest of us embarked upon summer vacation, Pete commenced full-time employment at the Porter General Store. The business, which provided everything and anything from groceries to tools, toys to cosmetics, as well as all manner of sundries, thrived during the Depression if only because the nearest competition was over ten miles away. As the economy picked up during World War II, with gasoline subject to rationing, everyone in Grand Falls shopped at the General Store. Sam's father, among the town's wealthiest citizens, constantly assisted those in need, sometimes with a job and others with credit. Pete was no exception. Daytime he worked at the General Store while his mother cared for Laura. When the fall came, Pete resumed his weekly, thirty-hour schedule while attending school part time, enough that he could graduate with our class. Though he remained a member of The Guys, rarely did he join us either on or off campus. One such occasion was in late August 1944, a picnic at Dalmer Glen, shortly before the start of our senior year. Even then, Pete stayed for little more than an hour.

Most of us arrived at Dalmer around three. We swam in a small, circular pond, about 12-feet deep near its center. The idyllic waterhole lay along a creek between two levels of otherwise steeply sloping, rocky terrain. The creek's precipitous, 15-foot drop from the rocks leading down to the pond created a narrow waterfall. With about four feet of clearance between the rocky wall and the waterfall, one could swim between the two. Alternatively, one could brave the pounding onslaught of the relentless cascade. About ninety degrees from the waterfall was Perch Rock, an outcropping that provided a wonderful dive spot into the crystal-clear waters.

We had been partying for the better part of two hours, swimming and drinking beer, even though only two of us had turned eighteen, New York's legal age for alcohol at the time. Except for Sam and me, everyone had made the 10-foot dive or leap from Perch Rock. Pressure, the taunts of peers, mounted.

"How 'bout it?" said Sam.

"I don't know," I said.

From the far side of the pond, Lefty Lucinski yelled, "Unless I'm mistaken, membership in The Guys requires a leap from Perch Rock."

"Yeah, it's in the bylaws," said Larry Babbitt, who was dog paddling in the middle of the pond.

Sam jabbed me in the side. "If we don't take the leap, they'll cause us to weep."

His poetic quip sucked, but his point had merit. As a poor swimmer who abhorred heights, I had no desire to take the plunge. I shrugged.

Sam started up the short, windy path that led to the Perch. Trapped between peer pressure and fear, I hesitated.

Babbitt yelled, "Looks like Geeko is a chicken."

I glanced his way but said nothing. What could I say?

"Can't hear you," said Babbitt.

"He went 'cluck, cluck, cluck,'" said Lefty.

A chant of "cluck, cluck, cluck" rang out among the others.

Sam's earlier point, one I had all but conceded, grew increasingly evident. Reluctantly, I climbed the trail. Short, slow steps, a device to delay the ordeal, reaped nothing more than escalated anxiety. When I reached the top, Sam was standing on the Perch. A new chant, "jump, jump, jump," erupted.

"Sam, you don't have to do it," I whispered. The truth be known, I was concerned for myself. Sam was a better swimmer than I. He had ascended the Perch when I had sought to stay below. From all indications, my fear dwarfed his. But if he balked, stepped back from the brink, there would be two of us refusing. The aphorism regarding strength in numbers applied. Admittedly two was tiny, but next to one, it was huge, a 100% boost.

Sam looked back my way. "Gotta do it...Here goes nothing." Moments later, he jumped.

I moved forward, not in preparation for a leap, but to see how Sam had fared. He rose to the surface and waved his arms...not in desperation, but triumphantly. He swam to shallower waters, looked up my way and yelled, "It's fun, like that big roller coaster we rode three years ago at the state fair."

The evocative memory flashed into my mind. With both excitement and dread raging, we had stalked the demonic ride for twenty minutes, taking in the screams of those who braved it, eavesdropping on their comments as they deboarded. With approach-avoidance rampant, we had debated. In my case, *anguished* more accurately describes my thought process. Our friends knew we were going to the fair. Doubtless, they would ask if we had ridden the vaunted coaster. Having to confess that we chickened out was intolerable, especially when the alternative would confer bragging rights for conquering the twisting track. And so, we climbed on board. As cranking gears slowly dragged our car uphill to its zenith, trepidations abounded. White knuckles evidenced the grip that locked my hands onto the safety bar. All too soon, our car reached the peak. It surged downward, the whim of gravity snowballing its speed. I shut my eyes and screamed. Terror reigned. Not until we halted did I open my eyes. Only then did I slacken my sweat-ridden grip.

When we stepped off the ride, Sam said, "That was incredible!"

"Yeah," I said, nausea permeating my stomach.

"Wanna go again?"

My bragging rights had been etched for posterity. I had endured the ordeal. However daft I may have been, no way would I board the monstrosity again. Atop Perch Rock, déjà vu reigned. The climb to the spot bore the same apprehension I had experienced ascending the coaster's initial hill. Once again, gravity, the capricious force that pitted my tiny body against the power of the massive Earth, would hold sway. But unlike the coaster, standing above the pond, I had no safety bar. I was on my own.

Babbitt yelled, "Okay, Geeko. It's your turn."

All eyes focused on me. A chant of "jump, jump, jump" resounded.

I longed to run. That was out of the question. I inched forward so my toes were tangent to the edge of the Perch. It was the first time I had drawn so close. From down below, the Perch had looked high, but from its summit, far higher. Perhaps it was the addition of my height, all 5'9" of it, save the several inches from my eyes to the top of my head. Perhaps it was the change of vantage point, looking down from the Perch, not up at it. Regardless, my fear compounded. I stood at the precipice, both figuratively and literally. The more I dawdled, the louder the chant grew. I had to jump. I forged a plan. A count of three and I would make the fatal plunge. Slowly, silently, I recited, "one...two...three." A statue of stone, I failed to budge.

Screams of "chicken," "cluck," and "jump" peppered me.

Almost as if external forces consumed my body, I leaped. Even before I hit the water, my arms began flailing. Terror consumed me as my feet struck the water. My slim frame sliced through the sparkling liquid, plunging me deeply beneath the surface. (Candor forces me to admit that at no time was my head more than three feet below the waters' apex.) With hysteria superseding rationality, my arms thrashed. My legs kicked. I rose so half my head was above the surface. Panic prevailed.

Pete Longley, who had just arrived on the scene and was standing in street clothes on the near bank, leaped into the water. Seconds later, he grabbed hold of me.

"I've got you. You're fine." With one arm around my waist and one stroking the water, he moved us diagonally about fifteen feet toward the bank where the water was shallow enough that we could stand with our heads well above the surface. "You okay?"

"Yeah, I...I guess," I said, relieved, but mortified. "Uh...thanks for coming to my rescue." My expression of appreciation, voiced as an afterthought, uncloaked mixed feelings.

"It looked as if you were struggling. I jumped in to help. I didn't mean to embarrass you, but I couldn't take the chance you might drown."

"No, I'm grateful. I might not have made it on my own."

Several others, most of whom had been near the waterfall or on the far bank, hurried our way.

"You all right?" said Lefty.

"Sorry," said Babbitt. "Goading you into harm's way was not our intent. I assure you."

The voiced concerns, far better than the ridicule I had anticipated, mitigated my discomfort. "I'm fine. I...uh..." Painting my leap with an intrepid brush was absurd. Acknowledging that I had panicked had no appeal. I shrugged as I climbed from the pond.

Buster pointed upward at the Perch. "If it's any consolation, you now have bragging rights."

For an instant, the point was palliative. But second thoughts countered. A quaking leap into a pond requiring rescue bore no basis to boast. If anything, I preferred to bury the incident.

Once it became clear that I had survived and was fine, attentions shifted to Pete, whom most had not seen the entire summer.

"How things going?" said Lefty.

"Pretty good." A nondescript tone left doubt if his response was a statement of fact or a convenient way of saying nothing. Someone tossed a towel Pete's way, which he used to dry off, not that it altered the state of his wet clothes.

"Have you been – "

"Jeez," said Buster. "Before you start with the third degree, let Pete get some eats."

"Hot dog or hamburger?" said Lefty, as we headed toward the grill and picnic table.

"Give him one of each," said Buster.

While Lefty laded a plate with a hot dog, a hamburger, baked beans, and coleslaw, Sam pulled me aside and whispered, "You okay?"

"Yeah, I guess."

"You ready to jump again?"

I shot him a look.

"Bad joke. Only teasing. And for that matter, I'm sorry."

"For what?"

Sam shrugged. "I don't know. Putting you on the spot. Once I jumped, you were left – "

"Don't apologize. It wasn't your fault."

We joined the others who surrounded Pete at the picnic table. From all sides, questions bombarded him.

"It's different, being a father. You look at this beautiful little girl, so innocent, and know that she's depending on you. Your world has changed." Pete took a bite of his hot dog. He glanced at his watch. "I can only stay a little while. I wouldn't have come at all, but my mom pushed me, insisted I come and see you guys at least once before the summer ends."

For one whose summer had been the proverbial lark, Pete's words were sobering. No way could I picture myself, yet to turn seventeen, assuming adult responsibilities, being a man of the house, working, and caring for a baby. I glanced at the others. Though some were more mature than I, not one was ready for the onus Pete was shouldering. It crossed my mind that before our senior year concluded, in less than twelve months, some of us would suddenly be yanked into adulthood. With World War II raging on two fronts, the draft would presumably dictate our lives. A newsreel of soldiers slogging through the mud and freezing in the bitter cold of Europe's winter popped into my head. I could all but hear the rat-a-tat-tat of machine guns and the booms of cannons. An image of a dying soldier, guts ripped out by the blast of a grenade, turned my stomach, an organ still dealing with the aftermath of my panicked leap. Unable to handle a frolicking jump from the Perch, how would I handle battle...bullets, blood, and death? Would I freeze? Might I run or worse yet, curl up and cry like a baby? Where previously I had worried that the draft might frustrate my plans for college, my brush with adversity minutes before added a new perspective, a terrifying one.

"You coming back to school in the fall, Pete?" said Babbitt.

I welcomed the distraction, though my mind, like the war, occupied two fronts.

His mouth full, Pete garbled, "Plan to...part time. I'll be working about thirty hours a week. My mom is gonna babysit Laura while I'm at work and school." Pete grabbed another bite, its alacrity indicative he needed to gobble his food. "Don't know if I can juggle everything. If not, school gets the axe. Down the road, there's always the possibility of a GED, that new high-school-equivalency test my school advisor mentioned."

I surveyed The Guys. Their eyes and ears were glued to Pete. His absence throughout the summer provided a reason. But that explanation was a longshot, as likely as my afternoon including another leap from the Perch. In all probability, like me, they were having thoughts, sobering ones, maybe not with blood and guts, but hardly filled with food and frolic.

Lefty handed Pete a bottle of Ballentine.

"Damn, I haven't had one of these in weeks. He snatched a church key and popped the top. He took a swig. "So, what's new with you guys?"

"Baker went down to the draft office last week and enlisted," said Babbitt. The draft applied to those who had turned eighteen, but enlistment was possible at seventeen.

"You signed up?' said Cooper, giving Baker a wide-eyed look.

"School has never been my thing. I figured, what the hell. It's now or later."

I whispered to Sam, "Did you know that Baker had enlisted?"

"News to me."

"What branch did you join?" said Pete.

"Army. I'll be heading down to Fort Bragg for basic training in a few weeks."

Just as the focus had shifted from me to Pete, it moved again, this time to Baker and his expectations. The inquiries reflected more than a casual interest. The possibility that any or all of us could face military service in the war was inescapable.

The other guys in our homeroom all knew Baker better than I. That included Sam, having tutored him in math early in our junior year. Baker and I had rarely spoken to one another, and those times were brief. We were never in the same class. Where I was taking college preparatory courses, Baker was traveling the vocational route. Academics were his Waterloo. Despite membership in The Guys, Baker and I were barely acquaintances, almost strangers. Little did I imagine that the picnic would be the last time I would see him. Just four months later, Baker's parents received a beautiful American flag, the worst of Christmas presents. Private Donald J. Baker had been killed in action in Germany. The Guys numbered twelve.

***

The grass is greener on the other side of the fence. From a distance it often seems that way. But up close, what previously appeared to be a verdant lawn may reveal itself as a weed-begotten mess. Objectivity, plus a willingness to scrutinize the lots of others, can vanquish jealousies. It can also foster an appreciation of one's own lot.

As the 1944-45 school year commenced, two worlds grappled within the minds of us seniors. Our behavior communicated that senioritis held sway. Rampant carefree attitudes proliferated. But beneath devil-may-care bravado, fiery coals of war raged. For some in our group, the magic age of eighteen lay just around the corner. An invitation from the draft board might be on the horizon. Sentiments regarding the draft varied. Some, like me, dreaded it. A few were blasé. Others, gung-ho, enlisted before the school year ended. Many planned to join up once they had their diplomas in hand. Among them, some fretted that conscription might short circuit their graduations. For others that risk sparked minimal concern. If a draft notice came before *Pomp and Circumstance* played, so be it.

Having been born in November, my eighteenth birthday was still fourteen months away, but the window until that milestone would quickly close. For me the draft was an unnerving monster whose odious head constantly reared. Fear of the battlefield churned. It did not, however, supersede my duty to serve. If called, I would step forward. About that, I had no doubt. How many others shared my views remained unclear. With support for the war widespread, I kept my reservations to myself. I suspect others did so as well. What I do know is that Sam shared my reluctance. His upcoming eighteenth birthday at the end of the ensuing August, what otherwise would have been a celebratory occasion, loomed ominously.

Speedy viewed it differently. Until 1943 Negroes had been exempt from the draft. The need for more soldiers, not a push toward equality, altered the law. But for Speedy, the conscription amendment bore no consequence. All along, he had planned to enlist.

Among The Guys, Pete Longley's situation was unique. When the draft was enacted in 1940, it excluded men like him. They were classified III-A, as "men with dependents, not engaged in work essential to the national defense." But in 1943, the need for soldiers, 200,000 per month, narrowed the exception. A father whose children were born prior to Pearl Harbor who was the sole support of the family remained exempt from conscription. Because Pete's daughter Laura was born after Pearl Harbor, Pete was subject to the draft. He would have been happy to serve were he not the breadwinner of his family, were he not needed by his mother and daughter. He hoped the draft board would let him be. If called, he planned to appeal. That would impose an uphill battle. He lacked both the time and funds. Compounding the difficulty, he would face the legal burden of proving that the draft board's action was arbitrary.

With his distinctive schedule, rarely did I see Pete at school. Homeroom had been stripped from his program. Classes requisite to graduation consumed his limited time on campus. Even when our paths crossed in the building, his time constraints permitted little more than a passing hello. Fraternizing was foreign to his busy timetable.

As hard as Pete worked, his part-time job was insufficient to provide for his mother and daughter. Within a short time, Pete realized that either he would have to quit school and work full time or his mother, who for years had been a homemaker, would need to get a job. Determined that Pete get his diploma, his mother, Millicent, rejected the former alternative.

With many workers off to war overseas, jobs at the local leather mill were plentiful. Still there was the issue of baby Laura's care. My mother, who a decade before had developed a close friendship with Millicent, offered to watch Laura on the days that Millicent worked, enabling her to accept a position at the mill three days per week. Many days when I arrived home from school, Laura was still at our house, and so, I often helped babysit her. Some days Pete would pick her up, while others, his mother did. On those when Pete came to get her, he and I frequently chewed the fat for ten or fifteen minutes, what for Pete was a rare oasis of relaxation in what had become a life of continuous responsibilities. Our confabs amplified our friendship. And too, it made me appreciate my good fortune. Where Pete was on a proverbial merry-go-round, I was free to fool around with my pals, listen to my favorite radio programs, *Sergeant Preston*, *The Lone Ranger*, and *The Shadow*, and on weekends take in ballgames or enjoy the amusement park at Caroga Lake.

A balmy, late-September day found me on the glider of our porch with three-month-old Laura asleep in my arms when Pete arrived to pick her up.

"Did Laura behave herself today?" Pete said, as he approached.

"She was an angel, as always."

He took his daughter from me and started to leave.

"Have a seat. Take a few minutes."

He glanced at his daughter, who was still asleep. "Just a few." He parked himself alongside me on the glider.

"How was work today?"

"No complaints...For that matter, how could I with a boss as nice as Mr. Porter. Even assuming I could have found a job elsewhere, it would have required me to quit school. He, on the other hand, works my hours so I can finish my education. Find another boss who would do that." Pete looked down at Laura and smiled. "I'm one lucky guy...Damn lucky."

His comment triggered a recollection from my late grandfather. Quick to praise whatever I did and never one to

72

criticize, he rarely gave me advice. An exception was one phrase that he repeated on several occasions. "Jim, my boy, count your blessings every day...find reasons to be grateful." I tried...but only irregularly. All too often I complained about little nothings: homework; a mean teacher; my few chores; a bad bounce on the golf course; the weather; or whatever. Never, however, did I grumble when Pete was in earshot. How could I? He had lost his father, become the man of his house, and father to a baby born out of wedlock. He was shouldering responsibilities beyond my comprehension. He did so stoically, even voicing gratitude. My reluctance to carp when with him was hardly noble. Whining would have made me look and feel like a fool.

"Is it hard to squeeze your schoolwork into your schedule?" I said.

"Less so than I expected. Between you, me, and that maple on your front lawn, the teachers are giving me a break."

"How so?"

"The tests they give me – a few have been oral – include loads of softballs. And when they grade my answers, they're anything but tough."

Where on other occasions a pang of jealousy might have nettled me, with my grandfather's words fresh in my mind, I was happy for Pete. If anyone deserved a break, he did. I said, "I'm glad they do." Ironically, my magnanimous comment, intended for Pete's benefit, lifted me. My grandfather's message, in the past a platitude with little impact, had finally found a resting place in the portion of my brain where it mattered. The lesson had shaped my conduct.

Chapter VI:
Larry (George) Babbitt

To one passing through a rural American town, its population may appear homogeneous. Perhaps it is. But ask the people who live there, and expect disagreement, if only because they differ from their neighbors, who are diverse from one another.

Most every high school class boasts a Larry Babbitt. Even before we formed The Guys, we tagged him with the nickname "George." Five of us, including Larry, had read Sinclair Lewis's classic novel *Babbitt* in English class. With a last name matching that of George Babbitt, the novel's title character, a link to Larry was logical. But the similarities ran deeper. At 5'8" with a paunchy midsection, Larry, whom I will generally refer to as Babbitt, except when it could cause confusion with the literary character, embodied a younger version of the novel's banal real estate man.

Atop a flabby, unathletic body, Babbitt sported a round face with big cheeks and a fleshy nose. He belonged to the Future Businessmen's Club, an organization with only five members, that he co-founded during freshman year. He also participated in the Travel Club, a group notorious for talk, not action. Over two years their lone journey was a day trip to Blue Mountain Lake about eighty miles to the north.

Like golf, tennis was a sport that few at Grand Falls High School played. For Babbitt, who possessed limited athletic skills, tennis offered the perfect opportunity to project himself as a "regular guy," with all that term connoted in Sinclair Lewis's world of conformity. Senior year, Babbitt made the tennis team as last man. Serendipity begot his achievement. Eight students tried out for the eight-man roster. With no one

74

cut, a pulse, not tennis talent, captured a spot on the team. Babbitt played only doubles. In a league replete with feeble teams, Babbitt and his partner never won a match. For that matter, they never won a set. A 2-6 shellacking was the closest they ever came. Babbitt's serve enjoyed renown. Word had it that the weapon had racked up the most points in the league. Unfortunately, those points, incessant double faults, facilitated his opponents' path to victory.

Like high school classes across the land, ours voted for its "most" whatever in a wide range of categories. We tapped Babbitt most likely to succeed, though his meager plurality, a total of thirteen votes, reflected that his name was just another among many. Prone to clichés, Babbitt was himself a cliché, a conservative white male destined to succeed in business, especially by those who measured success in Machiavellian terms, appearances and results, rather than methods and reality. As Sam pointed out more than once, Babbitt's future success, whether large or small, would likely be achieved at the expense of ethical principles.

Where most would have resented the "George Babbitt" tag, Larry relished the moniker, deeming it a badge of honor. A successful white male who fit in characterized his life's ambitions. But unlike Lewis's character, who evolves into a hollow incarnation of prosperity, Larry was determined to parlay his success into bigger and better things. As he phrased it, "My classmates naming me most likely to succeed proves I'm on the right track."

Larry Babbitt was a racist, at least that is how I viewed him. Others may have disagreed, though doubtful anyone would have labeled him inclusive. He had proved the point when The Guys had been formed. As previously indicated, I was not among the few who created the group. My knowledge of those events came compliments of Buster who filled Sam and me in on the details after we were made eligible. The idea to form the group was Babbitt's. That alone afforded him a seeming measure of influence over the early proceedings. Looking to elevate his own status, he invited Lefty Lucinski, Buster Brady, Pete Longley, and Ronald Cooper to join him in an exclusive club comprised of our homeroom's jocks, cool guys, and others of so-called importance. The "riffraff," Sam, Speedy, and I, plus several others, were to be excluded. As mentioned earlier, Buster demanded that Sam be included, and Sam stuck up for me, making us a package. Buster may not have been the intellectual paragon of our class, but physically strong and quarterback of the football team, he was a savvy leader, adept at exerting leverage. When Babbitt balked at Sam's and my inclusion, Buster convinced Lefty to abandon Babbitt's group and form one excluding Babbitt and those concurring with him. When Longley learned of the new plan, he went Buster's way. That left Babbitt and Cooper on an island. Babbitt, ever the shrewd businessman, proposed a compromise. He would lead a more inclusive group. Buster's response: "Not gonna happen! Eleven of us are forming a club. You and Cooper can suck wind."

Buster never intended to exclude the duo, but unwilling to let Babbitt wield power, Buster out-foxed the wheel-and-deal negotiator. He forced Babbitt and Cooper to beg for inclusion. Guided by Buster, the eleven of us admitted the pair as probationary members, arguably second class. Were they shoved into a second tier? Not really. But in the first months after the group's formation, even Sam and I had greater sway. By Thanksgiving, the eggshells on which the pair had to walk faded. All thirteen of us enjoyed equal status, at least in theory. Differences were settled the democratic way, with a vote. Even so, certain members, jocks such as Buster and Lefty, exerted greater power. Their voices, hinting which way the wind was blowing, influenced the votes of others. Such was how our group formed and developed.

On the final Friday of September, the initial month of our senior year, the twelve of us – Pete Longley had no time for our carefree activities – gathered at Rizzo's Pizza on Route 29. We traveled there in two cars, six in each vehicle. Speedy was last to pile into Lefty's heap, a souped-up Ford, Model-A Sedan, or as Lefty and other hotrodders dubbed it, an A-bone. A supercharger, which Lefty had added to his car's water-cooled, forty-horsepower engine, enabled him to top end at over eighty miles per hour. Despite a stodgy, squared-off frame, Lefty's additions, whitewalls, a polished chrome ornament, and red stripes on the black frame, gave it style. Given a choice, Sam and I would have opted to ride with Lefty, but with his car full, we had been consigned to the rear of the Babbitt family Oldsmobile. Though the latter was more expensive, Lefty's wheels were cooler.

When our group arrived at Rizzo's, more a joint than a restaurant, the two long tables toward the center were occupied. Lefty's six, who had arrived first, saved three booths, all back-to-back. Sam and I were the last to reach the booths. Two were full, and the third, in the rear corner, had two vacant seats. Where or with whom we would sit had been determined by default. We approached the booth occupied by Cooper and Babbitt, their backs to the wall.

Cooper pointed backwards over his head. "You two get the outdoor seating, the smelly dumpster out back."

Ignoring the jibe, Sam slid into the booth opposite Cooper and Babbitt. I plopped down in the spot next to Sam. Though Cooper had punctuated his remark with a smile, I suspected that malice, rather than good-natured ribbing, adulterated it. If he had his druthers, Cooper would have picked different tablemates. For that matter, Sam and I would have as well. It was not that Cooper and Babbitt disliked Sam and me, or vice versa. Very simply, Cooper and Babbitt had much in common. The same could be said for Sam and me. As for the respective pairs, no way. That all members of our group were not close friends was predictable. Such is the nature of most groups. And given the disparate composition of The Guys, its sole commonality, a shared homeroom, varied affinities were to be expected.

Cooper, stocky, but not with the paunch of Babbitt, looked across the table and said, "How many pieces of pizza do you two plan to eat?"

With each table splitting a rectangular, twelve-cut pizza, I assumed that Cooper wanted to grab more than his share. No way would I let him. "Three for me," I said.

"At least two, but more likely three," said Sam.

"Damn," said Babbitt. "Doesn't make sense that skinny dweebs like you eat as much as Coop and me."

"We're active," said Sam. "We have high metabolisms. We burn loads of calories."

Babbitt frowned. "Whatever."

"I got a question," said Cooper. "Who's the greatest baseball pitcher of all time?"

Without a moment's thought, Babbitt said, "Cy Young. The 511 games he won far outpaces all others. No one will ever come close to breaking his record. It's safer than the Babe's sixty homers in a season."

"I disagree," said Sam. "Not about the records. They're likely to stand forever, especially Young's, given that pitchers today take the mound less. But as for the best pitcher, Christy Mathewson merits that honor. A 2.12 lifetime ERA backs me up." Sam looked my way. "What do you think?"

I had pondered the matter before. Nevertheless, I lacked a definitive answer. "It's a close call between Mathewson and Walter Johnson. I don't have the Big Train's ERA at my fingertips, but it wasn't much more than Mathewson's. And Johnson strung together ten straight twenty-win seasons, not to mention a hundred-plus career shutouts."

"Coop, you asked the question," said Sam. "Who's your pick?"

Cooper shrugged. "Definitely not Young…Mathewson, I guess."

"There's another pitcher who may prove better than any of them," said Sam.

"Really?" said Babbitt, his condescension undisguised. "And who might that be?"

Owing to a prior discussion, I knew whom Sam was referencing.

"Bob Feller."

"Jeez," said Babbitt, "comparing Feller, a Johnny Come Lately, to Young and Matthewson, is like equating the town's new Elks Lodge to the Empire State Building."

"Well, Feller may not have the statistics of the others, and with years lost fighting in the war, his career numbers may never match up, but pitch for pitch, game for game, he's got the potential to be the greatest. And for whatever it's worth, he's the fastest ever."

"No doubt, he's good…damn good," said Cooper, "and no doubt he's got potential. But until he chalks up a slew of mound-dominating seasons, mentioning him in the same breath as Mathewson and Johnson is ridiculous."

"You ask me," said Babbitt, "Feller ranks with the likes of Satchel Paige."

"Just what does that mean?" I said, though Babbitt's punctuating sneer had negated what otherwise might have been thinly veiled ambiguity.

"What – I need to spell it out for you?"

"Please," said Sam. "We'd love to hear it."

"Fine. I'll give you the score." Babbitt leaned back with arms folded across his portly chest. "Feller's the kind of guy who'll do anything for a buck. His barnstorming tour against Paige's team of Negro League all-stars proved that."

"You suggesting that makes him less of a pitcher?" The more sinister side of Babbitt's remark, not Feller's pitching, triggered an edge in my voice.

"It doesn't affect his pitching one way or the other," said Babbitt, "but it says a lot about him. To line his pockets, he'll sell out our American pastime."

"You care to amplify that?" said Sam.

Babbitt turned to Cooper. "Are these geeks so green that I have to explain the obvious?" Babbitt refocused on Sam and me. "There are those who wanna integrate our country. If they had their way, schools, hotels, restaurants…everything would be wide open. Baseball is a stairway to integration. These games between white and Negro all-stars are a step in that flight."

I laughed…sardonically…for two reasons. The first: Babbitt had evidenced his racism. For the moment, I left that on the back burner and addressed the second: the irony that Babbitt was seemingly complaining that Feller was a progressive. I said, "You're aware that Feller, owing to past comments, has been labeled a racist."

"Yeah, and that proves my earlier point. Regardless how he feels about integration, the bastard will do anything, rape an angel or yank his grandmother's gold tooth, just to snag a buck."

Though I doubted Feller was a racist, Babbitt's point had more merit than I had anticipated. Rather than debate it, I redirected my attention to the first reason behind my earlier guffaw. I said, "I'd love to hear your reasons for opposing integration."

"Because no one should be forced to mix involuntarily."

"You deem it fair that Negroes who are risking their lives defending this country are treated as second class when they come home from the battlefield? Of course, that assumes they make it." Though I checked the urge to raise my voice, my indignation, indeed ire, was evident. Were my words directed at the physically strong Cooper, instead of the buffoonish Babbitt, I might have tempered my temerity.

Babbitt glanced at Cooper. "Apparently Geeko's nose is in a knot."

When first I had gotten the nickname "Geeko," I had looked it up. I learned that it originated from a man who lived in the Isle of Jersey; that it was subsequently associated with a smart person. On balance, it did not seem terrible. But more and more, members of The Guys were invoking it to mock me. With the passage of time, my distaste for it mounted.

"Great student that you are, Geeko," said Babbitt, "I'm sure you recall what Mr. Willard taught us about race (Mr. Willard was our history teacher). The law of the land, the Constitution, as interpreted by the United States Supreme Court, is 'separate but equal.' No one is required to integrate."

"That may be," I said. "But as Mr. Willard also told us, schools, employment, housing, and other facilities are far from equal."

Babbitt shrugged. "Maybe so, but that ain't my problem. Negroes oughta fix up their homes and schools. And in case you've forgotten, Mr. Willard also taught us that the First Amendment guarantees the right of association. Folks can associate with whom they want. Our nation's founding documents entitle states to maintain segregation."

"Well, now that we've added the subject of segregation to baseball," said Cooper, "anyone think our National Pastime will ever be integrated?"

"Won't happen. Not in our lifetimes," said Babbitt.

"Is that so?" I said. "Give me one reason."

"I'll give you two, the first compelling, and the second, a sure thing. An attempt to integrate the Major Leagues would lead to a revolt by many of the players. More important, the owners of the teams, greedy bastards that they are, would never allow it. Countless fans, the ones who butter the owners' bread, would desert the ballparks. Revenues would crash. Love of the almighty buck guarantees that the Major Leagues will remain lily white."

"And that's just the way you want it," said Sam.

Babbitt shrugged. "Yeah, you better believe it."

Our pizza arrived. Along with my tablemates, I grabbed a slice.

Babbitt, his voice lowered to a whisper, continued. "Back when we formed this group, I voiced my preferences – all white, among others. Had it been up to me, Speedy would be on the outside looking in."

The comment hit my ears just as my teeth bit into my slice. The hot cheese burned the roof of my mouth. Babbitt's message fired my temper. "Damn!" I barked, grabbing my Pepsi to ease the burn.

"When it comes to Speedy, it's not up to you, Babbitt," said Cooper.

Silence, palpable tension, punctuated Cooper's barb. Softly voiced, but emphatic, it surprised me. Though I had never heard Cooper express views about race, I knew that he, along with Babbitt, wanted the group to be exclusive. Based upon the newest tidbit, the duo's desire for a limited roster may have matched, but their motivations differed. Only Babbitt was a bigot.

Hostility might have persisted at our table, were pizza not so adept at mollifying testy teens. With a couple of bites, the delectable taste of baked dough, smothered with sauce, cheese, and pepperoni, vanquished any appetite for rancor. Within fifteen minutes, the four of us devoured the twelve-cut delight. The other two tables did likewise. Soon the bill arrived.

"Ship it over to Doc," said Buster. "For a change he can put his mathematical prowess to good use."

The check was relayed from booth to booth until it reached Sam, who mumbled calculations.

"Damn," called out Lefty. "I musta left my wallet at home. Someone wanna pick up my share. I'll pay you back in school."

"Just divide it eleven ways," said Buster.

Sam nodded. A minute later, he said, "Eighty-five cents apiece covers it. That includes a shade under twenty percent for the tip." He gathered up the money and delivered it to the waitress.

We left Rizzo's, climbing into the same cars as before. Babbitt drove us back into Grand Falls, arriving at Sam's house first.

"I'll get out here," I said. "Sam has some stuff from school I need to see."

Sam, who was next to me in the back seat, gave me a look. I jabbed my elbow into his side.

We said our goodbyes, thanked Babbitt for the ride, and climbed out. Babbitt drove off.

"What was that school stuff about?" said Sam.

"I wanted to talk...alone. Whad'ya think about Lefty, not having his wallet?"

"No big deal. The extra cost for the rest of us was less than a dime each...closer to eight cents."

"I know, but it's the principle."

"C'mon," said Sam. "He drove. He used his gas...close to a gallon by the time he drops everyone off. That's twenty cents, plus wear and tear on his heap."

"I suppose, but..." Were I with anyone other than Sam, I would have dropped the issue. I said, "Last month I saw Lefty borrow a buck from Charlie Wells. As of two weeks ago, he hadn't paid it back."

"Might have in the interim."

"Maybe...and maybe I'm making a mountain out of a mole hill. All the same, I hate to be his patsy."

"Understand, but...give Lefty the benefit of the doubt."

I nodded before bidding Sam goodbye. My acquiescence notwithstanding, the chance that I was a moocher's mark stuck in my craw.

***

A wise student ranks a good grade as priority number one. Understanding your teacher's views facilitates that goal. Playing devil's advocate, following Frost's less traveled road, may be wonderful when engaging in a bull session with friends, but once pen hits paper, stay between those straight and narrow lines.

As the month of October rolled along, chilly mornings heralded what lay on the doorstep. Where spring and summer materialized late in Grand Falls, autumn and winter appeared earlier than their designated dates on the calendar. Save for a few isolated days, once Labor Day passed, summer morphed into ancient history. Autumn, a short season, assumed command. The dulcet notes of summer songbirds, accompanied by the whisper of rustling leaves, became distant melodies. Air, no longer permeated with the wafting fragrances of wildflowers, grew cooler. Soon enough October stamped its imprimatur on the region. Forests, once green, transformed into impressionistic canvases suffused with gold, red, orange, and yellow, only to lie barren as the month retreated. Traces of snow, ephemeral invasions of icy precipitation, hinted that winter's curtain would soon drape itself over the Adirondack foothills.

We were seven weeks into our senior year. The teachers had tempered our epidemic of senioritis. Warnings that colleges would scrutinize our first semester grades when weighing our applications for admission forced us to keep our noses to the proverbial grindstone. Reminders that we needed favorable recommendations from our teachers constrained profligacy.

Near the end of Mr. Willard's American History class, he assigned us an essay, three hundred words assessing how well America had fulfilled the ideals enunciated in the Declaration of Independence and Constitution. He encouraged us to include suggestions, if any, to improve the nation. A classmate hoping to gain an inside track sought the popular educator's view on the subject. Normally open to questions, Mr. Willard declined to answer. He urged us to discuss the matter with our friends; cogitate its manifold pluses and minuses; and ultimately, draw our own independent conclusions.

En route to my next class, I sought the counsel of others. I would have discussed it with Sam, but our schedules piloted us in opposite directions. A brief chore in afternoon homeroom prevented me from discussing the matter with him there. By the time I caught up with him, the day's dismissal bell had rung. I found him talking to Babbitt on the walkway leading from the school's front entrance.

"Larry and I have been discussing Mr. Willard's essay assignment, trying to figure out the best approach. What do you think?" said Sam.

I preferred to hear their views first, but they had beaten me to the punch. At least I had the benefit of the thoughts of another with whom I had spoken earlier. I said, "I need more time to think about it, but of one thing, I'm certain. My essay will emphasize the positive, minimize the negative. The way I see it, as Americans, we should be grateful. Whatever else I say, that'll be my central theme. As for warts, I suspect I'll toss in a couple, if only to avoid appearing pollyannaish. But any such negatives will get short shrift. Assuming I can come up with some suggestions for the future, I'll add them…How do you guys see it?"

"With America in the midst of a world war," said Babbitt, "the last thing I intend to do is criticize our country. No doubt, I'll throw in tidbits from history. Mr. Willard loves when we do that. Maybe I'll compare our nation to others, past and present, to prove my point. Apart from advocating expanded presidential powers, I'll limit my suggestions for improvement. I'd rather focus on our country's many achievements, technological progress, and growing world leadership. America is the best of the best. Like a big locomotive cruising down a straight track, it should stay the course. Do that, silence the nasty Nazis and crummy Commies, and all will be well."

Babbitt's tack, consistent with his duly earned moniker of "George Babbitt," embodied no surprises. Like his literary namesake, he was adrift in a vacuous world, an endless ocean.

If ever he chanced upon an island, its beachhead would be invisible amidst the grains of sand. A shifting tide might catch his eye, but only as a repetitious pattern of monotony. Observations, even some purportedly astute, would be nothing more than parroted phrases commandeered from others. I was confident Babbitt's essay would be a sycophantic harangue that would drown in a plethora of superficial clichés. That said, to give the clod his due, when it came to history, his strong suit, he knew more than most of us. Indeed, he flaunted his knowledge whenever the opportunity presented itself. Were he not a pompous clown, I would have counseled him to rethink his essay strategy. "Interesting approach," I said, keeping my thoughts to myself. I turned to Sam. "How will you handle the essay?"

"Not sure, but I suspect I'll take a more controversial path."

The response intrigued me. I welcomed any idea that could help with the tricky assignment.

"Like you guys," said Sam, "I'll certainly laud America's superb experiment in democracy. I'll also acknowledge how fortunate I am to live in a nation that values freedom, prosperity, and equality. But I intend to call out what I see as shortcomings."

Nose in the air, Babbitt groaned. "The all-knowing Doc Porter will pontificate on the flaws of the finest country the world has ever seen."

"You believe America is above criticism?" said Sam.

"Definitely, if it comes from the likes of you." Babbitt paused just long enough to sneer. "Maybe you'd rather live in Hitler's Nazi Germany." Babbitt took a step forward and glared at the physically smaller Sam. "Enlighten us poor mortals what makes you an all-knowing guru, competent to critique America."

Sam held his ground as he took a moment to seemingly collect his thoughts. "Like most high school chowderheads, my knowledge is meager. And lest there be any confusion, I deem myself lucky to live in America. I love my country and the values enshrined in the Bill of Rights. But just as every individual is far from perfect, the same can be said for every nation. All people, all nations can strive to improve. America is no exception."

"Fine." Babbitt sneered again. "So, apprise us lowly peons of America's shortcomings."

Babbitt had thrown down the gauntlet. But if anyone in our class was equipped to back an argument with substance, it was Sam.

"People of color and women enjoy a lesser status than their white-male counterparts. Even as we speak, Japanese Americans, loyal to our country, are locked up in internment camps. America has a history of imperialism. The acquisition of Hawaii and the Philippines are prime examples. So too, is the country's expansion, its Manifest Destiny, the so-called will of God that our nation should inherit the continent. All too often, treaties have been trashed, as native tribes were repeatedly dispossessed."

Babbitt groaned dramatically before turning to me. "Did you know that your pal is a turncoat...or maybe a communist?"

Babbitt's failure to make a substantive argument might have been tolerable, but his personal attack on Sam provoked me. "Rather than spewing nasty epithets, tell us why Sam is wrong."

"It's simple. America has consistently corrected its errors. Doc speaks of imperialism. That policy was abandoned years ago. As for slavery, it was common throughout history, places like Greece, Egypt, you name it. Sure, it was part of America's founding, but to the country's credit, the nation banned it well before its hundredth birthday. Negroes were emancipated and granted citizenship. Thanks to the Constitution, they enjoy all the rights that white folks, like us, have. The truth be known, Negroes are lucky we brought them here from Africa."

"You actually believe that?" Sam's incredulity was palpable.

"Absolutely."

"Give me a break!" said Sam. "Your so-called equality is a myth. We have segregation, enforced in the South and *de facto* in the North."

Babbitt turned my way. "Your buddy here is supposedly the smartest guy in the class. Remind him what Mr. Willard taught us…that 'separate but equal,' per the Supreme Court, is the law of the land. Been that way since before the dawn of the twentieth century."

"Separate but equal," barked Sam, "is a lousy euphemism for – "

"Whatever the hell a *eupha* is, it's the law of the land." Babbitt folded his arms across his flabby chest.

For a second time, Babbitt's hubris overcame my preference to remain on the sidelines. "Your claim that Negroes enjoy equality is bogus. Their education and housing facilities are inferior. Their incomes are lower. So many of them languish in poverty."

"So what?" said Babbitt. "That's their problem. Don't blame it on me or those who founded and built this country."

"Why not?" said Sam. "They built it on the backs of Negroes."

Babbitt struck a pose and pretended to play an imaginary violin. "Your argument is outdated. In case you've forgotten, even though I just reminded you, slavery was long since abolished. Not my fault that Negroes don't measure up."

"You're a racist," said Sam. "A goddamn racist!"

"I rest my case," said Babbitt.

"You what!" shouted Sam.

"Rest my case…Unable to respond meaningfully, you resort to name calling."

"What about women?" I said. "Do they enjoy equality?"

Brow furrowed, Babbitt jerked back. "They have the vote. Their husbands no longer own their property…Of course, there are differences in the sexes. Men are physically stronger and breadwinners. On the other hand, women are nurturers and bear children. Would you suggest that America is guilty of discrimination because men can't bear children?"

The absence of logic in Babbitt's point dumbfounded me. I said, "You're a freakin' neanderthal!"

"Name calling…Rest my case again." Babbitt smirked before extending his arm and pointing at me. "Whatever our differences, tell me you don't agree that Doc's approach to the essay is a recipe for a bad grade."

Much as I detested Babbitt's bigoted contentions, his latest point had merit. An essay attacking America was suicide, a strategy begging a lousy grade. I said, "Not to give credence to any of your despicable claims, for purposes of our assignment, I admit that cataloging America's sins would be foolhardy. To paraphrase a trite adage, discretion is the better part of...folly." I turned to Sam. "Face it. Priority number one is to get a good mark."

Sam shrugged.

"You disagree?" I said.

He heaved a sigh. "I hear what you're saying, but..."

"You gonna stick to your guns...join our Jap enemies and commit academic hara-kiri?" Babbitt laughed.

"Maybe," said Sam. "I'll have to think about it."

***

America is a free country. The First Amendment to the Constitution affords its citizens freedom of speech. That said, you don't blaspheme God in church; you don't bring a foul mouth to a first date with the prim and proper girl upon whom you have a crush; and you don't present your teacher with a daft paper that begs he grade you down.

Before we handed in our essays, Sam and I had read each other's. He faced a rough ride. I would have told him so, but with class beginning, the time for rescue had expired. A revision, one bearing a wiser approach, was impossible. Regardless, I had previously spoken my piece.

One by one, Mr. Willard called us forward to read our essays aloud. Babbitt was among the first. When he finished, Mr. Willard said, "You take great pride in traditional America, don't you?"

"Absolutely...though more power in the executive, less in the other branches, would increase efficiency...But bottom line, I love America."

"I'm sure you do," said Mr. Willard. "I do too, though my essay would have differed from yours. That said, each of us is entitled to his or her own views. Such is the nature of a country which cherishes freedom of speech."

As Babbitt took his seat, I laughed to myself. Disaster dwelled on his doorstep. Mr. Willard had repudiated Babbitt's version of America, his predisposition toward the preservation of a society dominated by white males. Compounding Babbitt's difficulties, dogma, not reason, dominated his essay. Ironically, his outrageous perception of persons other than white American males accurately depicted his essay's content. It was second class.

Several more read their essays before Mr. Willard called my name. Less nervous than when I had given an oral book report in English class a week before, I stepped forward. Fear of drawing a blank, forgetting what I had planned to say, was absent. All I had to do was read my essay, one that reflected my finest writing. Just as I had rehearsed it before my bedroom mirror, I read my paper with modulated pace and volume, adding emphasis where apropos. My non-controversial endorsement of America played harmonious music in my ears.

When I finished, Mr. Willard said, "Very interesting. The prose was excellent."

As I returned to my seat, I was beaming. Mr. Willard's failure to voice any criticism indicated that unlike the ballfield where, at best, I celebrated an occasional single, I had knocked it out of the park. Consumed by my success, I barely listened as my classmates read their essays. Only when Mr. Willard called Sam's name did my detachment cease. Watching him walk forward, I feared for him, not the cliff over which his essay would take him, but the impact that would ensue.

Sam read his essay with exemplary elocution. Impeccable characterized his writing. Unfortunately, the content was...the content.

"Wow," said Mr. Willard. "You didn't pull any punches."

Rarely one to embarrass a student in front of the class, I wondered if Mr. Willard would do for Sam what Sam had failed to do in his essay, pull his punches.

"You certainly told us how you see it, Sam."

Sam shrugged.

Babbitt, who sat near me in the back of the room, leaned my way and whispered, "Hey, we tried to warn the dunce."

I voiced no reaction. Whether my face reflected sympathy for Sam, I couldn't say. I watched him return to his seat. If concern consumed him, he concealed it masterfully. I decided to keep my thoughts to myself. Later when we discussed our presentations, and no doubt we would, I would be diplomatic, complementing the quality of his writing and delivery. Both were excellent. Regarding its calamitous message, I would not opine.

***

A wise man's wisdom is...

The following day, just before the bell ending class, Mr. Willard handed back our essays. As he traversed the room, a buzz proliferated. One of the first to get his graded paper was Babbitt. I leaned over and caught a glimpse. Not surprisingly, it was replete with red marks. Despite an impressive vocabulary, Babbitt's writing enjoyed a well-deserved reputation for slipshod spelling, godawful grammar, and pitiful punctuation. At the top I could make out a red *B-*, a bit higher than I would have predicted. A handwritten red message in the margin was too small to discern.

A couple of rows ahead of me, Sam received his essay moments later. With his back to me, it was impossible to see his paper or his reaction. The absence of a visible celebration failed to prove that Sam had gotten a low grade. Never one to whine or brag, his stoic reaction was predictable. For that matter, all of us who got high marks knew better than to broadcast success. Playing it cool was the way to fit in. Appearing bookish was bait for the bullies.

Mr. Willard circled the room, back and forth. He was near the bottom of his pile when he handed me my paper. The red *C* at the top sledgehammered me. Expecting an *A*, a *B+* would have been disappointing. A grade of *C* was inconceivable. I did a double take. The horrific mark remained unchanged. I slumped in my seat, struggling to fathom the ineffable.

"How'd you do?" said Babbitt.

"Not great," I said, hiding my paper, which unlike his, lacked a plethora of red marks. How could Babbitt have gotten a *B-*, a higher grade than I. The impossibility sparked ire. I thought of Sam. My assumption that he also did poorly provided no consolation. It failed to improve my mark. I needed to speak with Mr. Willard, argue my case. But before I got ahead of myself, I had to calm my emotions, both shock and anger, and read the red-penned note that lined the right margin of my essay.

"Excellent prose. Attention to detail, grammar, and spelling is apparent."

"What the hell?" I muttered. Another glance at the top of the page instantly dashed a fatuous hope that I had misread my grade. I refocused, reading the remaining comments in the margin.

"Kudos aside, your essay disappointed me. Knowing you as I do, it was vapid." I stared at the unfamiliar adjective. Context conveyed that it was a slur. I continued reading Mr. Willard's critique. "I asked you to think hard, not pen what you thought I wanted to hear. I believe that if you reevaluate the issue, you will discover more substance than your essay displays. I know a *C*, far lower than your usual grade, must dismay you. There are two ways you can raise your mark. Feel free to rethink and resubmit your paper, in which case, I will mark it anew. Alternatively, convince me, either orally or in writing, that your essay reflects your beliefs, not hollow rhetoric. I don't mark a student down because his/her views differ from mine."

I reread the critique. I had a blueprint for earning a higher mark. Unfortunately, the critique proved the grade that had hammered me a minute earlier had hit the nail on the head. My *wonderful* essay was pointless, a sheet of 20-lb. bright white paper tarnished with a superfluity of worthless ink. It exemplified the meaningless discourse I had anticipated from Babbitt. I deserved my paltry mark. Babbitt may have been a lousy writer and a bigot, but he had penned a substantive essay, commensurate with that which was in his heart. I thanked my lucky stars that Mr. Willard had given me an opportunity to resubmit my paper. Not only would I take advantage of the chance, but in addition, the revision would be written with far more integrity. What at first blush had appeared to be a disappointing mark was a boon, an opportunity to critically examine the subject; earn a good grade; and most important, learn a valuable life lesson. I glanced at Mr. Willard. He was an excellent educator.

The bell ending class sounded. I got up from my seat and headed toward Sam. "How'd you make out?"

An abashed look on his face, he allowed me to view his paper. At the top was an *A*.

"You earned it."

"How about you?"

"*C*."

"C'mon, be serious."

I showed him my paper.

"That's not fair. You should discuss it with Willard."

I pointed at the critique.

Sam read it.

Once he finished, I said, "It rates a *C*."

Sam shrugged.

"We need to get to class," I said. We headed off in opposite directions.

***

"Money buys everything, except morality and citizens."
So said Jean Jaques Rousseau in 1750. But for some, morality and citizens mean nothing. Ergo, for them, money buys everything. For that matter, money is everything.

Even from an early age, Larry Babbitt was different. As we reached our teenage years, like the other guys, he displayed an interest in girls, not that Babbitt cut it with the fair sex. But apart from that link, Babbitt's interests forked. Where those in our group generally favored sports, cars, and goofing off, the almighty dollar consumed Babbitt. His focus, to make money, a lot of it, was evident.

Babbitt also craved recognition. An outwardly confident exterior shrouded a fragile ego. Fear of failure, the shame that accompanied it, lurked. As for academics, he displayed measured respect. He knew better than to ignore the books. Though never foremost, grades were a necessary device, albeit an inconvenient one, for achieving his goals. Apart from history, he exerted limited effort. Marks that could get him into college, one with a reputation a notch higher than Podunk, sufficed. Academic honors were never his aim, not that he possessed the intellect to win such awards. While most of the guys left their futures to the future, as early as tenth grade Babbitt began networking, making connections in the business world. Whom he got to know was paramount. Information, the kind garnered in the classroom, took a back seat. On the other hand, lessons illuminating artful angles commanded his attention.

After college Babbitt had no intention of working at an hourly rate. Even a salary would be nothing more than a temporary nuisance, a steppingstone to bigger things. As he put it, "The smart people make money watching others work." Contrary to the maxim that "talk is cheap," Babbitt viewed talk, a glib tongue, as the road to easy street. But Babbitt acknowledged that easy street would not come calling. The key was to find shortcuts, and that required unconventional methods. Robbing a bank or a Ponzi scheme fit the category, but Babbitt repudiated such rash routes. Admittedly they were roads to a fast buck, but they were laden with intolerable risks. Too often the law's unrelenting tentacles short-circuited such felonious methods, obliging the offenders to trade expensive duds for prison jumpsuits. But eschewing illegal tactics did not necessitate that one walk the straight and narrow. Shrewd schemes and clever exploitation were valuable tools. Bending and stretching rules, just far enough that they did not break, underpinned a pragmatic middle ground. Such Machiavellian machinations, akin to those invoked by wily politicians, was the wise man's method...according to Babbitt.

A methodology functioned as a compass, but financial success demanded more. Exceptional athletic, theatric, musical, or creative talent could fill the bill, but only for the extraordinary few who reached the acmes of their crafts' incredibly narrow pyramids. Babbitt was no athlete. He was clumsy. Babbitt was not destined for the stage. He had a monotone voice, two left feet, and a tin ear. Babbitt was neither brilliant nor creative. He had no great natural talent. Simply put, Babbitt was the proverbial "average Joe," in his case, "average George." As such, Babbitt needed to rely upon a different asset. That asset was capital. As Babbitt put it, "Capital begets capital."

Babbitt's family was well off, upper middle class, upper class by the standards of Grand Falls. The family resided in an imposing Victorian north of Main, among the nicest homes in Grand Falls. More than three thousand square feet, with four stories, including the finished attic and basement, the green structure with red trim, had a turret, wrap-around belly porch, and a profusion of gingerbread.

Like his big family home, Babbitt thought big. Thoughts were nice, but success required more, namely opportunity, and as noted already, capital. Babbitt's first door to financial success might have awaited adulthood had kismet not handed him an early key. Opportunity, complete with capital, came his way when, for his sixteenth birthday, his father gave him $100, what for a teen in the post-Depression years of the early 1940s constituted a veritable fortune. Babbitt wanted to immediately throw the money into the stock market. His father offered to cosign for him on a 50% margin account, provided Babbitt first educated himself about the market. While his classmates, including me, engaged in youthful frivolity, one evening per week during the second semester of junior year, Babbitt traveled to Utica where he spent two hours attending a night-school course on stock investing. The class, given by a local stockbroker, included fifteen men, lawyers, businessmen, and the like, plus a single teen, Babbitt. Even as we poked fun at him, our reactions were mixed. That we voted him Most Likely to Succeed evidenced a modicum of respect.

At the start of summer following junior year, Babbitt, with his father's backing and signature, put his acumen to work. He opened a 50% margin account. The approach, as he later described it, invoking the jargon of Wall Street, gave him leverage. He could make twice as much. The margin account, however, compounded his risk. Using his $100, he purchased $200 worth of stock, all in a small company, Electrodics, that was developing improved diodes for use in the burgeoning television industry. At $5 per share, he bought forty shares. A month after he bought the stock, the company signed a licensing agreement with Stromberg Carlson, a well-established electronics company that was entering the television manufacturing field. Electrodics shot up to $12 per share. Babbitt unloaded his stock, having parlayed his $100 into $480. By the end of September, the stock had drifted down to $8 per share. Babbitt bought back in, and again with his fathers' backing, did so on the 50% margin. That enabled him to purchase $960 worth of stock, 120 shares.

Around school Babbitt's disclosures about his stock investing were strategic. Early on we knew he had dipped his toes into the market. What he had bought and how he was faring remained his secret. If his investments went south, he could remain mum. If, on the other hand, he picked winners, he could reap the bragging rights. With his investment having mushroomed to $960, he was in the latter boat. Lured by the opportunity to boast, he detailed his success to the editor of the school newspaper who penned a laudatory story. The article labeled Babbitt as "Grand Falls High School's Teenage Tycoon." Throughout the school, students and allegedly, some teachers began tracking the price of Electrodics, calculating Babbitt's net worth. He was pocketing the money he coveted. He was grabbing the ego-stroking recognition he craved. He briefly considered a run as our homeroom's student-council representative. He quickly abandoned the idea. Reactions, a lack of popularity, demonstrated that his candidacy would wax into a humiliating fiasco, perhaps yielding a vote total of one. Still, he was free to bask in the glory of financial success.

The Monday after the article appeared in the school newspaper, lunchtime found Coop, Sam, and I seated with Babbitt in the cafeteria. Passersby spewed repeated kudos his way. The bumptious Babbitt proudly held court.

"How did you know that Electrodics was poised to shoot up?" said Susie Maier, a perky cheerleader who had stopped to take in Babbitt's spectacle.

"Well, it's like this. I analyzed the company, computed its PE – that's its price/earnings ratio – scrutinized its prospectus and examined the industry's landscape. Superimposed on that was knack, my inherent flair for spotting potential. It's that last element which separates a stock picker from a washout. It's like speed or perfect pitch. Not something you can teach. Either you got it, or you don't. Sure, training can help, but you've gotta be born with natural talent. Slow Steve ain't destined to become Jesse Owens. Tone-Deaf Debby ain't the next Dinah Shore. And paraplegic Peter ain't steppin' into Fred Astaire's shoes." Babbitt pushed out his chest.

Behind his back – Babbitt was facing Susie – Sam stuffed a finger down his throat. A nauseated expression accompanied the gesture.

I winked. Our meal had already included several portions of the insufferable braggadocio.

"You know a lot about the stock market, don't you?" said Susie.

"Hey, I'm prepared. I attended night classes in Utica. I do my homework. It's…it's like that singing I referenced. Even Bing Crosby can't croon a tune without knowing the words."

"Could you help me make money too?" said Janey Jackson, whose father was a partner in a big Utica law firm.

"Maybe." Babbitt rocked his chair back onto its hind legs.

"Next time, could you tell me before you invest?" said Janey.

Babbitt jerked back further, nearly tipping over. "You gotta be kidding. That's like asking a poker player to show you his hand in the middle of a game. But I'll tell you what, next time, after I buy, I might clue you in on my purchase." He looked Janey in the eye. "You got money to invest?"

"I've got $57 in the bank. With the little interest they pay, I'd love to try half, $25 or $30, in the stock market."

Babbitt gave her a look. "Stocks are generally sold in round lots. Twenty-five dollars…"

"What's a round lot?" said Janey.

Babbitt groaned. "If you don't know the term round lot, you're too green for the market." He looked Janey in the eye. "You wouldn't take a trigonometry test without studying, would you?"

Janey sighed. "Uh...I did that a couple weeks ago. Well, I crammed for fifteen minutes the morning of the test."

"How'd you do?" said Babbitt.

Janey bowed her head. "*D-.*"

Babbitt spread his arms wide, much the way Jesus' arms extended on the cross. But unlike Jesus, whose tilted head bore the pained mien of torture, Babbitt exhibited a derisive expression. "Need I say more?"

***

"Is not the truth, the truth?" (Shakespeare, William, *1 Henry IV*, 2.4).

Much as I detested Babbitt's pomposity, I could not deny that my own jealousy influenced my feelings. A couple days a week I was checking the price of Electrodics. As September rolled into October, Electrodics creeped upward. By late October, it was priced above $11 per share. Babbitt's investment, 120 shares, had ballooned to a value of more than $1300. In just a few months, with no work, he had made roughly half of what one of our teachers earned in an entire school year. As one whose list of career possibilities included teaching, Babbitt's success was mind boggling.

Over the ensuing month, Electrodics's stock price remained relatively constant, oscillating between a floor of $10 and a ceiling of $12. Back when its fluctuation was greater, mainly upward, I checked it regularly. Once it settled into a narrow trading range, my interest waned. I checked it about once every two weeks.

The Monday after Thanksgiving break, about ten minutes before the start of school, I was in homeroom gabbing with Speedy and Sam when Buster, who had just arrived, approached.

"Did you guys happen to check Electrodics over the weekend?"

"Nope," I said, echoing the substance of the verbal response of Speedy and non-verbal of Sam.

"Late Friday it nosedived. It's down to 5½."

"Did you say 5½?" said Sam, his eyes wide.

"Exactly," said Buster. "Another company has applied for a patent on a diode that is smaller and cheaper than Electrodics's product."

"Damn," I said. "Babbitt just got a kick in the ass."

"More like someone jammed a diode up his fat butt," said Buster.

"Serves him – " I clipped my tongue. After the way Babbitt had bragged, I couldn't help gloating. But discretion dictated that I keep my feelings to myself. I eyed the other three. I would have laid money that they too were taking delight in Babbitt's comeuppance. If so, they were wise enough to keep their thoughts to themselves.

A minute later Babbitt arrived in homeroom. Whether any of us would have sought his reaction to the news is unclear. The matter became academic the instant Babbitt came through the door. Julie Burrows, the class gossip, called to him, loud enough for everyone in homeroom to hear, "Hey Georgie, what happened to your beloved Electrodics? Looks like it tanked."

I thought Babbitt might ignore her. I miscalculated.

"Big deal. So, it dropped to 5½. My 120 shares are worth $660. Damn good return given that I invested $100. Multiplying my money more than six times in only a few months ain't half bad. In case you've got doubts, compare it to a savings bond. The government-issued security would take a half-century to generate such growth." Babbitt folded his arms across his broad, though flaccid chest.

I was thankful I had forgone the opportunity to taunt him. Apparently, there were others of the same mind. No one reacted with a quick retort. Indeed, no one said a word. As for Julie Burrows, she silently melted into her seat near the back of the room.

In the weeks that followed, Electrodics inched back upward above seven. But after the first of the year, it began a steady slide. Technology, the announcement of even smaller and more efficient diodes, turned Electrodics's product into a dinosaur. From time to time, I checked the stock price of Electrodics. Speedy and Sam did so too. Conversations demonstrated that like me, they had no sympathy for the hotshot tycoon. By the middle of February, Electrodics's stock had sunk to $.75 per share. It had waxed into a penny stock relegated to the pink sheets.

Several of The Guys were eating lunch in the cafeteria when Spike Brawn, a 230-pound bully, who had been pushed along from grade to grade despite failing numerous courses, approached our table. Brawn grabbed Babbitt's shoulder from behind. "Hey George, you still flyin' high with Electrodics?" Spike winked. "Don't think so, given that it ain't worth a buck a share." Spike jabbed his index fingers into the sides of Babbitt's head. "Looks like you got *electrode-cuted*." Spike laughed diabolically.

Babbitt flashed Spike a cheeky smile. "Sorry to rain on your pathetic parade, but I sold Electrodics weeks ago at $7 per share. Made a sweet killing." Babbitt glanced back over his shoulder. "Spike, you enjoy your lunch...that crow you'll be eating."

Spike opened his mouth but said nothing. His abashed expression spoke volumes. The huge lug slinked away.

Babbitt refocused on those of us at the table. "Seems our brawny friend flew the coop. That tough-guy stuff he used to dominate the halls in junior high doesn't fly anymore. Twenty years from now, he'll be making a nickel over minimum wage...Well, good guy that I am, maybe I'll toss him a quarter when I pass him on the street. Who knows? Perhaps, I'll even throw him a bone, hire him to simonize my car or trim the gardens of my estate."

The possibility that Babbitt had lied about selling his Electrodics stock crossed my mind. With weeks having passed as the equity had declined, he had ample time to concoct his face-saving story. I considered challenging him. Discretion, as well as undeniable futility, scrapped the idea. Regardless of whether Babbitt had sold the stock, he would insist he had. Discerning the truth was an impossibility. As to one matter, however, no doubt remained. Babbitt had made mincemeat of the big gorilla.

My attention, indeed that of the entire table, shifted as Lucy Witherspoon sauntered past in a tight red sweater. Even without the benefit of the form-fitting garment, the hot looker would have garnered our attention, not that she would have given any of us a second look...for that matter, a first look. Much as I was sure that she savored the scrutiny, with nose in the air, she feigned indifference as her hips swiveled past.

"Man would I like a piece of that," said Sam.

"You wouldn't know what to do with it," said Pokey Paulsen.

"Even if you did, it would kill you," said Speedy.

"Maybe so," said Sam. "But what a way to go." He leered at Lucy once again.

My imagination running wild, I ogled her too, echoing the sigh that one of the other guys had breathed. I briefly closed my eyes. The musing of my brain delivered a conscious smile to my face. Ungentlemanly conduct, even words, could get one into big trouble. On the other hand, thoughts, no matter how lascivious, begot no repercussions.

We finished our lunch in relative solitude. Reverberations of Lucy's performance may have played a role, though more likely the brevity of our noon break was the prime mover. Dearth of time demanded we reserve our mouths for eating, rather than talking, lest we depart for class unsated.

Soon enough the bell for the next class rang. We got up, heading off in diverse directions. As Speedy and I headed for the west-side hallway, he said, "Whad'ya think? Was Babbitt lying? Did he really sell Electrodics before it crashed? You think he still owns it?"

I weighed the evidence, something I had started to do before Lucy had rudely...no make that pleasantly, interrupted my analysis. Apart from Babbitt's claim, I had no proof one way or another. Were it somebody else, I would have given him the benefit of the doubt. The Falstaffian Babbitt – only a fortnight before we had read Shakespeare's Henry IV in English class – grandiose and slippery, had forfeited that benefit. Admittedly, I had no evidence that Babbitt was lying. I said, "I don't know."

"Me neither." Speedy shrugged. "And for that matter, I don't give a crap."

Chapter VII:
Louis (Lefty) Lucinski

Swiss mathematician and physicist Daniel Bernoulli enlightened the world how the velocity of a fluid affects its pressure. His equation untangled the concept of lift, why airplanes fly. For Bernoulli, the knuckleball, mystifying to batters, would have been easy to explain. Unfortunately, for batters, that explanation, a conundrum of unpredictability, would have compounded their confusion.

Lanky Lefty Lucinski sported a knuckleball that was Gene Kelly. It danced. Lefty's knuckleball was Houdini. It mystified. Lefty's knuckleball was Bugs Bunny. It hopped. Lefty's knuckleball was a hummingbird. It fluttered. Lefty's knuckleball was a rebellious teenager. It defied reason. And Lefty's knuckleball drove batters, catchers, and umpires to distraction. With capricious blips and dips that stupefied even Lefty, batters waved at it futilely. Catchers hated how it sullied their statistics with countless passed balls, all the while turning their hands into gnarled meat hooks. Umpires, their eyes boggled by the pitch's mercurial motion, dreaded the screams of berating fans who labeled them blind. When Lefty pitched, efforts to steal the catcher's signs vanished. Even runners on second abandoned the opportunity. Everyone, the batter included, anticipated the upcoming pitch. But such knowledge was nugatory. No one, Lefty included, could predict the Jell-o ball's capricious course.

Using Bernoulli's Principle, Mr. Korman, our physics teacher, explained why a curve ball, with its consistent rotation, curved. He likened it to how an airplane wing with its curved upper side enjoyed lift, upward air pressure, which enabled it to fly. He explained that because the knuckleball had virtually no spin, interaction between the seams of the ball and the air was an irregular variable. Prognosticating which side of the ball would feel extra pressure causing it to hop in one direction or another was futile. Lefty did not take physics. He knew no more about Bernoulli's Principle than he did about Einstein's Theory of Relativity. But Lefty knew that his knuckleball made him a star on the baseball diamond. He had hopes it would transport him from the humble ballfield behind Grand Falls High School to the splendid stadiums of the Major Leagues.

Besides baseball, Lefty had two interests, girls and cars. Academics languished lower on Lefty's list. Apart from industrial arts, the first letter of the alphabet never appeared on his report card, at least not in the column listing grades. When Lefty was not in school or on the ballfield, he could be found with his hot rod. That isn't to say that he put cars ahead of girls. The two went hand in hand. Either he was driving his vehicle, in which case, there was almost always a girl alongside in the front passenger seat, or he was fine-tuning the engine, generally with a girl handing him his tools.

Senior year, Lefty's first car, a souped-up A-Bone jalopy, had given way to a flashy hot rod. The bright yellow 1930 Buick Rumble Seat Roadster convertible, with fold-down windshield and six-cylinder overhead valve engine, gleamed as it had in a dealer's showroom fourteen years earlier. Skills and money earned at his part-time job at Gorman's Garage enabled Lefty to supercharge the flashy wheels with power and speed that dwarfed its original capacity. Around Grand Falls High School, there was no doubt who ruled the road. Few students had their own cars. Those who did, the lucky exceptions, sported unreliable heaps that were no match for Lefty's racer. He was king of the highway, as well as the diamond. Add good looks, and Lefty had it made with the girls. Rumor claimed that come spring he was an odds-on favorite to add a third level of royalty, senior-prom king.

The fall spectacular had slipped past its peak two weeks earlier. Trees whose leaves had been ablaze with color were barren. Shortly after dismissal for the day, a half-dozen of The Guys, including me were hanging out near the street that fronted the school. A red convertible with black and white lightning bolts on the sides pulled up along the curb. The driver, along with his passenger, hopped out.

"You guys know Lefty Lucinski?" said the driver, a squat, but tough-looking punk.

"What's it to you?" said Buster, who along with his teammates had a rare day off from football practice.

"Before your butt breaks, chill," said the driver, holding up a calming hand. "Word says Lucinski has a hot car. Claims he can beat anyone." The driver gestured at his vehicle. "My 1940 Chevy Street Rod, all 350 cubic centimeters of its eight cylinders, says otherwise." He displayed a trio of ten-dollar bills, splaying them like a poker hand. "These three crisp sawbucks are beggin' to test him on the quarter-mile. Tell him – assumin' he ain't chicken – he can dial me, Cliff Carter, at 2378 in Little Falls."

Sam grabbed a pen from his bookbag. "What's that phone number?"

"2378." The driver motioned to his pal to climb back into the car. As he did, he glanced back. "Thirty bucks, quarter-mile...winner takes all." He revved his engine before driving away.

"Whad'ya think?" said Speedy.

"Lefty can take him easy," said Buster.

I watched the red rod travel toward Main Street. Whatever power lay beneath the hood remained concealed. I doubted the hotshot's car could back up his mouth.

"Pretty sure Lefty is down at the gym," said Buster.

All six of us circled to the school's rear entrance, to the gymnasium, where we found Lefty firing knuckleballs at a cloth target that hung from a wood frame with broad feet. An area typifying the size of a batter's strike zone was cut from the cloth.

Buster laid out Carter's challenge for Lefty.

"You gonna take the bet?" said Speedy.

"Maybe...You fellas want in?"

"Whad'ya mean?" said Buster.

"Thirty dollars split thirteen ways among The Guys would be two dollars and...whatever each," said Lefty.

"Uh...$2.31, with three cents left over," said Sam.

The sum was no fortune, but it was hardly chicken feed. Ambivalence kept me silent.

"I've got an idea," said Buster. "Len Wright moved to Little Falls two years ago. How 'bout we contact him? See if he can feed us the inside scoop on Carter's wheels."

The idea, a device to gain a leg up on Lefty's odds of winning, drew resounding approval. Three days later, Wright reported back. He tabbed Carter's car a pig that took sixteen or seventeen seconds to turn a quarter-mile. Armed with the information, we all accompanied Lefty to a quiet road where he ran the designated distance. Three runs produced times of 14.1, 14.4 and 13.9. Lefty was a sure thing.

Except for Pete Longley, who had a family to support and could ill-afford to gamble, the other twelve of us were all in. We split the cost to cover the bet twelve ways, $2.50 each.

"Suggestion," said Speedy. "Suppose we split our winnings thirteen ways, include Pete for a $2.31 winner's share. It'll cost the twelve of us...just under twenty cents apiece."

"Why should Longley get a share?" said Cooper. "If the piker wants a piece of the pie, he should ante up."

Glares shot Cooper's way.

He shrugged. "Fine, do it however you want."

"Once we win," said Babbitt, "we should celebrate."

Arms flailing dramatically, Buster feigned an effort to maintain his balance. "Wonders never cease! George may have a good idea." He focused on Babbitt. "So, what kind of celebration?"

"We could take in a movie with popcorn, followed by burgers, fries, and soda at the diner." He turned to Sam. "How far would that set us back?"

Sam mumbled audibly, "Movie, 25 cents; popcorn, 10 cents; burger, 30 cents; fries, 20 cents; soda, 10 cents...plus a 15-cent tip. If we toss in another dime for a double-dip at Arctic Freeze...the whole shebang will run a buck-twenty each. Subtract that from our winnings, and each of us walks away with a buck and change, plus our ante."

***

Benedict Arnold confirmed that we have the horses to win.

One week after Cliff Carter had issued his challenge, we gathered on Quaker Road about five miles outside of Grand Falls. Lefty and Carter had agreed on the location during a telephone conversation in which Lefty had accepted Carter's bet. The spot, a section of Quaker Road that ran between two farms, was ideal for the race. The quiescent, straight, flat stretch of freshly paved two-lane highway punctuated at a dead end less than a half-mile beyond the finish line. Any doubts whether Lefty's car had the muscle to win had been dispelled during the intervening week. Additional practice runs had produced great times. If that weren't enough, he had fine-tuned his roadster to what he termed perfection.

On race day, apart from Buster and Cooper, who were at the starting line with Lefty, and Pete Longley, whose family responsibilities precluded participation in the high jinks, all The Guys were a quarter-mile down the road at the finish line. Directly across the highway, a cadre of Carter's buddies had gathered. The pair of polished vehicles, Carter's red 1940 Chevy Street Rod and Lefty's yellow 1930 Buick Roadster stood side by side, ready to go.

Down at the finish line, we were all abuzz. On our side we were looking forward to our movie, eats, and ice cream, plus a few shekels in our pockets. Across the way, one of Carter's supporters waved a twenty-dollar bill high in the air. "I've got four fins that says Cliff scorches that yellow piece of junk on your side of the road. Which of you birds got the guts to take my side bet?"

We looked at one another...blankly. None of us was carrying that kind of dough. For that matter, some of us didn't have that much at home or otherwise.

"Chickens!" yelled the guy who offered the side bet. He turned toward his pals. "After the race we'll have to put the fowl back into their pens." He pointed in the direction of the farmhouse on his side of the road. "They lack the – "

The rev of an engine drew everyone's attention. A moment later, the familiar roar of Lefty's sleek machine replied. On both sides of the road, the finish line hushed. All eyes transfixed on the starting line, a long par four, 440 yards away. Both red on the right and yellow on the left glistened in the bright sunshine. The starter stepped out into the center of the highway just ahead of the two cars. Both engines revved again. The starter raised a green flag. A moment later, he snapped it down. The two racers surged off the line. Lefty, the quick-reflexed athlete, got the jump.

A conscious smile lit my face. Carter's only hope, a fantastic start, had been obliterated. The outcome had been etched. Our scouting report of Carter's hot rod proved the pig had no chance to catch Lefty's hare.

Shouts of encouragement bellowed from both sides of the road. Halfway to the finish line, Lefty held the lead, though it remained slim. The duo drew closer. The lead narrowed. A question mark materialized as Lefty's lead dissolved. Certainty yielded to the impossible...ambiguity. The red hot rod roared past the yellow roadster, crossing the finish line twenty yards ahead of its competitor.

The gang across the way cheered as they raced to catch up to their victorious leader. On our side, blank looks accompanied slumped shoulders. No one said a word. How, I wondered, had Carter blown past Lefty? Doubtless, the rest of The Guys were wrestling with the inexplicable outcome.

Finally, Speedy, who had brought his stopwatch, broke the painful silence. "I don't get it," he said.

His comment drew all eyes.

Speedy held up his stopwatch, not that I was close enough to read it. He glanced at it again before shaking his head and saying, "Lefty turned the quarter-mile in 13.6. That's his fastest time yet."

"Let me see," said Babbitt, grabbing the stopwatch. He eyed the timepiece. "What the hell?"

A suspicion about what had transpired crossed my mind. Whether or not my guess was valid, one thing was certain. Like the rest of my buddies, I could forget the big celebration and anticipated pocket money. I was out $2.50. I kicked the ground.

Our group headed toward the spot where the racers had pulled off, about 150 yards down the road. Those from both teams who had been at the starting line hurried to join us. Carter's supporters gathered around him next to his car. The Guys surrounded Lefty's roadster. Still in the driver's seat, he sat crestfallen.

"Tough luck," said Buster, who had just arrived, along with Cooper.

Lefty shook his head. "It's crazy. My roadster ran like a top. I'd swear I rang up a terrific time."

"You did," said Speedy. "13.6 seconds."

Lefty went wide-eyed. "Then how the hell did I lose?"

I viewed it differently. *How did we lose?* Each of us was out $2.50. The race was about more than Lefty. I looked around, wondering if anyone else was harboring such uncharitable thoughts. Regardless, I had no intention of sharing mine. The imprudence of coming across as a self-centered sore loser kept me silent.

A rusty Ford pickup pulled up behind Carter's hot rod. Len Wright, along with a guy big enough to be a tackle in the NFL, climbed out. Carter hopped out of his rod, holding a five-dollar bill high in the air. He walked over to Wright, handing him the bill. He slipped an arm over Wright's shoulder.

Wright yelled to us. "These days I go to Little Falls High. Too bad, suckers."

Confusion explaining the loss vanished. Wright had fed us phony information about Carter's car. We had been duped.

Cooper turned his back to Carter's group. He held up a fist close to his chest. "We oughta give the bastards a taste of this."

Babbitt jerked back. "Not a fight. We...uh...gotta keep our heads."

The reaction from the gutless braggart was no surprise. Still as I looked around, his point had merit. While we numbered one or two more than Carter's crew, the big goon who accompanied Wright was a match for Sam, Speedy, and me...together. I sensed that if a fight ensued, whichever side prevailed, I would be the worse for wear. Adding injury to insult, along with financial loss, was not a route I wanted to travel.

Though no one voiced strong opposition to Cooper's call for fisticuffs, no one supported it either. Enthusiasm for a rumble, momentum sufficient to incite violence, failed to eventuate. A brief silence ensued. Lofty expectations, which had peaked five minutes earlier when the racers had left the starting line, had yielded to a dispirited debacle. Nevertheless, I found an iota of solace knowing that I was not alone, that my misery enjoyed company. The setback, because it was shared with others, was easier to bear. That said, the defeat was still a defeat. The pain was palpable, particularly in my body's tenderest nerve, the pocketbook nerve.

"Not to make it a total loss," said Buster, "we could still get ice cream at Arctic Freeze."

Admittedly, the cones – we opted for them – were a poor substitute for our pre-race expectations. The elation that would have followed a win was unmistakably absent. On the bright side, the ice cream mitigated our letdown. And too, from my standpoint, the treats were an exceptional alternative to a rumble.

***

A hopping knuckleball is a ticket aboard the train to fame and glory.

Seated with Speedy in the small grandstand behind home plate, I watched Lefty take the mound against the Herkimer High Magicians. Several seats to our left, one row below, sat Rip Ryman, scout for the Cleveland Indians. Ryman had served a brief stint in the Major Leagues, hurling a meager seventeen innings, way back in 1907. Upon learning that the scout would attend the game, we had unearthed his statistics, a lifetime record of one win and two losses with an ERA of 6.23. Admittedly, the paltry numbers were nothing to crow about, but to impressionable high school students, anyone who had pitched in the Majors warranted celebrity status. While Ryman had come to scout Lefty, we were scouting the former major leaguer, hoping for an autograph.

The game was Lefty's third start. In his two previous outings, he had allowed only one run. That occurred in the former and was unearned. In the latter he had hurled a no-hitter. With Lefty on the mound, our own Grand Falls Eagles took the field in the top of the first. The leadoff hitter for the Magicians, a diminutive kid, stepped to the plate. After watching two strikes sail past with the bat on his shoulder, he swung and missed the third. The next batter struck out as well. The third, well over six feet with shoulders twice his trim waist, strode to the plate. He fouled the first pitch straight back, suggesting he could get around on Lefty. Whether he could make solid contact was another matter. The second pitch dipped into the dirt, bouncing past the catcher all the way to the backstop. A borderline called strike on the outside corner brought the count to 1-2. The batter banged his spikes with his bat dislodging any dirt. He dug in. Everyone, the batter included, anticipated a knuckleball. Where it was going, no one could predict. Lefty stared in at home plate. He shook off the catcher's sign. He shook off another before finally nodding.

Speedy whispered in my ear. "It's a pretense. He has the batter guessing. It'll be the knuckleball."

Lefty wound up and launched his pitch. The batter stepped forward with his left foot, unleashing a staggering swing. The offering, a knuckleball, sailed into the catcher's glove as the batter, losing his balance, crumpled to the ground in a heap. As he climbed from the dirt and slinked away from home plate, Lefty jogged to the home dugout, accompanied by the crowd's chant, "Lefty, Lefty, Lefty!"

Speedy and I leaned forward, attempting to eavesdrop as Ryman spoke to Lefty's father, who sat alongside. Others nearby were trying to hear as well. Owing to the din of the crowd, only those immediately adjacent had any chance. I asked the man just to my left if he was able to hear. He shook his head before leaning forward and tapping another man, one row ahead.

A minute later, the man to my immediate left said, "Ryman says he likes what he sees…that Lefty has great stuff."

The game progressed. Lefty continued to mow down the Herkimer hitters.

"You know why these guys call themselves the Magicians?" said Speedy.

I shrugged.

"One after another, they magically disappear."

I laughed, slapping Speedy on the back.

Inning after inning, the pattern continued. Lefty made mincemeat of the Magicians. As the top of the seventh, the final inning, commenced, Lefty was spinning a one-hitter, a broken-bat single that had gone halfway down the first baseline. Lefty had advanced his own cause with a double that had driven in one of four Grand Falls runs. Already with a dozen strikeouts, Lefty closed out the game, sandwiching two more KOs around an easy, unassisted ground out to first.

In the stands our eavesdropping continued. But once again, we had to wait until the man next to us passed on third-hand information. "Ryman labeled Lefty 'an excellent prospect.' He thinks the Indians might sign him to a farm team straight out of high school. Once he has been seasoned, he might get a shot at the Majors. Knuckleballers are valuable. With less wear and tear on their arms, they can pitch more often, both starting and relief. Because their pitches are unpredictable, they're effective against batters on both sides of the plate. Managers like that. Less need to use the hook." The man started to get up but stopped. "I assume you both go to Grand Falls High."

"We do," said Speedy.

"Have Lefty autograph a baseball for you. Down the road, it could be valuable." The man got up and left.

"Wow," I said. "In a couple years, Lefty may be pitching in the big house."

"Prison?"

I shot Speedy a look. Certain though I was that he knew what I meant, I said, "The big house, the one that Ruth built, Yankee Stadium. Or maybe, the Indians' home, Cleveland Municipal Stadium."

Speedy's brow furrowed.

"Hey, a big-league scout just labeled Lefty 'an excellent prospect.' Who knows? He might be a future Hall of Famer."

"Jeez, don't get carried away."

"Hey, you never know," I said. "A decade from now, we may be saying we knew Lefty when."

Speedy shook his head.

"What? You disagree?"

"Yeah. We're not just anybody. We're members of The Guys. Ten years from now, we can say we knew him then...and *we know him now*."

On the last point, I was less sanguine than Speedy. If Lefty made it big, he was apt to cultivate a new circle of friends: baseball players, movie stars, and the like. Knowing Lefty, high school pals like Speedy and me would be akin to an old baseball glove, discarded and forgotten.

***

In the hand of a golden arm, a baseball can be more powerful than a gun. But during times of war, convincing Uncle Sam of the notion poses a problematic issue. Even if one does, aspirations for fame and glory may explode. Uncle Sam may commandeer the golden arm, utilizing it to hurl grenades.

Around the hallways of Grand Falls High, Lefty Lucinski was a big man on campus, arguably the biggest. A dozen colleges, one as far away as Florida, had exhibited interest in the southpaw. However, none from the Ivy League had come calling. Lefty's grades barely met the standards of the least selective schools.

Lefty hardly fit the mold of the proverbial dumb jock, which, like its counterpart, the dumb blond, was often nothing more than a convenient stereotype. That said, standardized tests evidenced that Lefty, a master mechanic, was not the swiftest piston in the engine. Ability wise, he fell somewhere in the middle. But his performance in the classroom tended lower than his potential. Teachers termed him lazy. The description was a half-truth, its veracity a function of the endeavor. Lefty maintained a sharp dichotomy, separating that which he liked and disliked. He attacked the former with intensity and persistence. The latter enjoyed short shrift. Schoolwork fell into the latter category. Baseball and cars occupied the former.

In the classroom Lefty devoted more time to girls, snacks, and naps than participation. Though he handed in most of his homework, he employed indecorous methods for completing assignments. Copying from another student topped the list. Plagiarism was popular too. Occasionally, one of Lefty's girls did it for him. Seldom were his submissions purely the fruits of his own labor.

Even when there was no baseball practice, once the dismissal bell rang, Lefty raced to the gym where he engaged in a demanding exercise routine, followed by a lengthy stint hurling knuckleballs at the baseball team's catcher. When his human backstop was unavailable, his homemade mock-up of the typical strike zone substituted. Immediately after his workout session, he gobbled down a peanut butter and jelly sandwich and drove his souped-up Roadster to Gorman's Garage where he worked part time. Well after nine, when the lights went out by the gasoline pumps and the establishment closed to customers, Lefty could be found polishing his Roadster or tinkering with its engine. Around Grand Falls High some teased him that he came directly from the garage to school without going home for the night. Few would have had the courage to voice the contrived accusation, were it not apparent that Lefty welcomed the quirky reputation.

An inordinately warm, late-October evening inspired Speedy and me to ride our bikes to Arctic Freeze, a chance to savor a final ice cream cone before the iconic stand shuttered for the season. We might have driven, but our junior licenses barred us from driving after dark. As for taking the family car without permission, having done that once, reprising the deed had no chance. Convincing Speedy would have been impossible, not that I wanted to embark on such a cretinous course. Lunacy had its limits.

Once we arrived at Arctic Freeze, we purchased our favorites, mint chocolate chip for Speedy and coffee for me. I was relishing my sweet treat when I noticed that Speedy bore a disquieted look, atypical of what accompanied licks of his beloved flavor. "Something wrong with your cone?"

"No." His face bore a surprised look. "What prompted that?"

"You look as if you're eating rancid sardines."

"Oh, that. No link to the ice cream. I was distracted, contemplating the day after tomorrow. I gotta give an oral book report in Shorter's class. God, I despise public speaking. I'd rather eat those rancid sardines you referenced. For that matter, I'd rather square off against the feral hyena that attacked the hero of my book. Anything is better than an oral presentation."

Instinct cajoled me to tell him it would be easier than he anticipated. Instead, I licked my cone. If I felt as Speedy, silence would be preferable to a vacuous platitude minimizing my apprehension.

Once we finished our cones, we pedaled for home. As we approached Gorman's Garage, located on Main a short distance from Arctic Freeze, Speedy said, "My back tire is low. Mind if we stop for air?"

We pulled into the service station where Lefty was pumping gas and washing a customer's windshield. Speedy filled his tire. I topped off both of mine. The car that Lefty had been servicing drove off. He came our way.

"What's up guys?"

"Not much. Just a visit to Arctic Freeze," said Speedy.

Lefty shook his head. "Some enjoy the easy life, while others slave tirelessly."

I assumed Lefty was kidding, but unsure, I suppressed a sarcastic retort.

"I stopped off at home before coming here after school," said Lefty. "My mailbox contained good news and bad news. On the bright side, the University of Delaware offered me a baseball scholarship, a full ride…tuition, plus room and board."

"That's great," said Speedy.

"Unfortunately, my draft board sent me a belated birthday present. They classified me 1-A. Invited me for a physical."

Unlike most of us seniors who would not turn eighteen until the next calendar year, Lefty had recently hit the magic number.

"You think they'll yank you out of school?" I said.

Lefty shrugged. "From what I've heard, it's a local issue. It depends upon the bodies available to fill the local quota. Draft boards have a bunch of rules that tell them who to take first. Single males, not in school, with no dependents top the list. How it goes after that, you got me. My old man claims that rich kids with political connections can beat the system. Don't know if that's true, but it wouldn't surprise me." Lefty shook his head. "If things were different, I'd be as willing as the next guy to grab a gun and go. But damn, does a war have to screw up my chances for a college scholarship or better yet, a possible contract with a signing bonus? Not fair."

Some would have condemned Lefty for viewing the universe as if he were at its center. With all the lives lost fighting to preserve freedom, there was ample basis to pillory him. Top major leaguers had stowed their gloves and spikes. They had voyaged across the oceans to battle Germany and Italy in Europe and Japan in Asia. Much as the point had merit, I was in no position to voice it. If I were in Lefty's shoes, my attitude would mirror his. Duty would demand I go. No way would I be eager. I was thankful to be among the youngest in the class, that more than a year separated me from my eighteenth birthday.

"If you do get drafted," said Speedy, "you think they might put you on a military baseball team?"

"Doubt it," said Lefty. "From what I've heard, that's common in peacetime, but not war, especially a world war. And from what I've seen in the movie newsreels, famous people are flying the planes and filling the trenches…alongside the no counts."

Unlike a minute before when self-reproach justified my failure to call Lefty out, his latest remark begged castigation. I might have if Lefty, rather than being an esteemed jock, were a geek…or among the "no counts" he had referenced. I opted for silence. So too, did Speedy. His failure to speak, contrary to mine, bore ample justification, a systemic structure of intolerance dating back more than three centuries.

Chapter VIII:
Samuel (Doc) Porter

Some trips around the world are free of fettering strings. Some take sojourners over the falls. Unfortunately, such trips are perilous. Those who take them risk calamitous fates.

Sam and I were hanging out in his backyard on Waverly Place, spinning our yo-yos. Like me, my long-time pal's growth spurt came later than many of our counterparts. As a result, we were always among the shorter boys in our class. Sam was neither handsome nor homely. With a humble nature and nondescript face, including brown eyes, ordinary nose, and narrow mouth, he termed himself the frontrunner if ever our class bestowed an award for most likely to go unnoticed.

More than a year had passed since we had played with our yo-yos. Had we been in a location where our schoolmates could observe us, the playthings would have been stowed. Only a high school senior soliciting ridicule would be caught wielding the puerile toy.

Back when Sam and I were in junior high, we regularly challenged one another to yo-yo contests. Besides performing the usual tricks, Half Moon, Loop d'Loop, Over the Falls, Around the World, and Rock the Cradle, we developed combinations for which we coined our own names. A favorite was Rock the World. After Rocking the Cradle, we would go directly into a full circle of Around the World. The trick demanded agile maneuvering, plus a perfectly tuned yo-yo with just enough twists in the string that it could sleep long enough to complete the two tricks.

"I've still got it," said Sam, punctuating a successful Rock the World. His crowing disregarded the fact that the feat only ensued after a half-dozen failed attempts.

"Congratulations. Try celebrating your success beyond your yard's shrubs. Unlike the jocks who get letters for their sweaters, not to mention the hottest chicks, you'll be showered with taunts."

"Well, my cousin – he graduated Columbia and is working for IBM – says that we'll have the last laugh. According to him, most of the cool guys from high school wind up in blue-collar jobs. Geeks like us, the kind they mocked in school, are their managers."

I launched my black Duncan Tournament straight out, snapping it back – Half Moon. I said, "You feel closer to that management job or your yo-yo days?"

Sam jerked the string on his sleeping yo-yo, causing it to rewind. He shot me a look. "What prompted that?"

"You painted a picture of us in management. But here we are playing with yo-yos."

Sam shrugged.

I waited a moment. "You didn't answer my question, whether we're closer to management or yo-yo spinning days."

Sam briefly eyed his Royal Monarch. "Given the current scene, I'd say it's obvious. But in case you have doubts, simple arithmetic confirms it. We're what…maybe three years past the prime of our yo-yo playing childhood. On the other hand, management is much further away. Take yourself. You have four years of college on the horizon. After that you're likely to get an entry-level job. You'll have to work your way up. Management is probably a decade away. In my case, assuming I go to medical school, the way I've always planned, what with internship and residency after my education, it'll be longer yet before I'm in charge of anything."

"So, we're still kids. Right?"

"I guess so." Sam knocked my yo-yo string, causing my sleeping Duncan to go awry. "Where the hell are you headed with all your crazy questions?"

The inquiry forced me to tackle the unsettling issue that was driving my probe. "Given that we're still kids, why are they ready to ship us off to war? Me in about a year, and you, sooner yet."

"I don't know. Maybe it's a matter of numbers. They need bodies."

"Dead ones?"

"C'mon," said Sam. "You know what I was saying. Don't hard time me, not when I'm trying to respond to your inane jabber."

His remark had too much efficacy to quibble. "Fine. Explain this. The law says we're too young to vote until we're twenty-one. Why then can we be drafted at eighteen?"

Sam shrugged. "Maybe because voting takes judgment. Being drafted, on the other hand, requires nothing. Standing at attention and looking stupid is sufficient." A smirk tacked an exclamation point onto his glib reply.

"Then tell me this, Mr. Smart Ass. What about the gun they give you? Learning how to use it is hardly child's play."

"Whad'ya mean? Even a five-year-old knows how to pull a trigger." Sam laughed uproariously.

I gave him a shove. "Be serious."

"I don't know. The politicians in Washington establish the rules, often without rhyme or reason. According to my father, much of the time, it's because some lobbyist is paying them off." Sam looked me in the eye. "All these questions. You must be headed somewhere...Where, I have no idea."

I cast my yo-yo, doing one of our best combos, Half Moon, followed by Around the World. All the while I debated whether to be up front. Finally, I said, "I'm scared."

"Scared?" Sam jerked his yo-yo up into his hand. "Of what?"

"The war...being drafted...shot at." The opaque but attentive expression that greeted my eyes induced me to continue. "That newsreel we saw at the movies last week got me thinking, especially at night when I'm alone in bed. Those soldiers in their foxholes taking fire in the mud and cold of France...I can't get it out of my head, knowing I could be in that foxhole a year from now...I'm not ready for it."

"If it's any consolation, you've got company. But I assume they'll get us ready...basic training...before they ship us off to the war front."

That Sam was afraid provided solace, but only a little. I said, "Gimme your best guess, the odds that we'll get drafted."

Sam heaved a sigh. "Ninety-some percent."

The estimate exceeded what I had conjectured. Consolation acquired a moment earlier evaporated. My fear elevated to a new high. "So, all our plans for college and beyond are pie in the sky?"

"No. We'll still be young with plenty of time for them after we come back."

"What if we don't come back? Many don't."

Sam flipped his yo-yo, spinning it around his hand doing Over the Falls. As it looped back, he fumbled the catch. "If that happens, we won't need to worry about college or the rest of our plans."

"Yeah...we won't need to worry about anything." The cogent point left me empty. It also tied my stomach into a knot. The misery associated with such vexation was all too familiar. Countless times I had grappled with a dreadful tangle in my yo-yo string, one so calamitous that the twine needed to be cut and deposited in its grave, the dumpster.

***

Amidst a pile of junk, riches sometimes emerge. Most of the treasures are concrete. Occasionally, intangible concepts, unexpected abstract notions, materialize amidst dross. Such nuggets can be sweeter than the most mouthwatering ice cream.

Armed with the Porter family wheelbarrow and my rusty red wagon, Sam and I nervously rang the first-floor doorbell of our initial target on Fairlawn Street. Following considerable debate, we had selected the residential thoroughfare for two reasons: It was densely populated with two-family homes set on narrow lots. It terminated only two hundred yards from the salvage drop-off point.

A school assembly the day before had inspired our venture. Unlike many earlier lessons of responsibility, the assembly's message had struck a chord. People everywhere were supporting the war effort. Women were staffing the factories that men had vacated as they battled on far-off fronts. Senior citizens had turned flower gardens into victory gardens, filled with all manner of vegetables. Children were collecting cooking grease in cans. Sam and I were on a mission, helping the nation fend off Axis evil.

A woman in her thirties opened the door, only halfway. "Yes," she growled with a jaundiced eye.

"My friend and I," said Sam, "are collecting scrap metal, tin cans, rubber, and the like for the war effort."

"Good for you." She swung the door wide open. "My youngest brother is in Europe defending our freedom. I'm all for anything we can do to support our troops. You said rubber...right?"

"Yup," said Sam.

"I got a pair of old tires out back in the garage. Bring your wagon around and I'll meet you there." She gestured to the near side of the house. A minute later she came out the back door and opened the unattached garage. She pointed at two tires leaning against the wall. "They're all yours."

We loaded the tires into my wagon.

"Could you use an old axle?" She pointed toward the corner.

"Sure," I said.

"Add it to your collections."

Sam and I put the axle into his wheelbarrow.

"Thank you, Ma'am," I said, with Sam echoing the sentiment. We started to leave.

"Really nice what you boys are doin'. Back in the roarin' twenties, when I was young, the older generation called us lazy and spoiled. Not that way today. Young people, still in their teens, are carryin' guns, riskin' their lives to save freedom. And here on the home front, school kids like you – I assume you boys are in school..."

We nodded.

"Admirable that you and your generation are lendin' a hand. The more who join the – " The woman put her hand over her mouth. "Last thing you boys need is a lecture, not when you're doin' such good work. My prattle slowin' you down doesn't help. On your way, and good luck."

We thanked the woman. Once we took the wagon around to the front, we rang the doorbell for the upstairs flat. The elderly man who answered, eager to help, gave us several tin cans.

We continued up one side of the street. Though many greeted us with a wary eye, once they learned our purpose, most were happy to help. Some who had no available salvage materials apologized for their inability to contribute. One woman followed up such regrets by offering fifty cents.

Sam eyed me blankly.

His look echoed my thought. I said to the woman, "I'm not sure whether the salvage place wants us collecting money." We thanked her and went on our way.

As we moved on to the next house, Sam said, "Should we have taken her contribution?"

"Probably, but before we do, maybe we should check at the salvage office." I pointed at our collections. "The wagon and wheelbarrow are nearly full. Once we do these next few houses, we can unload at the office. While there, we can check on cash contributions."

Several minutes later, we arrived at the office. We got the okay on cash and headed out for another load. Early reticence, attributable to shyness, as well as a lack of door-to-door experience, had diminished. In less than an hour, confidence had grown.

"This salvage-collecting thing isn't half bad," I said. "Easier than I expected."

"Yeah, it's almost fun," said Sam.

"Fun?" I furrowed my brow. "Let's not get carried away. It's not baseball or a cone at Arctic Freeze."

"True...but knowing we're doing something to help the country feels good. The praise and thanks we get from strangers is rewarding."

Sam's comment sparked an insight that had previously escaped me. The positive reactions we had received had influenced my feelings. Had potential donors been grouchy and told us to get lost, the experience, my emotions, would have differed.

Over a four-hour stretch, Sam and I covered six streets, filling the wheelbarrow and wagon four times. It was nearly 1:30, and we had just unloaded.

"I'm starved," said Sam.

"Me too. Suppose we call it a day, head home, and eat."

"You have any money with you?"

I reached into my pocket and pulled out two nickels and three pennies. I displayed my thirteen cents.

Sam checked his pockets, producing twenty-two cents.

I read his mind, at least I thought I did. I gestured at the salvage office. "Okay…if you can part with twenty-two, I can donate thirteen."

"Make it seventeen for me and eight for you."

Unable to comprehend his mystifying mathematics, I tilted my head with a contrived look of puzzlement.

"That'll leave us each with five cents, enough for a single dip at Arctic Freeze."

With my stomach growling, the image of the treat, better than a nourishing lunch, brought a conscious smile to my face. "You know," I said, "contrary to public opinion, now and again, you have a good suggestion."

Sam shrugged. "Damn. Wish I could say the same for you."

Another time, I would have met the dig with more trash talk. Instead, I directed my brain to ice cream. We returned to the salvage office where we deposited our excess change into a large donation jar on the counter.

Sam displayed the nickel he had saved. His tone abashed, he said, "We each kept five cents for an ice cream."

"After donating your time, adding your own money to the cause…mighty generous." The man reached into his pocket and drew out two nickels. "You've each earned a double dip. Second one is on me."

I glanced at Sam. Once again, I read his face, this time correctly.

"The cost of a second dip would be better spent on the cause," said Sam.

"You sure?" said the man.

"Absolutely," I said.

The man reached over to the donation jar. He dropped his two nickels into the cap's slot. "This is what America is about. I fought in World War I. Still have shrapnel in my bum left leg. The greed of the 1920s, followed by the Depression, had me wondering if our country had lost its way. Seeing today's soldiers and young people like the two of you justifies the sacrifices of my generation." The man looked us each in the eye. "You boys enjoy those ice cream cones. You've more than earned them."

***

Winning is wonderful. Losing is painful. But now and then, losing is as rewarding as winning...arguably better.

It was autumn 1944. All nine homerooms in our 224-student high school nominated two classmates to compete in the annual general knowledge contest. Our homeroom chose Sam Porter and Mary Wheeler. Sam, the odds-on favorite for class valedictorian, was a no-brainer. Mary and I tied for second choice. But with one male on the team and Mary, the smartest girl in our homeroom, she was an excellent selection. And the truth be known, regardless of sex, she was the better pick. An avid reader, she had more fact-based knowledge than I. She may have been smarter as well.

Because we were both in accelerated classes, she and I had most of our classes together. A brunette with a nice figure, the understated Mary drew scant attention. Her round, wire-framed glasses, common before women's styles became bolder after World War II, imparted a studious look. Some stamped her as plain. I disagreed. Her ordinary exterior mantled a lovely young lady, one with class.

In lieu of last period, the entire high school gathered in the auditorium for the contest. A rivalry, decreasingly homeroom based, had evolved. To be sure, individual bragging rights garnered attention, but the competition among the three grades had acquired precedence. Not since 1939 had an underclassman prevailed. To the seniors, having a junior, or God forbid, a tenth grader, a callow freshman, emerge victorious would be a badge of infamy. Preserving the streak was paramount.

And so, with that perspective abiding, the contest commenced. Principal Armstrong read the first fifteen questions aloud. The contestants wrote their answers on a sheet of paper, while we in the audience listened and silently played along. Many of us kept our own score, albeit to seek a meaningless claim to fame that we beat the best. Once the fifteen questions were completed, the scores of those on stage were tallied. The six high scorers, along with any ties, advanced to the finals. Both Mary and Sam qualified. So too, did another senior, Zelda Bushmeier, two juniors, and one freshman. One by one, the finalists were asked questions which they answered aloud. Two misses resulted in elimination.

By the time the fourth round ended, three of the six, the lone freshman, one of the juniors, and Mary Wheeler, were out. In the fifth round, Ellen Turcotte, the remaining junior, suffered her second miss when she identified Andrew Jackson, rather than Martin Van Buren, as the nation's eighth president. We seniors, guaranteed our bragging rights, cheered her mistake.

"We'll have none of that," barked Principal Armstrong. "We applaud correct answers; wrong ones demand decorum."

With the primary goal, a senior victory, ensured, the competition came down to individual bragging rights, a battle between Zelda and Sam. With no misses to Zelda's one, Sam was a heavy favorite. I silently booked him at ninety percent.

The introverted Zelda, short and plump with coke-bottle glasses, responded correctly with George Gershwin, when asked for the composer of *Rhapsody in Blue*.

Principal Armstrong shifted to Sam. "What river did Julius Caesar cross when he uttered the famous words, *"Alia acta est…*The die is cast?"

For Sam, a fellow fourth-year Latin student, the question was a gift. Second year Latin had been all about Caesar's Gallic Wars. The crossing of the Rubicon was notorious.

"Caesar crossed...the Tiber River," said Sam.

I disbelieved my ears.

"That's incorrect," said Principal Armstrong. "It was the Rubicon."

"Oh, that's right," said Sam, shaking his head.

"The competition is now tied," said Principal Armstrong. "Both Miss Bushmeier and Mr. Porter have one wrong answer. The next error will determine the champion.

Principal Armstrong focused on Zelda. "What document of rights was agreed to by King John at the Runnymede Meadow in 1215?"

Zelda was briefly pensive. "The...uh...Magna Carta?"

I had no idea if the noncommittal answer was right, and Principal Armstrong was slow to provide confirmation.

"Miss Bushmeier...your answer is...correct!"

The pressure moved to Sam, as did Principal Armstrong's attention.

"Mr. Porter, tell us, who is the winningest pitcher in baseball history with a total of 511 victories?"

The question was Brer Rabbit in the briar patch. Just a couple days before, Sam and I had again been talking about Cy Young's incredible record, that it would never be broken. Pitchers did not pitch often enough to do so.

Sam remained mute.

His delayed response, a pretense of searching his memory, may have fooled the throng, but not me. After the assembly, I would give him the raspberries, mocking his phony dramatics.

"Your answer, Mr. Porter."

"Uh...Walter Johnson."

Walter what? I did a double take. The question was as easy as if Sam had been asked his own name. What was going on?

"Incorrect," said Principal Armstrong. "We have a winner! Miss Zelda Bushmeier!" Following a round of applause, he handed Zelda a small box. "I present you with this Parker Pen, emblematic of your victory in this year's general knowledge competition. Congratulations." He shook her hand before turning back to the audience. "You are all dismissed for the day."

I got up from my seat and headed to the rear of the auditorium. I heard a girl just behind me say, "Can you believe that? Zelda Bushmeier took top prize…Guess she's the best."

I checked the urge to dispute the assessment. Doing so might have provided visceral satisfaction, but it would have made me look small. I exited the auditorium and waited by the doors for Sam.

A minute later, when he arrived, I grabbed his arm. "What the hell is going on?"

"Hey, you win some and you lose some."

"Bull crap! Maybe you can fool everyone else, but not me. Missing the Rubicon was implausible. Cy Young? Impossible!"

Sam gave me a blank look.

I shook my head. "You're not talking to Johnny Came Yesterday. You and I spoke about Cy Young's 511 wins only two days ago. You knew the answer. You've known it for years."

Sam looked around where lots of students were milling about. He whispered, "Let's go outside. I'll explain."

Once we were away from the building and by ourselves, Sam said, "Up there on stage, when it came down to Zelda and me, I got to thinking. Over the years I've gotten several academic and citizenship awards. On the other hand, Zelda…invisible Zelda has never won anything. Recognition, she's never had any. In class, she sits there quietly. Friends, she has few, if any. Once it came down to the two of us, and I knew that senior pride had been assured, mixed feelings stirred. Yes, I wanted to win…but I wanted Zelda to win even more." Sam bowed his head. "I know. I was wrong to throw the contest, but…" He looked me in the eye. "I'm sure you think I'm a jerk."

I shook my head. "Just the opposite. I'm proud of you." I looked him in the eye. "Sam Porter, you're one helluva guy."

PART II

Chapter IX

History is a collection of mundane facts of negligible consequence. The proposition furnishes a convenient reason to treat the past as irrelevant. However, examination of those purportedly boring facts yields remarkable insights about the present. Just as an individual learns from his/her accomplishments and mistakes, especially the latter, political entities of all types acquire understanding and vision from the past. Ignoring that which has preceded is a formula for preserving the ignorance of infancy and duplicating the errors of earlier eras.

As I entered Mr. Willard's American History class on the Wednesday before Thanksgiving, I had little desire to contemplate the pros and cons of Reconstruction, the topic we had begun discussing the day before. My thoughts revolved around the upcoming four-day recess. Images of the wonderful turkey-day dinner, especially my mother's gloriously gooey, sinfully sweet pecan pie, danced in my head. Plans of how I would spend the extended leisure time supplanted any thoughts of events following the Civil War. Little did I imagine that the class, the last of the shortened school day, would impact the balance of my life.

Four minutes earlier, the bell for the passing of classes had rung. Ordinarily with Mr. Willard, who ran a tight ship, we were seated and quiet when the ensuing bell sounded and our class period commenced. But pre-vacation restlessness found us milling about the room. Jabbering groups dotted the normally disciplined space.

"Settle down. Get to your desks," said Mr. Willard. "Let's get started."

Alongside the windows a group of girls gabbing and giggling ignored the instruction. Two guys tossing a pen back and forth, playing keep-away from its owner, Benny Morse, continued their game. I headed to my desk, but with the security of widespread disobedience, spurned my seat. I soaked in the intriguing scene. Much like toddlers, we were testing authority. A united effort could alter standards. Like the start of English class, perhaps American History could be delayed a minute or so each day. The chance for a small gain, a tiny erosion of institutional power, had presented itself. Such an opportunity was too appealing to forgo.

I glanced at Mr. Willard, surprised that the master disciplinarian had not backed his original call with a more decisive demand for compliance. Instead, he strolled to his file cabinet in the corner, where he removed some paper. He headed down the first row, placing a sheet on each desk. As he reached the second row, Lucy Smoltz said, "What's this?"

"The paper on which you'll write your answers to today's test."

His response grabbed the full attention of the class. It launched me into panic mode. Eager for the Thanksgiving hiatus, I had neglected to read the homework assignment from the day before. That many of my classmates were likely in the same boat offered little solace. An *F* averaged into my grade would drop it dramatically.

"You never warned us about a test today," said Denny Golden.

Numerous others echoed Golden's reaction.

"Astute observation," said Mr. Willard. "But where is it written that I'm prohibited from giving an unannounced test? I don't recall seeing it in the Constitution...The same goes for the Bible."

"But you've always told us in advance," said Mary Lou Kaine.

"That I have. And speaking of the past, you've always been in your seats and ready to work within seconds after the bell. But not today. Even when I chided you, your arrant disregard persisted." Mr. Willard gave us the slow once over.

"I'll tell you what. Against my better judgment, I'll give you a second chance. No test today – "

A cheer pervaded the room. It lasted barely two seconds. Mr. Willard's halting hand, decisively raised, delivered silence.

"I'm granting you a reprieve today. But that reprieve comes with conditions. Full cooperation today, and henceforth, you will always be in your seats and quiet the moment the bell sounds. And to erase any risk of confusion, understand that if you're not, a pop quiz, a challenging one, will ensue."

Like my classmates, I breathed a sigh of relief, thankful the unexpected test had been scrapped. At that moment, I failed to recognize Mr. Willard's canniness. Time evinced it. For the balance of the school year, we were in our seats, ready to work, the instant the bell rang. When anyone delayed, others attacked the transgressor, demanding immediate compliance, lest we face a test. Never again did Mr. Willard need to police our conduct at the start of class. He had a roomful of dedicated deputies. Hindsight provided me with a better perspective regarding the episode. On the pre-Thanksgiving Day when we had avoided the test, we students had celebrated. We had won the battle, at least we thought we had. The truth be known, Mr. Willard had won the war, and for that matter, the battle as well. As for the wonderful opportunity for us to usurp a scintilla of our teacher's power, it had been a figment of my imagination. We students were playing tic-tac-toe. Mr. Willard was engaged in chess…in three dimensions.

The class that day continued…with the full cooperation of everyone. Mr. Willard said, "Let us leave Reconstruction for next week. Another matter, which will become part of this course's curriculum and bears significance to your lives, merits discussion. I'm referring to the war in which the world is currently engaged. Many of you have relatives serving in the armed forces. Some, fighting overseas, will not be at your Thanksgiving tables. By this time next year, some of you will also be fighting on behalf of our nation. Understandably, that concerns you. So, let us address the matter, but as we do, keep in mind that your comments may be consequential to your classmates. Accordingly, please voice them with due respect.

With that admonition, let me begin the discussion by asking how many of you anticipate enlisting in the military?"

A few hands shot up immediately. From my seat in the back, it was apparent that many were interested in the reactions of their neighbors. Several more hands gradually rose. A quick count indicated that from our class of twenty-four, seven males and one female expected to enlist.

"We thank you for your willingness to serve," said Mr. Willard. "While the importance of such service is in some respects self-evident, would any of you wish to voice your personal feelings or views regarding such service?"

Compared to the questions that Mr. Willard normally asked, this one appeared easy.

"Yes, Charles," said Mr. Willard, who called us by our given names, never nicknames.

Seeing Speedy, who despised public speaking, volunteer, might have surprised me, but not given the subject. He had strong feelings about the war. He had voiced them to me numerous times. Few questions asked in class would be easier for him.

"Germany and Japan want to dominate the world. America didn't seek this fight. Japan brought it to us when they bombed Pearl Harbor. They attacked our nation and our democratic way of life. Germany has charged through Europe crushing Poland, Czechoslovakia, Belgium, and France. The Axis must be stopped."

"Does anyone disagree?" said Mr. Willard.

Not surprisingly, no one raised a hand. If by chance someone disagreed, which was unlikely, he/she remained mum. Only a masochist begging ridicule would have put such unpatriotic misgivings on public display.

"Let me modify my question," said Mr. Willard. "Even accepting that our nation needs to stop German and Japanese aggression, does anyone believe that fascism is preferable to democracy?"

Once again, I assumed that no one would take the bait. My expectation proved wrong. Larry Babbitt raised his hand. A smattering of hisses and boos, plus a cry of traitor, greeted him.

Mr. Willard moved his disapproving eyes over the class. "Either my admonition that we will treat everyone with respect has slipped your minds or worse yet, you've chosen to ignore it. Whatever the case, alter your thinking. Courteous and constructive criticism is welcome. Deriding others, either before or after they have expressed their views, will not be tolerated.

I was happy to give Babbitt the floor, watch him commit rhetorical suicide, dig himself an inevitable grave. He may have been one of The Guys, but he was not one of my favorite guys. His comeuppance would cost me no sleep.

"So, tell us Lawrence, why do you believe that fascism is preferable to democracy?"

"First off, understand, I support America. I despise Hitler and his Nazi Germany. My cousin is fighting for this country in Europe. But like numerous noted Americans, I believe that democracy will lead to industrial socialism. Democracy breeds political parties and leaders whose compass is a quest for votes and ultimately, power. They pander to voters who make outrageous demands. All kinds of benefits are enacted. Ever increasing inefficiency, as well as bureaucratic hurdles, creep into any democratic system. Sooner or later, these burdens cause the system to collapse of its own inefficient weight."

The cogency with which Babbitt had articulated his view stunned me. Even so, I was certain he was wrong. He had to be. But I was ill-equipped to fashion an effective counterargument. Fortunately, I had no need.

"Very interesting," said Mr. Willard. "It appears you've thought about this matter before. Is that right?"

"Yes, my father speaks about it often. It's among his favorite topics. My comments echo the very phrases he has repeated many, many times."

"I see." Mr. Willard pawed his chin. "Before we go any further, let's be sure we all know what we're talking about. What do we mean when we use the term *fascism*?" A hand went up near the front of the room. "Yes, Marie."

"It is the opposite of democracy. It is an authoritarian form of government, generally accompanied by nationalism and forceable repression of opponents."

Mr. Willard nodded. "Clear, substantive, and succinct." He turned back to Babbitt. "Lawrence, earlier you indicated that notable Americans have supported fascism. Can you name any?"

"Charles Lindbergh. In the 1930s he was a strong advocate of Nazi-party principles. Later in the decade, when the war began, he opposed American involvement. But once America entered the fight, like my father and me, Lindbergh supported our country. And there is William Randolph Hearst, the country's foremost newspaper publisher. He has used his platform to promote a positive image of the Nazi party. Oh, and of course, Henry Ford."

Suggestions that such prominent Americans had been Nazi sympathizers shocked me. It rankled me as well. I wanted Mr. Willard to negate Babbitt's claims.

"What you've said Lawrence comports with my understanding." Mr. Willard moved toward the window, facing the class diagonally. "Lawrence mentioned Henry Ford. In 1938 he was awarded the Grand Cross of the German Eagle. It is Germany's highest award for non-Germans. Yes, the award preceded the war, but its advent did not stop Ford's efforts on behalf of Germany. Ford, like General Motors and Chrysler, was and is a multi-national corporation with far-flung subsidiaries, including plants in Germany and Japan. General Motors and Ford have built most of the trucks that Germany and their Axis allies are employing in the war, along with countless engines for their jets and bombers. While these companies have converted themselves here at home in support of America's war effort, their subsidiaries across the Atlantic are arming our enemies. You might say, these companies have hedged their bets. If America wins, wonderful. On the other hand, if the Axis powers prevail, these great auto manufacturers will prevail as well. With the coin in the air, they are willing players. Heads they win. Tails...they win."

The message dumbfounded me. A pall draped the room. How could this be? The greatest of American companies were two-faced. They were selling out the country we loved.

"It's shocking. It's appalling. And it's seemingly illogical," said Mr. Willard. "But allow me to put it into perspective." He gestured east, out the window, as if he were transporting us across the broad expanse of the Atlantic. "Picture the plants in Germany. Were these companies not willing participants, Hitler would demand and command that they support his war effort. But such arm twisting is superfluous. People in Germany, both labor and management, have embraced Hitler's propaganda. They cheer his demagogic nationalism and fascistic rants. They wallow in his assertions of Aryan superiority. Folks manning the German automotive plants willingly do his bidding. And so, our nation's great auto manufacturers arm both sides. Such is the nature of..." Mr. Willard pursed his lips and shook his head. "I'll leave it to each of you to select an appropriate predicate."

Mr. Willard walked to the back of the room. An otherwise eerie silence accompanied his footsteps. "Questions, comments," he said.

I had none. The lightning bolt he had delivered had flummoxed me. Apparently, it had shocked my classmates as well.

"Perhaps you've read in the newspapers about the concentration camps and allegations of gas chambers that Hitler's regime is employing to eliminate those he deems undesirable, particularly Jews, the mentally infirm, and others not of his so-called Aryan master race. Another American company, International Business Machines, fashioned the devices and data bases used in that endeavor. Hitler awarded Thomas J. Watson, the founder of IBM, a medal for this work."

A tentative hand rose...halfway.

"Yes, Mary."

"I...I don't get it. Why do these people and companies do these things?"

I welcomed her question. I might have asked it myself had my time in Mr. Willard's class not educated me about inquiries infected with confusion. They tended to boomerang. Eager to make us think, Mr. Willard often invited us to answer our own questions. Sure enough, he afforded Mary the opportunity.

"You tell me," Mr. Willard said.

"I don't know," said Mary. "Money maybe...Power?"

"Good answers," said Mr. Willard. "It can be lots of things. Self-delusion, lack of integrity, narcissism, egomaniacal motivations, rationalizations...and even good faith, but misguided intentions." Mr. Willard walked up the center aisle to the front of the room. "Lawrence, earlier you told us why you believe democracy is destined to fail. You indicated that you favor fascism. Can you tell us why?"

"Well, I can offer one of my father's favorite examples, if that's okay?"

"Absolutely," said Mr. Willard.

"My father is not a fan of President Roosevelt's progressive policies, but he likes the president's style. Roosevelt has been labeled a socialist. In many ways he is. Admittedly, Roosevelt opposes communism, as well as that form of capitalism developed by the great moguls of industry, men like Rockefeller, Carnegie, DuPont, and Morgan. But in many respects, Roosevelt is a would-be fascist."

Though I knew little of the matter, attaching the egregious label to our president stunned me.

"Can you explain further?" said Mr. Willard.

"Much of President Roosevelt's so-called 'New Deal' was inspired by the programs of Italy's Fascist Party leader Benito Mussolini. The National Industrial Recovery Act, which was declared unconstitutional, is a prime example. It authorized the president to set wages and prices to stimulate economic recovery. To gain greater control of the judiciary, President Roosevelt also sought to pack the Supreme Court. He recognizes that democracy is cumbersome and messy, that politicians utilize their positions to expand their influence and line their pockets. All too often, power and money, not concern for the nation, drive them. Lobbyists take advantage of the politicians' greed. They buy the politicians. To overcome these pitfalls and be effective, a leader must seize control. President Roosevelt understands this point. Using the authoritarian playbook, he grabs the bull by the horns. As I said, my father likes the president's style, though not his policies. I agree."

Mr. Willard surveyed the class. "Would anyone like to challenge Lawrence's view?"

No one moved a muscle. Like me, they may have disagreed, but they lacked the courage, as well as the ammunition, the logical arguments, to articulate the point.

"Before I respond to Lawrence's position, I want to commend him. He has acquired considerable information. He has made an informed judgment. That's more than most can say. And in advance of responding to his arguments, let me make two critical points. First: No system of government, be it fascism, communism, democracy, or whatever, is a panacea. Governments are created and led by people. People are imperfect, sometimes evil. Ergo, governments are imperfect, even immoral or oppressive. Second: The points I am about to enunciate include opinions...my opinions. Treat them as such. In no event should you take them as gospel."

Mr. Willard moved forward, so he was front and center in the room. "Here is why I oppose fascism. Admittedly, a fascist leader can promote wonderful programs. He or she can even be benign. And all that is great. But most fascist leaders exercise power in a manner that promotes their own interests. They do whatever is necessary to preserve their power. They install 'yes men' who do their bidding. They manipulate the media, eliminating a free press. They silence those who dare voice contrary views. Carefully controlled propaganda replaces an open exchange of information. Freedom evaporates. Repression pervades. History, the conduct of countless autocrats over many centuries, bears this out. Repeatedly, unchecked leaders, be they titled king, fürer, emperor, dictator, or whatever, have wreaked oppression. Checks on their power is imperative lest fundamental freedoms, such as speech, assembly, press, etcetera, vanish. As I previously indicated, democracy is far from perfect. It is hard. It is, as Lawrence said, 'cumbersome and messy.' It demands effort. It invites dissention. What's good for the goose is bad for the gander. Benefits, whether they involve social programs, education, infrastructure, or whatever, have costs. Many, particularly those who don't benefit from such programs, oppose their costs. Society requires rules. People disagree about them. Their lists of differences are seemingly endless. Admittedly, an all-powerful leader mitigates the constant delay and contention inherent to democracy. But the trade-off, forgoing freedoms, fairness, and a voice as to the scope of government's power, comes at a humungous cost. That price forges a compelling argument in favor of democracy. Nevertheless, the matter is hardly black and white. It involves tricky shades of gray. The functioning of government, efficiency, necessitates that the executive branch enjoys broad powers. Determining the limit of those powers provokes thorny issues. Regardless, I, for one, am thankful, particularly in this season of Thanksgiving, that I live in a republic that cherishes democratic values."

As Mr. Willard circled behind his desk, a hush, interrupted only by his footsteps, pervaded the room. The silence, indicative of his singular ability to capture our undivided attention, was familiar. He said, "I reiterate. My comments represent my opinions. You should form your own. Keep in mind that no one has a corner on the truth...that is, assuming such so-called truth exists. Also, keep in mind that whatever system of government you deem best, one of the aforementioned, a hybrid, or an entirely new concept, you have not reached the end of the road. You have merely taken a fork along that path. For example, suppose you come down on the side of democracy. You still have miles to travel. You need to educate yourself about the many issues confronting a democracy; evaluate them in the context of the experiment we call America; draw both analogies and contrasts to past nations, their successes and failures, as well as the causes underlying such outcomes; read and listen to the views of those who disagree with you; make informed judgments about the issues; and once you are of age, exercise your franchise...vote."

Bearing a thoughtful pose, Mr. Willard moved his gaze over the class. The hiatus, presumably calculated, allowed us to digest his message. "There is one last matter that I want to mention – Thanksgiving. Indeed, it is a holiday, but it should be more than that. It should be a time for reflection. You and your generation have had it far from easy. Most of you were two years old when the stock market crash of 1929 abruptly ended the high-flying days of the roaring twenties. You have lived through the Depression and now World War II. It has been an uninterrupted period of sobering challenges. Still, as I look around the room, I see individuals who come from good homes, secure with the knowledge that your basic needs will be met. Compared to many young people around the globe who live in fear and poverty, your childhoods have been relatively carefree...Your homework over the Thanksgiving break is – "

A groan draped the room.

A quick look from Mr. Willard halted the grousing. "Your homework is to contemplate your reasons to be grateful and to do so in the context of your family, community, and the system of government that guides our nation. Discuss these matters with your parents; listen to their views; and most of all, count your blessings. Until the bell rings, please contemplate these issues silently at your desks...Happy Thanksgiving."

Amidst the quiet suffusing the room, my thoughts drifted to World War II. Apart from worrying about the draft, in the past my reflections about the conflict had been limited. They were also superficial. The matter was simple. The Allies were the good guys, and the Axis, the bad. Like the westerns shown in movie theaters, we wore the white hats, and the enemy donned those of black. That principle still abided. But applying it through the eyes of others, perceptions altered. Most Germans, Italians, and Japanese viewed themselves as wearing white hats. They deemed their cause just. Convenient though it may have been to dismiss their claims out of hand without any analysis, that approach was disingenuous. Mr. Willard had demonstrated that the landscape was far from black and white, that like the theater newsreels, manifold shades of gray abounded. The mere idea that we might be wearing other than white hats irked me. Addressing nuanced shades was complicated. But the need to do so was patent. Admittedly, I remained reluctant, arguably, incapable. That said, I had made progress. A fragment of my ignorance had chipped away.

I looked across the room at Larry Babbitt. In many respects he was a jerk, a pompous one at that. But I had to give him his due. With parental influence at play, he had explored the issues. His views may have been misguided, but they were the product of informed analysis. That was more than I could say for myself.

My gaze shifted to the front of the room where Mr. Willard sat at his desk reading. The man in the suit and tie had gotten me to think. In a matter of minutes, he had altered my view of history. It had always been an endless list of events, dates, and places, a conglomeration of information associated with a narrow purpose, earn a good grade on my report card. History, dating back to ancient civilizations, had suddenly become a meaningful collection of experiments in which human beings had endeavored to create better societies. How *better* was defined varied. Often it focused on the few, not the masses. Each society had its pros and cons. Apart from the most recent, they had one thing in common. Despite successes along the way, sooner or later, all had succumbed. Understanding the mistakes that had caused them to collapse was important lest the blunders of the past be duplicated.

An odd thought popped into my head. Adults often asked me what I wanted to do with my future. I always gave the same answer: A shrug, followed by a statement: "I'll figure it out when I get to college." Mr. Willard had caused me to rethink my response. The next time I was hit with the question, I might respond differently. I might mention the possibility of teaching history. That I would pursue such a career remained a longshot. Still, the idea, daft fifty minutes earlier, sounded a harmonious chord.

***

Christmas comes in November.

Thanksgiving Day, I slept in late. My mom had been preparing the holiday dinner for several days. My dad, who had arrived home after seven o'clock the preceding evening, having worked a couple hours of overtime, had slept in as well. Where I would enjoy a four-day weekend, my dad, as always, would work Friday at his regular job at Utica Power, as well as five hours Saturday at his second job, cutting hair at the local barbershop. I had just finished setting the dining room table with our best china, my tiny contribution to our family's

Thanksgiving celebration, when my mom added a dish of Waldorf Salad to each plate.

We seated ourselves with my dad at the head of the table, my mom at the end nearer the kitchen, and I on the side closer to the living room. As my dad reached for his fork, with Mr. Willard's message from the previous day still fresh, I said, "May I say a few words before we eat?"

My dad eyed me oddly. "Uh...sure."

Ever since I had gotten up, I had been rehearsing my little speech. "In the past Thanksgiving has meant a break from school with great food, especially Mom's apple and pecan pies." Her glowing smile rewarded my glance her way. "This year, Thanksgiving means more to me. I'm beginning to understand how fortunate I am." I turned to my father. "Dad, you work so hard, not just at your jobs, but as our plumber, electrician...whatever our home requires." I refocused on my mom. "You cook, clean, do laundry, and so many chores that make our home and lives comfortable. Both of you treasure education. You've inculcated that value in me. When you were my age, financial pressures precluded you from getting a college education. To afford me that opportunity you sacrifice. You have given me a safe and loving home in which I have enjoyed a wonderful childhood. Your demands on me are few. Rarely do I acknowledge these things. Most times, I take them for granted. Maybe it's because it's all I've ever known, not that such an explanation is satisfactory. Regardless, I appreciate all you have done and continue to do for me. I am grateful for our family, that we can enjoy this wonderful Thanksgiving celebration in a country that cherishes freedom."

With her napkin, my mother wiped a tear from her eye.

My father nodded slowly. He said, "Christmas has come a month early. I have received my gift." He circled to other end of the table and pecked my mother on the lips. "See – it's all worth it." As he returned to his end of the table, he paused and gave me a hug. "I love you, Son." Coming from the normally stoic man, the message was all-the-more meaningful.

As my father reseated himself, he said, "This is what Thanksgiving is about. This is the best Thanksgiving ever...Amen." He smiled broadly.

My mother, teary eyed, smiled as well. "Let's eat," she said.

I dipped my fork into the Waldorf Salad but paused to savor the moment. I was lucky...very lucky. Mr. Willard popped into my mind. I hoped he was enjoying a superb Thanksgiving. He had earned it. His homework assignment, an unpalatable chore when announced, had provided my parents and me with a singular moment. I took a bite of salad, savoring the sweet flavor of apples and raisins. "It's delicious, Mom," I said, conscious of the extraordinary meal that lay ahead, especially the luscious pecan pie. Even more so, I reveled in what was certain to be a treasured memory.

Chapter X

The keepers of the faith have a God-given right to tell others whom they may love. So say the sacrosanct laws of bigotry, along with those who enforce them. That said, some have the temerity...or perhaps courage...to challenge those laws.

Christmas vacation had come and gone. The New Year had arrived. Across the Atlantic, the Battle of the Bulge, having begun on December 16, 1944, raged amidst the forests that lay between Belgium and Luxembourg. The German offensive, calculated to cut off the Allies' access to the Port of Antwerp and to divide, encircle, and destroy the Allies' forces, persisted for more than five weeks. Hitler, who had taken personal command of the German army, believed success would impel the Allies to sue for Western Front peace on terms favorable to the Axis. The German army, overstretched by conflict on dual fronts, could then focus on the Soviets and the Eastern Front.

In the halls of Grand Falls High, we heard reports about the fighting, but our knowledge of particular battles was scant. Our grasp of the war's overall complexion remained vague. Among my senior classmates, more and more, schoolwork was taking a back seat to merriment. For those who were headed to college, applications and transcripts had been submitted. Admittedly, there was a need to complete one's courses and earn a high school diploma, but attention to grades had diminished. The possibility that war's horror lay only months away could have magnified our interest in the conflict, but instead, we used it to justify kicking back and allowing high jinks to prevail. Simple statistical logic indicated that for some, identities yet to be determined by the kismet of battle, second semester of senior year would be a last opportunity to check off items on bucket lists whose formulations had barely begun.

Accomplishing everything was impossible; a portion, imperative.

Numerous times I had heard adults speak of the purported invincibility and immortality that exemplified the teenage mentality. Whether the concept had merit in typical times, in the context of World War II, it bore little validity. My classmates and I hoped we would see many years beyond the war. But were we sanguine in that hope? Absolutely not. The ever-present reality that we might not make it out of our teens, never enjoy the fruits of adulthood, loomed.

Among my classmates, risky behavior and rejection of rules rose. An observer might have viewed the conduct as evidencing hubris, but inability to control our fates played a greater role. While most of us were still months short of eighteen, what was New York's legal drinking age when we were in high school, consumption of alcohol escalated. With each passing month, the quantities climbed. Speedy, Sam, and I were the last of The Guys to yield to the bottle. Compared to most, our consumption was paltry. For that matter, I disliked beer. Placed side by side with a cherry Coke, the bitter liquid paled. Why then did I opt for the illegal beverage? Peer pressure would be an easy explanation. Indeed, it was a factor, but only secondary. Failure to imbibe never posed a risk of ostracization. Booze became a means, admittedly bogus, to voice my objections to global circumstances. In a world where events in distant locales could dictate my life, disdain for rules conferred a semblance of control, albeit specious. Rebellion represented a source of power, as well as a device to release pent-up emotions.

The extent to which defiance, rather than experimentation and/or other factors, precipitated individual conduct is open to debate. Speedy, who followed the rules as much as anyone, provided the quintessential example. During Christmas vacation he began dating Lisa Raines, a Caucasian junior. Interracial dating was not an issue in Grand Falls. Its non-existence, not open-minded liberalism, explained what otherwise would have been an anomaly. As noted earlier, Grand Falls included only two Negro families. Each had two children. Speedy had a sister, four years younger. The other

Negro family had two children, a daughter, age ten, and a son, fifteen. In Grand Falls there were no Negroes for Speedy to court. His rare dates were either out-of-town fix-ups or girls from his family's church in Utica.

We were in homeroom the afternoon of the second Friday in January. From his desk adjacent to mine, Speedy leaned my way and whispered, "You available after school? I need a favor."

"I think so. What's the favor?"

"I'll tell you once the bell rings."

A few minutes later, the dismissal signal sounded. The classroom emptied. Once we were out in the hall, Speedy said, "I'm meeting Lisa Raines at the Village Library in fifteen minutes. I need cover."

"And..." I said, despite a notion as to my role.

"We want to spend a little time alone. If this were summer, the wooded area in the park would fill the bill. With the temperature barely ten degrees, we need a place inside. Both our mothers are at home. The tiny conference room in the Village Library seems our best bet. It's always available. But if the librarian, old lady Gandes – you know what a gossip she is – sees me come in with Lisa, she'll suspect something. She might demand we keep the door open. Even if she doesn't, snow to sludge she'll advertise our rendezvous all over town."

"So, where do I fit in?"

"If you come along, the picture will appear innocent. We can cover it as a school project. Naturally, we'll keep the door closed, so we don't disturb others in the library. Once the three of us have the conference room, you can step outside...for fifteen minutes, while Lisa and I make out. You could do your homework while keeping watch at the table just outside the door."

The idea was half-baked. On the bright side, if something went wrong, it would be Speedy and Lisa's necks, not mine. "Okay," I said.

"Thanks a million. I owe you." Speedy eyed the wall clock. "We better go. I'm due at the library in eleven minutes."

The two of us arrived just before the appointed time. The small structure, a converted bungalow, was all but deserted.

145

The conference room was available. Soon Lisa joined us. Speedy went to the reference section, returning with a volume of the World Book Encyclopedia. Lisa selected a couple of random books. I stepped out and took up watch. My job, a simple one, became even easier when a man entered and sought help researching Vermont's ski slopes. Miss Gandes welcomed the opportunity to assist him. Fourteen minutes after I had begun guard duty – I was checking my watch regularly – I tapped the conference-room door, the agreed signal that in one minute, I would be coming in. Lisa and Speedy came out just before I opened the door.

Speedy winked at me.

"Thanks," said Lisa.

The three of us left the library. I glanced at Miss Gandes. The portly prig was none the wiser.

***

Indoctrination, the device one generation uses to inculcate its cherished values into its progeny, is wonderful. Without indoctrination a nation's youth might stray from essential tenets and abandon its ancestors' prejudices...God forbid!

A sock hop in the gymnasium was scheduled for the second Saturday following Lisa and Speedy's library tryst. Back during freshman year, I had invited Speedy to accompany Sam and me to a school dance. He declined. Though he gave no reason, pressing him was superfluous. We both knew why. He would be the sole Negro. What would he do there? Ask one of the girls to dance? That would be a recipe for ruin. Best case scenario, he would be refused. A *yes* would be worse. Both he and the girl would face repercussions from school authorities, as well as their parents. Technically, there were no rules banning interracial dancing. They were unnecessary, but only because they were implicit.

Speedy, Sam, and I were eating lunch in the cafeteria on the Monday before the dance when Speedy said, "You guys going to the hop this Saturday?"

"Yeah." I would have asked him to accompany us, but certain that he would refuse, I avoided putting him on the spot.

"Mind if I join you?"

Though I suspected he was joking, I said, "Be glad to have you."

"How do you think people will react?" said Speedy.

I doubted that his attendance at the affair would, by itself, cause a stir. But if he invited a girl to dance, the presumed reason for attending the event, he best follow it up with a *quick step*, a bolt for the door, not the dance. I said, "Do you plan to dance?"

Speedy shot me a look. "Did you think I intend to play croquet?"

The inanity of his response underscored the absurdity of my question. Much as I wanted to explore the matter, my need to be circumspect was undeniable. Speedy and Lisa had been anything but open about their relationship. As best I knew, I was the only one aware. Both Speedy and Lisa were certain their parents would disapprove. Remaining discreet was imperative.

"With whom do you plan to dance?" said Sam.

"I assume that's a rhetorical question," said Speedy. He puffed out his chest. "You impressed with the way I used *rhetorical*, the new word we learned this week in English class?"

"Not really," said Sam. "Not when it's a camouflage to duck my inquiry. But just to refresh your memory, I'll repeat it. With whom do you plan to dance?"

"Obviously, a girl."

"You gonna bring a date?" said Sam.

"Whad'ya mean? I'm going with you guys...No offense, but neither of you is my date. And for that matter, dancing with either of you has no appeal."

Sam gave me a look.

I shook my head. "You opened this can of worms. You do the fishing."

Sam turned back to Speedy. "Not that it matters to me with whom you dance, but have you weighed the ramifications?"

147

"Ramifications?"

Sam heaved a sigh. "Fine. I'll spell it out. All the girls at the dance will be white. You're Negro."

"Really?" Speedy's eyes were cantaloupes. With feigned dramatics he stared at his arm. "My God! Shock of shocks! You're right! I am!"

"You're making fun," said Sam. "But have you thought about how the school administration will react to interracial dancing?"

"Unfortunately, yes. But that's their problem. New York is not one of the many states with an anti-miscegenation statute."

"What the hell is that?" said Sam.

"It's a law prohibiting whites and Negroes from cohabiting."

Sam looked my way. "Is he right? The school can't stop him from dancing with whomever he wants."

I shrugged. "Don't ask me." I turned to Speedy. "Even assuming whites and Negroes can cohabit in New York, we've always been told that the school administration stands *in loco parentis*, that they can make rules governing our conduct. What about that?"

"I don't know. But maybe I'm about to find out." A devilish smile decorated Speedy's face.

"How do your parents feel about you dancing with white girls?" said Sam.

"Got me, though I suspect they'd object. As for me dating white girls, that would be way over the line."

"So," I said, "aren't you worried that your parents would back the school, assuming it takes exception?"

"Yeah."

Contrary to my expectation, Speedy failed to clarify.

"You're taking a big chance," said Sam.

Lips pursed, Speedy stared into space. "What can they do? Suspend me? Or my parents could ground me...Big deal."

Had the cavalier reaction come from one of the school's truants, it would have been no surprise. But Speedy did not fit the mold of the profligates. Like me, his worst-ever deed was taking his father's car to Arctic Freeze. Apart from that rare aberration, he walked the straight and narrow.

"Six months from now, I'm gonna be wearing a uniform. Even if the school expels me, you think the military would refuse me? Whatever I do, short of a felony that lands me in jail – and dancing with a white girl is no felony – I know my destiny. I'll be serving my country. The nation needs my body. And like it or not, there's a risk that body may come back in a box...On second thought, it may never come back."

A hiatus ensued. Perhaps Speedy was awaiting a reaction. His sobering words, however, had silenced both Sam and me.

"If someone wants to punish me for dancing with a girl, let them have at it...If the powers that be can ask me to give my life for my country, I oughta be able to enjoy a few dances first."

His point underscored the potential inequity he faced. I had nothing to add. I doubted that Sam did either. But Speedy had a question, one that discomfited me.

"I know that when our club, The Guys, was created, a couple of the fellas wanted to blackball me because I'm Negro. Did – "

"That...that wasn't Sam or me." My defensiveness, a blaring horn, evidenced my discomposure.

"I know," said Speedy. "But that's not the issue. Does the color of my skin play a role in our relationship?"

I longed to say *no.* That was the easy answer. But Speedy had asked a consequential question, one begging a soul-searching response. I asked myself: What if I had a younger sister? How would I feel if Speedy dated her? The truth be known, it would make me uncomfortable. Exactly why was hard to discern. Viewed in a vacuum, apart from society and its strictures, the idea seemed okay. That said, the hypothetical stirred consternation. Perhaps it was due to the taboo associated with interracial dating, my concern that others, owing to their prejudice, would look down on my family and me. But maybe my own bigotry played a role. Whatever the reason, claiming that I was color blind would be a lie. The admission was upsetting, indeed shameful. It magnified the need for me to be forthcoming. I said, "When we're together, our racial difference doesn't matter. In school, at the ballfield, Arctic Freeze, wherever, I never think about it. But much as I wish I could tell you that I'm color blind, I can't. If I had a sister, having you date her would trouble me. I can't pinpoint why. Maybe it's because society, as well as my parents, would object. That's not a good reason. I don't have one." My last comment echoed in my ears. There were no good reasons. The painful concession prompted yet another question: How and when had my bias evolved? Likely it had commenced from the time I was a baby. Society, my family included, had shaped my views, instilling their biases. I might have voiced the explanation were it not a rationalization, a means to deflect my own responsibility. Whatever I had been told by others, I had free will. I could reject the prejudice they had tried to inculcate. I said, "I apologize."

"No need to...And for that matter, I appreciate your honesty." Speedy looked skyward and chuckled.

"What's so funny?" I said.

"My parents, your parents, Lisa's – " Speedy clipped his tongue.

I stole a glance at Sam, wondering if he had noticed Speedy's misstep, if he had put two and two together, that Speedy wasn't merely looking to dance with any girl. A specific girl was part of his intrigue. Regardless, I had no intention of saying anything. If Sam tried to explore the subject with me later, I would play dumb. I would suggest he direct his inquiry to Speedy.

***

One man's crime is another's righteous civil disobedience. But rules are rules. Conventions must be preserved. Change, however sound, is no excuse for sullying hallowed traditions....Justice be damned!

Saturday night, Speedy, Sam, and I arrived at the dance, a two-hour affair, shortly after its seven-o'clock start. Per usual, the girls lined up on the right side of the gym and the boys on the left. No protocol dictated division of the sexes, let alone that each occupy a particular wall, but tradition, inhibitions, or some form of justifiable illogic guaranteed the positioning. The three of us shuffled down to the middle of the boys' wall. A minute later, two more of The Guys, Ronald Cooper and Larry Babbitt, joined us.

"What's up?" said Sam, as the duo approached.

"Nothin' much," said Babbitt. "How's the flock across the way?"

"Look for yourself," I said. "You've got eyes." My new cardigan sweater, decorated with the letters *GF* that I had earned playing on the golf team, armed me with inordinate confidence. Like Buster and Lefty, I could be cool, at least with the likes of Babbitt. Let a hot cheerleader approach, not that such a happenstance would eventuate, and my bravado would evaporate.

"Almost nobody dancing." Cooper gestured at the thinly populated gulf that divided the males and females.

"Whad'ya expect?" said Sam. "Only a llama or some such beast could dance to *The Trolley Song.* Don't know why we gotta have Miss Horrigan spinning the discs."

"Were many dancing earlier?" said Babbitt.

"Doubt it, not that we know," said Speedy. "We arrived just before you."

"You planning to dance tonight?" said Babbitt, directing his sarcastically inflected inquiry to Speedy.

"I might. You never know."

"Sure," said Babbitt. "And I'm going to sleep with Grandma Moses this weekend."

"You would, if you could," said Cooper. "But she wouldn't have you."

Babbitt gave Cooper a look. "Since when did you become a prick?"

As slick as a showroom-waxed new car, Cooper ignored the gibe. He pointed to the farthest corner where four or five girls surrounded Lefty. "God, Lucinski has it made. A freakin' harem, all slobbering over him."

"Hey, if you had big league scouts sizing up your arm, the chicks would be chasing you too," said Speedy.

"Lefty's not the only one with a good arm," said Babbitt. "Coop has one too. Perfect for cleaning latrines." Babbitt punctuated the barb with a smirk.

Brow furrowed, Cooper shot the literary cliché a dismissive look.

I soaked in the droll interplay. Babbitt could identify his worst enemy with a mirror. For him to trade barbs with Cooper was as foolhardy as me picking a fight with Joe Bell, the biggest lineman on the football team. Just as Bell could swat me away with one hand, Cooper, merely by ignoring Babbitt, could brush him aside like an annoying gnat. I anticipated Babbitt might be dippy enough to beg for more. Instead, he shut his mouth, not that the ensuing conversation was any less inane.

Finally, Cooper said, "I thought we came here to dance." He headed to the far wall and found himself a partner.

Babbitt followed. Whether he found a partner, I didn't notice. Sam eased a short distance down our wall, apparently to get a better view and/or map strategy. I whispered to Speedy, "I don't see Lisa. Is she here?"

"Not yet. She had a prior family commitment. Said she'd get here around 8:30."

"You still planning to – " I stopped mid-sentence as Sam rejoined us.

"Next slow song, I'm making my move," said Sam. "Gonna ask Julie Trackman."

A half-minute later, a slow number, an unfamiliar one, played. As Sam headed toward Julie, I spotted Mary Wheeler standing alone. I started across the gym. I was ninety percent of the way when, from off to my right, Bernie...what's his name...swooped in and asked Mary to dance. I did a self-conscious U-turn, certain that numerous eyes feasted on my debacle. I rejoined Speedy on the sidelines.

"Sweet ballet," said Speedy.

"Ballet? What are you talking about?"

"Your suave pirouette a moment ago."

I shrugged. "I was about to ask Mary Wheeler when some jerk got to her first. Next song, I'm dancing."

Another song started, a rumba or mambo or some such Latin music.

"Well," said Speedy, gesturing at the far wall.

"C'mon, give me a break. I can't do this. I don't even know what it is."

As we waited for the next song, Sam returned. The announcement of a Sadie Hawkins dance, girls' choice, altered whatever plans I had. I began talking about the Montreal Canadien's hockey game from the night before when, from behind, I felt a tap on my shoulder.

"Would you like to dance?" said Mary Wheeler.

"Sure," I said, even before I knew what was playing. Fortunately, the slow song, *It Had to be You*, was one I could handle. I guided Mary to the center of the floor where we swayed and glided, now and then exchanging a few words. As the dance ended, I said, "Would you like to do another?"

"Glad to."

A few seconds later, the zany tune, *Dance with a Dolly (With a Hole in Her Stocking)* began to play. I gave Mary a look.

She shrugged. "We could do the penguin stomp to it."

"Uh...I...uh...don't know how."

"Not surprising, given that I just coined the name." Mary smiled broadly.

"You wanna get some punch?" I said.

"Better than the penguin stomp."

We headed to the refreshment table where we got our beverages. Unlike the libation that filled the punchbowl at the dance a month earlier, no alcohol spiked the sweet pink liquid. A teacher stood guard ensuring that it remained low octane.

With our drinks in hand, we conversed while watching the few who had tried to dance to the song about the dolly with tattered hose. Finally, the quirky selection yielded to Glen Miller's *In the Mood.*

"Look over there." Mary pointed off to her right. "Speedy Jackson is dancing with Lisa Raines."

"So he is."

"You don't seem surprised."

I was not. But not wanting to breach Speedy's confidence, even if he was arguably going public himself, I said, "Well, it's just a jitterbug."

"Just a jitterbug?" Mary eyed me. "When was the last time you saw a Negro and a white dancing here at Grand Falls High School?"

I shrugged.

"I rest my case."

I looked around the gymnasium. Speedy and Lisa had drawn widespread attention. Off to our left, Principal Armstrong and Mrs. Tillis, the Spanish teacher, were mixing animated conversation with repeated glares at the mixed-race duo. I could only imagine what the imperious chaperones were saying. That begged the question whether they might step in and separate the couple.

The fast number concluded and the next song, a slow one, *Till Then*, by the Mills Brothers, commenced. Several couples began to dance. Most attention remained on Speedy and Lisa, awaiting their next move. Would they return to their separate sides? Might they simply stand in place and talk? Or might they dance?

About a half-minute into the song, Speedy took Lisa into his arms. Cheek to cheek, they floated to the second verse:

> *Our dreams will live though we are apart*
> *Our love, I know we'll keep in our heart*
> *Till then, when all the world will be free*
> *Please wait for me.*

The next verse no sooner started than Principal Armstrong marched toward the couple. The moment he arrived, they separated. Some conversation ensued, and about the time the record ended, the three went their separate ways: Speedy, to the boys' wall; Lisa, to the girls'; and Principal Armstrong, to his station at the head of the gymnasium.

Curiosity lured me to immediately collar Speedy. A desire to maintain Mary's company demurred. A suggestion that Mary and I go together to Speedy would have covered both bases, but putting Speedy on the spot in front of a third party was unthinkable. I decided to bide my time. Mary and I finished our punch. We danced to the last two songs of the evening. We thanked one another for a nice time and headed to our respective walls, both of which had begun to empty.

I hurried to Speedy and said, "What happened...with Armstrong?"

"The louse ordered us to stop dancing. He said that if we didn't, he'd contact our parents and I would be suspended from school."

"Why just you?"

"Lisa asked that very question...Damn, that took guts on her part."

"How did Armstrong react?"

"It took him back. First, he stammered some double talk, but then he shifted, saying that I bore primary responsibility because I asked Lisa to dance. He claimed I put her on the spot because it would have been discourteous for her to decline. Armstrong said – "

Speedy clipped his tongue as Sam approached.

"Man, did you turn the gym on its head," said Sam.

"Whad'ya mean?" said Speedy, his veil of feigned ignorance fruitless.

"C'mon. Dancing with Lisa Raines, your bodies pressed together. You gotta be kidding."

Speedy shrugged.

"So, what did Armstrong say?" said Sam.

"He ordered us to quit. He threatened me with suspension if we didn't."

"You gonna – "

"Let's get out of here." I interrupted Sam to help Speedy elude an inquiry I presumed he preferred to evade.

The three of us left school and started for home. As we reached Waverly Place, Sam's home street, he detoured north. Once he was out of earshot, Speedy said, "Thanks for not letting on about my relationship with Lisa."

"No problem...but if your goal is to keep it secret, why did you advertise it?"

"Whad'ya mean?"

"Gimme a break. Everybody and their uncles watched you and Lisa dance."

"So, we were dancing."

I shot him a look.

"If anyone asks, we're just good friends. People can't complain about that."

"You believe that?"

"Maybe yes...and maybe no. But at least it'll give us a chance to spend more time together. Otherwise, we're limited to a few stolen minutes." Speedy heaved a sigh. "I know. It's risky, but sometimes you gotta gamble. And for that matter, why should we kowtow to the rules of bigots? No school administrator, least of all a meatball like Armstrong, should dictate whom we date." Speedy looked me in the eye. "You agree, don'tcha?"

"Yeah...not that the school or any of its administrators give a hoot what I think."

Speedy sighed again. "Unfortunately, my view matters even less." He kicked a stone, sending it bouncing into the street.

Chapter XI

Magic...allure...rapture...Oh, those initial voyages into the world of love.

As the month of January concluded, news arrived from Poland that the Soviets had liberated the Auschwitz concentration camp. With 1,100,000 of the camp's deportees, including 960,000 Jews, having been exterminated or otherwise succumbed, one might have expected immediate shock across the globe. But the Germans had taken pains to hide their evil. Before the Soviets had arrived, the Germans had opened the mass graves and burned the remains, turning them to ashes. Prisoners still alive were removed on death marches in the dead of winter. Auschwitz had been liberated, but the magnitude of its atrocities remained camouflaged.

At Grand Falls High, sheltered in the cocoon of our small town, we embarked on second semester. I had taken Mary Wheeler out on two dates. The first we had doubled with her cousin from Herkimer, whom Mary had fixed up with a friend from her church youth group. We had seen the movie *Return of the Ape Man* with Bela Lugosi. Never had I imagined that such a predictably trite horror movie could be so appealing. Despite its dreadful acting and poorly written script, its scary moments had Mary cuddling close. By the time the heroine had collapsed in the arms of the ape man, Mary and I had shared our first kisses. The evening taught me a not-so-subtle lesson: in my teenage world, a stinko film with a great date dwarfed an Oscar-winning production. Two weeks following the ape man, I had taken Mary ice-skating, after which we had enjoyed burgers, fries, and ice cream sodas at the diner. We had walked back to her house, a fine white Dutch colonial with green trim, where, in the finished basement, we had spun records, all of which were slow. Dancing soon yielded to a wonderful session of necking. I had my first girlfriend. Over the summer before junior year, I had dated one girl twice, but terming her my girlfriend would be delusory.

Among the senior boys, an interesting pattern emerged. Serious relationships evolved quickly. As raging hormones intersected with the awaiting perils intrinsic to the war, going steady, even talk of marriage, escalated. From all we could surmise, albeit unscientifically, the expansive conflict was inducing couples in our class to accelerate their lives. Mary and I were an exception to this pattern. If anything, war's uncertainty magnified our caution. Our self-perceptions also came under a microscope. Candid moments betrayed recognition of our immaturity. Like me, having a girlfriend-boyfriend relationship was a first for Mary. Much as we were a couple, both of us valued our independence. Neither of us was ready for an all-consuming connection. Though never voiced in so many words, our mutual reluctance to be tied down was tacit. Because we were not "going steady," technically we had the right to date others, but neither of us did. We continued, however, to spend lots of time with our respective friends, Mary with her girlfriends, and I, with The Guys, especially Sam and Speedy.

Hindsight demonstrates that our relationship progressed at an ideal rate. For Mary and me, equally inexperienced in the world of love, time allowed us to savor romance, even as sexual desires remained unrequited. We had been dating for more than a month when I arrived at Mary's house for a combination study session and make-out opportunity. The former was how we described the get-together to our parents; the latter reflected our primary purpose.

Down in Mary's finished basement, we did our Advanced Algebra homework for Monday and quizzed each other on the details of the Spanish-American War. About an hour after I had arrived, I shut my book. "Shall we dance a little?" My use of the word *dance* was literal. It was also figurative. When we were alone, it was an invitation to make out, as well as dance.

Mary closed her book and went to the record player, a step up from the phonograph we had at my house. On the bright side, her record player could repeat the same record. On the negative side, it could only hold a single disc and played exclusively seventy-eights, each lasting three or four minutes. It was great for dancing in the literal sense, lousy in the figurative sense. It demanded that passion be interrupted every few minutes. The one way around the drawback was to pick a single record, allowing it to endlessly repeat. Mary shuffled through her records before drawing one from its paper jacket. She placed it onto the turntable. After a few scratchy seconds, the nasally tenor voice of Rudy Vallee crooning *As Time Goes By* emerged from the shellac platter.

Lights turned low, Mary's perfume luring, and youthful desire burning, we embraced one another, slow dancing through two renditions of the seductive song. Steps grew shorter. Motionless feet yielded to a passionate kiss. Nervously, I slid my right hand around from the back of Mary's tight pink sweater, pausing just below her breast. Inching higher, my palm cupped the lower portion of her magnificent contour. A final assent, and I fully embraced the fount of my desire. Glorious hallmarks of the female figure, oft eyed, were mine to hold. Unlike Moses who only viewed Canaan from a distance, I had reached the promised land.

Several wonderful minutes passed before I circled my hand around to Mary's back, sneaking it under and up her sweater until the tips of my fingers touched her bra. I slid my other hand around to her back, slithering it upward so my fingertips met. Intentions manifest, I waited, fearing repercussions. None ensued. Nerves abounding, but thrilled and titillated, I made my move. I unlatched the strap. As its connecting ends parted, I caressed Mary's velvety skin. With awaiting grandeur consuming me, I pressed my lips to Mary's, kissing her tenderly. My left hand drifted around her lovely body, meandering upward until it encompassed the fullness of her breast.

"I love you," I said.

"I love you too."

Mary's whispered words resounded as we kissed more passionately. Allure, so often eyed, a figment of my fantasies, had materialized. I was living past dreams, and reality eclipsed imagination.

We drifted to the couch where our passion continued. Temptation cajoled me to dispatch my hand wandering again, this time south to the furthermost border of Mary's gray skirt. Judgment, commingling with fear, nixed the move. The golf course had educated me about risk and reward. Going for a water-guarded, par-5 green from long range stirred visions of an eagle. More likely it invited a big number, even a snowman, a dreaded eight. The offbeat analogy, arguably dubious, checked my hand's urge to rove. Admittedly consummate rewards lay below Mary's waist, but the risk of spoiling ineffable ecstasy was greater yet, especially knowing that postponing the bounty did not demand it be forever forsaken. A future day could see it realized.

***

Nobility springs from curious places. But curious minds also spring from such places. And boys will be boys. So, beware.

With the school day due to start in twenty minutes, The Guys were holding our biweekly meeting. With the thermometer hovering near zero and the wind howling, we had opted to gather in the hallway outside our homeroom, rather than the front yard of the school. Our meetings were less formal than the term might imply. With no officers, no call to order, and not even a request for old or new business, the only thing that made them meetings was that we labeled them such. Most of what the group did was accomplished on an *ad hoc* basis.

"Pipe down," said Buster, quelling the conversations occurring among the ten of us. Three were absent. Pokey Paulsen was out sick; Pete Longley was at work supporting his family; and Don Baker, who had died on the battlefields of Germany, was in the great kingdom in the sky.

"Yesterday, Coop hit me with a good idea," said Lefty.

"Cooper having a good idea is an oxymoron," said Sam.

160

"What the hell is an oxy…whatever?" said Babbitt.

"A self-contradictory statement," said Sam.

Babbitt's face was blank.

"For example," I said, *"jumbo shrimp, icy hot…*or *Babbitt-like modesty."* The gibe Sam had hurled at Cooper moments before had emboldened me to add the final example.

"Screw you, Geeko," said Babbitt.

"Enough," said Buster. "Let's hear Coop's idea."

All eyes shifted to Cooper.

"It would be nice if we put up a bronze plaque in memory of Don Baker. I ran the idea by Armstrong, but with other school alum having died in the war, he was reluctant to honor just one. Next, I tried Walker's Drug Store. As you probably recall, Don worked there part time for two years. I spoke with Mr. Walker. He welcomed the idea. Said he'd put the plaque on the front wall."

"How much would it cost?" said Babbitt.

"Thirteen dollars for bronze, six inches by a foot," said Cooper. "Mr. Walker offered to contribute three dollars toward the project. We could do it for under a dollar apiece."

The proposal drew positive reactions. Objections, if any, were not voiced.

Speedy whispered to me. "This is the best thing The Guys have ever done. Makes you feel good, doesn't it?"

"Yeah, it does." The point had escaped me until Speedy had made it. I turned to Cooper and said, "Great idea. Thanks for coming up with it." It was the nicest thing – perhaps the only nice thing – I had said to him since the dust-up after the golf match against Dolgeville.

Cooper offered to collect the needed money and purchase the plaque.

With the matter of the plaque set, Vic Dolan said, "Anyone interested in skating at the park this Saturday afternoon? We can go to my house afterwards. My mom will make hot chocolate and cookies."

"Some of us don't skate," said Babbitt.

"You can sleigh ride on the hill adjoining the pond," said Dolan.

"Can we bring dates?" said Cooper.

"The more the merrier," said Dolan. He turned to Lefty. "Maybe you could bring some extras for us less fortunate souls?"

Lefty shrugged. "Yeah, I can probably share."

"Make sure you bring Lucy Wendell. Word has it she's enough action to warm everybody up. And she definitely has the right equipment." Fingers spread wide, Cooper held his hands out in front of his chest.

"Speedy, you plan to bring Lisa?" said Buster.

Speedy was wide-eyed. "What are you talking about?"

"C'mon, you're not fooling us," said Buster. "We all know that you and Lisa are an item."

"Then you know something I don't."

Had the conversation occurred five days earlier, Speedy's denial would have been false, but in the interim, he and Lisa had broken up. The problems associated with interracial dating may have played a role. Both were certain their parents would be irate once they learned of the relationship. But mainly it had terminated for a simpler reason, one common to many teenage romances. Like a star bright at night, the fling, an early experiment in the complex world of love, had evanesced with the advent of morning. From all I had observed and from what Speedy had told me, mutual consent had ended their time as a couple. They remained friends.

"So, you're telling us that the rumors about you and Lisa are false?" said Cooper. "What about you two at the dance a few weeks back? Or was that a hallucination?"

"Big deal. I danced with Lisa. For that matter, most of you left the wall and cut a rug with some of the girls on the other side. Does that mean you're going with them?" Speedy eyed his inquisitors defiantly.

"Well, it's your loss," said Cooper.

"Loss? What are you babbling about?"

"C'mon, I'm sure you've noticed that Lisa has a great body...built like Mount Rushmore, if you get my drift. I assumed you were getting a piece, but apparently not. Well, like I said, it's your loss...Maybe it's the same with your buddy." Cooper turned my way. "Geeko, with all the time you've been spending with Mary Wheeler, walking her to class and carrying her books, I presume you two are a couple."

"We're dating."

"Are you dating?...*or are you dating?*" said Lefty, his reiteration of the question followed by a puckish grin.

"What the hell does that mean?"

"Fine, I'll spell it out," said Lefty. "Like Speedy, who it turns out was only dancing on the dance floor, are you doing more than carryin' Mary's books and sippin' a malt at the diner?"

"That's for me to know and you to find out."

"That's exactly what we're trying to do," said the normally taciturn Shadow Sherwood. "Find out...all the juicy details." Sherwood rubbed his hands together.

"C'mon," said Cooper, "you can share with us. We're your pals." He shifted his focus away from me to the group. "What base do you think Geeko is on...second, third...or maybe...maybe he's hit a home run?"

The entire group refocused on me.

That they were all intrigued with my love life, that they thought that I might be getting action, a boon most of them could not claim, was exciting. Temptation might have wheedled me to brag, but sagacity subdued imprudence. Regardless, boasting was unnecessary. My silence had them wondering. Admittedly, affirmative statements trumped mystery. Nevertheless, I refused to wag my tongue. How far our relationship had progressed was between Mary and me. Chivalry demanded that I keep my mouth shut. So too, did self-interest. Satisfying my buddies' curiosity would rightly invite Mary's ire. It could risk my relationship with her. Now and then, I demonstrated a lack of judgment – none worse than the time Speedy and I had taken his parents' car to Arctic Freeze – but stupid, I was not. In love for the first time, no way would my ego inveigle me to jeopardize the best experience of my young life. The Guys were great, but next to Mary, inconsequential.

***

A double negative yields a positive. Ergo, two falsehoods equal truth. Well, maybe not...but occasionally, justice.

"Hi Mary," I said, as I approached our homeroom for the start of the school day.

"Can I talk with you?" Mary, who had been standing just outside the doorway, moved to a quiet spot in the hall.

"What's up?"

"Did you discuss our relationship with that little club of yours, The Guys?"

"Yeah, the subject came up."

"And what did you say?"

The pointed nature of Mary's questioning, coupled with a frosty tone, suggested that something was amiss. "Nothing...really."

"You tell them you scored with me?"

"No way." I looked her in the eye. "What makes you think I did?"

"On the way home from school yesterday, Sheila Smith said that Janey Jackson told her that she spoke with Ron Cooper who said that you told The Guys you made it with me."

"That son of a bitch! Excuse my French...And to answer your question, no way did I say anything like that. Yeah, the guys asked me, and I told them it was none of their business."

Mary appeared to study me, presumably judging my credibility.

"Has Cooper arrived yet?" I pointed at our homeroom.

"Not that I know of."

We went to the doorway and confirmed he was not in the room.

"Let's wait here and corral him when he arrives. I'm gonna confront the snake." A triggered temper had me displaying a fist, not that I planned to use it. A fight with Cooper would be a double loser. I would wind up on the short end, and to make matters worse, as the aggressor, I could anticipate a suspension from school. That Cooper, the winner of the fisticuffs, might be booted as well would be no consolation.

Minutes later, we spotted Cooper coming our way. We intercepted him as he approached the doorway.

"Coop," I said, temporarily containing my ire, "Mary and I would like to speak with you."

"About what?"

"Did you or did you not tell Janey Jackson something about my relationship with Mary?"

"Yeah, I may have. What about it?"

Exhibiting uncommon pluck, I stepped closer to the brawnier Cooper. "Did you tell her that Mary and I were having sex?"

"Not in those exact words."

"But you led her to believe that, didn't you?"

Cooper shrugged. "Yeah, so what?"

"A whole lot when you had no basis."

"What do you mean, no basis?"

I feared that Cooper was about to lie. Out of the corner of my eye, I saw Mary bristle. I said, "When you guys asked what Mary and I were doing, I said it was none of your damn business. And you know it!"

"Yeah...but two and two makes four."

"So, the truth is," said Mary, "what you told Janey, you made up."

"Hey, c'mon," said Cooper, "I drew a reasonable conclusion."

"Baloney," I said. "You started a damn rumor, one that you're gonna correct right now." I pointed toward our homeroom. "You're gonna march in there and tell Janey in front of Mary and me that you fabricated the story and that I told you absolutely nothing."

"Screw you, Geeko!" Cooper held up his middle finger inches from my face. "Since when do you tell me what to do?"

"Since you don't want everyone in Grand Falls High to know your impotent." Mary punctuated her remark with a diabolical sneer.

"What the hell you talkin' about?" said Cooper.

"It's like this," said Mary. "If you don't do as Jim said, I'm going in there and tell everyone that a girl I know from Little Falls, who asked that I not repeat her name, said that you and she were petting and you couldn't get a hard on...that you're impotent!"

"Jeez, you...you know that's not true."

"Maybe so, but it'll teach you not to lie." Mary glared.

Cooper grumbled inaudibly. "Damn! You don't play fair."

"Look who's talking." Mary gestured at our homeroom. "You've got ten seconds to get in there and confess. Take a second longer, and I go into action. And if I do, I'll supplement my narrative with prevarications that will make the tidbit about your impotency seem like your privates...minuscule potatoes."

"Okay...calm down." Cooper entered our homeroom, with Mary and me following close behind. He went directly to Janey Jackson and told her that he had made up the story about me scoring with Mary and that he knew no details about our relationship. A half-dozen others were close enough to hear the confession.

As Mary and I headed to our desks, she said, "Thanks for not feeding your ego at my expense. Knowing you, I'd expect no less...Oh, and by the way, I think we're progressing at a perfect pace."

"Thanks," I said, glad that I had used good judgment both in what I had not disclosed and what I had not tried the last time we were alone in her basement.

As Mary slipped into the chair behind her desk, I whispered, "Would you have really told that story about Cooper being impotent, along with whatever other embellishments you had in mind?"

Mary shrugged. "I doubt it. For that matter, I'm amazed I made the threat...I even feel a little guilty."

"Hey, you fought fire with fire...and the rat deserved it." The adage, *Two wrongs don't make a right*, reverberated in my brain. The bromide had merit, but injustice warranted draconian medicine. And the bottom line, Cooper's lie, the first wrong, was laid bare, while Mary's fabrication, what would have been the second wrong, never saw the light of day.

***

An avid fan of Roy Rogers and the Lone Ranger, in moments of fantasy, I longed to have a horse, a magnificent palomino like Trigger or a fine white stallion like Silver. The closest I came to realizing the fatuous aspiration was on the basketball court. Combining a lack of touch with unwavering inaccuracy, over time I had acquired a huge herd, each member indicative of my ineptitude.

Only days before, the front page of our local newspaper, the Grand Falls Gazette, had borne the photograph that had graced newspapers across America, the image of six U.S. Marines raising Old Glory atop Mt. Suribachi on the island of Iwo Jima. Capture of the Pacific patch of land, roughly 800 miles off the coast of Japan, had strategic significance. American planes could use the territory as a launch strip to attack Japan. Though the event was nothing more than a tiny step in war's long slog, the iconic picture abounded with symbolism. America's standard stood high over land theretofore held by the Axis enemy.

Where the overall status of the war was a vague conglomeration of ebb and flow, territory gained and territory lost, such was not the case on the first Wednesday of March as I competed with Sam in an after-school game of *HORSE*. Throughout the contest, the exact amount of his lead, established from the get-go, was easy to identify. With my failure to match his easy layup, I earned a game-ending *E*. I immediately demanded a rematch. Before starting the new game, Sam and I took a few moments to watch Lefty, down at the other end of the gym, hurling knuckleballs at Frank Carlo, the team's catcher.

"I swear he has upped his speed this winter," said Sam.

"Maybe," I said, wondering if the resounding smack when his pitches hit Carlo's mitt, much louder than when he was on the mound outside, created the illusion that his deliveries were faster.

"You ask me, he's got major-league speed."

"Like Feller?" Any suggestion that Lefty was comparable to the fire-balling pitcher would earn Sam an argument.

"Of course not. Lefty's a knuckleballer. You can't expect him to have Feller's speed. But I'll bet he's as fast as knuckleballer Ted Lyons. The White Sox hurler has notched over 200 wins."

As well as I knew my baseball, next to Sam I was a piker, especially when it came to the game's history and statistics. Sam was a walking encyclopedia.

"You really think Lefty will get a contract?" I said.

"Look at his record here at Grand Falls. One loss through his freshman and junior season, including seven shutouts and two no-hitters. Tack on an ERA of .76, and you've got the hottest commodity from Albany to Buffalo. Major League scouts don't travel here to pick the wild blackberries that grow in the woods beyond the ballfield."

I would have balked if Sam had based his case solely on Lefty's statistics, numbers racked up against small-school, rural competition. But his reference to Major League scouts preempted my argument. If anyone knew how to evaluate potential prospects, the scouts sported the credentials.

I began our *HORSE* rematch with a hook shot that got nothing but...air. Sam followed with a two-hand set shot that rattled off the backboard into the hoop. I was about to take my shot, hoping to avoid a quick *H*, when Larry Babbitt approached.

"Glad I caught you guys. Friday night at seven, I'm having a get-together of The Guys at my house. You know where I live. Right?"

I had never been inside Babbitt's home, but I knew the impressive Victorian. "You're on the corner of Forest Avenue two blocks north of Main...Right?"

"You got it," said Babbitt. "So, I'll see you both Friday night."

Sam and I thanked Babbitt for the invitation and confirmed our intention to attend. Babbitt headed down to the far end of the floor to Lefty, presumably to invite him to the party. Sam and I returned to our game of *HORSE*. His hot shooting from our earlier contest fizzled. The door for me to even the score and force a rubber game opened. Unfortunately, I turned ice cold. Well, the truth be told, I hit my typical paltry percentage. We departed the gym with Sam having recorded back-to-back victories. My notorious herd had grown by two.

***

White snow can cast a black cloud. So too can voices of conscience.

Thursday morning, I departed for school at the usual time. Speedy was outside waiting to join me for the walk. Pleasantries exchanged, I said, "Nice of Babbitt to invite The Guys to his house for a party tomorrow night."

"First I'm hearing about it."

"Well, he only mentioned it to Sam and me in the gym after school yesterday. The rest of the invites will probably come in school today. I'm sure you'll get one."

"Maybe," said Speedy.

His ambiguous response introduced doubt into what a moment before had seemed certain. It reminded me that Babbitt had tried to blackball Speedy when The Guys had been formed. Were it not for Buster, Speedy would have been excluded. That Babbitt might snub Speedy ceased to be farfetched. It begged the question: how should I react? I could press for Speedy's inclusion. I could boycott the party if Babbitt snubbed him. Maybe Sam would join me in the protest. I realized I was getting ahead of myself. Two years removed from the club's formation, odds were Speedy would be invited. Crossing the troublesome bridge would be unnecessary.

Once Speedy and I arrived at school, we went to our homeroom. Shortly after, Babbitt entered. He approached several of The Guys. I surmised he was issuing more invitations to the Friday get-together. I watched him, as well as the clock, hoping that he would approach Speedy. With only a minute remaining until the bell, Babbitt took his seat. I hurried to his desk and said, "I'm looking forward to tomorrow night. Are all The Guys coming?"

"Uh…yeah."

"On the way to school this morning, I mentioned the get-together to Speedy. I assumed he had been invited. He indicated he hadn't."

Babbitt's lips briefly pursed. "The rest of The Guys are coming."

"But you're excluding Speedy?"

"I didn't invite Pete Longley either."

"That's because he works Friday evenings supporting his family. No way could he come."

Babbitt glared. "This is my party at my house. I'll decide who comes. When you have a bash at your place, you can pick and choose."

The bell commencing the school day sounded. Its mandate sent me racing to my seat to avoid a tardy mark. With hindsight, the otherwise unwelcome chime, a restriction on my right to roam and ramble, was a blessing. Going off half-cocked was a tactic thirsting for trouble. I needed time to ascertain the smartest strategy. I eyed Speedy. His nose was buried in a book. The challenge of being Negro in America confronted me again. Unfortunately, I had never addressed the matter, certainly not in a meaningful way. It was simply the way things were. But looking at Speedy, knowing that he was being excluded because of his race, the issue fell squarely on my doorstep. I tried to imagine the disconsolation that would rack me were I in his shoes. Pondering theoretical torment differed from experiencing it. But certain aspects were clear. Teenage years, a time when peer acceptance was critical, bore inherent difficulties. Superimpose intolerance and exclusion, and wounds to one's psyche were all but inevitable. Emotional pain, permanent scars, could be expected. The egregious picture was evident; how I should handle it, problematic. The easy way might have been to turn a blind eye, but incipient pangs of conscience hinted that I would rue such a course. Speedy was my friend. Partying, while he was victimized by discrimination, would spawn guilt...deserved guilt. Initial analysis dictated that I do something substantive to mitigate the inequity. That begged the question – what?

I gazed out the window adjoining my seat. I recalled a point that Mr. Willard had made in history class when we had studied the Civil War. He had read a particular sentence from our textbook, allowing a moment of silence to follow the reading. I reached for my textbook and searched out the sentence, "The entrails of slavery...racism...remain extant."

I reread the sentence several times. I glanced at Speedy. Equality was at our nation's core. Our founding documents proclaimed the principle. How then did the nation embrace slavery? Why after the abomination was abolished were Jim Crow laws, devices to maintain a segregated, two-tier society, endorsed? The institutions of our country – accommodations, schools, employment, means of transportation, etcetera – were replete with deep-rooted, systemic racism. The Guys, the most insignificant of organizations, was a potential perpetrator.

I snapped my history text closed, loud enough that several people turned my way. I ignored their reactions. No way would I attend Babbitt's party. I would press Sam to skip the affair. I would urge Buster, one with more sway, to boycott as well. Change the world, I could not, but I could stand up for my friend. I could be one tiny brick paving the long path to equality.

The instant the bell to pass to first period rang, I raced to Sam. "Babbitt is excluding Speedy from his party."

"How do you know?" he said, as we headed into the hall.

"The bastard told me so."

"Is he excluding anyone else?"

"Not really, assuming you don't count Pete Longley."

As we entered the room for Advanced Algebra, Sam said, "What do you think?"

"We should boycott the party."

"It would have been fun, but you're right...You think we might get others to join us?"

"Yeah, if Buster buys in."

Sam chuckled. "Unfortunately, you're right again. Unlike us, he's got clout."

As it turned out, Buster stood up for Speedy. Others followed, with more threatening to do so. Babbitt refused to budge. Sam, whose parents knew the Babbitt family from their church, speculated that Babbitt's parents, strong opponents of integration, may have put the kibosh on a mixed-race party.

Admittedly, evidence supporting the supposition was absent. Regardless, with the bash fast becoming a non-event, Babbitt announced that he had to cancel, owing to a forecast of snow. The weatherman had predicted up to two inches. Such a paltry accumulation would never lead to a cancellation of anything in Grand Falls, least of all a party in the finished basement of a large Victorian home.

***

Confrontation, coupled with the last word, spawns satisfaction...maybe.

Over the weekend I pondered whether to let the matter be or confront Babbitt. Common sense told me the party's cancellation was an adequate victory. Indignation prodded me to pursue the issue. My conscience provided additional impetus. Knowing that I had ignored discrimination in the past, I was determined to improve my record. I debated with myself, seeking an opportune time and manner to challenge Babbitt. Morning homeroom where others could overhear what was apt to become a heated exchange was impolitic. Catching Babbitt following homeroom at the end of the day made better sense. I contemplated how to broach the subject, rehearsing suitable patter.

Monday afternoon, as we left homeroom following the dismissal bell, I collared Babbitt. "You have a couple minutes? I'd like to talk." I gave no indication of what was to ensue.

"Yeah, I guess."

"How 'bout we go outside? That way we can start for home."

"Fine by me."

Anticipating reluctance, his willingness was welcome. It enabled me to say my piece in relative privacy.

Once we departed the building, Babbitt said, "Let me guess...you want to apologize for screwing up my party."

His acquiescence moments earlier had been clarified. We inhabited distant planets. His gall, an expectation that I should

172

beg his pardon, infuriated me. Likely my face reflected my emotions.

"What then?"

Stupefaction superseded sagacity. Ire annihilated objective. Tactful remarks I had formulated over the weekend decomposed. My tongue transformed into a feral instrument. I said, "I'll be blunt...You're a racist!"

"Screw you, Geeko, you scurvy scumbag!"

"That the best you can do?"

Puzzlement glazed Babbitt's otherwise choleric countenance. "What the hell does that mean?"

"You proved my point. Knowing my allegation is true, you resorted to a nasty slur."

"Bull crap!...Whad'ya expect after you slander me? A thank you? And just for the record, I'm not a racist. I simply believe in separation of the races. That's my constitutional right!"

"Constitutional right?" I reiterated his words with all the sarcasm I could muster.

"Apparently, you didn't listen too well in Willard's class. The freedom to associate with whom you want flows from the right to assemble and the due process clause. A geek like you oughta know that."

I shook my head.

"You disagree?"

"It's not a matter of disagreement. It's a matter of decency. Let me phrase it in a way that even a cretin like you can comprehend. I'll refer you to another tidbit from Mr. Willard. The First Amendment protects hate speech, but it's still hate speech. Yes, you have the right to use it. But when you do, you prove you're a racist...despicable."

Babbitt laughed.

"You find that funny?"

"Yeah, in a way. It explains what my parents mean when they talk about moronic, bleeding-heart liberals, the danger they present." Babbitt looked me in the eye. "If idiots like you get your way, our town, as well as our country, will wind up in the sewer. Property values will plummet. Good white folks will move out. Slums loaded with freeloaders demanding government handouts will be rampant."

The bigotry enraged me. I said, "Babbitt, you're a lousy piece of shit! Go fuck yourself!" I stormed off, having gotten the last word. But the vile epithets left me empty. Even visceral satisfaction was absent. Rather than voicing a well-grounded argument, I had succumbed to rage. I had stooped to Babbitt's level. For that matter, I had slipped lower yet. His points may have been repugnant, but the son of a bitch had scored the last *substantive* word. The admission sparked remorse, especially knowing that in advance of ambushing him, I had spent a weekend preparing.

I turned and looked back. Babbitt had disappeared, presumably around the corner. "Damn you, you bastard!" I directed the epithet at Babbitt…but even more so, at myself.

Chapter XII

One need not be an Einstein to know that many things are relative. But when it comes to luck, the notion can yield very peculiar conclusions.

With the daily edition of the Grand Falls Gazette spread wide, my father sat at our hard rock maple kitchen table. As I joined him for breakfast, he said, "Appears one of your classmates had a rough go this weekend."

"Who?"

My father flipped back to the front page. "Look for yourself." He pointed at a photograph of a mangled Buick Roadster convertible, passenger side down, in a culvert. He passed the newspaper to me.

Despite the black-and-white photograph, I recognized the vehicle as Lefty's yellow hot rod. A glance at the story's headline, "Star Hurler Flips Car," confirmed my assessment.

"The article indicates he was taken to Little Falls Hospital," said my father. "Appears speed was a factor."

Knowing Lefty, the last point was no surprise. I read the brief article. It indicated that Lefty had lost control of his car on a curve on Route 29A near Wheelerville. Apart from stating that his injuries were not life threatening, the details of his condition remained unknown. No mention was made whether alcohol contributed.

"You'd think a kid with so much talent and opportunity would show better judgment." My father shook his head. "On second thought, if he's anything like his old man, lousy judgment comes naturally."

"What makes you say that?"

My father hemmed and hawed.

"C'mon, that's not fair. You make a suggestive remark, and then you leave me in the dark."

My father muttered. "I should have kept my mouth shut." He heaved a sigh. "Okay. Here's the score. Lucinski's father is a big talker who loves to carouse. His driver's license has been suspended more than once. Folks who knew him when he was young say he was too big for his britches, an annoying jackass."

I had met Lefty's father a couple of times. Now and then he had come to watch Lefty pitch. On one occasion he had sat in the stands with The Guys. Apart from exchanging pleasantries, I had never spoken to him, but I had been close enough to observe his style. A flashy dresser with a big ring and fancy gold chain around his neck, he was brash. Still, he seemed like a decent guy.

I would have torn the article out of the newspaper and brought it to school were I not sure that others would. I finished my breakfast and headed out to meet Speedy. I no sooner turned onto Elm than Speedy hurried down from his stoop.

"Did you hear the news?" he said.

"About Lefty?"

"What else?...You know anything more than what's in the newspaper?"

I shook my head. "Maybe once we get to school, we'll learn more."

"You think Lefty will be there today?"

I shrugged. "Don't know, but given that he was taken to the hospital, I doubt it."

When we arrived at school, not surprisingly, Lefty's accident was the talk of the halls. Because Speedy and I were members of The Guys, students probed us for information. We knew nothing more than they. The situation repeated itself in homeroom. Everyone was talking about the accident, but the newspaper account was as much as anyone knew.

The bell beginning the school day rang. Lefty was absent. Homeroom ended. The morning schedule of classes came and went. Still no Lefty. Sam, Speedy, and I had just finished lunch and were about to head back to class when we spotted Lefty at the far end of the hall. He had a large bandage on his head, and his left arm bore a cast. We hurried his way where others had already surrounded him.

"...a laceration requiring seven stitches." Lefty pointed at his forehead.

"What about your arm?" said a girl.

Lefty groaned, giving his cast-covered arm a look. "I broke my wrist. That's what they told me."

"When will you be able to pitch again?" said Chip Rider, a junior who had just come onto the scene.

A disgusted look painted Lefty's face. "The ER doctor guessed it would be eight weeks, give or take. Even then, I'll have to strengthen my arm before I can take the mound full speed. On the bright side, at least from the doc's view, it could have been worse, a compound fracture."

"You think you'll be able to pitch again this season?"

"Maybe the tail end...the playoffs, if we're lucky enough to make 'em."

The question on my mind, and I suspect others, was how it would impact his shot at a professional baseball career. The inquiry's negative aspects, as well as its impertinence, kept me from asking. My curiosity, however, did not go unsated.

"Will your broken wrist hurt your chances to make the big leagues?" said Chip.

"Doubt it. According to the doc, a fracture like mine should fully heal. He expects I'll be good as new...Of course, a two-month layoff does me no good."

"How's your car?" said Janet...what's her name.

Lefty rolled his eyes. "I'm yet to get the final verdict, but totaled is – "

"C'mon, break up the confab!" said Assistant Principal Milano, hurrying toward us. "You've got one minute to get to class, unless you want detention."

Even before he finished his warning, we dispersed, with Sam and me climbing the stairs, two at a time, racing to Physics.

We entered the room, beating the bell by seconds. "Looks like Lefty was fortunate," said Sam.

"I guess, if you deem a broken wrist, a bunch of stitches in your head, and a racked-up hot rod as good luck."

"Hey, all those things beat getting killed."
As Sam and I slipped into our adjoining seats, I digested his remark. "When you put it that way, you have a point."

***

Great news affords a reason to celebrate...perhaps.

After walking home from school with Speedy on the last Thursday in March 1945, I lingered at his house to toss a football. Though remnants of snowbanks from previously plowed snow persisted, spring hung on the horizon. Indeed, the calendar testified that it had already arrived. But tell that to Mother Nature. In the foothills of the Adirondacks, predictably, she disdained the calendar.

Going deep on Elm Street, with my arm fully extended I tipped the bomb that Speedy had hurled, pulling in the pigskin after a precarious bobble. The sterling catch, my day's crowning achievement, accorded the perfect conclusion to what had been a paradigm of incompetence. After moving closer, I tossed the football back to Speedy. I yelled, "On that last glorious note, I'm calling it quits. See you tomorrow morning." I grabbed my bookbag and headed home. Once I entered, I picked up the mail that lay on the floor inside the entranceway. Like many houses, ours had a mail slot adjacent to the front door. I dropped my bookbag and shuffled through the envelopes. The last, the only one addressed to me, was from the New York State Teachers College at Albany. I went to the kitchen, laying the mail, except for my letter, onto the table. I felt the envelope, gauging its heft and thickness. Around school, conjecture, the antithesis of statistically verifiable analysis, claimed that rejections came on a single sheet, while acceptances included enclosures. My feel test hinted at bad news.

I took the envelope into the living room where I plopped down into my father's favorite easy chair, a large, padded rocker. If I had to bear bad tidings, I preferred to do so comfortably. I held the envelope up to the adjacent table lamp. The scrutiny added nothing to my earlier examination. I peeled back the flap and opened the envelope. Knowing that my destiny, as determined by the military's whim, was other than college, the letter's contents mattered less. Whatever it said, whether it contained an acceptance or rejection, would not dictate the course of my life. Events across the world's two greatest oceans would determine my fate. I unfolded the letter and read its body:

> We are pleased to inform you that you have been accepted for admission to the New York State Teachers' College at Albany for the school year commencing Wednesday, September 12, 1945. We will be sending you more information about the curriculum, housing, and other relevant matters.
> No later than May 15, 1945, please inform us if you wish to become a member of the college's class of 1949.

With a conscious smile, I slipped the letter back into the envelope, putting it onto the arm of the chair. I leaned back with my hands behind my head. Mixed emotions stirred. Being accepted to my college of choice, at least when financial considerations were incorporated into the equation, was wonderful. But it meant little. Assuming I started my college career in September, by the end of the calendar year, odds were I would be joining the United States Military, preparing for war. Whether I would ever return, let alone get a college education, was questionable. I strongly supported America's cause, defeating the Axis. I deemed it righteous. Nevertheless, qualms kindled. The possibility my college experience might be brief, that my adult life would never eventuate, hamstrung any urge to celebrate terrific tidings.

***

The tortoise and the hare have taught us that appearances can be deceiving. Slow and steady can subdue stunningly swift. But when time is limited, one must be a hare. A tortoise has no

---

chance of reaching the finish line. But beware, haste makes waste.

The new month, its advent marked by April Fools' Day, unleashed a plethora of tricks. Most were stupid and spur-of-the-moment, but harmless. Perhaps the best came from our Advanced Algebra teacher, Mrs. Aiken. Once we were seated at the start of class, she handed out papers, face down on our desks.

"On your desk is a test...and stop moaning." Before a burgeoning mutinous reaction could gain momentum, Mrs. Aiken's admonishment had stifled it. "Do not turn your papers over until I tell you to begin. Follow the instructions. You will have ten minutes...Begin."

Already unnerved by the unanticipated exam, I flipped the paper over. Six complex word problems confronted me. Completing them demanded a half-hour. Sweat, indicative of my panic, subsumed me. Unable to afford time for my emotional or physical concerns, I dove into the first problem. About two minutes into the effort, as I set up my first equation, a smattering of laughter erupted. Surmising its precipitant entailed no brilliance. Forget about completing the entire test in the allotted ten minutes. Half was impossible. That said, I could ill-afford to participate in the guffaw. Not a second could be squandered. Full devotion to the problems was imperative, not that it could help me achieve a passing grade, 65%. My only hope was that Mrs. Aiken would mark the abomination on a curve. If so, scoring higher than others might bail me out.

Finishing the first problem, I checked my watch. Four minutes had elapsed. The laughter mounted. My stomach knotted. I glanced around the room. Those laughing, a tiny few, had apparently waved the white flag, yielding to the vain task. Stupid them, I thought. But all the better for me if there was a curve. I continued to race through the problems. The laughter grew even more pronounced, not to mention distracting. I had just begun writing an equation for the third problem when Mrs. Aiken called out, "Time's up. All pencils down."

I desperately tried to do a little more.

"Anyone I see continuing to write will receive a zero!"

180

At the wrong end of a loaded shotgun, I dropped my weapon...my pencil.

"Leave your papers, face up, on the upper left corner of your desks," said Mrs. Aiken. "I'll come around and grade them." She went to the storage closet and got a paper bag. She walked down the first aisle, the one farthest from the window. She paused at the first desk, just long enough to shake her head and scowl. She exhibited an identical reaction as she passed the next two desks. At the fourth, muttered disgust complemented her non-verbal negativity.

The harsh reactions flew in the face of her normally clement manner. Having allowed us a fraction of the time required to solve the problems, what did she expect?

Mrs. Aiken reached the last desk in the first aisle. She nodded repeatedly, displaying a broad smile. "Excellent!" she said, pulling a big *Snickers* bar out of her paper bag. She placed the treat on Nancy Cole's desk.

Nancy Cole? How, of all people, could she, who was failing Advanced Algebra, do this impossible test in ten minutes? What the hell was going on?

Mrs. Aiken continued up and down the aisles, mostly shaking her head and scowling. Now and then, she delivered praise, followed by a *Snickers*. At last, she reached my aisle, the one by the window. She paused alongside my desk. A shake of her head, followed by a displeased sigh, and she was on her way, visiting the final desks.

Mrs. Aiken returned to the front of the room and said, "Please read the instructions at the top of your papers."

I eyed the paper. At the top it said, "Instructions: Do not do any of the problems that appear below. Write the word *Snickers* at the bottom of your paper. Then lay your pencil down and sit quietly in your seat for ten minutes."

Laughter pervaded the room. We had been had...well, all but a few of us.

"Happy April Fools' Day," said Mrs. Aiken. "But this was more than an April Fools' joke. This exercise boasts a purpose, one that I believe merited ten minutes of our time. Instructions are important. They must be absorbed and heeded, not just here in math class, but in all your classes. They're equally important when trying to put something together, working in a job, trying to get from one place to another, or performing other tasks. The aphorism, *Haste makes waste,* has merit. May today's exercise be a lesson for the future...And to compensate for the stress of the surprise test, I have mini-Hershey bars for all of you." She handed another paper bag to Ellen Marsh who sat in the front row. "Please give one to everyone...And now, let's refocus on Advanced Algebra."

Before my mind redirected to mathematics, I jotted a note, a device guaranteeing that the consequential exercise, the need to check for instructions, not join the junk heap of countless past lessons. Unlike my past New Year's resolutions, the tutorial did not morph into a quickly forgotten good intention. Before long it became a habit. Little did I realize how soon the lesson's value would be realized. And when it was, I remembered Mrs. Aiken...fondly. She was an excellent teacher.

***

Statistics offer a valuable tool for setting odds, predicting future outcomes. But some predictions are too appalling to countenance.

Following school on April Fools' Day, The Guys met at the benches behind the building. As usual, our meeting was an informal, agenda-free get-together. Ten of us were present, including Lefty. He would have been at baseball practice, but for his broken wrist. Pete Longley was working and supporting his family. Buddy Slack was out sick. And of course, Don Baker was roaming the big paradise of the sky, having given his life on the battlefields of Europe.

"I've got some good news, something that oughta interest all of you," said Cooper. "My uncle – he's on the area's draft board – says they have enough recruits and draftees that they won't need to pull any of us seniors out of school before graduation."

The disclosure buoyed much of our group, but for those who would turn eighteen in the second half of the calendar year, after graduation, Sam and I included, it made no difference.

"Show of hands, how many plan to join up once school is out?" said Lefty.

Pokey Paulsen, Buster, and Speedy raised their hands.

"The rest of you gonna wait till you're drafted," said Paulsen. "From what I hear, if you enlist, you may get input on your assignment."

"May have been that way a few years back," said Babbitt, "but my cousin from Albany – he's an ensign in the Navy – says that became ancient history, ever since we entered the war. They ship you where they need you. A body is lucky to get lip service, let alone a choice."

"So, you plan to wait till you're called?" said Buster.

"I expect to go to college…in Utica." Babbitt bore a smug look.

"He'll be going to Utica all right," said Vic Dolan. "But it won't be college. George will be attending that big institution manned by the men in the white coats. Last I heard, they called it an insane asylum."

"Laugh now," said Babbitt, "but I'll get the last one when the Geris are hammering you with lead and I'm guzzling beer at a frat party."

"What makes you so sure you won't get drafted?" said Sam.

"I've got heel spurs," said Babbitt.

"And you think that's gonna keep you out of the military?" said Sam.

"I not only think so; I know so. Doc Sullmer – he's a friend of my dad from Syracuse – said he'll write me a letter saying I couldn't handle basic training and that I'd be a drag on my unit."

"No doubt you'd be a drag," said Lefty, "but it ain't due to heel spurs. It's 'cause you're a spaz."

"Call me names. See if I care." Babbitt shifted his focus from Lefty to the entire group. "Anyone else going to college?"

"I plan to attend the State Teachers' College in Albany, at least until Uncle Sam yanks me out." I gestured at Sam. "And Doc has been accepted to both Dartmouth and Cornell."

Cooper turned to Sam. "Porter...the Ivy League? What's this? A belated April Fools' joke?"

His tone apologetic, Sam said, "Well, they both accepted me. I plan to go to Cornell, but odds are Uncle Sam will come calling early in my freshman year. Chances are, I'll be carrying a gun before the calendar year ends." He looked around. "Anyone else plan to start college this fall?"

The question drew a brief silence.

"Here's another question," said Cooper. "How many of us will be dead a year from now?"

Like its predecessor, the question drew silence, but this one was eerie.

I could have speculated as to the number...maybe one or two...or even three. But the question was better treated as rhetorical. Answering it demanded I cross a bridge too far. No one else ventured an estimate. Likely, they too deemed it beyond the pale.

***

Sharing good news is enjoyable, though less so when inquisitive interlopers intercept the information.

"I'll get it!" I yelled, racing from my bedroom to our living-room telephone. The two short rings indicated the call was for our house, not Mr. Thorton's. I picked up the receiver. "Hello."

"Hi Jim."

"Hi Sweetie," I said, upon hearing Mary's voice. "What's up?"

"Good news. Skidmore accepted me. I just opened the letter."

"Congratulations...Now you'll have to make a decision, Mount Holyoke or Skidmore." A week earlier Mount Holyoke had accepted Mary.

"I've made it already."

"Really? I thought you were vacillating."

"Well...deep down I wanted Skidmore, but in case they turned me down and I had to settle for Mount Holyoke, I didn't want it to feel like a consolation prize. Now that Skidmore has given the thumbs up, no need to think twice."

"I'm glad you got your first choice. I'm happy for me as well. Skidmore is closer to Albany than Mount Holyoke, at most an hour on the bus."

"That's one of the reasons I'm opting for Skidmore."

Mary's response, confirmation that she wanted our romance to continue after high school, brought a smile to my face. I said, "I hope Uncle Sam doesn't put an ocean between us." I thought I heard someone pick up the receiver on another telephone. With our two-party line a constant source of suspicion, I said, "Mr. Thorton, do you think the military might station me in Albany?" If our party-line neighbor had begun listening in, I had no illusions that he would respond. The purpose of my question was twofold: first, to let the eavesdropper know I was aware of his prying; and second, to warn Mary that our conversation had ceased to be private.

"We'll talk more in school tomorrow. Okay?" she said, verifying she grasped my message.

"Sounds good."

A receiver clicked. The ensuing dial tone indicated that the person who had initiated the call, Mary, had hung up. I said, "Have a nice day, Mr. Thorton." I waited for more than a minute for a click. None occurred. Finally, I hung up. Though I lacked certainty, the evidence gainsaid that Mr. Thorton had been eavesdropping. Regardless, the call had terminated without personal revelations.

***

In the Big Apple annoying horns constantly blare. Such noise rarely racks rural towns. But occasionally events kindle cacophony in the most bucolic locales.

Where so many events of World War II had drawn little attention from us students at Grand Falls High, the month of April 1945 altered that trend. Headlines reporting death by all manners imaginable were difficult to ignore. On April 6th the American forces entered the Ohrdruf subcamp of the

Buchenwald concentration camp in Germany. There they found the remains of Nazi barbarity. Emaciated bodies with bullets in their heads smoldered in a state of partial incineration. Six days after the discovery, Supreme Commander of the Allied Forces, Dwight Eisenhower, who subsequently termed the scene "conditions of indescribable horror," ordered photographs of the evil released. Though the world was yet to learn the full scope of Germany's horrific savagery, denial ceased to be possible.

On the same day that Eisenhower directed release of the Ohrdruf photographs, President Roosevelt, who had been inaugurated for his fourth term less than three months earlier, died of an intracerebral hemorrhage. Before the month was out, Adolph Hitler and his wife Eva Braun each committed suicide. And in Italy, Benito Mussolini, along with his mistress Clara Petacci, were shot and hanged by their feet in Milan.

Where death dominated April, a different aura populated May. Tuesday, May 8, 1945, a day that began like any other, saw Speedy and me negotiating our usual route to school. As we turned onto Main, the horn of a car passing in the opposite direction bellowed. We were on the sidewalk, nowhere near the vehicle's path. No other car or person was within one hundred yards.

"What's his problem?" I said.

"Got me," said Speedy.

We continued down Main. Halfway to Bridge Street, where the school was located, another car passed with horn honking. An arm extending from the passenger-side window waved an American flag.

"Is today some kind of holiday, maybe a birthday of one of the presidents?" said Speedy.

The only ones I knew were Washington and Lincoln's, and those had stuck with me because we got them off from school. "Not that I know of," I said, "but if people think the day is worth celebrating, they ought to turn it into an official school holiday, one that we get off."

"I like the way you think."

As we drew closer to the school, a couple more horns honked. Several students on the lawn in front of the building were waving small American flags. "Did we miss something?"

"No clue," said Speedy.

We crossed the street to the school side where we caught up to Penny Pender, a fellow senior. "Any idea what's happening?" I said.

"You haven't heard?"

"Heard what?"

"Germany surrendered. The war is over in Europe."

"Really?" I said, shock, not disagreement, occasioning my reaction.

"I heard it on the radio, just before I left the house," said Penny. "They interrupted *Portia Faces Life*, my mom's favorite soap opera, to announce it."

Speedy and I continued into the building where a rapt atmosphere prevailed. "You know what this could mean?" I said, as we headed up the stairs to our homeroom.

Speedy stopped. Following a moment of apparent rumination, he shrugged. "What?"

"We might not get drafted. Even if we do, we won't be fighting a war."

"Not necessarily," said Speedy.

I shot him a look. "Come again?"

"Nobody said the war in the Pacific ended."

The point was salient. Regardless, I refused to let it spoil my excitement. "Maybe so, but it's terrific news."

"Absolutely, though…" Speedy turned pensive.

"Though what?" I said, when Speedy failed to clarify his apparent qualification.

"I doubt it'll affect my plans. I'll probably still enlist."

A fellow senior, Nick Prosper, passing in the opposite direction, slapped me on the back. "Great news, isn't it?"

"Got that right!" I said.

Speedy and I were approaching our homeroom when I spotted our history teacher two rooms ahead doing hall duty. I gestured toward him and said to Speedy, "Before going in, maybe we can get the full scoop. No one will know better than a history teacher." We hurried his way. "Mr. Willard, we heard that Germany surrendered. Is that right?"

"You know as much as I. But that's my understanding, and if so, it's wonderful."

"You think the entire war might be over?" Wishful thinking prompted my inquiry.

"Doubt it. There's still the Pacific Theater. Nothing I've heard suggests that Japan is ready to call it quits. Given their stoic determination, good chance they'll fight to the last man. I suspect we'll hear more in the next day or two." Mr. Willard glanced at his watch. "You two need to get to homeroom."

Speedy and I hurried there. Surrender-spawned enthusiasm reigned. Though little was added to what we already knew, the repetition reinforced the credibility of what we had heard. Anticipation of fathers, mothers, brothers, sisters, uncles, aunts, cousins, and friends coming home from the European warfront was rampant. So too was conversation about our futures. Might those of us who were reluctant to enter the military be free to pursue our lives as we wished? Optimism abounded. Throughout Grand Falls High School, everywhere in the sleepy town, and across the nation, folks celebrated.

Trumpeting to us students the magnitude of the event was superfluous. Even so, school officials underscored the point with rare leniency. They dismissed us for the day shortly after the noon hour. Walking home from school, drivers tooted their horns. Passengers, as well as people on the street, shouted and waved American flags. Everyone, strangers included, exchanged joyous greetings. An atmosphere more festive than the 4th of July parade down Main Street prevailed. I reveled as much as anyone, and part of my joy resulted from the expectation that come September my chances of pursuing my college education had mushroomed. Even assuming only half the war had ceased, logic dictated that the number conscripted would dramatically decline. For an instant, a pang of guilt interrupted my celebration. My improved opportunity to realize my dreams had come at the expense of the many who had given their lives. Their sacrifices gave me pause. My guilt, however, was fleeting. Admittedly, I had never been eager to serve. But I had never been called. I had never refused. Never had I intended to dodge the draft. That timing, serendipity, accorded me a reprieve was my good fortune. Such was the nature of war, indeed life. My celebration resumed, albeit with heightened gratitude.

Chapter XIII

Hurling a baseball is akin to fighting a war. Each time a batter steps to the plate to face a pitcher another battle ensues. But unlike war, where the game is for keeps and many participants die, pitchers and batters live to face one another again. A bad outcome can be redeemed in the next battle. Glory may be just around the corner. Unfortunately, it may be ephemeral as well.

Despite the good news associated with Germany's surrender, ambiguity how the war would unwind persisted beyond May 8th. The Pacific Theater remained a bloody tableau. My hope that I would not be conscripted elevated when, just two days after V-E Day, the Department of Defense announced that veterans would begin returning home based upon a point system. Still, in the ensuing months new soldiers were drafted at the rate of 100,000 per month. But we senior males at Grand Falls High School became increasingly convinced that we would not be pressed into service. The truth be known, we reinforced one another's beliefs, breeding a premature false sense of security. Whether similarly situated males around the nation shared a like perception, or if we, living in the bubble of a rural area, were more sanguine, arguably naive, I have no clue. Regardless, such was the mindset among my classmates and me. Day by day, the pervasive shadow that war had cast over our conversations and plans faded. Senioritis, which had long been percolating, exploded. We felt free to party hearty for the balance of the school year. Those of us who would soon be off to college in the fall anticipated that we would be able to continue our high jinks during the upcoming summer, after which we could pursue our futures as we wished. And so, the weeks of May rolled blithely past.

It was the last Friday of the month, the last baseball game of the season, when Lefty Lucinski, his arm finally healed, returned to the mound. Over the course of the season, without him pitching, the team had compiled a mediocre .500 record. While the outcome of the game meant little in the team standings, the game was consequential to Lefty's career. A Brooklyn Dodger scout had come to watch him. The outing would offer insight into the oft-repeated question: Would Lefty, the flashy knuckleballer, re-emerge with past promise extant, or would the aftereffects of his injury divert him from the road to renown into the dustheap of high school heroes who once had big-league potential?

Speedy, Sam, and I arrived at the ballfield early. We grabbed seats two rows behind Johnnie Markem, the Dodger scout. During the school day we garnered whatever we could about Markem's career. As best as we could tell, Markem had made it to spring training twice in the 1920s, once with the Pirates and once with the Dodgers. A shortstop, he had never played in a regular-season Major League game.

As Lefty warmed up, we focused on every comment Markem made. Seated next to him was our junior varsity baseball coach, Tom Peters. With the stands yet to fill, we were able to hear their conversation.

"Looks good," said Markem. "His ball's got hop...and decent pop. Question is, can he keep the damn thing in the strike zone?"

"Before his injury Lefty averaged just 1.1 walks per game," said Peters.

"Yeah, I seen his numbers. But any hurler worth a nickel can get high school kids to swing at junk a foot from the strike zone. Ain't that way in the bigs...not when guys like DiMaggio and Gerhrig are swingin' the lumber. Don't get me wrong. I ain't tossin' him in the dung pile, just sayin' that till he shows somethin' against big-time bats, he's a longshot."

"If that's how you see it," said Peters, "why you here?"

"'Cause watchin' him, I can tell if he's got a chance. Of every four I see – they all look great on paper – three are no counts. One first-hand visit, and it's obvious, they ain't got what it takes. Of the other twenty-five percent, most get contract offers, almost always startin' in the minors. Two-thirds of them never make it to the Majors. Throwin' a baseball ain't the same as the hundred-yard dash where a stopwatch and less than a dozen seconds tell the whole story."

The umpire shouted, "Play ball!"

Bentlyville's leadoff batter stepped to the plate. Lefty fanned him on three pitches, two of which the hitter waved at futilely. The next two batters met a similar fate, though they managed to run the count to 2-2 and 1-2 respectively, before striking out.

Lefty added a pair of strikeouts in the top half of both the second and third innings. Grand Falls broke the scoreless tie in the bottom of the third, plating four runs. Speedy, Sam, and I tried to eavesdrop, but Markem said little, and what he did was inaudible owing to crowd noise, which was much greater than pregame. With one out in the top of the fourth, Bentlyville nearly got its first hit, a broken-bat Texas Leaguer that appeared destined to hit the grass until Dick Gray, a speedster who had spurned track for baseball, snagged it inches from the turf.

"Lefty's still hurling a perfect game," said Sam.

"Jeez," said Speedy. "Don't you know it's bad luck, talking about a possible no-hitter while it's going on."

"C'mon," said Sam. "That's a ridiculous wives' tale. Be one thing to mention it to the pitcher. That could up the pressure. But folks in the stands mentioning it to one another has no effect."

Speedy shook his head. "Tradition says that mum's the word…And if Lefty loses his no-hitter, I'm blaming you!"

While Speedy and Sam bickered, Lefty fanned another Bentlyville hitter, retiring the side. He got through the fifth inning easily. With two outs in the top of the sixth, he threw a wild pitch, running the count to 3-2 on the Bentlyville hitter, a huge guy who sported a .389 average. Lefty followed with a rare curve, one that appeared to hook into the strike zone, leaving the befuddled batter frozen. The umpire bellowed, "Ball four!" Boos streamed from the stands, as the dubious call robbed Lefty of an otherwise perfect game. The next batter struck out on three straight knuckleballs ending Bentlyville's time at bat.

Grand Falls added two more runs in the bottom of the stanza extending the lead to six runs.

In the top of the seventh and final inning, Lefty breezed, sandwiching two strikeouts around an easy roller back to the box. Lefty had recorded an impressive no-hit victory that included fourteen strikeouts.

The stands began to empty. Speedy, Sam, and I stayed in our seats, once again monitoring the back and forth between Markem and Peters. As the seats emptied and the din of the crowd slackened, conversation between scout and coach grew audible.

"The kid has good stuff. Better than I expected," said Markem. "Knuckleballs ain't my cup of tea, but that Mexican jumping bean he throws is somethin' else. His curve ain't bad, and he has enough speed to keep batters off balance. Surprising control for a knuckleballer. Just one walk, and that owin' to an ump who's blinder than a dead mole at midnight...Damn impressive."

"So, you think he has a good shot?" said Coach Peters.

Markem nodded slowly. "Yeah, I suspect he'll get an offer. Assumin' he does, we'll see how he fares in the minors against real hitters. That's where the rubber starts to meet the road."

Markem got up from his seat. Coach Peters followed close behind. They headed down to Lefty. Though they were out of earshot, the arm that Markem put over Lefty's shoulder, coupled with the conversation we had just overheard, hinted at what the scout might be saying.

"Looks like Lefty is destined to be a professional ballplayer," said Sam.

"Betcha he makes it to the Majors," I said.

"Markem didn't seem so sure," said Sam.

"But he seemed impressed," said Speedy. "Wouldn't surprise me if Markem was curbing his enthusiasm. Knowing his club will have to negotiate with Lefty, he needs to play it cool."

"If Lefty makes it to the Majors," I said, "we'll be able to say we knew him when…that we were in an exclusive club with him." Even as I made the point, I knew it was hyperbolic. The Guys, which included every male in our homeroom, hardly qualified as exclusive. I glanced in Lefty's direction as I climbed down from the grandstand. I made a mental note to have Lefty sign a baseball for me. For too long, the task had remained undone.

***

Insurance is self-contradictory. You purchase it, hoping never to use it. But on those occasions when you need it, even as you rue the events that made it necessary, you thank your lucky stars you have it.

The first Friday of June found Grand Falls High seniors at Dalmer Glen enjoying the newly established senior-class picnic. While the freshmen and juniors had regular classes, the seniors were given the afternoon off for the cookout. Many had hoped the event would include swimming in the pond, complete with leaps from Perch Rock. An inordinately cool June day, light-jacket weather, all but eliminated water activities. Bathing suits had been left home. Only a few brave souls waded ankle deep into the crystal-clear, numbing creek. While most lamented that conditions were inapt for swimming, I was an exception. Eliminating the risk that my buddies might badger me into another leap from the Perch more than compensated for forgoing a swim.

With the pond all but empty, the activity centered around the pavilion in the main picnic area where a fare of hot dogs, hamburgers, chips, coleslaw, potato salad, and baked beans, plus cookies, cupcakes, and soda, awaited. Beer was also popular, but it was discretely stowed in coolers kept in car trunks. Though many had already celebrated their eighteenth birthday, rumor had it that openly providing alcohol to all could kill the picnic for future classes.

I had gotten my driver's license in early April, but only on rare occasions did I get the family car. The senior picnic was such an occasion. I had driven my father to work in the morning. He had arranged a ride home with a friend. For the first time I had driven to school. From there, following early dismissal, along with Mary, I had driven to the picnic. We had opted for a separate table where we could enjoy some time by ourselves. Much as I liked my pals, spending time alone with my first girlfriend had its advantages. And too, I had a surprise for her.

We had eaten an ample portion and were polishing off bottles of Pepsi when Mary said, "Can you believe it? In three months, we'll be off to college."

"I can hardly wait, not that I'm wishing away the summer." I had lined up my first real job, stocking shelves and bagging at the grocery market in Little Falls. The chance to earn a weekly paycheck excited me. The grocery had worked my hours so I could travel to and from work consistent with my father's schedule at the utility plant. My forty-hour workweek left me with ample time to goof off. The self-satisfaction and compensation of a job, coupled with the ease of teenage freedom, forecast a fabulous summer.

"I finally decided on a major," said Mary. "I've chosen biology."

"I thought you were leaning toward English."

"I was, and I'll probably minor in English. But I looked at careers. I'd like to have one, and I think biology will give me more options. I might do research. If that doesn't pan out, I can always teach."

"How's the biology program at Skidmore?"

"Excellent. A couple of professors there have won recognition in the field."

No longer willing to postpone my planned surprise, I got up from my seat. "Wait here a minute. I'll be right back." I hurried to the parking lot where I got my ivory cardigan bearing my golf letter from the car's trunk. I returned to the picnic table where Mary waited. I handed her the sweater. "This is for you."

She held it up with the front facing her. "I love it...Thank you."

"Try it on." I proudly helped her.

Mary admired the sporty garment, running her fingers over the *GF* that was stitched to the lower left front. Though I was four inches taller than Mary, the sweater looked great on her. She filled it out better than I.

"Does this mean we're going steady?" she said.

Where many viewed "going steady" as implying a committed relationship, only a step short of engagement, around the halls of Grand Falls High, "going steady" merely meant that a couple was dating exclusively...for the time being. Often it was no more than a few weeks. Our relationship had long since exceeded that length. I said, "I think so." I leaned forward and kissed Mary, more than a peck, but far from passionately.

"So, neither of us will date anyone else. Right?"

"Absolutely...And unless I'm mistaken, it's been that way for several months."

Mary furrowed her brow. "You mean you didn't know about the fellow from Utica and the one from Little Falls...and the – " Mary clipped her tongue, perhaps because she observed my umbrage. "Only kidding. I haven't dated anyone but you." She kissed me.

I put my arm over her shoulder. "Let's get a cupcake. I want one with blue frosting, not that it'll be as sweet as you."

Mary smiled. "Flattery will get you everywhere."

"Everywhere?" I punctuated my drawn-out utterance with a devilishly contrived smile.

She winked. "Everywhere!...Though not everything."

I pecked Mary on the cheek. Someone eavesdropping might have found our dialogue perplexing, but I knew exactly what Mary meant. She was a strong believer that sexual intercourse should await marriage. Risking the possibility of pregnancy at age seventeen was foolhardy. Much as my hormones disagreed, having seen how it had changed Pete Longley's life, judgment prevented me from arguing.

We went to the pavilion for our cupcakes, chocolate with yellow frosting for Mary and vanilla with blue frosting for me. We were finishing the delights when Speedy approached.

"The Guys are gonna meet in ten minutes, near the Susan B. Anthony Monument," he said.

I looked at Mary. "I can skip – "

"Go ahead. It's fine. I'll hang out with the girls."

"Thanks. It shouldn't take long." Along with Speedy, I headed to the monument.

Past the parking lot, near the ballfield, we reached the spot where The Guys had gathered, mainly around Pete Longley, who was accompanied by his eleven-month-old daughter Laura. She was hanging onto Pete's index finger as she took several wobbly steps.

"She just started to walk this week," said Pete.

"Dada...ju-ju," said Laura.

Pete handed his daughter a sippy cup. "She's really smart. She began speaking almost a month ago. She understands lots of words and can say about ten. The doctor says she's a couple months ahead of most."

Watching Pete, I made several observations. He was a proud father. He differed from the Pete I had known when he was a full-time student. It was as if he had leaped forward into his twenties. He was at a different stage of his life. Impressive as it was, I was thankful I could still be a typically immature high school kid. Accountability for myself was challenging enough. Responsibility for the health, needs, and welfare of a toddler was inconceivable.

"Pete...what a pleasant surprise," said Lefty, who came our way with a six-pack of Utica Club in hand. "Didn't expect to see you here."

"Working umpty hours a week, I figured I could take one afternoon off. Even lowly peons get a bit of free time now and then."

Though I knew his comment was rife with hyperbole, the gratitude I felt being able to savor my youth amplified. I grabbed a bottle of brew. With a church key, I popped the top and imbibed the bubbly liquid. It was as distasteful as ever. But when you are with The Guys, you do what The Guys do.

"Okay, let's get this meeting to order," said Buster. "What's on the agenda?"

Blank looks, coupled with some shrugs, par for the course, greeted the inquiry. Our years of high school had proved that The Guys was a clique rarely with a plan or goal.

"Anymore of you thinking of signing up with Uncle Sam?" said Pete.

"Speedy plans to," said Sam.

Pete groaned. "I knew that a year ago. Tell me something new. The group must have a few exciting tidbits."

A brief silence followed. It highlighted our fruitless existence. The point might have been disconcerting had it not been long apparent. Belonging, being accepted, was sufficient.

Babbitt, who had gone to the parking lot minutes before, delivered another six-pack, this time Schlitz.

Buster, who had grabbed one, looked my way. "Get 'em while you can. They're gonna go fast."

"Still got some," I said, my bottle three-quarters full. Odds were my first would be my last. The more I drank the bitter beverage, the worse it tasted. I wondered if any of the other guys shared my view. Apart from discussing the matter with Sam and Speedy – the former liked beer while the latter didn't – I kept my thoughts to myself, lest I make a public proclamation reminding everyone I was a dork. I sipped my brew, ever so slowly, likely slower than Laura slurped her juice.

"Doc," said Babbitt, "you did a paper last semester on the Spanish-American War, didn't you?"

"Yeah," said Sam, who was sitting on the ground cross-legged, his back against a big maple.

"You have Willard. Right?"

"Yeah. So what?"

"I've got Raines this semester. I got a paper due the end of next week. Can you bring yours on Monday?"

"What? So, you can copy it?"

"What else? To read it?" Babbitt laughed.

Sam shook his head. "You'll stick us both in a jackpot."

"C'mon, nobody will be the wiser. Hell, ever since Raines was passed over for department head in favor of Willard, she barely speaks to him."

"It'll be just my luck that they talk, and my ass, like yours, will be grass...with Willard the lawnmower."

"Jeez, Porter, don't be a prick." Babbitt moved closer, so he stood high over Sam.

"You're not getting my paper." Sam folded his arms defiantly.

Babbitt kicked the shin of one of Sam's folded legs. The shot, though far from full force, was sufficient to smart.

"Leave him alone," I said.

Babbitt, roughly my height, but forty pounds heavier, turned my way and shoved me. "You and who else is gonna make me, Geeko?"

I suspected that alcohol was fueling Babbitt's aggressiveness. How many bottles he had consumed was anyone's guess. I held my ground, standing as tall as possible. I checked the urge to shove him back. A fight was the last thing I wanted. Though Babbitt was hardly tough, with a body far outweighing my skinny frame, odds were he could lick me. But with everyone watching, no way would I back down.

Babbitt refocused on Sam. He kicked him again, about as hard as before. "You gonna give me your paper voluntarily, or do I have to make you?"

Buster came up from behind Babbitt and grabbed his shoulder, turning the stocky buffoon around. "You got a problem, George?" Buster moved closer yet, so he was in Babbitt's face. "Cause if you do, it's with me!"

"Uh, no...I...uh...was just hoping to borrow – "

"I know what you were doing. But now you're gonna set the record straight. Apologize to Sam and tell him you don't want his paper."

Babbitt turned back to Sam. "Uh...sorry, Sam...I...uh...I was only kidding." Babbitt slithered away, so he stood alone a few yards from the group.

"Thanks," said Sam.

"No big deal," said Buster. "You coulda handled it."

Sure, I thought...about as well as I could. I chuckled to myself. Babbitt should have known better. No one messed with Sam, not unless they had the guts to take on Buster. The job provided to Buster's father when he was out of work armed Sam with an insurance policy. The premiums were prepaid and its underwriter, reliable.

***

David A. Weiss

"What's in a name? That which we call a rose by any other name would smell as sweet." So said Shakespeare in *Romeo and Juliet (Act II, Scene II, lines 43, 44). Nearly two and one-half centuries later, little did Alexandre Dumas realize that the novel he was penning would someday taste as sweet, though not by another name. As for that sweet flavor, it only emerged long after Dumas had died.*

Friday, June 22, 1945, the last day of school, was a half-day. Apart from graduation ceremonies, for all practical purposes our high school careers had ended. Rather than full-length class periods, the day was divided into twenty-minute segments, all devoid of work. At roughly 11:30 we returned to our homerooms in advance of dismissal. Where ordinarily Mr. Thompson required that we find our seats promptly, he let us loiter several minutes until he directed us to settle down.

"Before we call it quits, a couple matters require attention."

As seniors who felt that summer had already begun, we deemed anything resembling delay unwelcome. We greeted the announcement with a moan, albeit feeble.

"I assume your reaction reflects disappointment that summer is on the doorstep. It couldn't possibly relate to the matters I mentioned." Mr. Thompson reached down and grabbed his leather satchel. He drew out a thick book and waved it in the air, not that we students could identify its title. "First order of business involves the wonderful characters created in this venerable novel."

With carping more pronounced than that which preceded, I joined the chorus of complainers. No way could Mr. Thompson be serious. Homeroom had been a place of decorum, but never work. Capping our last day there with intellectual pursuits was unfathomable. Compounding the absurdity, Mr. Thompson was seemingly dragging us into the world of literature. He taught science.

"Your assignment is to savor the wonderful characters contained in the pages of this book."

What? I disbelieved my ears. A brief academic divergence, a few comments about the work and its author, would have been distasteful. Assignment of the lengthy book, even a quick perusal, constituted an outrage. Had Mr. Thompson lost his mind?

Our whining turned mutinous. That our teacher had the gall to inflict such a burden defined the word *abomination*. No, it was worse than that. It was...beyond words. It violated the Constitution's Eighth Amendment proscription against cruel and unusual punishment, not that we had done anything meriting retribution.

Exhibiting a never-before-displayed fiendish scowl, the otherwise affable Mr. Thompson ran his gaze over the class. He marched to the first row, where, armed with his satchel and book, "The Three Musketeers," he paused just long enough to growl. From the satchel he drew out a big candy bar which he placed onto the first desk. His icy face evanesced into a broad smile. He continued down the row, putting a *Three Musketeers* bar onto every desk. He said, "Rather than reading, enjoy the sweet taste of chocolate and nougat."

Grumbling ceased. A cheer, accompanied by rousing applause, erupted.

We were devouring our candy, when Mr. Thompson said, "Second and last order of business involves information brought to my attention only ten minutes ago. Earlier today, halfway around the world, in Japan, where the sun rises thirteen hours ahead of Grand Falls, the United States forces defeated the last pockets of Japanese resistance on Okinawa Island, what has been one of the hardest and bloodiest battles of the Pacific Theater. Perhaps it presages the beginning of the end on the war's remaining front."

Unlike many other bits of news regarding world events, the disclosure excited me. The possibility that I would be called up for service, something that had dramatically diminished in recent months, dipped further yet. The probability that events on distant foreign soil would delay my college education had become minuscule.

"Do you think the Japanese will surrender soon?" said Shadow Sherwood.

Mr. Thompson heaved a sigh. "I'd love to say *yes*. But I don't really know. The Japanese are legendary for their extraordinary aversion to capitulation. They deem it shameful. I understand that the commander of the Japanese forces on Okinawa committed suicide rather than yield. If that's any indication, all-out defeat may be necessary to end the war."

The assessment reined in my earlier sanguinity. Still on balance, the totality of information buoyed me.

The final bell rang.

We started to get up from our seats.

Mr. Thompson held out his arms and said, "Please...please indulge me a few additional seconds."

We remained at our desks.

"I've enjoyed having all of you in my homeroom the past three years. As you embark on your adult lives, I wish you success and happiness. Have a wonderful summer, followed by a joyous and rewarding future...Class dismissed."

I got up from my desk, waiting for Mary to do likewise.

She said, "Mr. Thompson just referred to us as adults. I like that."

"Yeah," I said, digesting her observation. Until that moment, I had viewed myself as a kid. My behavior, as well as that of my friends, evidenced a puerile status. But we had reached a crossroads. We were moving into adulthood. Unlike Pete Longley, who had made the leap in a flash, and Don Baker and Carl Blake, two classmates killed in the war, we were entering a period of transition, one in which we would, in some respects, be kids, but others, adults. No longer were we purely the former. I took hold of Mary's hand. "You're not just beautiful, Sweetheart. You're also very smart."

Mary pecked me on the cheek. "Not sure what prompted that...but far be it from me to refuse such a lovely bouquet."

Chapter XIV

When "Pomp and Circumstance" plays, diplomas and prizes are bestowed upon the graduates, but the highest awards belong to their parents who reap the fruits of years of sacrifice.

Saturday morning, along with my parents, I headed to school to gather one last time with my fellow seniors, seventy-three of us, for graduation. Until that morning, I was hardly excited about commencement ceremonies. They represented little more than a necessary inconvenience. But observing my parents as we drove to school, I recognized the importance of the event, not for me, but for them. Their parents, my grandparents, had come to America from Europe, specifically Ireland and Austria, with little more than the clothes on their backs. They had forged a better life for my parents. That said, my grandparents fell short of their goal, achieving the American dream. My father found it necessary to leave school shortly before his fifteenth birthday to contribute to the support of the family, which included five younger siblings. Though my father's formal education was cut short, he continued to educate himself. My mother, an avid reader, had the good fortune of completing high school, but even as she did, she worked part time. At the age of twelve she began delivering newspapers. Throughout her high school years, she waited tables at a greasy spoon. Despite achieving excellent grades, her options never included college. Even if it had been financially viable, which it wasn't, in the patriarchal, misogynistic universe of her father, higher education was a male only prerogative.

Unlike my immigrant grandparents, who had left the poverty of war-torn Europe with nebulous aspirations, my parents' dreams for me were more specific. From an early age they emphasized the importance of higher education. Even in elementary school, they voiced hopes that my future would include college. Occupations such as accountant, teacher, lawyer, engineer, and architect were bandied about. In pursuit of that future, my parents scrimped and saved. Meager comforts were luxuries. My graduation, commencement of my life beyond high school, was their reward for years of sacrifice.

As we climbed out of my dad's freshly waxed, black 1939 Chevrolet Master Deluxe 4-door sedan, just under $700 when new, I said, "Mom, Dad, stand by the driver's door. I'll take your picture." Armed with our family's Kodak box camera, I snapped a shot. "Stay right there," I said.

I latched onto Mark Herman, a fellow senior. "Do me a favor and take a picture of my parents and me." After handing him the camera, I stepped between my mom and dad, putting my arms around them.

Herman took the photograph and returned the camera before heading toward the building.

"Just before we go in," I said, "I want you to know how much I appreciate all you've both done to give me a wonderful childhood with countless opportunities that neither of you had. Though I've seemingly taken it all for granted, I assure you, I appreciate your sacrifices."

"We know," said my mother. "But it hasn't been a sacrifice. Your future, your success, is worth more to us than a few material items."

My father looked me in the eye. He hugged me. The gesture, uncommon for the reserved man, spoke volumes.

We entered the building where my parents took their seats in the auditorium, while I joined the other seniors in the alphabetical line forming in the hallway. Twenty minutes later, dressed in our caps and gowns, with *Pomp and Circumstance* playing, we marched into the auditorium, taking our seats in the front four rows.

Following the Pledge of Allegiance, the singing of the school song, and some platitudes from Superintendent Tompkins and Principal Armstrong, Sam was called to the lectern to deliver the valedictory. He unfolded the paper that housed his speech and laid it on the lectern. After adjusting the microphone, his focus shifted to the assembled throng.

"A month ago, when they told me that I would be delivering this address, I spent hours searching for a message worthy of the honor. I hit upon ideas with seeming potential. Unfortunately, once pen met paper, they morphed into vacuous rhetoric on crumpled masses deposited into my waste basket. Hard as I tried to summon words of wisdom, advice I could share, I managed no better than trite and presumptuous phases. Repeatedly, I asked myself: *Who am I to tell my classmates how they should live their lives?* Next, I tried humor. Rather than clever wit, I produced lines destined to reap deflating silence. Worse yet, some had the potential to come across as invective meriting condemnation. I considered lauding my favorite teachers. I dismissed the idea knowing that my picks differed from others. I contemplated anecdotes from our high school years. One after another, I rejected them because they singled out the same individuals who have always garnered recognition. All these vain efforts left me with a stark reality: I had a speech to deliver, but I had no message. With that in mind, the need for brevity mounted."

Sam's odd, but honest concession rattled my brain. Far from profound, it outstripped a hackneyed, supercilious, or boring homily. I scanned the audience. Sam had their full attention. His well-modulated, carefully paced delivery was easy listening. Though far from a showstopper, it rated a good grade.

"Befogged, but knowing I would have to say something," said Sam, "gratitude seemed apropos. Each of us has arrived at this day thanks to others. From birth, roughly eighteen years ago, the kindness and generosity of others have paved our paths. All of us have parents or caregivers who not only met our basic needs of food, clothing, and shelter, but also provided the love and guidance requisite to our development. Doubtless, we can all name teachers who paid for materials from their own pockets; stayed after to school to clarify a lesson; or offered encouragement when we were confused or downcast. In far-flung reaches of the globe, American soldiers have fought the Axis in order that we might receive our educations and enjoy our formative years amidst freedom. Dozens of those soldiers graduated from this very institution that today awards us diplomas. Others from our class would be with us today were they not currently serving. And two more from our class, Carl Blake and Donald Baker, have already made the ultimate sacrifice. All of us enjoying this day of celebration owe these benefactors a huge debt of gratitude. That we can repay them is unrealistic. What we can do is give our time, knowledge, and support to those who come after us.

"Beyond these walls lies a fascinating world. Futures replete with boundless potential await. Living in the most successful and advanced democracy in history, our opportunities are unlimited. May we avail ourselves of those opportunities, always keeping in mind our benefactors. A decade from now and for decades thereafter, may we all return to Grand Falls proud of our accomplishments, not just successes and affluence, but deeds that have benefited our neighbors, communities, and country. To you, my fellow classmates, I say, May God speed, guiding you along a path that features morality, kindness, and charity." Sam folded his paper crutch, one he had eyed not once. He headed back to his seat in the third row.

Just before he turned into his row, he appeared to glance my way. Perhaps he glimpsed the thumb I raised in front of my chest.

Superintendent Tompkins stepped to the microphone. "Wonderful thoughts, well delivered…a fine embellishment on a momentous occasion…The time for awarding diplomas has arrived. Principal Armstrong will read the names of our graduates, and I will hand out the certificates. We ask that you withhold your applause and cheers until the last graduate has received his…excuse me…her diploma."

One by one, we stepped forward when called. If history repeated itself, 85% of us had ended our formal educations. Whether the end of World War II, assuming that soon eventuated, would alter the future numbers remained to be seen. I glanced back over my shoulder. For many parents in the audience, perhaps a third or more, their child was the family's first to achieve a high school diploma. They had ample reason to be proud. It justified the choice that they or their ancestors had made when coming to this country. They were living out the American dream, building a better life for their children and grandchildren.

My musing halted when our row, the last to receive our sheepskins, got up and formed a line to the right of the stage. I stole a peak at my parents. My mom displayed a subdued wave, her hand no higher than her shoulder. She was no different than many other parents. She focused on her own offspring.

I climbed the four stairs that took me onto the stage. Darlene Vance shook the hand of Superintendent Tompkins. Principal Armstrong announced my name, James M. Ward. An unexpected surge of adrenaline filled my body. As I shook the superintendent's hand and received my certificate, undeniable pride, more than I had anticipated, materialized. I climbed down the stairs on the far side of the stage. I eyed my ribbon-wrapped parchment. I had done well. I had laid the foundation for my future. And far better than the preceding Christmas, when I had given my mom a scarf and my dad a tie, for once, I had given each a meaningful gift.

Moments later, Lucille Zalinski received her diploma. As she returned to her seat, senior members of the orchestra joined their freshman and junior counterparts on the rear of the stage. The recessional played, and we marched out into the June sunshine where we tossed our caps skyward.

Speedy came my way. "Did you hear the news about Lefty?"

"Don't tell me he racked up another car."

"No, but last night he got a contract with the Chicago Cubs."

"Holy crap! Lefty is headed to the Majors?" I pounded my fist into my cap as if it were a baseball glove.

"No, the Cubs' organization. He'll be joining the Hagerstown Owls in the Inter-State League. It's B level."

With A, AA and AAA between B and the Majors, Lefty would be far from the bigs. But a minor league contract at any level was impressive. "Where is Hagerstown?" I said.

"According to Lefty, it's in Maryland, just south of the Pennsylvania border, about fifty miles northwest of Washington D.C."

"Did he sign your yearbook?" I said.

"Yeah, and I'm gonna have him sign a baseball. Could be worth real money...someday."

"You think he'll make it to the Majors?"

Speedy shrugged. "Hard to say, but I wouldn't bet against him."

My parents joined us on the front lawn. They congratulated both Speedy and me, after which he headed off to find his parents.

"We're going to the Inn at Nick Stoner's for a prime-rib dinner," said my father.

"Wow," I said. Rarely did we eat out, and when we did, it was at the diner or the Blue Plate, a stand that specialized in burgers and fries.

"On a special day like this, nothing is too good for the Ward family. Your mom and I have a son who graduated high school and is on his way to college." My dad puffed out his chest.

Our golf team had played matches on the hilly links that adjoined the impressive three-story, wood-frame inn, but apart from post-match sodas from the beverage machine, I had never dined at the fine establishment. Named for Nicholas Stoner, a renowned Adirondack hunter and trapper, who had served in both the American Continental Army during the Revolution and with the American forces in the War of 1812, the imposing structure was emblematic of the region's rich history. With four stately dormers, it bore an august stone chimney that rose from ground level to an apex well above the rooftop.

Twenty minutes after we left the graduation ceremonies, my dad pulled our Chevrolet Master Deluxe into Nick Stoner's parking lot. As we climbed out of the vehicle, he ran his hand over the car's polished surface. "It looks showroom new, doesn't it?"

"Sure does," I said.

A satisfied smile on his face, my dad gestured at the tires. "The whitewalls are as spiffy as the finest white dinner jacket."

We entered the restaurant, where the maître d' greeted us.

"Reservation for the Ward family," said my father, seemingly standing taller than his 5'7" height.

The maître d' guided us to a table adjacent to a huge, multi-paned window beyond which lay the fairways and greens, rolling hills and woods of the beguiling links. The maître d' helped my mother to her seat and one by one, handed us our white cloth napkins. Following the lead of my parents, I placed mine in my lap. More than a year had elapsed since my cousin's wedding, the last time my lap had borne such an adornment.

The maître d' filled each of our goblets with water. He said, "Maurice, your waiter, will be with you shortly."

A minute later, Maurice came our way and placed a basket of rolls onto our table.

"We're ready to order," said my father. "We'll have three prime-rib dinners. Two, medium rare, and rare for me. They come with baked potatoes and Yorkshire Pudding. Right?"

"That they do," said Maurice.

"And we'll start with three shrimp cocktails. We're celebrating. Our son here (my father gestured at me) graduated high school today. He's headed for college in the fall. First in our family."

Maurice looked my way. "Congratulations." He heaved a sigh. "Wish I went that route. Not till I got out into the workin' world did I discover the importance of an education. Unfortunately, back when I was in school, I preferred brews to books." He gestured out the window in the general direction of the golf course. "Out there they give a fellow a mulligan now and then. Ain't that way in life." He headed off.

"Really nice eating dinner in a fancy place like this," I said, conscious that the pricey meal was way beyond my family's normal budget. "They even serve dessert with the main course."

My mom's brow dipped. "Dessert?"

"The pudding. I wonder if it's vanilla or butterscotch or what?"

My mom laughed. "It's not that kind of pudding. It's a popover generally made from eggs, flour, milk, and the drippings of roast beef."

"Oh." I breathed a relief-bestowing sigh, thankful I had stemmed the urge to ask Maurice the witless question regarding the pudding's flavor. A guy headed to college had no need to showcase his ignorance. I reached for the breadbasket, pulling back the napkin that covered the warm rolls. Unlike the diner where we got slices of white bread, I observed three kinds. I held the basket out so my mom and dad could select theirs, after which I opted for a twisted salt stick. Hungry as I was, the dense bread, which I amply slathered with butter, was tantamount to a dessert. I was savoring the final bite when Maurice delivered a trio of shrimp cocktails, served in small glass bowls supported by fancy metal bases, possibly silver. Each bore four jumbo shrimp laden with sauce, resting on a bed of lettuce with a lemon wedge on the side. I had occasionally eaten shrimp, but never any so large or elaborately presented. The odd little accompanying fork, the likes of which I had never employed, counseled that I procure instruction on how to eat the delicacy. I watched my mom, duplicating her lead. *So, this is how the millionaires dine.* I glanced at my father. He was relishing his shrimp cocktail. Even more so, he was reveling in the opportunity to engage his family in the lap of luxury. His quiet, but patent delight dispelled my doubt whether the cost of the inordinately expensive meal was justified.

For the ensuing hour we dined in blissful leisure. At times conversation grew sparse. Still rapture was omnipresent. A message from my late grandfather just two months before his death popped into my head. "Now and then throughout life, you will encounter special moments. Treasure them, inscribe them, so years later when you're my age, you can relive them. Too often when we're young, we take future memories for granted. Down the road, and that road is shorter than we think, those memories become invaluable. They give meaning to our lives. They manifest the merit of our days on Earth." At the time I had failed to comprehend the gravity of my grandfather's words. His solemnity, however, had compelled me to listen closely. Seated with my mom and dad at Nick Stoner's, my grandfather's message resounded, not just his words, but their import. Repeatedly, I made a conscious effort to imprint every detail of the special occasion. Years later, deep into my days, I would again savor the flavors of the glorious experience...not merely the delectable cuisine, but also everything associated with the special day. I reached for my water goblet. "A toast to the most wonderful parents a kid could have. Thank you both for all you have done for me, all the sacrifices you have made on my behalf...I love you Mom and Dad."

***

Not all mushrooms are ambrosian. Some are poisonous. Others rise in humongous clouds, wreaking utter destruction. But those same mushrooms can erase the exigent shroud clouding the lives of others. Thus, one man's bomb of utter ruin is another's ticket to a brighter future.

The summer following graduation from high school was great. With my plans in place for the next four years, a seeming eternity for one still months short of his eighteenth birthday, life was a lark. That said, it was hardly a summer of sloth. I worked full time at the grocery market in Little Falls. So too, did Mary. Thanks to the store's owner and boss, Mr. Case, we often worked as a team, cashier and bagger. From the outset, Mr. Case emphasized that if our working together, a privilege, proved unproductive, it would cease. Not wanting to forfeit the advantageous circumstance, Mary and I were conscientious. We strove for efficiency, constantly endeavoring to please customers. The arrangement provided an unexpected bonus, an excellent learning experience with valuable corollaries. I discovered that a boss can earn respect with benevolence; that such benevolence can pay dividends to both employer and employees; that appreciative workers are better workers; and that management and labor need not be enemies. Cooperation can transform a work environment into a win-win situation. Unlike a poker pot, it need not degrade into a zero-sum game.

My last observation resulted from a digression, one of many, by our Advanced Algebra teacher, Mrs. Aiken. She had constantly encouraged the use of knowledge outside the discipline in which it was acquired. Shortly before Easter of senior year, Mrs. Aiken had linked a facet of our curriculum to principles that had been recently propounded by renowned mathematician John Von Neuman. Without Mrs. Aiken's detour into Von Neuman's work on the win-win concept and zero-sum games, my understanding of our supermarket employer-employee relationship would never have come into focus.

Just a week into my job at the market, another of Mrs. Aiken's non-mathematical lessons came to the fore. I was sweeping the building's entranceway when a co-employee indicated that a truck had delivered boxes of product to the storeroom and Mr. Case wanted me to stow them. I went directly to the area. I started to move the first box but halted. The possibility there might be established procedures associated with the assignment crossed my mind. Ever since the April Fools' Day test that required us to ignore the problems and lay our pencils down, I had checked for instructions before commencing a task. I returned to the store's main section where I collared a long-time employee, who, after accompanying me to the storeroom, demonstrated the procedure. He explained that Mr. Case wanted stocking done in the reverse of the accounting process known as *LIFO*, "last-in, first-out." The goal, ensuring that older product did not remain stuck in the storeroom, required that items coming in first went out first. To accomplish this, product already on the shelves needed to be pushed aside; new product stored in the rear; and older product placed in front of new.

Once the employee educated me in the technique, he returned to his post. Alone in the storeroom, I tackled the job. I had been doing it for the better part of an hour – I was more than half done – when Mr. Case entered the storeroom.

"Hold up, Jim." With a look of concern, the boss shook his head.

Steeling myself for trouble, I laid the box I was holding onto the floor.

"We're gonna need to rearrange everything. But don't worry. It's not your fault." Mr. Case gestured at himself. "My mistake."

Whatever the problem, I welcomed the news that I was not responsible for the screw-up.

"Before you started, I should have told you that the new boxes go in the back."

"I've been putting them there," I said. "I make sure the older ones are up front."

A puzzled look on his face, Mr. Case eyed me. "How'd you know? You clairvoyant?" A chuckle muddied his words.

I shook my head. "Suspecting there might be a procedure, I checked with John before starting. He was kind enough to help me...show me the ropes."

"Impressive." Mr. Case drew closer and patted me on the back. "Obvious. You're a self-starter. You use your noodle; find out what's what; and attack a job properly." He headed toward the door of the storeroom but stopped. "Down the road, if you ever need a recommendation, let me know. Be my pleasure." He displayed a broad smile before leaving.

I rapped a fist against the palm of my other hand. "Score one for the good guys." I eyed the box that lay at my feet. "Thank you, Mrs. Aiken," I said. Her April Fools' joke, a nerve-racking interlude, had afforded me a valuable lifelong lesson. I resumed my work stacking the goods onto the shelves. My mind remained focused on what had transpired with Mr. Case. Mrs. Aiken would be pleased. That which I had learned in my Advanced Algebra class was not restricted to mathematics. The principles, win-win and follow instructions, could be employed in diverse situations. The same could be said for what I learned elsewhere. Lessons gained in any class, be it English, science, math, or whatever, or from anyone or at any time could be employed in manifold circumstances. The concept acquired new meaning. Back when Mrs. Aiken had voiced it, I had listened and absorbed it. Seeing it in action was an epiphany.

My first chance to tell Mary what had occurred in the storeroom with Mr. Case came at the end of our shift. I also shared my subsequent reflections. Mary gave them credence, though admittedly, her enthusiasm was more muted than mine.

We headed to the parking lot and Mary's Pontiac, actually her mother's. Unlike my family that had only one car, Mary's parents boasted two. Many days they allowed Mary to use the Pontiac. Armed with wheels, we sometimes stopped after work for dinner, typically pizza or burgers. Our summer may have included jobs, but we had loads of free time. That we worked at the same site with the same hours enabled us to spend lots of time together, including many romantic evenings. With both of us starting college in September, manifold common interests dominated our conversations. Topping the list were apprehensions and excitement associated with the challenges, responsibilities, and independence that would soon be ours. Occurrences at the market were another popular subject. The war found a place as well. It cast a shadow, though not so dark or long as before. Germany's surrender had stirred optimism. It had also lessened the risk that the draft might dismantle my future. Nevertheless, the possibility remained. At the end of July that concern magnified briefly when Japan rejected the Potsdam Declaration requiring that it surrender. The potential for persistent war in the Pacific loomed. Ensuing events, however, quickly erased that worry.

On the 7th of August 1945, President Truman issued a statement informing the nation that an atomic bomb had been dropped on Hiroshima. Two days after the announcement, a second atomic bomb was dropped on Nagasaki. The Manhattan Project, the secret program that had developed the nuclear weapon, transformed the landscape both literally and figuratively. Six days after the second bomb, on August 15, 1945, Emperor Hirohito, Japan's leader, announced his nation's surrender. The war finally ended. Worries about the draft ceased. The nation celebrated. So too, did I. In a mere month I would be off to college, embarking on my future. With the lifting of the burden so long encumbering my life, in the interim, I was free to luxuriate.

Chapter XV

All that glitters is not gold. Ask the prospector whose strike, when assayed, turns out to be iron pyrite, fools' gold. He might tell you that life on the road is a curveball.

Friday evening, immediately following work, Sam, Speedy, and I embarked in Sam's mother's car for Allentown, Pennsylvania, a drive of roughly five hours. The hastily planned trip had originated at the suggestion of Sam's father. He had learned that Lefty was scheduled to pitch an away game for the Hagerstown Owls against the Allentown Cardinals on Saturday afternoon. Wednesday evening, after Sam finished work in the family store, his father posed the idea. Sam's mom offered her car for transportation. Sam immediately called Speedy and me. The parental resistance that Speedy and I anticipated failed to materialize. Perhaps our parents recognized that in a couple weeks we would be on our own, Sam and I at college, and Speedy, Fort Bragg, North Carolina. That Mr. Porter had proposed the trip was likely influential. Regardless, we had the blessing of our parents for the impromptu adventure. Within an hour the trip had evolved from pipe dream to reality. We had reserved a cabin for Friday night, seven dollars, split among the three of us.

"Man, can you believe we're actually doing this?" I said, moments after Sam picked me up following my shift at the supermarket. Sam had already picked up Speedy, who was riding shotgun in Sam's mother's cream-colored Studebaker Champion.

"I can't believe our parents gave us the okay...and without an argument," said Speedy.

215

"Apparently, they trust us." The observation was satisfying. "Good thing they didn't know we took your parents' car to Arctic Freeze before you had a license."

"Speedy, you took your parent's car for a joy ride…before you had a license?" Sam's hands shot up off the steering wheel. They were back in place before I could chastise him.

"Not the smartest thing we ever did," I said. "Fortunately, we didn't get caught."

"How come you never told me about it?" said Sam.

"Speedy and I swore each other to secrecy…no exceptions. Nothing personal, but we realized that if we didn't keep our traps shut, how could we expect those we told to do so?"

Amidst relatively light traffic, we cruised south. About an hour into the trip, Speedy said, "Anytime you're tired, I can take the wheel."

"Not a problem. I'll do two hours. We'll make a pit stop and grab a bite. That should refresh me for a second stint."

From my seat in the rear, I tapped Speedy on the shoulder. "Did the army clue you where you'll be headed after basic training?"

"No, but the recruiter said that with the war over, enlistees like me have a decent chance of getting their preference. I'm hoping for something involving electronics."

"But no guarantees about your choice?" said Sam.

"Nah…and I know, it may have been a sales job to get me to sign up." Speedy heaved a sigh. "Given that I had already decided to put my John Hancock on the dotted line, it was no big risk…I'm hopin' that down the road my service may help me get a higher education, that Congress will enact veterans benefits. A guy my dad works with says his cousin – he knows our local Congressman – heard it's possible. And once again, I know, it's pie in the sky."

"Either of you ever travel anywhere without your parents?" said Sam.

"I took the Greyhound to Albany for my college interview," I said.

"I mean a real trip…overnight."

The qualifier drew silence.

216

"How 'bout you, Sam?" said Speedy.

"Does a pup tent in my backyard count?"

The response underscored that the trip was a huge deal. Given that we would soon be off to college and the military, arguably it should have been less consequential. But don't tell that to three guys venturing forth on their maiden exploit.

Both time and miles slipped by easily. Following a stop at a roadside joint for burgers and shakes, plus a chance to relieve ourselves, we were again rolling along on the highway. At Speedy's insistence, I took a turn at shotgun, while he sprawled out for a nap on the back seat. A reenergized Sam remained at the helm, all the way to Allentown.

Just after eleven, we pulled into our destination, The Pines, a half-dozen cabins and office along rural route 145, about five miles north of the city.

As Sam parked near the office, I eyed the small, weather-beaten structures, each with a center gable. "Not the most impressive accommodations."

"What? You were expecting the Waldorf Astoria?" said Sam.

I repressed a sarcastic retort. At just over two bucks apiece, I could hardly complain. And given my druthers, cheap and crummy beat pricey and posh.

"You think they have any objections to Negroes?" said Speedy.

Until that moment, the issue had never crossed my mind. The mere fact the possibility needed to be addressed nonplused me.

"We're in Pennsylvania, north of the Mason-Dixon Line," said Sam. "Can't imagine it's a problem."

"Just in case, I don't want to screw things up." Speedy handed Sam $2.35 to cover his share of the stay. "You guys sign in for the three of us. Okay?"

"Good idea." I no sooner spoke the words than I regretted them. Indeed, it qualified as a good idea, but acknowledging that Speedy should remain outside and invisible was grossly insensitive.

Inside the office an elderly gentleman checked us in. We settled into our cabin, one with two beds and a cot. We matched coins for the cot. My tail against a head for each of Sam and Speedy rendered me odd man out, earning me the second-rate accommodation. Tired as we were from the long day of work and travel, anything resembling a bed sufficed. Sleep came quickly, especially for me.

Saturday morning, we were up and out quickly. We found a diner down the road from the cabins. Once again, the possibility of discrimination loomed. I suspected that Speedy and Sam envisaged the issue. No one mentioned it, least of all, me. No way would I reprise my impertinence from the prior evening. The three of us walked into the establishment. A Caucasian woman greeted us cordially. She guided us to a booth without incident. My concerns dissolved. On the suggestion of our waitress, we all ordered flapjacks. Speedy and I went wild, topping ours with strawberries and whipped cream, while Sam added sausage. By nine o'clock we had finished eating. We had a few hours to kill before the players would take the field for pregame warmups in advance of the two-o'clock contest.

"What's the plan till game time?" I said.

Sam pointed to a telephone booth in the restaurant's back corner. "How 'bout we check the yellow pages. In a city like Allentown, oughta be something…an arcade, bowling alley, or a roller-skating rink."

"Yeah, let's look for a bowling alley," I said. "Better yet, we can ask the waitress if there's one nearby. Maybe she can give us directions to the ballpark as well."

The waitress recommended Lucky Lanes on Route 145, about halfway to the ballpark. We killed a couple hours rolling three games. Speedy's 465 triple crushed both Sam and me who finished in the mid-300s. A spare in the last frame with a nine-pin count gave me runner-up bragging rights as I edged Sam's three-game total by two. Tempted as we were to grab a bite at the alley, patience prevailed. No way were we about to spoil our appetites for ballpark franks.

Our bowling done, we drove south on 145, zigging onto Lehigh Street, which we followed for less than a mile to Fairview Field, where Sam parked in the largely deserted lot.

Climbing from the car, I surveyed the exterior of the sketchy ballpark. I said, "Reminds me of Jimmy Jucko's place." Jucko operated a Grand Falls junkyard for wrecked cars and tires.

Speedy shook his head. "Good thing Jucko can't hear you. He'd be insulted."

"C'mon," said Sam. "We knew we were coming to the minors, Class B at that. You can't expect Yankee Stadium."

When I was twelve, my father had taken me to the House that Ruth Built for a game against the Cleveland Indians. The day, arguably the most exciting of my life, had indelibly stamped my memory with images of the iconic stadium. No way was I expecting that the home of the Class B Allentown Cardinals would measure up to the renowned Bronx ballpark. But I had envisioned something akin to Doubleday Field in Cooperstown, about an hour from Grand Falls. I had been there twice, once when my father took me there for the annual Hall of Fame game and once on a day trip with Sam. With a fine brick entrance that covered the section that wrapped around home plate and extended partway down the first and third baselines, the small, but quant Cooperstown ballpark screamed of class and character. I turned to Sam. "Is this what you anticipated?"

Sam shrugged. "Well…not really. Maybe it's better on the inside."

We bought our tickets and passed through the turnstile. Uncovered wooden bleachers, taller behind home plate than down the first and third baselines, exhibited wear. Fences with faded advertisements enclosed the park. A well-maintained infield and baselines evinced a touch of class, but a brown and barren outfield, akin to Nick Stoner's parched fairways in a drought-stricken summer, rendered the diamond a scant oasis in a desert.

"Can't believe we travelled 250 miles for a dump like this," said Speedy.

"C'mon," said Sam, "we're here to watch Lefty pitch, not admire a ballpark."

"But one would – " I clipped my tongue. Sam had a point. Like our cabin, the ballpark's ambience was secondary.

"Now I know what my dad meant when he said that sports are like show business, a very narrow pyramid," said Sam. "Only those at the peak partake of the high life. Guys in the minors are like roustabouts in a traveling circus."

"You suggesting that Lefty is a nobody?" An edge crept into my voice.

Sam shook his head. "Not at all. Just that for now, he's only a somebody in Hagerstown and Grand Falls. To be a real somebody, he's gotta make it to the Majors, get his picture on a baseball card."

The unappealing assessment had too much validity for me to argue. I said, "Let's get some eats."

We went back near the entrance, to a small food stand. The menu, if one could term it that, had four items: hot dogs, beer, bottled soda, and bags of peanuts. Each of us opted for everything save the beer. Sam and Speedy chose Coca-Cola, while I opted for Hires Root Beer. After squirting mustard onto our hot dogs, we headed for the bleachers on the third-base line.

Famished from bowling, I bit into my frankfurter. The heavenly flavor of mustard-laden meat and roll consumed me. "Can't beat a hot dog at the ballpark."

"It's even better than Howard Johnson's," said Speedy.

"Maybe we should go back for a second," said Sam.

"Suppose we wait for the seventh-inning stretch?" said Speedy.

Absent my bag of peanuts, extra sustenance to tide me over, I would have balked.

We seated ourselves in the bleachers which, with the game still more than an hour away, bore only a handful of patrons. Out on the field, the Allentown Cardinals were conducting pre-game warmups. I guesstimated that the ballpark held a maximum of four thousand.

"Two ninety-nine to left, 418 to center and 310 to right," said Speedy, reading the large numbers printed on the outfield walls. "Hardly a cracker box, but not the easiest place to pitch either."

"Not so different from Yankee Stadium, 281, 490 and 295 from left to right." Having known the numbers ever since my father had taken me to the Bronx icon, I proudly recited them.

"That 490 figure in the Stadium," said Speedy, "turns the field's middle-45 degrees into what they call Death Valley. Loads of home-run balls in other parks end up as loud outs. Over the course of a season, it can save a pitcher fifteen or twenty home runs."

Coming from a guy who played the outfield in a local summer league, the astute point shut my mouth. I focused on the Allentown players who finished their warmups. The Hagerstown Owls took the field.

"Anybody see number 59?" said Speedy.

"I think that's Lefty over there," said Sam, pointing to the far side of the field. "Hard to tell with his cap on, but before he turned around, it looked like 59 on his jersey."

The players began their pre-game stretching.

"How 'bout we circle to the other side of the bleachers to get a better look. Maybe we can get his attention." We negotiated our way to the first-base side of the ballpark, where we stood along the rail.

"Hey Lefty," yelled Sam.

"What the hell you doing?" I said, giving Sam a shove.

Lefty peered our way and waved. "I'll catch you guys in a few minutes." He continued his calisthenics.

Once they finished and the players began batting practice, Lefty jogged our way. "Hi guys. Great to see you. I can only talk a minute. Gotta get to the bullpen and warmup. I'm startin' today."

"We know," said Sam. "That's why we're here."

"Hope I don't disappoint. Better get a move on or the pitchin' coach will be on my ass." Lefty hustled to the bullpen, down the right-field line beyond the end of the stands in foul territory. We returned to our seats along the third-base line, directing much of our attention to Lefty as he warmed up about a hundred yards away. Hitters at home plate pounding ball after ball, as well as fielders flashing leather, garnered our interest as well. The Owls completed their pregame practice and vacated the field. Shortly thereafter, the two teams emerged from their respective dugouts. The crowd, less than a thousand, stood for The Star Spangled Banner, after which the Cardinals took the field.

The Owls opened the game with three quick outs, an infield pop-up, a called third strike, and an easy grounder to the first baseman. As the teams traded places for the bottom half of the inning, Lefty strode to the mound. He threw several warmup pitches.

"He looks good," said Speedy.

"Sure does," I said, not that I could distinguish good from bad.

The leadoff hitter for the Cardinals stepped to the plate. After falling behind 1-2, he hit a grounder to short for an easy out. The next hitter struck out on three pitches, the last of which had him waving awkwardly at a knuckler that bounced off home plate.

"Lefty's making monkeys out of these guys," said Sam.

"You got that right," I said. "His knuckleball is dancing more than Jell-o on a freight train."

The third Cardinal batter came to the plate. Lefty went into his windup and fired the ball. The batter swung, the crack of his bat launching the sphere down the left-field line faster than it had been thrown. The frozen rope sailed past the third baseman's glove hitting *terra firma* in fair territory, where it bounded into the corner. By the time the left fielder retrieved the ball and threw it to the infield, the batter stood on second with a stand-up double.

Speedy looked my way.

I shrugged. "No big deal. Lefty needs just one more out."

Speedy pressed his hands together and glanced skyward. "Easier said than done."

The Cardinals' cleanup hitter stepped into the batter's box. Lefty shook off a couple of signs before delivering a knuckler on the outside corner for strike one.

"Chances are those shake-offs were decoys," said Speedy. "He did that back at Grand Falls to cross up opponents...make them think he was gonna slip in a fastball or curve, rather than the expected knuckleball."

Lefty went into his windup but spun and fired the ball to second base where the runner had taken a gigantic lead. Lefty's attempt at a pickoff might have succeeded, except his throw sailed high over the leaping shortstop's outstretched glove into centerfield. The runner advanced to third.

Ball back in hand, Lefty stepped onto the rubber. He went to the stretch, glancing over his right shoulder to check the runner. Lefty looked him back before making his next offering. The batter drilled the rare fastball into rightfield for an RBI base knock. Allentown led 1-0.

The next Cardinal hitter worked the count to 2-2. Lefty checked the runner on first. He delivered his pitch. The batter swung. The thunderous blast left no doubt. From the instant bat met ball, its destination over the centerfield wall was inevitable. Even Yankee Stadium's Death Valley could not have contained the massive shot. Lefty did not even turn to watch the soaring sphere. Shoulders slumped, he stood with bowed head.

"Not a very auspicious start," I said.

Sam turned to Speedy. "Your buddy here is a potential rocket scientist." Sam looked back my way. "Any other brilliant deductions?"

"Hey, don't blame me. I didn't throw the gopher ball."

"He's got a point," said Speedy, ignoring Sam's unreceptive reaction. "Think about it. If Ward were on the mound, no way would he have given up a homer…not when he could only throw the ball two-thirds of the way to home plate."

"Screw you, Jackson," I said, unable to muster substantive repartee.

Speedy laughed and refocused on the game. Lefty got the third out on an easy grounder to second.

The top of the second saw the Owls get a baserunner on a Baltimore chop. The runner was quickly erased on a bouncer to short that produced a double play, 6 to 4 to 3. A strikeout and the Owls returned to the field.

A bunt single, followed by a clean base hit to right center, had Cardinal runners at the corners. The manager of the Owls strode to the mound.

"You think he's gonna yank Lefty?" I said. Having him pulled with just over an inning in the books would be tough for Lefty. For us, having traveled 250 miles, it would be crushing.

"Hope not," said Speedy.

"That's not very reassuring," I said.

"If I tell you he's sure to keep Lefty on the mound, you think that'll improve our pal's chances of keeping the ball?"

The response proved where Lefty's tenure hung...on the manager's whim.

A moment later, when the manager plodded back to the dugout, like my two buddies, I breathed a thankful sigh.

The next Cardinal batter, a left-hander, stepped to the plate. A knuckleball from Lefty froze the hitter. A second drew a clumsy swipe.

"Lefty has this guy's number," said Sam.

"Sure enough," I said. "My money says he'll pitch out of this jam."

Lefty went to the resin bag. He stepped onto the rubber and after going into the stretch, let his next pitch fly. The batter swung. The ball rocketed down the left-field line. The Owls' leftfielder, who was playing just in front of the warning track, raced toward the line. An awe-inspiring dive, an indomitable effort to spear the ball, came up empty. The vain effort left the fielder prostrate on the ground. The fair ball caromed off the wall toward left center. With the centerfielder having shaded toward right and no one able to quickly retrieve the ball, only one question remained: Would the Cardinals' hitter get a rare inside-the-park home run. As it turned out, he stopped at third with a stand-up triple. But two Cardinals had crossed the plate, running the score to 5-0.

Once again, the manager of the Owls climbed from the dugout. As he reached the top stair, he gave the hook sign to the bullpen. Upon reaching the mound, he took the ball from Lefty, who, head down, trudged to the showers. His outing, an abbreviated one, had ended ingloriously.

I turned to Sam. "Not what we had hoped to see."

Sam shrugged. "Well, look on the bright side."

I eyed him incredulously. "Bright side?"

"Five runs, with only one inning complete, gives him an ERA of 45."

"You call that 'the bright side?'"

"Yeah, if the runner on third had tried for home, he would have beaten the throw. That would have upped his ERA to...54."

"It still may be," said Speedy. "With no outs, that runner on third remains Lefty's responsibility."

The detail highlighted the futility of Lefty's performance. With him out of the game, we had inherited a contest between the Allentown Cardinals and the Hagerstown Owls, two minor league teams about which we could not care less. Allentown added three more runs in the bottom of the second, upping the count to 8-0. If doubt about the outcome remained, five more Allentown runs in the bottom of the fourth dispelled any such ambiguity. Second hot dogs, midway through the seventh inning, did little to mitigate the game's rancid flavor. Most of the fans had already left when the Owls made their big comeback in the top of the eighth, plating an unearned run with the aid of a two-base Allentown throwing error.

Four more Allentown runs in the bottom half of the inning widened the gap to 17-1, what turned out as the final tally. Along with about fifty other fans, we stayed for the ninth. With the stands all but empty, we relocated ourselves in front-row box seats, where we had a near highlight. The leadoff Owl hitter launched a bloop foul in our direction. Sam got a hand on the ball, but fumbled it, allowing a lady in the adjacent box to snag it.

"Nice catch, Doc," said Speedy.

Sam eyed the bruised hand that had blown the chance for the sought-after souvenir. "Damn, did they have to add injury to insult?"

"You did that yourself," I said. "Give credit where credit is due."

Sam shot me a look but following a beleaguered sigh, nodded.

The slaughter ended, albeit unmercifully, when the Owls' leading hitter watched a called third strike for the final out. The misery of the Owls, as well as ours, had concluded...On second thought, that is not entirely true. The Owls still had a despondent bus ride back to Hagerstown; and our drive, far longer, was sure to be equally uninspiring.

The players departed the field. The few remaining diehard fans exited the ballpark. Lefty came our way. "Didn't have my best stuff today."

Disputing the gross understatement defined impossible. I searched for words to adorn the tattered rag with a silver lining. Nothing came to mind. I said, "We're gonna grab a bite before we head back to Grand Falls. Wanna join us?"

"I'd like to, but I'd miss the team bus back to Hagerstown. Appreciate you guys coming. Wish I coulda put on a better show."

"Hey, you tried your best," said Speedy. "That's all any athlete can do."

"I suppose." Lefty peered off into space. "Lot different from high school. No easy outs nowadays. All these guys were stars back in their hometowns. Two of our players, one who had a half-season in AAA ball and another who spent spring training with the Cubs, say the competition gets even rougher up above." He shook his head. "Today's loss makes my record 1-4. It raised my ERA to 6.87. After I was yanked in the second inning, I updated it. That math I learned in high school is good for something." Lefty eyed the big clock on the scoreboard. "Gotta go." He heaved a sigh. "Life on the road in a bus and second-rate hotels ain't glamorous…Thanks again for coming."

We bid Lefty goodbye and headed to the parking lot. "Professional baseball isn't all it's cracked up to be," I said.

"Not when you're at the bottom of the heap," said Speedy.

"Never saw that version of Lefty," said Sam.

"Version? Whad'ya mean?"

"You ever remember a time when Lefty was anything but cocky?"

I searched my recollection for an occasion that would contradict Sam's assessment. No matter the circumstances, self-assurance oozed from the big man on campus. "You think he'll make it to the big leagues?"

Neither Speedy nor Sam answered my question. Then again, maybe they did. Their silence, a telling testament, resounded.

***

In times of battle, a flag freely fluttering in the breeze can buoy a floundering force. But when that flag turns white, spirits sink. Capitulation is at hand. Even so, without a white flag, guns gone mute may signal surrender.

Sunday morning following our big excursion to Allentown, I slept late, getting up at ten. Attired in my pajamas, I found my mother and father in the kitchen. The former stood at the stove, while the latter sat at the table, reading the Sunday newspaper.

"Pecan pancakes are on the way," said my mother. "They'll be ready in two minutes." She flipped flapjacks already on the griddle. "You'll find a pitcher of fresh-squeezed orange juice in the fridge."

I fetched the pitcher and poured myself a glass, after which I seated myself across from my father.

He lowered his paper onto the table. "How was the trip?"

"Pretty good." Before heading home to Grand Falls, we killed a couple hours hanging out at Allentown's City Center. On the route back, we stopped for dinner. It was well after eleven when Sam dropped me off. My parents had already gone to bed.

"Lefty win?"

"Nope. Allentown drove him to the showers before he notched a single out in the second inning. He allowed five runs...six, including the one charged to him after he was yanked. He picked up his fourth loss against just one win."

"How'd he look?"

I eyed my father incredulously. The numbers I had provided conveyed the consummate critique of Lefty's impotent outing.

"Hey, the runs could have resulted from cheap hits and errors."

"Nothing cheap about Allentown's hits, and their runs were all earned." I turned to my mother who had just placed golden brown pancakes, along with a bottle of Vermont Maid Syrup, in front of both my father and me. "Thanks." I spread my flapjack with butter and doused it with syrup. I took a bite. "Pancake is delicious, Mom. A lot fluffier and tastier than the cardboard I had yesterday morning."

My mother smiled.

"Wonderful. Like eating dessert," said my father. He refocused on me. "You fellows get a chance to talk with Lefty?"

"Briefly. From what we could tell, his stint in the minors has been no walk in the park."

My father's nod hinted at an unvoiced reaction.

"You don't seem surprised."

"Not really...not that I had an expectation one way or the other." He sipped his coffee. "Potholes line the road from high-school hotshot to big-league stardom. Most local heroes languish on the low rungs of life's ladder. Physical attributes, what dominates among young teens, yield to mental skills. Out in the world, gray matter, not muscles, spawns success. Your mom, having graduated high school, can tell you better than I. Mildred, what do you think? How was it with the girls in your class?"

My mother laid her spatula alongside the stove. "Don't really know. Few girls in my class had big careers. Some became teachers and nurses, as well as secretaries. I can't recall any who went into business. And for that matter, at my last reunion there were no female lawyers, doctors, or engineers. One of my former high school friends is a CPA. She's the rare exception." My mother reclaimed her spatula and flipped some pancakes. "Junior and senior year in high school, good students seemed to draw increasing recognition. But the pretty girls, the cheerleaders, garnered more, especially from the good-looking, muscular guys. But things were different at our twentieth reunion last year. Many of those cheerleaders had lost their luster. Hourglass figures were ancient history. And beer bellies predominated among the one-time athletes. From what I observed, plain Janes, rather than sexy Susies, wore the wedding rings of the professionals. But understand, I'm speaking anecdotally, based on a tiny sample."

"Tiny sample or not," said my father, "your assessment mirrors what I've observed. In the long run brains, not brawn, prevail. Things work out the way they should. The smart men of the world rule."

My mother spun around from the griddle. "I beg to differ."

"With what?" said my father, his eyes wide.

Once my mother shoveled several pancakes onto a plate, she said, "Admittedly, men rule. Whether they're smart merits debate. Even more dubious is whether they should rule. Leading is a matter of judgment, intelligence, talent, and temperament. In all those categories, women's abilities equate to men's." My mother looked my way. "You observe any difference between the intelligence and competency of the girls and boys in your class?"

The unexpected question challenged me. Sam, our valedictorian, immediately came to mind. But Mary had edged me out in the classroom. Cumulatively the girls had compiled averages exceeding those of the guys. But when it came to leadership, the guys exhibited their mettle. Forget about Grand Falls High School. The world corroborated the point.

"Mildred, you're joking, aren't you?" said my father.

My mother shook her head.

"What? You disagree that nature gave men and women different roles?" said my father.

"Well, perhaps that was true in the age of cavemen. But in today's world, society has become increasingly responsible for defining the roles of the sexes."

My parents' unique exchange intrigued me. I was happy to remain a silent observer.

"What? You think men bear children the same as women?" My father punctuated his comment with a smirk.

The sarcasm, rare for my father, especially when speaking to my mother, stunned me.

"I'm not talking about childbirth." Spatula still in hand, my mother put her hands on her hips. "I'm referring to the working world."

My father looked my mother in the eye. "You tell me. If you were in court, who would you want representing you, a man or a woman?"

"Whoever was more capable. The attorney's sex would make no difference."

My father looked my way. "Next thing she'll suggest that women can be truckdrivers, firemen, and soldiers."

"That's exactly what I'm saying...well, with one exception, they'd be firewomen, not firemen."

My father eyed my mother in disbelief. "Are you serious?"

"Very."

"What – you're saying you dislike being a housewife?"

"Not at all. I choose that role. But other women who feel differently should be free to choose any occupation they wish. Ability, not sex, should dictate."

My father appeared flummoxed. It was understandable. My mother, his best friend, the woman he knew so well, had blindsided him.

"Since when did you reject the traditional roles of the sexes?"

"In recent weeks at my garden club, I've been speaking with Dinah Crane. She's single and teaches high school mathematics in Little Falls."

"So?" said my father.

"After listening to her, I've reevaluated my perspective as to how the sexes are treated. Dinah graduated magna cum laude from Smith. She aspired to be an actuary. When she graduated, she applied for a dozen jobs. Men with weaker backgrounds beat her out. More than once, she was told it was a man's field. At one interview, in Pittsburgh, she was asked about football, whether she was a fan. When she responded *no*, the interviewer shook his head. He indicated that the company's six actuaries all had season tickets to the Pittsburgh Steelers. Needless to say, Dinah didn't get the job."

"Well, you can't blame the employer. Having a staff with camaraderie – common ground that helps them bond – is a legitimate interest."

"Not when it results in discrimination." My mother turned to me. "You were in the debate club at school. What was the makeup of your team?"

"Whad'ya mean?" Despite having an inkling where my mother was headed, I preferred my place on the sidelines.

"How many boys and how many girls were on your team?"

"Three boys and two girls."

"More than once, you've told me that Mary was the best debater. Right?"

"Yeah."

"If the five of you were graduating law school and applied for a job, you think Mary would get it?"

I shrugged. "How should I know?"

My mother gave me a look. "C'mon."

My response had merit. I knew nothing about law school, let alone jobs for young lawyers. Unfortunately, my mother's point had greater merit. Logic, coupled with the makeup of society, indicated Mary would lose out.

"Are you suggesting that we turn the working world upside down so Mary can get some hypothetical job that she probably wouldn't want?"

My father's question, presumably rhetorical, wafted vacuously in the air. Ironically, it underscored the inequity of his misogynistic view.

"Dear, you're putting an unseemly spin on my words," said my mother. "Just to clear things up, I'll reiterate. Opportunity should be based upon ability, not sex."

My father shook his head. "If we follow your logic, we'll destroy our economy."

I had no idea what led my father to the perplexing conclusion. Apparently, my mother was equally confused, though the tone of her "pardon me" suggested she accorded his Byzantine reply little credence.

"Think about it," said my father. "If women flood the workforce taking traditionally male jobs, rates of pay for those jobs will sink not only owing to supply and demand, but also because employers can pay women less. Worse yet, men who are breadwinners will lose their jobs. Families, not just men, but their wives and children, will lapse into poverty." My father leaned back folding his arms across his chest. His smug smile negated any doubt whether his exposition was self-satisfying.

"Would you like another pancake, Jim?"

"Sure," I said, surprised my mother was yielding to my father's arguments.

As she served me another pancake, my father winked at me. He redirected himself to his newspaper.

Several quiescent seconds ensued before my mother said, "Not all women are housewives."

Her comment drew not just my attention, but my father's as well.

"Dinah Crane is unmarried," said my mother. "So too are many widows and single mothers. They have homes. They have families. They need to eat. They have as much right to a job as a man, even more if they're more qualified. As for the idea that they should be paid less for the same work, that's an insult draped in ignorance. Men asserting it, like the proverbial emperor, beg a new suit of clothes. Simply put, paying lower wages based on sex is unfair. For that matter, it should be illegal."

Silence, a booming silence, punctuated my mother's words.

I glanced at my father. He consumed the final bite of a syrup-laden pancake. He wiped his mouth with a fresh white paper napkin. He said nothing. Apart from subjects such as food, gardening, and the like, he always enjoyed the last word. His failure to respond was stunning. In a curious way, it mirrored events around the globe. Like Germany and Japan, my father's gun, his mouth, had gone silent. He had waved his white flag and surrendered.

***

Moving to a bigger stage is a double-edged sword. Opportunity knocks. But on the other side of the door, failure lurks as well. Opening the portal and stepping through is a gamble. But with resolve and dedication, one can shift the odds, flip them upside down.

Shortly after Labor Day, 1945, my mom and dad drove me from our Grand Falls home eighty miles east to the New York State Teachers' College at Albany. The trunk of our family car, as well as the entire back seat, save the portion I occupied, was loaded. A sunny, early September day provided ideal conditions for moving into my dormitory on Western Avenue in the state's capital city. We arrived around noon, and even before my roommate appeared, unpacked my things. We ate lunch at a small restaurant on nearby Madison Avenue, after which my parents drove me back to the urban campus. My father parked along the curb, and the three of us climbed out of the car.

"I think the time has come," I said. Gazing into my mother's moist eyes, a lump stirred in my throat. I hugged her.

"Our little boy departs the nest. Today he is a college man." My mother heaved a sigh as she released me.

My father stepped forward and hugged me. "Study hard but enjoy yourself as well. I know you'll make us proud."

"He already has," said my mother. "He's the first in our family to go to college." She hugged me again.

"C'mon, Mildred," said my father. "Time we let our son begin college life." He brushed a tear from his cheek.

I opened the car door for my mother, who climbed into the passenger seat. My father circled around to the driver's side. My mother rolled down her window. Last goodbyes exchanged, seconds later, they drove away with her still waving.

I watched the car disappear around a corner. I surveyed the entire area before directing my focus to my red-brick dormitory home. My childhood faded into the past. I was embarking on my adult life. The moment was as scary as it was exciting. I thought of Lefty. Back in Grand Falls, he had been a big fish in a small pond. Once he moved up to higher echelons, he was just another fish, arguably one of the smaller ones. Was I about to confront an analogous destiny? Formerly a small fish, was I transmuting into a minnow? Every freshman, each member of my class, was a high school graduate who, like me, had been accepted to the New York State Teachers' College. Many came from large cities, New York, Rochester, and Buffalo. Likely they were academically more advanced than I. Perhaps they were also more worldly, less provincial. Maybe they had been big fish in big ponds. Perhaps they were destined to be big fish in this new pond. The observations provoked disquiet. Little did I realize that hindsight would prove the disquiet ironically beneficial. During the initial days of my college career, self-imposed pressure, apprehension that my competition might be better prepared, motivated me to work extremely hard. Where many of my classmates reveled in their new-found freedom, abusing it to the detriment of their studies, my books took precedence. Unlike the slackers, I got off to a solid start. Gradually I eased up, slipping into a sweet spot, one that gave academics the attention they demanded, while also including ample time for bull sessions, playing ball, and getting together with Mary. Though only an hour apart, long-distance telephone fees limited the length and number of our calls. On the other hand, cheap bus fares and the ability to study during the ride, as well as when we were together, facilitated frequent weekend visits.

As the first semester of my college career edged forward, initial concerns evanesced. An opportune balance of work and play positioned me for a positive experience, one in which I could enjoy the present while laying the foundation for a fruitful future. Fears that I would face the horrors of the battlefield had long since dissolved. My life as an adult had commenced. I was in an excellent place, both literally and figuratively.

PART III

PART III

Chapter XVI

Architects draft meticulous plans before commencing construction. Wisdom counsels one to emulate the architects' blueprints, especially if one is risk averse.

Nearly a quarter-century had elapsed since I had begun my college education at the New York State Teachers' College at Albany. In the interim, the world had changed dramatically. Technological advances were rampant. Television, in its infancy in 1945 and found only in the homes of the wealthiest, had become an accouterment of almost every household. Satellites traveling seven miles per second had astronauts circling the globe in an hour. Expectations ran rampant that man would walk on the moon before the upcoming summer ended. Computers were altering everything. But in some respects, the world remained the same. War, this time in Vietnam, again dominated the news. However, the world viewed the current conflict, including America's role therein, very differently from World War II. In 1945, America's leadership against the Axis had rendered it the darling of democracies around the globe. By way of contrast, Vietnam had tarnished that image, earning the nation disdain, not only abroad, but also at home. The direct impact that each of the two wars had on my life also differed. Where the World War II draft had insinuated persistent uncertainty into my life, at age 41, conscription for Vietnam, an unrelenting bane for much of America's youth, posed no threat to me. So too, my sentiments regarding the two conflicts differed. Back in the 1940s, even as I dreaded the draft, I supported America's fight for freedom; not so, it's involvement in Vietnam. I rejected the Domino Theory, as well as the Gulf of Tonkin Resolution. I deemed the former a misguided gambit to fight communism and the latter a shameful pretense to mire America in a distant Asian civil war. I did, however, support and sympathize with our unfortunate troops who fell victim to the rash enterprise.

Mary and I had become engaged the summer after our junior year in college. By the time we had completed senior year, we had each lined up a teaching job for the fall: Mary, teaching biology in Little Falls, and I, history in Grand Falls. We were married shortly after our college graduations on the first Saturday in July. We opted for a small wedding, after which we honeymooned for two weeks, flying to Colorado and driving from national park to national park in a rented camper. Thanks to my parents' generosity, supplemented by my summer and part-time jobs, I graduated college with no debt. Mary's parents had paid for her entire college education, and she had saved over four hundred dollars from summer jobs. We commenced our life after college on the plus side of the ledger.

During the first three years of our marriage, both of us taught full-time. Each summer we attended a summer program in Utica, where we earned our masters. Our first child, Lisa, was born days before our third anniversary in July 1952, at which time Mary became a stay-at-home mother. Two years later, a week after Mother's Day, our son Jerald was born.

During our first three years of marriage, we lived on my salary and saved Mary's. We managed to put away over $6,000. The July preceding Lisa's birth, we moved from our small apartment to a twenty-year-old bungalow that we purchased for cash, using all but $500 of our savings. Living on a teacher's salary might have been tight, but because we paid neither mortgage nor rent, we managed comfortably.

Over the ensuing sixteen years following Lisa's birth, life was good for the Ward family. Admittedly, we were far from rich. We needed to watch our budget, but we never did without. The source of our next meal never kindled apprehension. Our paid-for home, just a seven-minute walk from school, afforded comfort. Transportation costs were minuscule.

As the years rolled past, Mary and I fashioned a plan for retirement. When Lisa graduated high school, Jerry would be finishing tenth grade, two years from his diploma. Once Jerry began college, Mary would return to teaching. With two incomes, we would be able to assist our children with their college educations. An inheritance that Mary had recently received from a bachelor uncle would make up the difference, allowing our kids to finish college debt free. Once they graduated, Mary and I, having two salaries, would have sufficient funds to travel during our unencumbered summers. Our joint income would allow us to increase our savings. We anticipated that Mary would remain in the classroom for seventeen years, at which time she would have a total of twenty years, including the three she had worked before we had children. I would have 40 years of teaching. Both of us would be within months of our 62nd birthdays. We could retire with two pensions from the very well-funded New York State Teachers' Retirement System. Each of us would become eligible for social security benefits shortly thereafter. We had mapped out our American dream. We were living it.

Both Lisa and Jerry were excellent students, near the top of their respective classes. Neither displayed exceptional athletic talent, but each played a sport. Lisa earned a spot on the girls' tennis team and Jerry, the boys' golf team. Both were good citizens, volunteering on weekends at the local soup kitchen. Lisa always watched out for her younger brother, and Jerry looked up to his sister. Sibling rivalry was minimal. Disparate interests and skills partly accounted for it. Lisa was a fine artist, while Jerry showed great promise on the trumpet. That Jerry was a stronger mathematics student than Lisa might have provoked jealousy, but he acknowledged that her help underpinned his success. Jerry's exemplary achievement furnished Lisa with a badge of honor. Her mentoring, coupled with his success, resulted in a win-win situation.

In the Ward home, win-win, a concept that Mary and I had learned years earlier from Mrs. Aiken, was an omni-present goal. For example, summer vacations were planned with that principle in mind. Mary and Lisa both loved the beach. Jerry and I liked to play golf and paddle the family canoe. Lisa wanted to play tennis. Everyone in the family liked to hike and swim. Several summers we rented a small cabin for a week in Lake Placid. Admittedly, it was not the ocean, but it allowed us all to enjoy our favorite activities. To be sure, our family, individually and as a group, had its share of flaws and issues. We also had our moments. Both Lisa and Jerry faced the inevitable ups and downs, joys and crises, particularly those associated with the teenage years. Like Speedy and me, and our infamous joy ride to Arctic Freeze, I suspect that Lisa and Jerry engaged in mischief they concealed from Mary and me. But in many respects, we were the Andersons of *Father Knows Best* and the Cleavers of *Leave It To Beaver*, at least to the extent that such fanciful families existed.

***

When cars collide, well-sewn pillows can cushion a crash, at least for those in the vehicles. Bumpers, headlights, and fenders, as well as egos and truth, are another matter.

It was six o'clock on the second Thursday of February 1969, when I arrived home after staying late at school and stopping at the local seamstress to pick up two throw pillows she had fashioned from material matching our drapes. After putting the car into our unattached garage, I went through the mud room where I found Mary in the kitchen. I held up the pillows before handing her one.

"They came out nicely. Don'tcha think?" I said.

"Seems so. Let's see." Mary took a pillow into the living room and put it kitty-corner at one end of the couch.

I placed the other at the opposite end.

Mary stepped back, eyeing the couch and the drapes that hung from the large front window behind the couch. "They go perfectly." She looked my way. "What…you don't agree?"

"No, they look great."

"Based upon your face, I'd never have known it."

I heaved a sigh. "It's not the pillows. I had an accident, just a minor one, on the way home."

"You…you okay?"

"Absolutely. Not a scratch. As I said, it was minor, a tiny fender bender. I barely felt the impact. It happened a few blocks north of Main, at the intersection of Sparrow and Blake. I was going south on Sparrow when this jerk coming from my left on Blake blew through a stop sign. I slammed the brakes. I was only going about five miles an hour when my front bumper hit his front fender. The other guy, who also hit his brakes, had slowed almost to a stop. Except for a small scratch to our bumper and a broken headlight, our car sustained no damage. The other car, a small, rusted-out junker, a Crosley – they stopped making them around 1950 – suffered a big dent in its right front quarter panel."

"But no one was hurt?"

"I don't think so, though the passenger in the Crosley never said much."

"You think the other driver will try to recover his property damage?"

"No way he can. When we exchanged information, he admitted he had no insurance. And as far as collecting from our insurance, he doesn't have a leg to stand on, not when he had a stop sign. Matter of fact, he asked if we could forget the whole thing. I told him I had to notify my insurance company and do whatever they say. I suspect they'll tell me to file an accident report...And that said, I guess I should give our agent a call." I went to the telephone and contacted our agent who arranged for me to come in after school the next day to fill out what he referred to as motor vehicle form MV-104.

***

Though folks with Tarot cards or a crystal ball might claim otherwise, prognosticating an individual's future is difficult. Nevertheless, clues, owing to personalities, intelligence, past behavior, and the like, allow for educated guesses. But enunciating hard and fast rules, reliable ones, as to what lies ahead is a fool's errand. An exception to this principle is noteworthy. One can always predict that the future will be full of surprises. Of course, that prediction, like any other, can only be proved with hindsight.

The last week of February 1969, with our group in its 27th year, those of The Guys who had remained in Grand Falls, eight of the original, met for our biweekly wintertime get-together. Once the warmer weather arrived and Nick Stoner's golf course opened, weekly gatherings on the links would resume.

Seated with brews at our usual large round table at Orton's Ale House, we awaited the arrival of our two eighteen-inch pizzas. As usual, one was a veggie and the other, pepperoni.

"I still can't believe the goddamn Colts," said Lefty. "How the fuck could they lose to Joe Namath and the Jets? The powerhouse of the NFL falling to some ragtag bums from the AFL. It's as bad as the NBA All-Stars succumbing to a bunch of Soviet commies."

Sam, seated immediately to my right, whispered in my ear. "It's been weeks since the Superbowl, and Lefty is still whining."

I looked across the table at the one-time jock. With a hairline that had drifted backward and a paunchy mid-section forged from an exorbitant consumption of beer, he was a shell of the big man on the high school campus who had visions of a Major League baseball career. Three seasons in the minors, none with a winning record, had proved the knuckleballer lacked the talent required for the big leagues. I whispered back, "Apparently, you didn't hear the latest news. The Yankees are secretly begging him to join their staff."

"What? They need a jock washer?" Sam smirked before sinking his teeth into a piece of pizza.

"You think Nick Stoner's might open for play by the first day of spring?" said Pete Longley.

"Sure…for snowmobiling," said Ronald Cooper, who had been elevated to Superintendent of Schools the preceding year. He pointed out the window. "In case you haven't noticed, a foot of snow coats the ground."

"Well, it could melt." said Pete.

"More likely, we'll get another foot between now and then," said Cooper.

"Jeez," said Pete. "You really know how to dash a guy's optimism, not to mention his appetite." Pete looked around. "Can't one of you galoots offer a rosier forecast?"

"You mean irrational?" said Speedy. "This isn't the foothills of the Smokies. In case you've forgotten, we live at the base of the Adirondacks. Snow is known to fall in May."

I jabbed Speedy. "Who appointed you Minister of Misery?"

"Somebody has to do the important jobs." Speedy capped his quip with a broad smile.

"Not to change the subject (Lefty never hesitated to invoke the self-justifying phrase), but we're demanding a spring rematch of last autumn's four-on-four flag football game. Ain't gonna wait till November."

"Bring it on. We're ready anytime you want," said Buster, who like Lefty, quarterbacked one of the two squads. The pair of jocks also captained the teams. The gridiron contests had begun in the early 1960's, a consequence of watching the Kennedy family at their Hyannis compound. Back then when we chose up sides, Buster picked Speedy. Lefty, who got the next two picks, responded with Cooper and Longley. Buster followed with Sam and me, leaving Babbitt for Lefty. The beefy Babbitt was a better blocker, but Sam and I were faster than the buffoonish blob. Whether Buster chose Sam and me because he deemed us more valuable than Babbitt or out of deference to Speedy was hard to say. Babbitt's antipathy for Speedy may have moderated over the quarter-century that had elapsed since his attempted blackball, but terming the two friends would torture the term.

After graduating high school and serving his enlistment in the army, Speedy had worked for a decade at the General Electric plant in Utica, earning an associate's degree at night. In 1958 he purchased Grand Falls Hardware from its retiring founder, Wilber Hopkins. Virtually everyone in town shopped for their hardware at Speedy's small establishment. Babbitt was the rare exception. That said, Speedy, like me, bought his insurance from an agency in Utica, rather than Babbitt's Grand Falls office.

"Next time when we square off on the football field, we're gonna whip your asses," said Lefty. "I'm installing trick plays that'll make the flea flicker and fumblerooski look like a quarterback sneak."

"Yeah, sure." Buster rolled his eyes. "And you're gonna win baseball's Cy Young award this year."

"That's a low blow." A smile on his face, Lefty shrugged before taking a swig of his brew.

I eyed him. Despite his protestation, he had taken the jab in good spirits. Undeniably, he was a blowhard who lived in the past and loved to talk trash. But in the face of ridicule, a happenstance that had grown more common over the years, he maintained good humor. Even so, a quick diversion, his *modus operandi*, was predictable.

Lefty turned to Speedy. "When you gonna marry that little looker you been dating for what...102 years."

"Actually it's 107," said Speedy. "But as for marriage, it's none of your damn business."

Speedy had been in a committed relationship with a bi-racial nurse from Little Falls for over a decade. For whatever reason they had declined to tie the knot. Speedy never said why, and I never pried.

Our pizzas finally arrived. Food pilfered the focus of our famished flock. Bubbling brews blunted blather. Piquant pizza pruned prattle. Trash talk tapered, as conversation localized, mainly tête-à-têtes between adjacent neighbors. About fifteen minutes elapsed, when Babbitt, ninety degrees to my right, said to Cooper, ninety degrees to my left, "Where do you think the school budget is headed? You expect the voters will give the thumbs down and the district will have to lay off more teachers?"

My ears perked up. The budget, as proposed by the school board, axed two teaching positions, art and Latin, plus a couple of extra-curricular activities. Those cuts represented a best-case scenario. My concern was that the budget might be voted down and additional cuts, including my position, would ensue. Around school, rumors abounded, but I had heard them in prior years, and those threatened doomsdays had never materialized.

"I assume matters will work themselves out," said Cooper. "In the meantime, I have to deal with the nonsense. Sitting at the top of the pyramid, all the headaches rain down onto my head."

With a salary double mine, it seemed fair that Cooper should bear those headaches. What he failed to mention was that if there was a shortfall, teachers like me would endure the pain. He would still enjoy his high-paying job as superintendent. On the bright side, I doubted that layoffs in the history department would eventuate. If, however, they did, and a position in the history department was axed, I would be the one to go. In a tiny department of long timers, I had the least seniority.

"When it comes to cuts, it's the board, not you, that controls the situation. Right?" said Pete.

"Yeah, on paper…but not in reality." Cooper chugged his brew.

"What kind of double talk is that?" said Pete.

"The kind our superintendent always gives," said Buster.

"Scoff all you like," said Cooper. "Between you, me, and the four walls, with few exceptions, the board is my echo. They have lives doing their day jobs." He leaned back and folded his arms. Though never short on hubris, the ample beer he had consumed elevated his hauteur. "Three of the five board members are in my back pocket. They look to me for guidance. Generally, I tell them to go with their own hearts and minds, but when something important pops up, when I want a result, I prod them. Yet to see the time they nixed a position I had pushed. Good CEOs are master puppeteers. Not to brag, but I'm a *good* CEO."

"Prove it," said Babbitt. "Produce a budget that cuts our taxes. And speaking of those taxes, they'd be a helluva lot lower and the school district wouldn't be in this mess if it weren't for the damn Democrats."

That the diehard Republican had thrown a political hand grenade into the conversation was no surprise. Babbitt blamed all the ills of society on the left.

"What nonsense leads you to claim that the Dems are responsible for possible layoffs in our schools?" said Sam. "The last time I looked, our local government, from top to bottom, mayor included, was Republican."

"Grand Falls happens to be in liberal New York State, which, in case you're unaware, is located in the United States of America." Babbitt's nose was in the air. "Just a month ago, our new president was inaugurated. Unfortunately, Johnson left him a horrendous mess. The mad Texan promised 'guns and butter.' He delivered neither. The crass bully mired us in an inane and endless Asian war. His policies brought chaos to the cities. All the while, he spent like a drunken hobo building his imaginary 'Great Society.' No surprise, the economy feels the strain, and we, the taxpayers, are paying through the nose. Fortunately, conservative competence has moved into the White House. Give Nixon a year or two, and the troops will be home and the economy humming."

"I'll believe it when I see it," said Sam.

"What – you hoping Nixon fails?" Babbitt garbled the quip, displaying an unappetizing mouthful of partially chewed pizza.

"That's not what I said, and you know it! Very simply, I don't trust Nixon. They don't call him Tricky Dick for nothing."

I looked around the table, a collection of four Democrats, three Republicans, and one independent. I could read the minds of my cohorts. With one exception, we had all learned to keep politics out of the conversation. Unfortunately, Babbitt, the exception, not only ignored the sage tack, but he also delighted in dumping gasoline and lighted matches onto volatile issues. Irrespective of whether the Democrats or the Republicans were on the right side of an issue, Babbitt's spin-laced, pejorative language inveigled even the most imperturbable listener to take his bait. In a word, Babbitt was a gadfly...Let me restate that in three words. Babbitt was a *condescending, infuriating gadfly.*

"Not to change the subject," said Lefty, but – "

"Then don't do it!" barked Babbitt.

"Babbitt, shut your trap!" said Buster. He turned to Lefty. "Change the subject, even a pitch-by-pitch recap of one of your illustrious mound exploits on behalf of our alma mater."

"I was gonna tell you about my new wheels, but if you want, I can give you a blow-by-blow of the sixteen Dragons I fanned junior year."

Amidst groans and cries of *spare us* and *God, no*, Lefty said, "Only kidding. What I was about to tell you was that I swapped my *mom's*...Trans Am for a bright red Corvette convertible." Lefty winked. "As you know, my mom loves hot cars." He laughed.

I read between the lines. Lefty was divorced. He had endured tough battles in Family Court over alimony and child support. Lest the judge raise his payments, quintessential Lefty, he had hidden his assets. He had registered his car in his mother's name. He had also worked a second job, off the books, getting paid in cash.

"Is it a new Corvette?" said Cooper.

"Almost. Only got fifteen-K on the odometer." Lefty, a car salesman, traded for a new ride roughly twice every three years. "Jim's got himself a new car too. He picked it up just three weeks ago."

All eyes turned my way.

"It's nothing like Lefty's Corvette. It's a Chevy Nova." Following my minor accident, rather than having the headlight repaired, I had traded up for a new car, something Mary and I had been talking about for months. I financed it over three years, with monthly payments of sixty dollars. The new car, a first for our family and the first I financed, was a big deal for us.

"It's a beauty," said Sam. "Baby blue."

"You drive it here tonight, Jim?" said Buster.

"Yup, it's out there in the parking lot."

"You'll have to show it to us when we leave." Buster turned to Pete. "How's your daughter doing? She still the tycoon of the fashion world?"

Pete shrugged. "She's doing well."

"That's an understatement," said Sam. "I saw the write-up in *Fashion World*, not that I normally read the publication. According to the article, she built a multi-million-dollar business, a small empire."

Pete shrugged abashedly.

"Ever the modest one," said Speedy. "We here in Grand Falls have bragging rights that she was one of our own."

"How old is she?" said Buster.

"Twenty-five," said Pete.

"But don't forget," I said, "she graduated high school at sixteen and flew through Vassar on a full scholarship in three years." I knew Laura's history almost as well as Pete. When Laura was still in elementary school, Pete's mother, his primary source of day care for Laura, died of a heart attack. Just as my mother had done when Laura was a baby, my wife Mary, then a housewife, stepped in. Each day after school Laura came to our house and stayed until Pete picked her up after work. Once or twice per week, when he worked overtime, Laura stayed for dinner. We deemed her a member of our family. Bright as she was and nearly a decade senior to Lisa and Jerry, Laura taught them to read even before they began school. She also taught them arithmetic. Years later, when Laura was in high school, she was a student in both my American and world history classes. A year after graduating college, she began her fashion design business. It took off like a rocket. In the four years that followed, she had become a millionaire.

Lefty got up from his seat and circled around to Sam. "Doc, would you take a look at this brown spot I have on my arm."

"Lucinski, you're a piece of work," said Buster. "Give Doc a break. He's a general surgeon, not a dermatologist. Between office hours and house calls, he puts in sixty hours. When he comes here – this is a pub, not a hospital – he's entitled to relax, not have a freeloader like you bombard him."

"Yeah," said Pete. "Just twenty minutes ago you bragged to me that last week was your best ever. To use your words, you're 'pocketing commissions faster than an IBM mainframe can count them.'"

"Oh, Doc doesn't mind checkin' me out. For that matter, a few months back he mentioned that he enjoys his rural practice because it allows him to do more than just surgery. He gets to see patients with all kinds of problems." Lefty turned to Sam. "You're okay with giving my arm the once over…Right?"

"When you put him on the spot, what do you expect him to say?" said Buster.

"It's okay," said Sam. "Here, roll up your sleeve, and let me see your arm."

With all of us watching, Lefty pulled up his sweater sleeve. "Eat your damn pizza. My arm is between me and Doc."

"Lucinski, don't tell us what to do," said Cooper. "You want privacy, pay for office hours."

Lefty ignored the jab, as he displayed his arm for Sam.

"It's a seborrheic keratosis."

Lefty's brow furrowed. "Is...is that bad?"

Doc smiled and shook his head. "Nah. It's a harmless growth."

"So, it's not cancerous?"

"No, it's round and uniform. That's the good news, but..." Sam suddenly became very serious. He breathed a beleaguered sigh. "Unfortunately, I see a different issue...really grim. Far as I know, it's not treatable."

Lefty's face flushed.

Lips pursed, Sam drew a somber pose. He shook his head again. "All these guys (Sam gestured around the table) will need to put up with you for many more years."

Apart from Lefty, we all roared.

"Go ahead, laugh." Lefty hurried to the head.

Once he was out of earshot, I whispered to Sam, "That was classic Lefty."

"How so?"

"Sponging on you. He's been doing it for years."

"Well..." Sam shrugged. "What can I say?"

"You needn't say anything. Far from the sponge, you're the victim." I reached for my pizza and took a bite.

"Hey, Pete," said Cooper. "I'd like you to seal my driveway. You got any time in the next week or two?"

Once Laura had headed off to college, Pete had cut his overtime and begun a sealcoating and paving business. Within a year or two, it had shown sufficient success that he had given up his day job. He earned a good living doing driveways, parking lots, and the like.

"I'm sure I can squeeze you in," said Pete. "I'll give you a call tomorrow, once I check my calendar."

"Coop, that big house of yours is only two years old," said Babbitt. "Did Buster build you a lemon?"

"It wasn't that good." Buster displayed the cheekiest of smiles.

His lack of defensiveness was no surprise. Self-deprecation had become a Buster hallmark. He could take razzing, especially that which veiled a compliment. Over the years, Buster, the youthful miscreant, had become a successful contractor. Throughout the surrounding area, he enjoyed an impeccable reputation for building quality homes. The region's wealthiest citizens, people like Superintendent Cooper, chose Buster when they built. Word of mouth, not advertising, was responsible for his reputation.

"My driveway, like my house, is *A-1*," said Cooper. "Buster builds the best. My attorney claims he's the only contractor from whom he doesn't demand an escrow at closing for unfinished details. When Buster says he'll do it, it's as good as done."

Buster pawed his chin and gazed melodramatically into space. "Apparently our good Superintendent is a dreadful judge of character." He reached for his brew and took a swig.

Our table grew uncommonly quiet. Mouths that had been rife with chatter focused on the taste of pizza. In the background the typical din of Orton's Ale House droned. I ran my eyes over my seven tablemates. The eight of us boasted a history extending back more than a quarter-century. When we first came together, could I have predicted how our respective lives would eventuate? The overall answer included some yeses, but as many noes. Sam was always destined to be a doctor. We knew it when we were kids. Babbitt was Babbitt. Whether he was a white-collar company man, realtor, insurance agent, or businessman, he fit his mold. Cooper was predictable, not that I anticipated him as our superintendent. But a significant position in government or industry was a solid bet. The other four were more surprising. Who would have thought that Speedy, who never seemed the entrepreneurial type, would own the local hardware store? A blue-collar job at a manufacturing plant seemed more probable. And Pete, whose life seemed doomed when he dropped out of school after getting a heroin-addicted girl pregnant, had not only built himself a seal-coating and paving business, but in addition, his daughter had become a wealthy businesswoman. As for Lefty, he was a mixed bag. In one respect, he was predictable, but in another, he was not. Back in the day, I believed Lefty would have a Major League career. My heart deemed it destiny. But my brain, the logic of statistical probabilities, would have bet against it. A brash salesman, always on the brink of easy street, merited better odds. Lefty may not have lived the dream, but he was no shock. Finally, there was Buster. Even fatuous dreams could not portray him as a field general in the National Football League. No Division I college programs had recruited him. Far from a great student, his path always bordered on the edge. If anyone in our group had booked a ticket on the train to trouble, Buster had that distinction. A prognostication that his résumé would showcase a stint in prison might have been even money. Lest there be any confusion, once I got to know Buster, I liked him. I valued his friendship, especially in our school days when, owing to Sam and his father, Buster sheltered me from would-be bullies. That said, back when we were in school, little did I imagine that the devil-may-care longshot would become a successful contractor with a first-rate reputation.

I bit the remaining crust of my second slice of pizza. I chewed the crisp dough, shifting my thoughts to the last member of The Guys – me. Had my life after high school followed a foreseeable course? The answer merited a resounding *yes*. Indeed, one could argue that except for Sam, I was the most predictable. Following graduation, I went to the New York State Teachers' College at Albany. Many who went there did not become teachers, but a career in education was an excellent bet. Marrying my high school sweetheart, though hardly a given, was no shock. Indeed, I bore all the earmarks of one likely to become a typical member of America's broad middle class. Where some might deem my life insipid, one teeming with ennui, I take exception. Admittedly, I was far from wealthy, but with a job I liked, a wonderful wife and children, and a comfortable home, my life was excellent. With our long-term plan, one that would provide a good retirement, Mary and I had a bright future. No doubt, several of The Guys had achieved greater financial success than I, but add up everything, quality of life included, and the assets stocking my portfolio equaled the wealth of the most affluent. I was indeed blessed.

***

A poor swimmer flailing in freezing waters has been known to panic. But another, equally inept, remains calm. People vary. They handle the same situation differently. Some exhibit optimism. Others focus on the dark side. Pessimism clouds perspective. Worry comes with the territory. But even worriers can occasionally appear phlegmatic in the face of dire circumstances.

Shortly after ten, I arrived home. A book in her lap, Mary sat in the living room.

"You had a nice evening with The Guys?"

"Yup."

"Anything new?"

I thought for a second. "Not really. The pizza, as always, was great. Trash talk abounded. Babbitt was typical Babbitt...irritating, not that anyone gave him credence. And of course, Lefty, having consumed his customary excess of beer, was bombastic Lefty...How was your evening?"

Mary heaved a sigh. "Peaceful...well except for Jordina. She nearly drowned."

"Jordina?" I searched my brain for the unfamiliar name. "Is she okay?"

"Oh yeah. Maurice dove into the icy waters and rescued her." Mary held up her book. "Jordina and Maurice are the principal characters. They're doing fine now, lying on a bearskin rug enjoying a roaring fire in a cozy cabin. They were on the verge of steamy romance when you interrupted."

"Sorry. I'll let you get back to your book."

"That's okay. Maurice and Jordina are incredibly patient." Mary laid her book onto the end table. "Did Cooper reveal anything new about possible layoffs?"

"Why – did you think he would?"

"Not exactly, but he is the superintendent. If anyone has inside information, he's the one."

"Well, the subject did come up. And based upon his bluster, he controls the board."

"So, did he give any hints which way the wind is blowing?"

"Not really...I suspect it's a reprise of many other years. Budget is tight. Layoffs can't be ruled out. The spenders and fiscal tightwads will push their positions until the eleventh hour when compromise will magically materialize. After months with a logjam, everyone will be copasetic. Isn't that how it always goes?" Not wanting to alarm Mary, I colored my assessment with feigned optimism. And too, I was trying to convince myself that things would work out. I said, "Lisa and Jerry in their bedrooms?"

"Lisa is. She went to bed early. Jerry is staying over at Don's house. They're doing a joint presentation for their biology project tomorrow. They anticipated staying up later than usual. They arranged for the sleepover...You want a cup of tea?"

"Sounds good." I followed Mary into the kitchen.

"When do you guys meet next?"

"Two weeks...the 10th of March. Not till the links open will we begin our weekly get-togethers. Babbitt proposed that we switch our golf from Monday to Thursday. The idea crashed faster than a B-52 with engines on fire and no wings. Monday is the quietest day at Nick Stoner's. It's the lull day after the weekend rush. Playing Mondays makes it easier for our two foursomes to finish nine holes before dark. Any other day would be iffier, especially in the fall when the sun sets earlier. Thursday would also be problematic for Speedy. It's the day the hardware store remains open until six. Though Babbitt never shops there, I'm sure he's aware. Possible Babbitt's real motive was to eliminate Speedy from the group...or knowing Babbitt, jerk Speedy's chain."

Mary set two cups of tea onto the table and joined me there. "You know that cut Lisa got on her leg while running the trail in the woods?"

"What about it?" I sipped my tea.

"It hasn't healed."

"It's only been a week."

"That's what Lisa said this afternoon. Claimed it's no big deal. But she said the same thing the day before, and I don't like how it looks. I'm concerned it might get infected. I put a call into Sam. His secretary indicated he was doing surgery in Little Falls but would be in the office tomorrow. I'll ask him to give it a look. And I know, I'm probably being overly cautious."

My assessment concurred. Chances were it was much ado about nothing. Regardless, I was glad Mary had opted for the prudent route. Like her, I was a worrier.

Chapter XVII

It is said that ignorance is bliss. But ignorance, dependent on luck, can beget disaster. Knowledge, on the other hand, is the fount of wisdom, the resource enabling the prudent exercise of judgment.

The day after The Guys had met, I arrived home from school shortly before five. I had been supervising the newly formed Chess Club. A half-dozen students had approached me with the idea, and once I agreed, a group of eight began meeting in my homeroom on a biweekly basis. Because we were an informal body, not established by a duly approved board resolution, my service carried no stipend. Whether that might change in the future depended in part on whether the club grew into a well-attended activity or fizzled out. Far more determinative, however, would be the dictates of the district's budgetary constraints. Fiscal concerns had steered extracurricular activities on a downward trajectory. Even football, the darling of Grand Falls, found itself battling for increases equal to what had become a pattern of persistent inflation. As for the school board appropriating funds for the chess club, a single pawn had a better chance to capture two rooks, two bishops, a queen, and a king.

After pulling into the driveway, I entered the house through the mud room adjacent to the kitchen. I no sooner opened the door than Mary said, "Good thing I took Lisa to see Sam."

Concern stopped me in my tracks.

"Relax," said Mary. "Lisa is fine. But her leg is infected."

"What does that mean?"

"Sam said he'll need to debride the wound. It's loaded with necrotic tissue."

The unfamiliar word unnerved me. "Necrotic tissue? What's that?" My eyes still on Mary, I laid my briefcase down.

"I don't know exactly, except that it's dead."

I shot Mary a look.

"I know what you're thinking. I had the same reaction, but Sam reassured me. Lisa will be fine. But he said it's good we didn't ignore it. The infection could have spread, in which case it could have become dangerous."

"So, it hasn't spread?"

"Not really. Sam cleansed the wound and treated it with antibiotics. He plans to debride it first thing tomorrow morning at Little Falls Hospital."

"Lisa needs to go to the hospital?" Increased volume underscored my mounting concern.

"That's where Sam performs the procedure. It's more sterile, plus it has facilities if by chance any unexpected issues arise."

"Unexpected issues?"

Mary held up a pair of halting hands. "Stop challenging the messenger. I'm only telling you what Sam said. And like me, you want Sam to do the procedure in the safest environment. Right?"

Her undeniable point quelled my acerbic propensities. "I'll go with you to the hospital in the morning, I'll call in at six and tell them to get a sub."

"Not necessary. No reason for both of us to go. Sam said so."

I looked Mary in the eye. "You sure?"

"I'm sure."

***

In the hardest of times, people welcome comfort foods like pizza and ice cream. Of course, people welcome pizza and ice cream most any time.

The moment the last of my morning classes ended, I hurried to the teachers' room and dialed home. On one level I knew that everything would be fine with Lisa. But nervous father that I was, all morning disquiet had obtained. Even as I taught lessons in American and world history, an impertinent voice from the depths of my brain fixated on Lisa. The telephone rang once…twice…three times. I grew more antsy when, following the fourth ring, from the other end, came Mary's *Hello.*

"How's Lisa?" I said, ignoring usual niceties.

"She's fine."

I breathed an audible sigh of relief.

"Sam said it was fortunate we didn't ignore the wound. It was infected, even more than he originally thought. Additional delay would have been dicey."

"But she's fine. Right?"

"Absolutely. Sam reassured me…more than once."

"What exactly did he do?"

"He surgically debrided the wound. From what he said, that involved probing with a scalpel and special scissors. He removed any infected and non-viable tissue, as well as what he referred to as – I wrote it down…hyperkeratotic tissue. Sam described that as skin that's thick and bearing pointed protuberances."

"So, it looks good now?"

"It's bandaged, so I can't say firsthand. But according to Sam, it's not pretty. You can't expect otherwise, not after six inches of her lower leg were surgically probed. But the important thing is that her leg will be fine. Sam also told me that scarring, requiring additional debridement, will be inevitable. But that's cosmetic and can be done over time."

"Is Lisa in any pain?"

"No. She's in the living room watching TV. How much discomfort she'll have later remains to be seen. When doing the procedure, Sam used an anesthetic, a local one, lidocaine to be precise. He said that once it wears off, her leg is sure to be sore. He prescribed a pain med, along with an antibiotic to protect against further infection. He termed both standard procedures."

"Anything else I should know?"

"Just that you should relax. Lisa is fine."

I welcomed the reiterated reassurance. "Can Lisa eat everything?"

"Sure."

"Good. I'll pick up a veggie pizza on the way home, along with a half-gallon of her favorite, Stewart's Star Gazer ice cream."

"You love that too."

"What can I say? My daughter has good taste. She takes after her father." I waited a couple seconds for a reaction. None was forthcoming. "I'll see you later. Love you."

"Love you too."

***

Anytime someone delivers a surprise, the possibility of a bonanza looms. But some surprises transcend others.

Seated in the living room on an early March evening, the ring of the doorbell drew me from the episode of *Bonanza* our family was watching. Upon opening the portal, I observed an unfamiliar man. "Can I help you?"

"Are you James Ward?"

"Yes. What can I do for you?" If he was selling something, I would bestow a swift heave-ho.

The man handed me some folded papers attached to a blue backer. "You are hereby served with process in the lawsuit of Casper Cuthbert against you."

"Casper who?" I said, reacting to the unfamiliar name.

"It's all in the papers." The man turned and walked away.

I briefly watched him, after which I unfolded the papers. Stapled to the blue backer, the top form, a half sheet, was a summons in an action entitled, "Casper Cuthbert, Plaintiff, v. James Ward, Defendant." Behind it were several typewritten sheets, a complaint bearing the same title as the summons. I shut the door, and stepping back into the hallway, I began scanning the document.

"Who was that?" said Mary, as I returned to the living room.

"A process server."

"A process server? What did he want?"

"He served me with papers in a lawsuit from…" I glanced at the complaint to refresh myself as to the name of the plaintiff. "Some guy named Casper Cuthbert. I have no clue who he is." A perusal of the complaint's initial paragraphs answered the question. "Appears he was the passenger in the Crosley with which I had that fender bender at Sparrow and Blake."

"I thought you said that no one was hurt."

"That was my understanding. The other driver, a guy named Steve Jones, insisted the accident was a little nothing. Maybe because he had no insurance, he wanted to forget the whole thing. He was ready to go our separate ways without even exchanging information."

I went to my easy chair, where *Bonanza* and the predicament facing the Cartwright family yielded to a more important matter, the blue-backed papers. Though extensive legal jargon inhibited a complete understanding, a closer reading shed light on the lawsuit. I said, "This Cuthbert fellow claims he hasn't been able to work since the accident, that he suffered permanently disabling injuries. He demands judgment for $250,000."

"What? You gotta be kidding," said Mary.

"I wish I were."

Lisa and Jerry, seated on the floor, had remained focused on the television, at least until my mention of $250,000, a sum roughly thirty times my annual salary. The outlandish number drew their attention, as well as their apparent concern.

I said, "This whole thing is garbage…a big nothing." I was less sanguine than my reassuring words.

"What are you going to do?" said Mary.

"Well, the papers indicate I have 20 days to answer the complaint. And Joe (Joseph Walker, the sole attorney in Grand Falls, was our family lawyer) has told me more than once to contact him immediately if I'm ever arrested or served with papers. He said don't wait for the next business day. So, I guess I'll follow his advice and give him a call."

I headed to our bedroom where we had a second telephone. As I looked up Joe's home telephone number, I harkened back to bygone days when as a child we had a single telephone and a party line. Important calls, such as the one I was about to make, risked an invasion of needed privacy. The hindsight stirred memories of the annoyance occasioned by a party line. Of course, back then, we were happy to have a telephone. And too, our perspective differed. We imagined the inconvenience of even earlier days when people lacked telephones, radios, cars, refrigerators, and numerous other conveniences. Difficult as those days may have been, they had advantages. Money-grubbing claimants and shysters trumping up phony lawsuits were yet to become the norm.

After rereading the complaint and thinking through what I would say to my attorney, I dialed his number.

"Hello."

"Hi Joe. It's Jim Ward. I…I'm sorry to bother you at home, but I was just served with a lawsuit, a claim for damages from a car accident I had a week or so ago."

"First off, no need to apologize. Many of my clients, despite my repeated admonitions, delay calling. You, on the other hand, got it right. You followed my instructions…So, the accident you had, was it serious?"

"No, just a fender bender…at the intersection of Sparrow and Blake. The other driver – he had no insurance – ran the stop sign on Blake. From what I knew at the scene, no one was hurt…just a broken headlight and a couple of scratches on our bumper. The other car had a dented front quarter panel. But now his passenger is suing me for a quarter of a million dollars."

"Par for the course."

"Par for the course? What does that mean?"

"When lawyers issue a summons and complaint in a personal injury action, they stick in big numbers. They cover all contingencies. If down the road, injuries turn out more serious than initially thought, they don't need to make a motion to amend their pleadings."

"Fine, but a quarter of a million?"

"What can I say?"

"Since the other driver – he had an old junker – went through the stop sign, I shouldn't have any liability. Right?"

"Well, yes and no."

"That's a very lawyerly response, but not a reassuring one." My comment echoed in my ears. After calling my attorney long after office hours, I needed to stifle sarcasm. Unfortunately, stress, attributable to being sued, superseded restraint.

"Let me explain…and relax. Your insurance company will defend you, and if by chance the plaintiff recovers, they will pay. What are the limits of your policy?"

"It's a standard 10-20 policy."

"Fine. So, you have $10,000 of coverage for any single claimant."

"But why should I have any liability when the other driver was at fault?"

"Good question. And I'm not saying you do. But here's why you might. New York is a contributory negligence state. There are bills in the Legislature to change it to a comparative negligence state, but that's neither here nor there. The guy who is suing you, a passenger, didn't cause the accident. He can recover his damages from anyone whose negligence contributed to the accident, even someone who was only a tiny percent at fault. Since your car hit the other car, a jury is apt to find that you had a small degree of responsibility. Earlier you characterized the other car as an uninsured junker. Apparently, the passenger is suing you because you have the deeper pockets. And unfortunately, juries are inclined to believe passengers more than drivers when it comes to finding fault for accidents. But all that said, I assume you'll be fine. As I mentioned, your insurance policy should take care of everything, a defense of the action and payment, if any, for damages."

"Anything I need to do?"

"Leave the papers in my office mail slot on your way to school tomorrow morning. I'll Xerox a copy for myself and deliver the original to your insurance agent. Make sure you jot down your agent's name. I'll notify him to keep me informed of whatever transpires with the lawsuit. My monitoring should require minimal time. You shouldn't run up much of a bill…Any questions?"

"No."

"Good. Then one last matter. Put your mind at rest. Okay?"

"Yes...and thanks." As I hung up the receiver, I felt better than I did before I called. That said, I felt much worse than when the doorbell had rung twenty-five minutes earlier.

***

Tuna fish, unlike pizza and ice cream, lacks a proven track record. When the vicissitudes of life brandish their savage teeth, a tuna fish sandwich fails to thwart the suffering. For that matter, even a pepperoni and sausage pizza, followed by a triple-dip sundae with all the toppings, lacks the necessary magic.

Three weeks had passed since Lisa had undergone her treatment at Little Falls Hospital. Her wound was healing, and the danger associated with infection had subsided. However, her lower right leg evidenced the ordeal. A thick, discolored, ugly scar was forming. Restoring the area close to its pre-wound appearance would require a series of debridement treatments. A check of my health insurance, a plan not nearly as comprehensive as that provided by larger school districts, confirmed the cosmetic procedure would not be covered. Brief research indicated the cost would run between $500 and $1,000, a heavy hit to our family budget. Regardless, Mary and I never thought twice about going forward.

En route to lunch on the third Friday of March, I stopped at my mailbox adjacent to the school's office. Most notices, the date for submitting grades, the schedule of events, and the like, came on a folded sheet of paper. Notices that were personal arrived in an envelope, and I had one. I suspected, indeed I feared, what it contained. I took the envelope from my mailbox, heading out to the largely deserted hall. I opened the message. It confirmed my prescience, not that such foresight inspired celebration. I was on notice that if the voters rejected the budget, my teaching position risked elimination. Though the threat was no surprise and I had faced it before, seeing it in black and white provoked angst. I headed to the teachers' lounge and removed my brown bag from the refrigerator, not that I had an appetite. I seated myself with Sarah Hayes, the French teacher, and Herb Smith, a mathematics teacher.

"Did you hear the latest about the district's budget?" said Sarah.

Being a first-year teacher, presumably she too had received a warning notice. I suspected that the lovely missile, a first for her, had precipitated her question. As I took my tuna fish sandwich from my bag, I said, "You referring to the possibility of pink slips?"

"Not exactly, but a tidbit linked to that subject. Word has it that several businessmen, along with numerous homeowners, met last night and formed a coalition to oppose the budget. They plan to print leaflets and go door to door urging people to vote down the budget."

"Just peachy." I turned to Herb. "Must be nice to have seniority, to be free of worries that you'll be excessed."

Herb displayed an abashed look. "Can't deny it. Knowing my job is safe from the chopping block sidesteps a load of stress. But that's not to say I'm indifferent to the potential cuts. I feel for those who may be excessed. And for that matter, the cuts will hurt those of us who retain our jobs. The quality of education here in the district will suffer. Class size will escalate. Even now, with twenty-five, it's hard to maintain discipline, let alone accord students needed individual attention. Add a few more, and..." Herb exhibited a troubled look as he grabbed the sides of his head.

"You think the taxpayers will nix the budget?" Begging a *no* to my question, I added, "From what I've seen, especially on parents' night, folks in our community care about education."

"Agreed," said Sarah, "when you refer to those who show up on parents' night. But they represent a decided minority. Include the majority who stay home and the ones who have no children or their children are grown, and our community's support for education warrants a low grade. Even more important, all these folks, even the ones who come on parents' night, care more about their pocketbooks. Times are tough. Unemployment in the area remains high. Raises, if any, are tiny. Add in annual inflation, a fraction over five percent, and folks feel pain. Their personal budgets don't add up. With the district proposing a three percent increase, less than what is required to maintain existing staff and services – forget about money for needed work on buildings – it's a formula for a rejected budget." Sarah heaved a sigh. "As one likely to get the axe, I'd love to be more optimistic, but facts are facts, numbers are numbers."

I chewed a mouthful of tuna on white, along with the points Sarah had made. The grim picture embodied more truth than the pollyannish response I had sought. I turned to Herb, hoping for a second opinion, one that was more palatable. "You're the math expert. You think the numbers are such that layoffs can be avoided?"

He finished chewing, and following a pause that included pursed lips, said, "I hate to be a herald of hopelessness, but given the arithmetic, the landscape looks bleak. You've got a budget that's already stretched to the limit. Add more expenses and a shrinking tax base and…it's like trying to make one plus one equal four because three already proved impossible. Bottom line, something has to give."

"True," I said. "But the district has faced budget shortfalls before. When push came to shove, it has always worked out."

"Yeah, I guess," said Herb, his concurrence lacking conviction. "Unfortunately, years with that pattern have exacerbated the situation. One can only tread so near the edge of a cliff before gravity takes over. All things considered, I suspect we're in freefall."

I drifted into my own thoughts, searching for a silver lining. My brain delivered nothing. I reached into my bag and extracted a big chocolate chip cookie that Mary had included. Its sugary flavor pleased my palette. It did not, however, gratify my appetite for a solution to the district's financial woes, one that would eliminate the threat to my job.

A pall settled in. We finished our lunches in silence.

I gestured at the clock. "I need to get back to my classroom…put some material on the blackboard prior to fifth period." I got up.

"Circumstances may not be as bad as they seem," said Herb. "As you said earlier, budget problems have a way of working themselves out. Maybe it'll all be fine."

Easy for you to say. You have seniority; your kids are out of college; your wife has a full-time job; and you're eligible to retire. I kept the thoughts to myself. Herb bore no blame for Sarah's and my misfortune. He was empathizing, not gloating, trying to make Sarah and me feel better.

***

Parents endeavor to inculcate their children with basic values and principles. Unfortunately, some children are excellent learners. They regurgitate what they were taught at the worst of times, hoisting their parents onto their own petards.

Mary laid a bowl of salad onto the dining room table before taking her familiar seat at the end nearer the kitchen. Seated at the opposite end, I added salad to my plate that already housed chicken parmesan, served over angel hair pasta. Lisa and Jerry occupied their usual seats to my right and left respectively. Dinner as a family had been a tradition ever since the children were small. As they had moved along in school, particularly in high school, their activities sometimes forced us to deviate. So too did my get-togethers with The Guys.

"How was school today?" said Mary. Hardly a day went by that she failed to ask the question.

Lisa, Jerry, and I all welcomed the inquiry. Though our reactions, frequently blasé, suggested otherwise, each of us relished the opportunity to share our successes: Lisa and Jerry, a high grade, and I, a productive day on the opposite side of the desk. We also appreciated the doorway to carp. Years earlier, Lisa and Jerry had learned that when their gripes related to one of their teachers – a tough test or an onerous homework assignment – the friendly ear lay at the end of the table nearer the kitchen. With few exceptions, I declined to criticize other teachers. Having my kids spread the word that I had labeled one of my colleagues an SOB was a tack begging blowback.

Lisa shared that she got an *A* on her Advanced Algebra test. Jerry complained that Moose Miller, who was spending a second stint in tenth grade, had threatened to beat Jerry up because he had looked at Moose the wrong way. I had a grievance of my own, the state of the budget, an entrée which had spoiled my lunch and subsequent afternoon. Not wanting to worry the kids, my grousing needed to await a second cup of coffee alone with Mary. Unfortunately, Lisa short-circuited my patient plan.

"Just before last period, Deanna Wilkerson – her mother works in the junior high cafeteria – spoke to me about the school budget. She said her mother would be among the first booted in the event of additional cuts." Lisa focused on me. "Possible layoffs don't affect you…do they, Dad?"

An admission that I, the family's breadwinner, might be unable to support my wife and children would be heartbreaking. But denying that reality would entail dishonesty. I swallowed hard. Threading a size-5 needle with heavy tex thread was oxymoronic, especially when Mary, not I, boasted the family's sewing skills. I said, "These budget issues crop up most years, and they're almost always resolved without significant cuts. If history is any indicator, we'll be fine." I had successfully threaded the needle, delivered truth without alarm…albeit ignoring realism.

"But Dad," said Lisa, "you, a history teacher, taught us that every situation is unique. You stressed the importance of history, the insights it provides, but you emphasized that it's never an end all. Current facts and circumstances, never identical to the past, must be scrutinized. That's what you taught us." Lisa looked me in the eye. "What do the facts say about this year's budget?"

My own words had come back to haunt me. Contrary to my earlier self-satisfied assessment, a second look revealed that my thick thread had deflected wide of the needle's narrow eye. I was in a tight spot. No way could I chide my daughter for heeding my lessons. Alarm remained unacceptable; a lie, worse yet. I hedged or more precisely, I sidestepped the question. "I don't have a crystal ball. We'll just have to see what happens."

"But if they cut your job, what will we do?" said Jerry. "How will we live?"

"We'll cross that bridge if and when we come to it," said Mary, invoking one my favorite adages. "We'll be fine."

I welcomed Mary's intervention. Without it, the needle I had endeavored to thread would have stabbed me.

***

A motor vehicle accident emulates beauty; it rests in the eye of the beholder. So too do liability and damages. Juries, one's peers, proffer prodigious prizes for pulchritudinous pictures.

Seated in an impressive conference room in the Utica law offices of Herman Pritchard, the attorney for plaintiff Casper Cuthbert, I had just finished my deposition, an Examination Before Trial, what the lawyers referred to as an "EBT." I had answered Pritchard's questions regarding the motor vehicle accident that had occurred in February. I had described the accident exactly as it had occurred, detailing how the other vehicle, the corroded Crosley, traveling west on Blake, had failed to stop for the stop sign at Sparrow; and how I, going south on Sparrow, had applied my brakes when I saw the Crosley, coming from my left, enter the intersection. I had testified that at the time of the accident I was going roughly five miles per hour; that I believed the other driver also applied his brakes because he skidded before the impact; and that at the time we collided, his speed was comparable to mine.

With my testimony completed, Marcy Wilson of Cantley and Willson, the law firm engaged by my insurance company to defend me, began her examination of Cuthbert, a burly fellow with a goatee and beer belly, who was wearing braces around both his back and neck. Wilson took Cuthbert through the preliminaries, his age, 35, his address, etcetera. Cuthbert indicated that Jones, the other driver, had given him a ride home after bowling in Little Falls.

"Did you have anything to drink while you were bowling?" said Wilson.

"A bottle of Utica Club," said Cuthbert.

"What about Mr. Jones? Did he have anything to drink?"

"A couple Cokes...though they coulda been Pepsis, whatever they serve at the lanes."

"What time did you and Mr. Jones leave the bowling alley?"

"'Bout 5:30, give or take."

"Was it light or dark out?"

"Dark...wintertime, you know."

"How were the roads and weather that evening?"

"Clear and dry."

Short, crisp answers hinted that Pritchard had taken pains to prep the otherwise inarticulate Cuthbert in advance of his testimony.

"What kind of vehicle was Mr. Jones driving?"

"A Crosley, 'bout 20 years old, a 1949 model, I think."

"And where were you seated in the car?"

"Right front passenger seat. The Crosley, real small, don't got much of a back seat."

"Did there come a time that the Crosley in which you were riding became involved in an accident?"

"Yeah."

"And can we agree that the accident occurred at the intersection of Blake and Sparrow?"

"Yup."

"Are there any traffic control devices, for example, stop signs or traffic lights, at that intersection?"

"Uh...yeah...stop sign on Blake. Nuttin' that I know of on Sparrow."

"On what street was Mr. Jones operating his vehicle, the one you were riding in?"

"Blake."

"And what direction was Mr. Jones going?"

"West."

"And do you know the model of the other vehicle?"

"Some sort of Chevrolet...but can't say the model."

"And on what street was that vehicle traveling when the accident occurred?"

"Sparrow...It wuz headin' south, comin' from my right."

"Can you please describe for me what happened from the time the Crosley approached the intersection until the collision?"

"Well, Steve...Jones, he slowed the Crosley and stopped at the stop sign...the one on Blake. Nuttin' wuz comin', least far as I could tell. So, Jones, he headed into the intersection when this here Chevy, no headlights on, skidded into the intersection and slammed into us...right on my side of the car, the front right quarter panel."

On a pad that Wilson had given me before the deposition, I jotted the following note: "I had my headlights on. I know because when Jones and I got out of our vehicles and exchanged information, one of my headlights was broken and the other was still on."

While I was writing, Wilson continued her questions. Once I finished, she glanced at my note and nodded, after which she resumed her examination, inquiries about the moment of impact, the speed of the cars, the damages they sustained, and the like. She said, "I see you're wearing braces around your back and torso. Did you wear those before the accident?"

"No, Ma'am. I wuz fine before the accident. Worked construction, handlin' 2 x 4's and 4 x 8's and wieldin' a sledgehammer. Can't do it no more."

"Have you worked at all since the accident?"

Cuthbert shook his head.

"You need to give an audible answer so the young lady can take it down." Wilson gestured at the court stenographer who sat next to Cuthbert at the corner of the large table.

"Oh, sorry...And no, I ain't worked since the accident, not a day."

"How much were you earning before the accident?"

"'Bout $300 a week."

"During the year prior to the accident, what did you average?"

"'Bout $300, like I said."

"How much of the time do you wear your braces?"

"Most all the time, 'cept when I sleep or shower, stuff like that."

"What, if any, pain or discomfort do you have?"

"Constant. Hate to complain, but I hurt right now. Hard to sit here. 'Course standin' wouldn't be no better. Both my neck and back ache, and the hurt runs down my right leg."

"Do the braces help your pain?"

"Ain't that they make it good. Just that widout 'em, pain gets worse, damn near unbearable."

"Besides the fact that you're unable to work, has the accident otherwise limited your activities?"

"Has it ever. Can't bowl or shoot hoops. Can't do much of anythin'. And...and my personal life with my girlfriend...if you...uh...get my drift...It ain't been the same since the accident."

"What, if any, treatment have you had for your injuries?"

"Well, I been seein' Doc Baker in Utica every week, plus physical therapy twice a week. The Doc prescribed some pain pills. Don't recall the name. I take 'em daily. Helps a little. Drops the pain from a seven to a three or four. That's outta ten."

Wilson examined Cuthbert for another ten minutes or so, more details about medical treatment and limitations. Once the questioning concluded, Cuthbert, his attorney, and the court stenographer left.

Wilson said, "So, what do you think?"

"Cuthbert couldn't have been hurt as badly as he claims. The impact was a little nothing. And he lied about my headlights being off. I'm sure because my right headlight, the one that wasn't broken in the accident, was still on after the crash, when I exchanged information with Jones."

Wilson nodded slowly but said nothing.

"So, what do *you* think?" I said.

Wilson stared off into space before refocusing on me. "Personally, I believe you. But history says that when a passenger sues a driver, the passenger wins. And not to cause you undue worry, but you're being sued over the limits of your insurance policy. I know you're aware because your personal attorney Joe Walker has contacted me. I know Joe well. He's a good guy. Very capable. Anyway, I've been keeping him apprised of everything. I'll be sending him a copy of the transcript from today's deposition, once I receive it."

"How much do you think the plaintiff might recover, assuming he wins?"

"If you're talking about a jury verdict, hard to say. Damage awards from a jury are a guessing game. Depends how the testimony shakes out. But if they believe the plaintiff is as bad as he claims, we're talking about a big number. First off are his lost wages. More important, his life has been changed. Can't do much, and he's in constant pain." Wilson reached into her file and took out a photograph. "Much as I think he's exaggerating, looking at the Crosley, its smashed-in front quarter panel (Williard pointed at the photograph) leads one to believe that the impact was worse than a fender bender. And I know, the Crosley was an old piece of tin, but, as people say, 'a picture is worth a thousand words.' The adage may be trite, but experience has taught me that when juries deliberate, the bromide holds true. And bottom line, the plaintiff, who comes across as credible, was a passenger. He didn't cause the accident."

I thanked Wilson and went on my way feeling worse than when I had arrived. Two hours earlier I was nervous about the deposition. Never had I testified under oath. But I found solace in the assumption that my insurance would cover any liability. Walking back to my car, earlier nerves had eased. Unfortunately, a far worse, depressing feeling prevailed. The possibility that I could have personal liability dwarfing my $10,000 coverage terrified me.

As soon as I arrived home, I dialed Joe Walker and filled him in on what had happened at the deposition. "So, what do you think?" I said, reiterating the same question I had asked Wilson, hoping for a more reassuring answer.

Walker heaved a sigh. "I'd like to tell you it's no big deal, but that would be disingenuous. It could be problematic, but that doesn't mean it will...How did the plaintiff, Cuthbert, present? Did he seem believable?"

"I guess so. Wilson said he came across as credible...Suppose he does get a big verdict, way above my $10,000 coverage, what would that mean for me?"

"Cuthbert would get a judgment that he could enforce against you."

"Could he take our house?" My stomach was churning.

"No, because you and Mary own it by what is called *tenants by the entirety*. I know because I drew the deed when you bought it. But the lien of the judgment would attach to your interest in the house and could be enforced against your share if you sold it. The judgment would also enable Cuthbert to garnish your wages, up to ten percent of your pay, until the judgment was satisfied. And he could execute on other personal property you own."

"If I understand, he could turn my life into financial Hell."

"Hold on. Let's not get ahead of ourselves. The case remains far from judgment, let alone a judgment above the limits of your policy. Focusing on a worst-case scenario will only wreak mental havoc."

"Fine. But are you confident such a scenario is improbable?"

A brief silence answered my question.

"Well, let's see how things progress...cross bridges when we reach them."

"I'll try," I said, though the familiar phrase did little to alleviate my concerns. If anything, they had magnified. The conversation ended. I went into the kitchen and opened the refrigerator. After staring blankly at the plethora of foodstuffs, I slammed the door. I had no appetite.

***

In days of yore, the prophet Jeremiah, his doubt manifest, questioned whether a leopard can change its spots (Bible, Jeremiah, 13:23). For centuries people have interpreted Jeremiah's message more categorically than its wording. The notion that some leopards, particularly those that walk on two legs, might change their spots is intriguing. Anecdotal evidence sheds light on the matter. For example, cosmetic producers proudly tout creams that magically mask spots. But the industry's ephemeral results yield inconsequential insight. That leaves the underlying question unanswered. Perhaps time, tougher tests on suitable leopards, will resolve the conundrum.

The second Monday in April, the Guys played our first round of the year at Nick Stoner's. Any possibility that the new season might open with different teams had been negated months earlier in the autumn flag-football game. Riding Buster's redoubtable right arm at quarterback and Speedy's nifty moves at flanker, Buster, Speedy, Sam, and I had snagged bragging rights, something we had unabashedly wielded throughout the winter. Eager to turn the tables, Lefty, Pete, Coop, and Babbitt demanded revenge sooner than the teams' next meeting on the gridiron. They insisted on a shot as soon as the links opened. As I detailed at the outset of my story, that demand, coupled with back-and-forth outcomes on the golf course, followed by a tie, established permanent team lineups, at least for the foreseeable future. But for the moment, let me focus on the season opener.

With our swings rusty, Nick Stoner's clay-based fairways still soggy, and the greens far from their velvety best, we opted for what is known as a *scramble*. The forgiving format, which erases the agony of appalling shots, works as follows: Each player hits a drive. Each team picks their best, and each player hits a second shot from that spot. The same procedure obtains for all subsequent shots. Even on the green, the team can select the easiest putt, taking four tries to hole it. A team that hits three horrific shots and one excellent shot is better off than a team that hits four good ones. Shanks, skulls, and other shoddy shots are skipped. As a result, pars come easily. Birdie chances are omnipresent.

Lefty's team teed off first and stayed about a hole ahead of ours. Once they finished, they ordered our eats, after which they waited for us at the clubhouse entrance. As our foursome climbed the hill from the ninth green, the sight of our opponents' glum faces stirred hope that our score, an ugly conglomeration of execrable play and blown opportunities, might steal the day.

"What'd you guys shoot?" said Lefty.

"Two under," said Buster. "What about you?"

Lefty held out his hand with three fingers pointing down. "Three under for us." His smug face augured that our menu, along with pizza and beer, would include a surfeit of crow.

Buster held up three fingers, his index, middle, and ring. I had no idea what he was signaling. I glanced at Sam. A shrug indicated he was equally befuddled.

"I thought you said your team was two under," said Lefty.

"I did."

"So," said Lefty, "what's with the three fingers?"

Moving the digital display closer to Lefty's face, Buster said, "Lucinski, read between the lines."

Speedy, Sam, and I roared. We may have lost the war, but Buster had purloined a skosh of satisfaction.

"Screw you!" said Cooper. "And just to rub a little salt into your wounds, Babbitt, of all people, drove the decisive nail into your coffin. He rolled in an eight-footer on the last green."

Babbitt bowed deeply, as much as his midsection, even more rotund than high school days, allowed.

"Damn," whispered Sam. "We'll be hearing this forever."

Though the pain would only last for a week, the detail hardly merited mention. I thought back to the seventh hole where we had blown four runs at a six-foot birdie putt, including two lip-outs, one of which did a 360. Tempted as I was to announce how close we had come, discretion silenced me. History had proved that whining about a bad break would evoke no sympathy. Instead, such misfortune would arm our enemies with a trash-talking weapon, grounds to tag us as chokers.

We seated ourselves at our usual large round table where we poured beer from two pitchers. A minute later, our two pizzas arrived.

"The course has a long way to go before it'll be in shape," said Pete.

"The guy wins," I said, "and he has the gall to bitch about the conditions."

"What – you're a fan of bumpy greens and plugged balls?"

Rather than respond, I bit into my pizza, knowing that frustration with our loss had driven my sarcasm. The briefest introspection had me chastising myself. Unlike a good-natured trash talker, a sore loser was *persona non grata.*

"You guys make any bogeys?" said Lefty.

"Never came close," said Speedy. "Our pars all came with tap-ins. Your team record any bogeys?"

"Second hole," said Cooper. "That stinkin' par 3. No one hit the green and a bunch of mediocre chips left us with a slippery, seven-foot left-to-righter. No one even grazed the hole."

Apart from a plethora of predictably painful jabs from the winners, conversation yielded to pizza and beer. We were nearly done eating when Lefty stood up and said, "I hate to leave this lovely party, but I gotta pick up my cousin at the bus depot in Little Falls." He headed for the door.

"That son of a bitch," I whispered to Sam. "Same as high school. He disappears just before the check arrives."

"Pisses me off," said Sam. "Especially when he has been boasting lately about record commissions. The guy has no compunctions. Bad enough his gloating has the flavor of stale sardines. Does he need to top them with castor oil?"

A part of me wanted to voice my grievance to the entire group. Judgment, the risk of coming across as a backbiter, restrained the urge.

"Coop," said Buster, "what's the state of the school district budget?"

The question grabbed my attention.

Cooper shook his head. "It's in the hands of the voters. Come the third Tuesday in May, we'll see what they say."

"If they vote it down, you really gonna lay people off?" said Pete.

"Gotta…unless someone can suddenly show me a new math that turns a dollar bill into $1.05."

"High time that educators discover that money doesn't pour from a spicket, one you open wider every year," said Babbitt. "Like the rest of us, they need to live within their means."

"Look who's talking," said Speedy. "The single guy with a successful insurance business who inherited a big Victorian and boatloads of money."

Seeing the soft-spoken Speedy blast Babbitt boggled my brain. I wondered what type of reaction his barb would evoke. Around the table, side conversations ceased. Eyes transfixed on Speedy and Babbitt, with everyone waiting to see how the latter would respond.

"Whoa…look who has suddenly become feisty," said Babbitt. He punctuated the remark with a condescending sneer. "Just to set the record straight, I pay some of the highest school taxes in Grand Falls. And with no children, what do I get for it? Nada."

"Unless you were a hallucination, my recollection indicates that you enjoyed thirteen years of Grand Falls education," said Speedy.

"I did indeed, and my parents paid ample taxes throughout those years."

"So, as a citizen of Grand Falls, you feel no obligation to fund the education of our community's current children?" Speedy's tone bore uncharacteristic contempt.

"You miss the point," said Babbitt. "I pay my school taxes. What I object to are lazy freeloaders constantly hocking me for bigger handouts."

"And pray tell, who are these freeloaders?" said Speedy.

"Calm down," said Babbitt. "I wasn't pointing a finger at you. That hardware store of yours is on the tax rolls. But a few of your friends, newer people in town, from the islands and Africa, many of whom don't speak English – "

"You racist son of a bitch!" Buster leaped from his seat, displaying a clenched fist.

"What do you want from me?" Babbitt displayed puzzlement, though I suspected it was feigned. "I'm merely reciting the facts. These damn newcomers, parasites, are straining our educational, health, and other services. They're the root of our skyrocketing taxes."

Buster shook his head before looking around the table. "Any of you agree with George?"

If so, they kept their sentiments to themselves.

"Appears this assembly includes only one asshole." Buster turned to Speedy. "On behalf of The Guys, save one, I apologize for that asshole. He's too dumb to do so himself."

"Screw you, Brady!" Babbitt grabbed his beer and sulked.

A palpable hush gripped the table as Buster reseated himself. Over the years we had gotten together many times. Pizza, beer, and good-natured trash talk had provided a great menu. One gathering mirrored the next. Not so, on this occasion. The outburst, the rancor it engendered, was unique. A pall prevailed.

Finally, Pete said, "Maybe we should get the bill." He gestured to our server, getting her attention. "Check please."

"Already taken care of."

Her words drew stupefied looks.

"The tall fellow, the one-time pitcher, paid it before he left."

I eyed Sam. "Lefty…Lefty picked up the tab?"

Sam shrugged. "Hey, what can I say? Wonders never cease."

***

Clubs, associations, cliques, whatever their names, are often short-lived. Disinterest, disputes, or inability to find people willing to do the tasks required to keep them alive are but a few reasons for their demise. Nothing is forever. Even the greatest of empires inevitably collapse. The question is never "if," only "when."

"How'd the golf go?" said Mary, as I passed through the mud room into the kitchen.

"Wonderful. We snagged the runner-up prize."

"That good?" she said, familiar with my multiple methods for gold-plating a defeat.

"We played a scramble format, same teams as autumn's flag football. The bad guys won by a stroke. Until we kick them off the mountaintop, they'll be rubbing it in."

"If I recall, your team did the same after last fall's victory."

"That was – " I stopped myself. Claiming our victory was different because it involved the annual flag-football game was a distinction without a difference. The only meaningful dissimilarity was that the newest rendition found our team on the short end.

Mary poured us each a cup of tea, decaffeinated, and we seated ourselves at the kitchen table. "Nice get-together after golf?"

"Yes and no."

About to take a sip, she halted. "My question was rhetorical, aimed at what I assumed was the bright side of your evening. Why the ambivalence?"

"The issue of the school budget came up."

A worried look draped Mary's face. "Let me guess. Our dear superintendent predicts it'll be voted down."

"No, the situation remains as ambiguous as before."

"So, why the negativity?"

"The discussion turned nasty. Babbitt got into an ugly dust-up with Speedy and Buster."

"That hardly sounds like Speedy."

"Well, he was merely an innocent victim, the recipient of racist comments by Babbitt."

"That lousy – " Mary cut herself off. She held herself to the standard she imposed on our kids. No swear words in the house. "So, what happened?"

"Well, to make a long story short, Buster stepped in on Speedy's behalf. He literally jumped out of his chair as he called out Babbitt's disgusting comments for what they were. For a moment, I thought he might deck Babbitt. He probably would have if Babbitt had continued his rant."

"Too bad Babbitt shut his mouth."

"What?" I stared at Mary in disbelief.

"Well, then Buster would have flattened Babbitt. The flabby blowhard deserves it."

I looked Mary in the eye. "Is that my non-violent wife speaking?"

She shrugged. "Can you blame me?...Anyway, thoughts aren't the same as actions."

"Point well taken, and yeah, it would have been nice if Buster had laid Babbitt out." Whether my comment was mere words or wishful thinking was unclear.

"Your group...The Guys (Mary dragged out the name) has been tight for years. Not all of them are your dearest friends."

"Well, there are a couple I never would have picked, not that they wanted me. But given how the club was formed, it's understandable. Location, not personal affinity, determined membership. Being male in our homeroom was the sole qualification. It added up to a mismatched amalgam. And those who remain, the eight who live in and around Grand Falls, mirror that."

"When you put it that way, it's remarkable the group has survived as long as it has."

I sipped my tea. Mary's assessment was well-founded. Given the diversity of our gang, not just racial and ethnic, but interests and personalities, our longevity was a testament to all of us. For that reason alone, it behooved us to overlook disagreements. Survival demanded civility. Civility allowed for affectionately traded trash talk. Invective-laced rancor was another matter. The latter would pave a path to oblivion.

Chapter XVIII

Teachers, armed with meticulously fashioned lesson plans, teach. But some of the most valuable lessons are delivered by people who not only lack preparation but also have no intention of teaching.

"I'll get it," said Jerry, hurrying to the front door in response to the bell. He opened the portal. "Laura...what a great surprise! C'mon in." He turned and yelled. "It's Laura Longley."

Mary and I, about to put dinner on the dining room table, hurried to the front door. Lisa came rushing from her bedroom.

"When did you get in?" Mary hugged Laura.

"Just this morning. I'm only here for the day. I spent the afternoon with my dad, but I couldn't leave without stopping to see all of you."

Lisa, Jerry, and I took turns giving Laura a hug and welcoming her.

"You have to stay for dinner," said Mary. Before Laura could balk, Mary added, "We won't take *no* for an answer." She turned to Lisa. "Set another plate."

As Lisa hurried off, Laura glanced at her watch, muttering to herself, "In a couple hours, the roads downstate will still be there, not to mention less crowded." She heaved a sigh. "Okay, you've twisted my arm, not that it took much as good as the cooking is here."

Jerry added an extra chair, adjacent to Mary's, on Lisa's side. Once dinner was on the table and everyone seated, Mary said, "So, tell us, is your fashion business expanding as fast as ever? You know that you're the star of Grand Falls."

An abashed expression painted Laura's face. "I can't believe how rapidly it has grown. It's a big challenge, but very rewarding."

"I'll bet it's fabulous, living in the Big Apple," said Lisa.

"It's exciting, but I miss the tranquility of Grand Falls, especially when I walk the streets. Rather than amiable greetings from people I know, I get bumped and shoved by madly racing strangers."

"Would you rather be – "

"Jerry, give Laura a chance to taste her salad," I said.

"It's okay. It's great to be here, having dinner with all of you. I loved the many times I ate here, both Mary's wonderful meals and your company. It meant so much to my dad and me. I don't know how we would have managed after my grandmother passed were it not for all of you. My dad would have had to cut his hours. No way was he about to turn me into a latch-key kid."

"It was a two-way street," said Mary. "You were a great mentor to Lisa and Jerry. Both are on the high honor roll."

"I'd expect nothing less." Laura started to take a forkful of salad but paused. "I wouldn't be where I am today if it weren't for all of you...I'm serious. Before I began coming here after school, I was treading water." Laura focused on Mary. "You were a great role model." She turned my way. "In school you motivated me and showed me my potential. The chance to mentor Lisa and Jerry increased my confidence. It was my first step in learning management skills."

"Do you go to many Broadway shows?" said Jerry.

"Now and then."

"What are – "

"Jerry, slow down," said Mary. "Allow Laura time to chew a bite."

"Tell you what," said Laura. "You kids fill me in on what you've been doing both in and out of school. I'll listen and eat."

Lisa and Jerry took center stage sharing loads of mundane updates. Mary brought out the main course, filet of sole, mashed potatoes, and green beans.

With entrees nearly finished, Laura said, "My dad told me that issues with this year's school budget are rampant. He said they seem more serious than usual. You think the budget might fail?"

I shrugged. "It'll depend on the voters, not that many turn out for school district budgets. If history is any kind of indicator, it should all work out."

"It always does," said Laura.

Not wanting the kids to worry, I welcomed her unconcerned response. I said, "So, tell us, what are your favorite Big Apple venues...Carnegie Hall, the Museum of Natural History, or maybe Madison Square Garden?"

"They're all nice." Laura chuckled briefly. "But busy as I am, I visit them about as often as a tourist. And for that matter, when I have free time, I prefer a relaxing picnic in Central Park. Don't get me wrong. I love a Broadway musical, as well as the museums, but in some respects, I'm still a small-town girl at heart."

I read between the lines of Laura's comments. Success on a bigger stage had failed to go to her head. She remained well-grounded. The observation warmed me. I glanced at Lisa and Jerry. Both were focused on Laura. I was an experienced teacher, as well as my kids' parent, but the paradigm that Laura exhibited was more effective than any lesson I could provide.

***

Machines, electronic gadgets, and sundry other devices seemingly display minds of their own. But nothing has a greater mind of its own than the mind. In times of stress, sleep, always important, becomes critical. Perversely, at such times, nightmares, linked to stress, deprive one of needed sleep.

"You okay?"

"Huh?"

"Are you okay?"

"Uh...yeah," I said, trying to gain my bearings.

"The past five minutes you've been thrashing about," said Mary.

"Oh, I was having a bad dream."

"Seems you've been having a lot lately."

I sighed, braced my pillow against the oaken headboard, and sat up part way. "These past few weeks, sleeping has been tough. The budget and my job, not to mention the lawsuit, gnaw. How will we manage if I'm axed?"

"We'll be okay."

The positive words might have eased my mind had the reality of our finances not demurred. "No, think about it. What'll we do if I lose my job?"

"You'll find another."

Amidst the darkness, I leaned Mary's way, giving her a look. "It's not that simple. Jobs for history teachers are few, probably non-existent within thirty or forty miles of Grand Falls. Let's assume I could find a position elsewhere in the state. Moving would be a nightmare. How could we drag the kids away from their friends…yank them from the only school district they've ever known? And what about housing? We love our home. After real estate commissions and moving expenses, can you imagine what we could afford in a more expensive market, a place like Long Island or Westchester? We'd have to settle for a closet, a tiny one at that." Though my assessment may have been hyperbolic, my underlying point was indisputable. "And what if that guy from the car accident wins a six-figure judgment? What'll we do then? File bankruptcy?"

"C'mon," said Mary. "What do you always tell the kids? Cross the bridge when you come to it."

"I'm at the bridge."

Mary, barely visible in the dusky room, looked at me askance. "You know that's not accurate. The budget hasn't been voted down. You haven't lost your job."

Her point, buttressed by my own words, was hard to debate. I said, "But going along blithely with our heads down while a guillotine looms above makes no sense."

"Well, if that's how you feel, you could check for opportunities in nearby districts, Dolgeville, Little Falls, Utica, etcetera."

The logical response bore scant appeal. I heaved another sigh. "We need to get some sleep."

Mary kissed me.

I turned over, slowly inhaling and exhaling a dozen times, hoping to nod off. My perturbed brain refused, regurgitating the familiar details of my uncomplicated past. Never in my life had I faced financial difficulties. As a youngster, though my family was never rich, neither were we poor. I never worried about my next meal. I played with Speedy and Sam. Life was secure. College was a given. My parents saved enough to send me to a state school. Some financial aid, coupled with part-time and summer jobs, allowed me to graduate debt-free. Thanks to Mary's parents, we started our marriage with a few dollars in the bank. A job offer from the Grand Falls School District my senior year in college guaranteed a steady income. With Mary working the first years of our marriage, we paid cash for our bungalow. By the time Lisa began elementary school, we were well down a prosperous road that would ferry us into our nineties, provided fortune let us live that long. Our familiar plan, one that in the past had been a source of peace and comfort, raced through my brain. After Jerry graduated from high school, Mary would return to work. Once the kids completed college, we would build savings which, by age 62, would supplement two excellent pensions. Add social security to the equation, and carefree golden years, replete with relaxation and travel, would follow. The blueprint was perfect; loss of my position would shred it.

Current circumstances compelled me to examine our great plan under a new microscope. Superb as it may have been, reflection unearthed glaring imperfections. Mapping our entire life had made wonderful sense, at least in theory, but only so long as a washed-out highway, fallen-rock zone, storm, or other road closure did not detour us onto an uncharted, wilderness path. Therein lay the rub. Most times, life's exigencies dictate forks. Flexibility is imperative. Dependence on a strictly plotted plan impairs one's ability to deviate. If forced to follow a mazelike course, replete with dead ends and pitfalls, could I negotiate my way out of the forest? Could I weather the challenges?

Having been a teacher my entire adult life, what saleable skills did I possess? None. A kid fresh out of college with a liberal arts degree would beat me out. Twenty-two years old and filled with energy bested mid-forties and unemployed. An image of myself flipping burgers at a fast-food joint popped into my head. The notion was nauseating. It was also terrifying. That I might be unable to provide for my wife and family tortured me. Forces beyond my control threatened to turn our secure and happy life into an arrant mess. A cold sweat engulfed me. Hopes for a tranquil night evaporated. Mary's voice, reiterating my own words to cross the bridge when I reached it, forestalled panic. But if I received a pink slip, any semblance of calm would vanish.

***

Too often success exemplifies the inequity of life. The person with integrity admits his/her errors and suffers the consequences, while the reprobate dodges responsibility even as he/she falsely takes credit for others' accomplishments. But now and then, justice prevails. That said, right and virtue are never guaranteed.

Owing to a rainout, the fourth round of our 1969 golf season was delayed until the second week of May. The first three matches had delivered one victory for each team, along with a tie. With the course in better shape, though far from mid-season condition, we had abandoned the scramble format following the first match. We had returned to our traditional formula, totaling individual scores to arrive at a team score. In the fourth contest, our team, Buster, Speedy, Sam, and I compiled a total of 169. Led by my 38, we knocked off the bad guys by four shots. My score, only one stroke off my record low, won me plaudits. I should have been in a great mood, but as I sat in Nick Stoner's clubhouse following the round, doldrums dominated. Lurking in the back of my mind was the unrelenting threat of the hammers that hung over my head. A judgment in the car accident or a pink slip at school could flip my world upside down. Worse yet, a double whammy could leave me bankrupt with no job.

Apart from the get-togethers with The Guys, I rarely crossed paths with Superintendent Ronald Cooper, the person most likely to have inside information regarding the school budget. Concerned as I was about the issue, the opportunity to pick his brain was tempting. Nevertheless, I was reluctant to raise the matter in front of the entire group. With curiosity and disinclination clashing, I got up from my seat and circled around to the opposite side where Cooper sat. My goal was a semi-private tête-à-tête.

"You kicked our asses, today, you sandbagger," said Cooper.

"I got lucky. I dropped a couple of snakes, one of which I pushed, but fortunately misread. It found the hole when it broke more than I expected."

"So, you come here to spit masticated mushrooms onto my pizza?"

Ignoring the barb, I leaned in and with voice lowered, said, "I was wondering if there's any new scuttlebutt regarding the district's budget."

"Hell, I've seen this crap before. Dissidents scream and yell. They stir up a bunch of whiners. But when push comes to shove, the people want their schools. They want all the courses and activities, especially football. Sure, there's lots of noise, but birdies to bogeys, when the ballots are tallied, the budget will pass."

The statement from the man in the know was reassuring. Under the proposed budget, two teachers, art and Latin, plus a pair of extracurricular activities, were scheduled to be axed. My greater concern was that the budget would be voted down and more positions, namely mine, would be eliminated. I said, "I hope you're right, though it's sad for the folks and activities that'll get chopped."

"Jesus, you're like all the rest. Gotta carp, even when you get your cake. Not enough to eat your own piece. You wanna dictate where the rest goes." He shook his head. "Day after day, all I hear are complaints. Whiners, whiners, and more whiners. You'd think when I offer positive info, I'd get gratitude, not grumbles."

Cooper's reaction nonplused me. "I…uh…don't mean to appear ungrateful. It's…uh…just that I feel badly for the kids and teachers who'll bear the consequences of the cuts."

Cooper looked me in the eye. "When you come here to play golf, enjoy a little pizza and beer, do I ask you to do lesson plans and grade papers?"

"Uh...no."

"You'd be pissed if I did. Right?"

"Yes," I said, uncertain where he was headed. One fact, however, had become clear. Ours had ceased to be a conversation between two cronies at the nineteenth hole of a golf course. Rank had been pulled. The discussion had morphed into a harangue by the corporate CEO, the Superintendent of Schools, reminding an underling on which side of the desk each sat. And lest there be any confusion, the surrogate site was his office, not my classroom.

"Well, it's like this," said Cooper, an ample consumption of beer fueling his fulmination. "Having to bear the biggest headaches of the district, I hardly appreciate argumentative parents, students...or *staff* interrupting my golf and meal. So, do me a favor. Take your bleeding heart back to the far side of the table and keep your carping to yourself...And by the way, if you have complaints about the proposed budget, take them up with the board members. They're the ones responsible for the spending plan."

You bastard! Wasn't so long ago you boasted that you had a majority of the board in the palm of your hand, that they did your bidding. You take credit for the wins, but no responsibility for the losses. My gut begged to shove the loudmouth's past braggadocio down his throat. But Cooper held the high hand. He could call my bluff, and if need be, draw a couple of aces from the bottom of the deck. I returned to my seat. I stole a peek at the dolt. He was guzzling another beer. As a so-called friend, even if he did nothing to help my cause, at least he could lend a patient ear. Countless times I had done that for students long after the bell for dismissal had rung. Never did I think of telling them to get lost because the official school day had ended. When asked by students to sponsor the chess club, I did so willingly. My consent was not preconditioned on a compensatory stipend. For several minutes I stewed, resenting the indignity of kowtowing to the blowhard. I eyed the lone, uneaten scrap of pizza crust that remained on my plate. It mirrored my ego. A thought about the budget intermingled with resentment. Cooper, the man in the know, despite his venom, had furnished information that suggested risks to my job were less than I had previously thought. The latter, more salient than transient wounds to my pride, mitigated umbrage. Another issue, one that needed to be addressed, popped into my head. I turned to Sam. "Lisa's scars are improving. The debridement treatments are working. You did a great job. Time you give me a bill."

Sam casually waved me off.

"What does that mean?"

"That if I'm not worried about it, you needn't be."

"It's fine that you're not concerned, but I am. You're entitled to payment."

"Consider it prepaid. More than three decades of friendship. And don't give me an argument because I'm one extremely stubborn doctor."

"You damn well are," I said. "And you're also a terrific guy." Sam's altruism lifted me. I imbibed my beer. I reminded myself to cross bridges when I reached them. I felt a bit better than earlier. Financial Armageddon might not be on the horizon. I eyed my scorecard. A 38 was damn good.

Pizza, beer, and an hour of boasts, beefs, and trash talk done, we headed for the parking lot. As I opened my Nova's door, Pete hurried my way.

"Nice wheels. Love the shade of blue." He ran his hand over the polished surface. "You got a moment?"

"Sure. What's up?"

"I'm glad you guys won today."

I furrowed my brow and said, "Okay, give me the punch line."

"No, I'm serious."

"Sure." I rolled my eyes. "Since when is anyone in our group pleased that bragging rights belong to the enemy?"

"Since someone on his team cheated...It happened on the eighth hole. Coop duck hooked his drive into the trees on the left. I found it for him, in weeds nearly a foot deep. Amazing I even spotted it. The lie was horrific. Only a fool would try to chop it out onto the short grass, let alone go for the green.

Anyway, I went to my ball – it was on the other side of the fairway – and hit my second shot. Next thing I knew, Coop delivers a stunner onto the putting surface. He two putts for a *so-called* par. Arnold Palmer couldn't have blasted that ball onto the green, not from that lie." Pete shrugged. "I thought about calling him on it, but afraid it would provoke a day-ruining brouhaha, I kept my mouth shut, at least for the time being."

"Time being?"

"Yeah. I waited until the teams matched totals and we knew who won. If our team prevailed, I planned to raise the issue. Fortunately, we lost, and a hellish confrontation was avoided."

"You think he's done it before?" Even as I posed the question, I knew the answer. Our high school match against Dolgeville years earlier proved the point.

"Sadly...yes. Last season he hit a ball on three that bounced hard off a baked-out downslope into the woods on the right. I was stunned when he found it along the edge of the trouble. It was possible his ball caromed off a tree, but unlikely given the spindly hardwoods in the area. I suspected he dropped another ball, but I gave him the benefit of the doubt. Today, however, having seen his horrendous lie, I had no doubts." Pete looked me in the eye. "Allowing Coop to continue cheating is intolerable. But how to handle it is tricky. I hoped you might provide some input."

I shrugged. "Well, knowing our superintendent, I'm not surprised."

"Really?" Pete's eyes were cantaloupes.

I related the details of our high school golf match years earlier.

"If I read between the lines, you're suggesting I should confront him."

"Well..." After debating with myself, I shook my head. "What the hell. Let it go for now. But keep an eye on him. If he cheats again, blast him. I'll back you up with his history."

***

Uncertainty obtains until the votes have been counted. But once the ballots have been tallied, the winners celebrate, and the losers...are losers.

In the days following my great round on the links, I did a decent job of reining in my apprehension. I constantly reminded myself of the optimism that Cooper had voiced about the budget. Nevertheless, my consternation ebbed and flowed. But on the third Tuesday in May, I was on pins and needles the entire day. The voters of Grand Falls were having their say whether the budget, as proposed by the school board, would be approved or rejected. On the way home from school, I stopped at the firehouse and cast my ballot. Mary had done so earlier that afternoon. The polls closed at seven.

Following dinner, I watched television, not that anything held my interest. I was in limbo, waiting for the eleven o'clock news when the results of school districts' budget votes would be announced. Needing to get up for school shortly after six in the morning, normally I went to bed in advance of the late evening news. But sleeping before I knew the outcome of the vote was impossible. Mary and I readied ourselves for the night. Propped by our pillows, lying side by side, we nervously awaited the news broadcast. In Grand Falls our local stations were all based in Utica. I opted for CBS.

Eleven o'clock finally arrived. The anchor opened with promos for the top stories: the day's events in Vietnam; a warehouse fire in Little Falls; and the area's budget votes. Regarding the last, the anchor indicated that most were approved, but two were voted down. Another time the teaser might have driven me to press the remote control and change the channel. The risk that flipping stations might cause me to miss the outcome of the vote in Grand Falls glued me to CBS. Finally, after enduring a lengthy wait, at 11:08 the anchor detailed the results of the area's budget votes. Grand Falls was one of the two communities that had turned thumbs down to its proposed budget. A pink slip was likely to find its way into my mailbox.

Mary and I gazed at one another. I heaved a sigh. Disappointment prevented me from voicing my feelings.

"It may not be as bad as it seems," said Mary. "The board can resubmit the budget, as is or revised, for a second vote next month. Perhaps the voters will change their minds."

Her words, intended to relieve my troubled mind, fell on deaf ears. Several weeks of aging would not magically rehabilitate a fetid, over-ripe cantaloupe into a delicious melon. The voters had spoken. Given a second chance, one could expect they would reiterate their distaste for the unpalatable budget. It was possible the school board would replace the rotten melon with a new one, propose an amended budget with reduced spending. Unfortunately, the additional budgets cuts would likely be distasteful for me. Odds indicated the changes would slash my position. If so, approval of the new budget, itself iffy, rather than solving my problem, would serve me a portion of acrid melon.

Mary cuddled close and kissed me. "We'll manage."

"I hope you're right." My ambiguous response masked pessimism. I pressed the remote control, shutting off the television. I had heard more than enough news.

We slid our pillows down from the headboard. "I love you," I said.

"Love you too."

I closed my eyes, exhorting myself to quell my propensity to catastrophize. Even as I did, one thing was certain. An unsavory menu of fitful sleep would dominate my night.

***

Two Union soldiers fight side by side at Gettysburg. A bullet hurtles in their direction. One soldier is struck and killed. The other walks away unscathed. Such is the serendipity of war. Golf, driving a car, and the game of poker bear little link to the Civil War...On second thought, perhaps the trio of activities have more in common with the great conflict than a first blush indicates.

Sleep deprived, my mind distracted, the morning after the budget had failed, I took out my first-period lesson plan as the students filed into the room. The bell beginning class sounded. A hand went up in the second row.

"Yes, Ellen?"

"Is it true, what they're saying, that your position will be cut because people voted down the budget?"

Rumblings, others voicing the same question, emerged. Comments that it was unfair echoed throughout the room.

The question and reactions were unexpected. But with years of experience in the classroom, addressing that which was unanticipated had long since ceased to be difficult. Now and again, students raised issues involving events throughout the school. I rolled with the punches. Occasionally a student carped about another teacher's alleged unfairness. I refused to get involved with such matters. They were beyond the scope of my classroom and the study of history. Whatever quirky items presented themselves, I handled them with relative ease. But this was different. I was the subject of the question. And unlike many others, I had strong opinions, which were undeniably influenced by personal interests.

"It's...it's..." I stopped myself. Voicing my feelings, the injustice I perceived, was contrary to what I had taught my students. I had preached that life is often unfair. When faced with inequity, one can whine and quit, or one can gird for the challenge and forge ahead. I had provided numerous examples. Two golf balls strike the same tree. One bounces out of bounds, while the other fortuitously caroms onto the green, inches from the hole. A plastered jerk, with three prior DWIs, or if you prefer, DUIs, going one hundred miles per hour, kills an elderly lady sitting on a sidewalk bench. Compounding the inequity, the drunken jerk walks away without a scratch. A poker player dealt a full house loses a hand to a bluffer who draws four cards to a straight flush. The player with the full house raises and calls a responsive raise, losing extra money because an extraordinary hand turns into a loser. Meanwhile, the bluffer, defying massive odds, walks off with a big jackpot. Along the way, each of us will be dealt bad hands. How many and how bad will vary. What matters is how we deal with those hands. Fairness is never a guarantee. I said, "I...I appreciate your thoughts and support. But those are matters to be determined by the school board and ultimately, the voters. Our task is to study history, specifically the Civil War...So, let us redirect our attention to Gettysburg's hallowed Pennsylvania battlefield.

***

He can dish it out, but he can't take it. Everyone has met someone who fits that description. For some that meeting occurs when gazing into the mirror. But often they fail to make the connection, which only proves...the imperfection of mirrors.

Over the weekend following the budget vote, the lack of viable alternatives to keeping my current job had grown increasingly apparent. I had checked and rechecked. Positions for history teachers within fifty miles of Grand Falls were non-existent. I had sent out several résumés, not that any of the targeted opportunities appealed to me. Their distance from Grand Falls ranged from one to two hundred miles. If I landed one of those positions, I might need to spend loads of time separated from my family. Requiring Jerry, who would be a junior in the fall, to change schools seemed unfair. Rather than move the family, I would likely commute home on weekends.

The first Monday after the budget vote found me at Nick Stoner's. Sunday evening, I had considered skipping the weekly golf match. With tough times on the horizon, saving money had become a priority. But Mary insisted that I play. Refusing to engage in enjoyable activities, permitting my job and the issues surrounding it to be all-consuming, would eat me up.

With back-and-forth outcomes on the links producing constant demands for rematches, all eight of us were happy to maintain the same teams. Our foursome teed off second. My teammates, Sam, Speedy, and Buster, eschewed the subject of the budget and my job. Their transparent efforts to shift my thoughts with mundane conversation failed to bridle my predisposed mind. My concerns constantly stirred. As I crouched to line up a three-footer on the last green, a slippery, downhill left-to-righter, I lacked focus. Failing to match the speed and break, I babied the putt, a pathetic effort, which left my ball dying short right. I tapped in the remaining six-incher. What total score the double bogey gave me I couldn't say, except that it was lousy. I headed into the clubhouse where I seated myself with The Guys. Babbitt totaled the cards. Our team lost by seven shots. My score, an abysmal fifty, my worst in two years, positioned me last among the group. I contributed nothing. On second thought, I keyed the victory...of our opponents.

Ordinarily, the high scorer of the losing team absorbed much of the day's trash talk. No such gibes came my way. Pete gave me a sympathetic pat on the back before seating himself.

"Next week will be better," said Sam.

From across the way, Babbitt said, "Ward, what happened to you today?"

"His play was better than his score," said Speedy. "Bad bounces and lip-outs added strokes. Let him be."

The usual vain chitchat ensued. For the most part, I focused on my pizza and beer, barely listening, often drifting into my own gloomy world. Shortly before we headed home, Lefty directed himself to Cooper. "Where do you think the school district's budget goes from here?"

The inquiry drew my attention.

"No guarantees, but I expect more cuts will ensue. Once the voters say *no*, the script is written. Rewrites or ad-libs are long shots. Even with a revote on a revised budget, and we'll have one, the story's outcome is predictable." Cooper gestured at Babbitt. "You might want to ask our insurance man. He's the kingpin of the contingent that stirred up folks to vote the budget down."

"What have you got against schools?" said Buster.

"Nothing," said Babbitt. "And don't try to paint me as the bad guy. The people of Grand Falls, the voters, spoke. They've had enough. They're tired of picking up the tab for freeloaders, lots of them immigrants and welfare recipients...progressives who spend like drunken sailors, bozos with no respect for law and order."

Babbitt's dog whistle, the kind Nixon had invoked in his appeal to his so-called Silent Majority, resounded. Quintessential Babbitt, it was no surprise. What was, however, was Sam's reaction.

"Babbitt, you're a bigoted bastard...a buffoonish one at that!"

The normally garrulous insurance man's jaw dropped. He sat silent.

"Cat get your tongue?" said Buster.

"Nah," said Pete, "it was a crow, the big fat one he just ate."

Teeth gritted, Babbitt stood up. He flashed the bird, something other than a crow, before storming out of the clubhouse.

"You think it might be something we said?" A sly smile communicated that Buster had no remorse.

"The guy asked for it," said Sam. "He dumps hot peppers and cow dung on dried liver...serves it up on a filthy plate, expecting us to eat it."

I wondered if anyone would go after Babbitt and salve his wounded feelings. If so, it demanded a quick move. Another minute and his car would likely be on its way. I looked around the table. No one, not even Babbitt's teammates, displayed an inclination to follow him. The truth be known, I felt no sympathy, not for a snake who was instrumental in the push to deprive me of my livelihood.

***

Some news is good. Other news is bad. Often news is mixed. Unfortunately, that can be horrific.

Having arrived home from school fifteen minutes earlier, I was relaxing in my easy chair, reading the newspaper, when the telephone rang. I reached for the receiver. "Hello."

"Hi Jim. It's Joe Walker."

"What's up?"

"I've got some news about the lawsuit."

"Good, I hope." I braced myself for the message.

"Not really good or bad. Just an update. Wilson, the insurance-company attorney defending you, called me today. She said the plaintiff has filed a Note of Issue. That's an indication that pretrial proceedings are complete. It puts the case on the trial calendar for the fall term. She said that settlement is unlikely. Negotiations show the plaintiff demanding six figures. The insurance company is at two grand. Talk about far apart. Tomorrow I'm sending a letter to Wilson demanding that they offer the plaintiff the policy, $10,000. They owe you a duty, as their insured, not only to pay damages up to the limits of the policy, but also to defend you and employ reasonable efforts to protect you from excess liability. If there's a big verdict, way above the policy limits, we could argue that their failure to negotiate in good faith exposed you to excess liability. We could demand that they indemnify you."

"Sounds good," I said.

"It is in theory. Just one problem: The plaintiff has shown no willingness to settle for anything even close to $10,000."

"If I read between the lines, you expect a verdict far in excess of ten grand."

"No, I'm not saying that…On the other hand, it would be foolhardy to rule it out."

Once again, I read between the lines. A big verdict, one that would destroy me financially, was a distinct possibility. Walker and I concluded our call. I put the newspaper aside. I was in no mood to read it. With my job in jeopardy and a lawsuit hanging over my head, my odds of dodging financial ruin had just grown longer.

Chapter XIX

Many with 20-20 vision are blind. They view themselves through rose-colored glasses. Delusions of grandeur vanquish reality. But often the overblown self-image is merely a façade, camouflaging feelings of inadequacy and failure.

I was about to sit down and watch *The Dean Martin Show* when the telephone rang. I lowered the television's volume and answered the call. "Hello."

"Hi Jim. It's Lefty. Did I get you at a bad time?"

"Not really. What's up?"

"With the...uh...issues surrounding the school budget, I...uh...thought I might be able to help. It's nothing much, so...uh...don't expect a lot. And...uh...before I go any further, if I'm out of line, tell me to shut up."

As one who was normally private, I was reluctant to involve anyone beyond my family and closest friends. But the adage, *beggars can't be choosers*, prodded me to think twice. Prudence counseled I listen. If I found the presentation invasive, I could react accordingly.

"This afternoon, I...uh...spoke with Charlie Tockler, my boss and owner of Tockler Motors. I told him how...uh...our school district's budget had been shot down by the voters and that your position is apt to be excessed. Suspecting it might be hard for you to make your car payments, I...uh...asked if there was anything we could do to help. I probably shoulda talked to you first, but I wanted to be able to say that it was strictly me, not you, asking. That plus I...uh...didn't want my dubious idea to give you false hopes. Anyway, I...I went ahead. Feel free to scream at me for not minding my own beeswax. I'll understand."

Realizing Lefty meant well, it was hard to criticize him. "I appreciate your effort."

"Thanks…Anyway, it turns out that Tockler's nephew, his sister's son, was a student of yours three or four years ago. His name is Jack Traynor."

"Oh, Jack. He was a great kid, an excellent student."

"So, I've heard. And according to Tockler, you were Jack's favorite teacher. You gave him a wonderful recommendation that helped him get into Hamilton. To make a long story short, when I told Tockler about your job, he was sympathetic. He's deferring your car payments for eighteen months, and no interest will accrue during that time. I know it doesn't save your job, but hopefully it'll reduce the pressure a little."

"Kind of you and your boss. One less worry is welcome."

"Least I can do for one of The Guys…especially given my history."

"What's that last phrase about?"

"C'mon, we both know that I've been a jerk over the years."

The uncharacteristic admission floored me. Its merit stifled exonerating words.

"Back during our school days when big-league scouts came to watch me, I was a big man on campus, full of myself. Around Grand Falls, folks gave me boatloads of attention. For years after my pitching career bombed, I lived in the past. I played the big shot, refusing to acknowledge I was a has-been high school hotshot, long on vanity, but short on a future. And because I was constantly dodging alimony and support payments, I rarely saw my son. A while back, I went to Poughkeepsie and watched him in a tennis match. He's a junior, first man on his high school team. But unlike me, he's an *A* student. His coach expects him to land a college scholarship. Anyway, after seeing him, I looked in the mirror. A revolting reflection, a lousy father, stared back. Given my history, my son had a mountain of reasons to tell me to get lost. But good person that he is – my ex did a great job raising him – he welcomed me. He treated me as if I had been a good father…gave me undeserved respect. I…I need to earn that respect." Lefty heaved a sigh. "I gotta do better. I...I wanna be a better person...I'm trying."

"Good for you. I believe you'll do it." My words, reflexive, echoed in my ears. A post-articulation assessment indicated they were heartfelt. "I appreciate your going to bat for me with Tockler."

"Least I could do. And thanks."

"For what?" I said.

"Lending a patient ear and tolerating decades of bluster."

"You're too hard on yourself."

"I doubt it...Regardless, it's necessary, lest nasty habits subdue better intentions."

***

When times turn tough and the chips hit the table, one's friends display their colors. Their support can ease burdens. Unfortunately, eliminating burdens is another matter.

Accompanied by Mary, I arrived for the public meeting being held a week in advance of the voters' second bite at the budget. Rather than submitting an amended budget with additional cuts, the school board was sticking with its original rendition. On the bright side, that meant the voters would be casting ballots on a spending plan that preserved my job. Unfortunately, the smart money said the voters, having already rejected the plan, would reiterate their opposition.

A crowd that I estimated at well over one hundred occupied the school auditorium. Mary and I seated ourselves in the back right corner. After brief opening remarks, a microphone centered in front of the stage opened to the public. A line of those waiting to speak had already formed. One after another they voiced support or opposition, but mainly with broad platitudes that likely swayed few in the sharply divided community.

About ten, a majority of whom endorsed a second thumbs down on the budget, had commented when Buster Brady stepped to the microphone. While he had waited in line, I had tried to predict what stance he would take. His personal history hinted he might advocate belt-tightening measures. Back in high school, the nifty quarterback had starred on the football field. In the classroom, his proficiency plunged. Whether ineptitude or indolence occasioned his academic performance was debatable. Regardless, Buster understood that his presence on the gridiron was conditioned upon academics, what he deemed a bureaucratically imposed inconvenience. Given that history, I doubted that he valued education, at least when we had graduated twenty-four years earlier. Prognosticating how his adult years as a successful contractor may have modified that view was a crapshoot.

Buster cleared his throat. "My fellow citizens of Grand Falls, like you, I dislike paying ever-increasing property taxes. For a contractor like me, they're a bane. They diminish the appeal of real estate, rendering it less salable. That hurts my business."

Buster had me squirming in my seat. Understandably, he needed to protect his business interests. That he would add a nail to my coffin, galling. I would have made the point to Mary, but I wanted to hear his every word.

"Back in my high school days, I was a woeful student. School, however, treated me well. As quarterback of the football team, I received more than my share of attention. I developed confidence. Left to my own devices, I might have chosen life's shortcuts, even ended up in prison. Fortunately, my coach and a couple of teachers kept me close enough to the straight and narrow that I dodged a ruinous path. They instilled a sufficient work ethic and sense of responsibility that I survived until judgment tamed immaturity...compunction contained conceit. Without that guidance, the contracting business I have today would never have materialized.

"Many around our community advocate that we nix the proposed budget a second time, a move that would force a contingency budget and inevitably, additional cuts. Don't let that happen. It would be a grave mistake. In recent years we have seen the best and brightest from our younger generation flee to greener pastures. Without quality schools our ability to attract new talent will evaporate. Failing to fund our schools today is shortsighted. In the long run, we will pay a price. Our economy will suffer. Our tax base will shrink. Our culture will degrade. The downward spiral of Grand Falls will continue. Please vote to approve the budget." Buster returned to his seat.

I whispered to Mary, "That was a pleasant surprise."

"Indeed. And coming from a respected entrepreneur and more important, a one-time local football hero, it could change a few minds."

The next two at the microphone, one pro and one con, added little with their terse, substance-free remarks. I focused on the man behind them, Larry "George" Babbitt.

A paper in hand, Babbitt began to read. "Ladies and gentlemen, the time has come that we, the citizens of Grand Falls, seize control of our community's finances. For years, liberal elites, featherbrained spendthrifts, have acted as if the many trees that decorate the forests surrounding our community bear leaves of gold, an infinite source of funds. They have saddled us with school budgets outstripping the pace of inflation. They have padded the costs of education with needless frills. Each time they do, your real estate taxes rise. For those of you who rent, they claim you reap the benefits of those increased taxes free of cost. That claim is an unmitigated lie. Free lunch is a myth. Landlords pass those taxes on to you, their tenants. They jack up your rent.

"As I walk the streets of Grand Falls, I have observed signs in several businesses urging you to support the budget. Most who own these businesses are financially comfortable. Unlike the vast majority who are struggling to make ends meet, these entrepreneurs can absorb the tax increases. Some of them are on our school board. They advocate a fiscally irresponsible budget. If we, the people, are to contain costs, enjoy financial health, we must send the cavalier nabobs a message. Boycott businesses with pro-budget signs. Let these arrogant school board members, who dig their dirty hands into your pockets year after year, know where you stand. Next Tuesday, reiterate your indignation. Vote the budget down again."

As Babbitt strutted to his seat in the front row, applause broke out. With a rap of his gavel, the board president silenced the stir. A woman who worked at the local convenience store stepped to the microphone. "Enough of this crazy spending!

Vote *no* on the damn budget!" Her comment, though voiced without reason, echoed Babbitt's grievance.

Pete Longley followed the woman to the microphone. "Back when I was in high school, I became a single father, destined to be a high school dropout, a burden on our community. Thanks to the administration and teachers of Grand Falls High, I was able to earn my diploma. I could provide for my daughter and guide her to a quality education. Today she is a successful fashion entrepreneur in New York City, and I have a sealcoating and paving business and enjoy a good life here in Grand Falls. All this good fortune would have been impossible but for the kindness and generosity of the family of one of our teachers, name to remain unmentioned."

Mary clasped my hand. A lump filled my throat.

"Roughly a decade ago, my mother died. The unthinkable possibility of turning my daughter into a latch-key kid confronted me. The aforementioned teacher and his family provided my daughter with a second home. At their own expense, they fed her when I worked overtime. This same teacher gave many students extra help after school. Without compensation he sponsored after-school clubs. Though far from wealthy, from his own pocket he purchased supplies for his classroom and students. He is emblematic of the wonderful teachers we have working in our schools. These teachers are one of our town's greatest assets. You, my fellow citizens, possess the power to preserve that asset. I beg you, please, in the name of all that's good in our community…vote to approve the budget. Vote to safeguard quality education in Grand Falls. Vote to save the jobs of our teachers."

As Pete returned to his seat, a buzz pervaded the room, a thoughtful one. His heartfelt words had been heard. That begged the question: Were the minds of the listeners too intractable to be swayed?

Behind the microphone the line evanesced. The board president said, "If no one else wishes to speak, we will close the – "

Speedy edged forward toward the microphone.

"Mr. Jackson, would you like to be heard?"

"Uh…yes." His tremulous reply was barely audible.

Speedy's diffidence was no surprise. His presence, however, at the microphone was. Back during our school days, he dreaded oral presentations. Their discomfort dwarfed that of an arduous test. When forced to do an oral report, he all but read it, even after memorizing the material. The years had not altered his attitude. Public speaking was Speedy's definition of the word *anathema*.

"I...uh...rarely...uh...never speak at public meetings, so...uh...I...hope you'll...uh...bear with me."

"Please speak louder...directly into the microphone," said the board president.

"Uh...okay. I'll try." A shake in Speedy's hand was visible as he adjusted the tilt of the microphone. "Uh...Growing up in Grand Falls, I...uh...was always different, the...uh...only African American in my grade. Several fellow students and...uh...some of my teachers made sure I was included. Playing on the football team, not that I...uh...was a standout, I found acceptance. Were it not for our local schools, I...I might have receded into a shell. Today, as owner of the hardware store, I operate one of the businesses that Mr. Babbitt urged you to boycott. Do that to me if you must, but please, I beg you, approve the school budget. Please, support our schools.

"The cuts that will ensue without such approval are more than mere numbers. They are teachers, custodians, and administrative personnel...individuals with families and financial obligations just like you. Most work far more hours than the school day. They stay after the final bell helping students. Evenings, they prepare lessons and grade papers at home.

"Coming to this microphone terrified me. Afraid of humiliation, I...I nearly skipped the opportunity. I longed to leave it to citizens with silver tongues. But to do so would shun obligations owed to those who helped me when I was a student. More specifically, I...I owe it to one of the teachers who could face layoff. Back when I was in seventh grade, my family moved to Grands Falls. With only one other African American family in the community and no other African Americans in my grade, discomfort was my constant companion. As a black boy in a white community in the waning days of the Depression, life was a challenge. Segregation remained the law in the South. Here in the North, in many respects, *de facto* segregation prevailed. Far from being inclusive, most whites ignored blacks like me. But that same teacher who could now lose his job broke the barriers that otherwise made me an outsider. From day one after I arrived in Grand Falls, he welcomed me. Every day he stopped at my house and walked with me to school. Back in junior high school, long before I played on the football team, he became my friend. He included me. Grand Falls has no finer teacher. Though I decline to identify him by name, he knows who he is. Please, I beseech you. Save his job. Save the jobs of the others who, without your support, will face the budget axe. Approve the budget." Head bowed, Speedy turned and returned to his seat on the far side.

A hush…a resounding hush pervaded the hall. As a speaker, Speedy may have been recalcitrant, but he was cogent. His heartfelt message furnished food for thought.

I looked at Mary. "That took guts. Speedy would sooner suffer a torture chamber than do public speaking…He did it for me. He's a helluva friend."

The president of the board gave the attendees one last chance to speak. With no takers, he banged his gavel and adjourned the meeting.

"Your pals, The Guys, really stepped up for you tonight," said Mary. "They hold you in high esteem."

I smiled. Inside I beamed. "Not all were supportive," I said. "Babbitt hardly went to bat for education, let alone me."

"Big deal. He's a narcissistic ass. Public concern, not to mention empathy, is beyond him."

Knee-jerk might have prompted me to defend a fellow member of The Guys. But Mary's point had too much merit. Regardless, Babbitt was an exception to the patella's otherwise involuntary reflex.

"I'm surprised our good superintendent stayed on the sidelines," said Mary. "You would expect him to encourage the voters to approve the budget."

Her point was valid, at least in a vacuum. But put into context, Cooper's silence was no shock. Golfer that Cooper was, before he played a shot, he threw up some grass. He checked which way the wind was blowing. But unlike the links, where some holes demanded that he play into inauspicious gusts or fight a tricky crosswind, elsewhere he circumvented such adverse circumstances. Guided by self-interest, rather than principle, he monitored the wind. Whatever the voters wanted was fine with him. No need to speak out, to add headaches to his life, and worse yet, put himself in jeopardy. The easy way, straight downwind, was the route Cooper traveled.

I looked around the auditorium, which had largely emptied. "Let's go," I said. We headed out into the darkness that had descended over the parking lot. Mixed feelings competed. Anxiety over my job persisted. Recognition and support from friends uplifted me. Only time…that, plus the will of the voters…would dictate whether I would keep the job I loved and maintain my ability to provide for my family. That said, history, my specialty, indicated that voters stick to their guns. Revotes rarely alter outcomes. Lloyds of London, willing to book a bet on anything, would have tagged me an odds-on favorite to join the line of the struggling unemployed.

***

Students abhor an invitation to visit the principal's office. Teachers detest it as well. But in either case, the offer cannot be refused. A previous invitation may suggest that the visit will end in disaster. But one should not jump to conclusions; rather, recall Yogi Berra's profound wisdom referenced in a previous chapter: "It ain't over till it's over." And that inspires another apt phrase from the bewildering catcher. "It's déjà vu all over again."

The Monday after the public meeting, one day before the second budget vote, a student in my afternoon homeroom brought me a note. I unfolded the message and read: "Please stop at the office at the conclusion of school today. Mr. Armstrong would like to speak to you."

Rarely had I received such an invitation. Nevertheless, my limited history provided grounds for worry. None had been the font of good news. The worst dated back to my days as a student when Buster had set off his infamous smoke bomb. I tried to imagine the reason behind the curious message. I had no clue, but bad tidings were an excellent bet. The critical question: How bad? On the bright side, my wait for an explanation would be brief. Less than five minutes later, the final bell rang, and my students emptied the room. I hurried to the office where the secretary greeted me.

"Mr. Armstrong is on the telephone. He'll see you shortly."

Rumor had it that the aging principal, in his late sixties, was planning to retire in another year or two. As far as I was concerned, his departure could not come too soon. Not having liked him when I was a student, my years on the opposite side of the classroom desk had done nothing to modify my feelings. Dictatorial exercise of power encapsulated his methods. Personality and warmth, hardly his forte, were never on display, even if only with lip service. Condescension foisted on teachers duplicated that which he inflicted on students. A colleague from the English Department described Armstrong as a real-life Scrooge, one yet to receive visits from the transformative apparitions. The depiction led another colleague to protest. He termed the comparison an affront to Scrooge.

I had just taken a seat when the secretary said, "Mr. Armstrong hung up. You may go in."

"You wanted to see me, Sir," I said, as I entered his office. As I student, I had called him Mr. Armstrong. As teachers, we enjoyed the privilege of calling him "Sir."

"Yes, James." Apart from my late grandmother, Armstrong was the only person who called me James. Far from a sign of respect, it highlighted the difference in our status.

"Please, shut the door." His deep voice, as always, was icy.

I did his bidding and took a seat.

"I have a bit of news, personal to you. It's only appropriate that you should hear it first, directly from me."

Though his officious formality was consistent with his *modus operandi*, it unnerved me more.

"A representative of a local bank has provided us with documents that impact your position."

Already apprehensive, the mention of a bank juxtaposed with my position, a link without logic, heightened my concern. It sent my brain racing. I had no mortgage. My credit card had a zero balance. My car payments were up to date, and to the extent I might be unable to make them in the future, Lefty had gotten me 18-months' forbearance.

"To clarify, an anonymous benefactor has deposited funds with the bank that are tied to your job."

Armstrong's purported clarification did anything but explain the connection between the bank and me.

"It seems this anonymous benefactor has pledged to pay your salary and benefits for the next two years."

I looked blankly at Armstrong. Indeed, I gawked, struggling to absorb the implausible message.

"There are certain strings attached to the pledge."

The word *strings* might have crushed my celebration, but yet to digest the news, no such celebration had commenced. I awaited the bad news.

"The pledge can only be used to pay your salary and benefits, not for any other purpose. To the extent that the voters subsequently approve funds for your position, that portion of the gift will lapse. Likewise, if you cease to teach in the Grand Falls School District at any time during the two years, the payments will cease." Armstrong eyed me. "Do you understand what I said?"

"I…I think so." I still feared I had missed something. "Is the school district okay with the terms?"

"Absolutely. The board has approved them. It was an offer they couldn't refuse. It's found money, a job saved…at a time when the district is in dire straits."

"So, irrespective of the budget vote tomorrow, I…I will still have my job?" Fearing I had misconstrued his message, I tenuously posed the question. With eyes tearing and voice choking, my words were barely audible.

"You will indeed."

"Who? How did this come about?"

"Got me. As I said, the donor is anonymous. Somebody out there...up there (Armstrong gestured skyward) likes you."

"Wow...Thank you, Sir."

"Don't thank me. I'm merely the messenger...Have a good evening."

About that, there was no doubt. I got up from my chair and bounded down the hallway. Waiting until I walked home to tell Mary was far too long. I hurried to the teachers' room and dialed our house. I gave Mary the incredible news. Her joyous bawling had me crying as well.

After stopping at my homeroom and picking up my briefcase, I headed out of school, literally whistling a happy tune, the song from my favorite musical, *The King and I*. I gazed up at the bright June sky. Heaven had shined on me. The job I loved was still mine. I could provide for my family. I remained the able breadwinner I had always been.

In the back of my mind, Cuthbert's lawsuit loomed. But I refused to let it quash my celebration. And on the bright side, even if Cuthbert won a judgment in excess of my insurance policy, according to my attorney, Cuthbert could only garnish ten percent of my salary. Though the judgment would be a lien on our house, he could not evict us from the premises. If we sold the house, he would be paid from the proceeds. Admittedly, that would be an unsavory result. But imperfect as it was, in the interim it would permit our family to enjoy life in our customary manner. Months earlier, such an outcome would have been unacceptable. But with what I had endured in recent months, with the dreadful repercussions I had been fearing more recently, the result was more than satisfactory.

I had barely left the school grounds when the question I had asked Armstrong reemerged. Who was my benefactor? It took only seconds before a compelling answer materialized. Doubtless, it was The Guys. Twenty thousand dollars, the rough cost of my salary and benefits over two years, was a lot of money. But several of my buddies were successful entrepreneurs. A momentary pang of guilt interrupted my celebration. Was it right for me to take their money? I told myself that they wanted to do it, that they could afford it. Pride might have inhibited me, except I had a family to support.

I was nearly home when I thought about the budget vote the following day. With my well-being no longer dependent upon its outcome, trepidations it had kindled vanished. But another pang stirred. Other teachers, most of whom I knew well, would likely be excessed. I had received my miracle. I longed for them to receive theirs as well. I stopped and stared upward into the firmament, a palette of blue, dotted with puffy white cumulus. "Please God, let the budget pass. As you saved my job, save those of my fellow teachers...please."

***

One wants to thank a benefactor. When the benefactor is anonymous, that becomes problematic. But canny detective work can solve the problem...sometimes.

After stopping home, briefly celebrating with my family, and grabbing a snack, I headed to Nick Stoner's for our Monday-afternoon golf. In recent weeks my rounds on the links and time with The Guys had lacked verve. But armed with my sudden good fortune, I had jumped to the opposite end of the spectrum. As I drove to the golf course, I contemplated how I should broach the subject. Logic indicated that my pals were responsible for my largess. But proof thereof remained absent. Even if my buddies were my benefactors, they might be unaware that Armstrong had given me the good news. Waiting until after the round, seeing what they said in the interim, made good sense. Perhaps they would confirm that they had indeed funded my job.

I parked the car and after removing my golf clubs from the trunk, headed to the first tee. All The Guys, except for Pete and Babbitt, were there. I greeted them, watching for hints that they were hiding something. If so, they kept it well disguised. A minute later, Pete arrived.

Lefty said, "Since our foursome has to wait for Babbitt, you guys go first."

We hit our tee shots. I began the round with a mood-matching drive, a beautiful baby cut that started down the left side of the fairway and drifted to the center. Our foursome left the tee and went to our drives. We looked back. No sign of Babbitt. There was also no mention of my job. We hit our second shots. Mine, a duck-hooked five iron, headed toward trouble left of the green. Perhaps my round might not duplicate my spirits. If so, that was fine. Numbers on the links paled when pitted against the superb news about my job.

Sam looked back toward the tee again before eyeing his watch. "Four-forty, and still no Babbitt. Wonder if he'll be a no-show."

"You'd think he would have given us a heads-up if that were the case," said Speedy. "Hope nothing happened to him."

"Maybe he's still pissed from last Monday," said Buster. "He stormed off without saying goodbye."

The idea that Babbitt would still be sulking seemed hard to imagine, but if any of The Guys were a candidate for an extended hissy fit, Babbitt boasted the résumé.

I hacked out of a bad lie, chipped on, and after two putts, carded a double bogey. I looked back again. Cooper, Pete, and Lefty had just left the tee. "Looks like they're playing as a threesome."

"Not much else they could do under the circumstances," said Buster.

We played the remaining eight holes. My score, 44, a sloppy safari that included several side trips to the sylvan sectors adjoining the fairways, warranted a prime place in the scrapheap of forgotten rounds. Nevertheless, I was flying high, even before the beer began to flow. In the back of my mind, the question whether The Guys were my benefactor percolated. If so, they concealed it masterfully. We went into the clubhouse where we placed our usual order. Ten minutes later, Cooper, Pete, and Lefty, still a threesome, joined us.

"No word from Babbitt?" said Buster.

Lefty gestured at the three of them. "What you see is as many as we had."

310

Normally, the comparison of scorecards took precedence the moment the second team arrived at the clubhouse, but having four against three put a hitch into the process. During the round, our foursome had weighed possibilities to deal with the situation. None were appealing.

Sam, who had gone to the pay phone, joined us at the table. "No answer at Babbitt's house."

"You think he's still stewing from last week?" said Lefty.

"We considered the possibility," said Buster, "but…who knows?"

"Hey, don't forget, you're talking about Larry *George* Babbitt," said Speedy.

Our server brought our pizza, adding it to the beer she had delivered minutes before.

Cooper said, "Our team totaled 128. Can you guys beat that?"

"How can we match scores?" said Sam. "We're adding four, and you've only got three."

"Details…Don't bother us with details." A smile confirmed that Pete was teasing.

"We could multiply our total by three-fourths," said Buster.

"Bad idea." I had already glanced at our opponents' scorecard and tested the idea. It would leave our team on the short end. "Seems to me, the team with a no-show loses by default."

"No way!" said Cooper.

"Let's decide it democratically," said Sam. "We'll take a vote whether the team with a no-show defaults."

"Not fair," said Lefty. "You guys are four, and we're only three."

"Okay. We'll make it secret ballot," said Sam.

"Yeah, sure," said Cooper. "Lotta good that'll do us…How about we call it a draw? No bragging rights."

Though the suggestion evoked apathy, a silent acquiescence hinted it was the final verdict.

With no one having broached the matter of my job's funding, I decided to do so…obliquely. I said, "You won't believe the terrific news I got yesterday afternoon. An anonymous benefactor funded my job at the high school for two years. Even if the budget doesn't pass, I'm still employed. Armstrong confirmed it."

A plethora of enthusiastic reactions emerged. Any hint of preexisting knowledge, let alone complicity, failed to evolve. Either they were genuinely surprised, or they were adept actors.

"So, this is the first that any of you are hearing this?"

My question evoked mainly affirmative verbal and non-verbal reactions. The lone exception was Cooper.

"I knew about it already."

The apparent implication defied credulity. Of all people, Superintendent Ronald Cooper had helped save my job.

"Yeah, I heard about the arrangement last Friday. Don't know the identity of the anonymous donor. It was made through a bank that contacted our school board president. Naturally, the board and I welcomed it. Found money, a gift horse, especially one not laded with dark surprises, is always welcome." Cooper looked me in the eye. "You are one damn lucky fellow."

I thought Cooper might indicate that he was happy for me. Perhaps his only interest in the gift was that it narrowed the budget shortfall, made his job easier. Regardless, his remarks explained his prior knowledge of the arrangement. I reached for my beer and sipped. My benefactor remained a mystery. Doubtful that The Guys, the entire group, was responsible. However, one or more remained possible. If so, an intention to maintain anonymity seemed apparent.

***

Spiders are equipped with a natural foot oil that neutralizes the glue of the sticky webs they weave. It enables them to evade entanglement in their own webs. But humans, who have no such oil, lack similar protection. If a man weaves a web, especially one of deceit, his own mendacity can ensnare him.

Following golf, as I walked through the mudroom into the kitchen, Mary hurried from the living room to meet me.

"Joe Walker called just before five this afternoon. He said he needs to speak with you. He asked that you call him at his home as soon as you return from golf."

In the weeks preceding the saving of my job, I had tried to bury the lawsuit in the distant reaches of my brain, not that the effort enjoyed appreciable success. Concerns about our source of income, only one of my dilemmas, more than filled my plate. I told myself that I could address the lawsuit in the fall when it came up for trial. Despite my good intentions, perhaps the issue was arriving sooner. Maybe it was at hand. I went to the telephone and dialed.

"Walker residence. Joe Walker speaking."

"Hi Joe. It's Jim. I just arrived home from the links. Mary said you need to speak with me."

"Yes, I have some news about your case."

The last time Walker had news it was supposedly neutral, neither good nor bad. That may have been accurate, but its implications were anything but good. That information had forced me to reassess my risk of being hit with a large judgment, one dwarfing both my insurance coverage and our family's assets. With an impending sense of doom, I said, "Do I need to sit down for today's news?"

"You might just as well...I'll give you a moment to get settled."

I parked myself in the chair adjoining the telephone. I said, "I've got my seat. Hit me with the haymaker."

"Haymaker?...Yeah, I guess it is, but I doubt it'll knock you out."

Were I still at Nick Stoner's with The Guys, I would have cleverly bantered, but delaying what was likely to be an unpalatable menu had no appeal. I opted for silence.

"I received a call this afternoon from Wilson. Your insurance company hired a private investigator, who took some wonderful home movies. They show Cuthbert, that pain-ridden, disabled plaintiff, who claims to require metal braces, playing basketball in Little Falls on two occasions. The guy is a helluva rebounder. He jumps high and bangs hard on the boards."

"That son of a bitch!"

"Yeah, that son of a bitch no longer has a leg to stand on. No pun intended. You might say he fouled out. The court, judicial, not basketball, will be shipping him to the showers. The investigator also learned from Cuthbert's former employer that he was laid off six weeks before the accident and had applied for unemployment. The employer said Cuthbert was never more than part time, typically earning an average of less than $100 per week, a third of what he claimed under oath. Wilson contacted Pritchard and showed him what she had. Pritchard got back to her. He indicated his client would accept the $2,000 the insurance company had previously offered."

"The crook doesn't deserve it, but the settlement will get me off the hook. Right?"

"It would, but Wilson countered that the insurance company won't pay a penny. She dared Pritchard to walk into court, indicating that Cuthbert would not only be bounced out, but Judge Graver – the case is assigned to the no-nonsense jurist – might also refer the transcript to the district attorney for prosecution. Following the conversation, Pritchard contacted his client who agreed to sign a Stipulation of Discontinuance ending the lawsuit."

"Wow, that's great!...All that remains is for you to send me your bill."

"About that...after I heard from Wilson, I called Pritchard. I told him that you now have a cause of action against Cuthbert for intentional infliction of mental distress; and that in my opinion, a jury would give a significant award of punitive damages against his client, owing to the gravity of Cuthbert's attempted fraud. I also mentioned a minor detail, that his client has caused you $400 of unnecessary expense, my legal fees for monitoring the phony lawsuit."

"Gosh...I don't want to sue Cuthbert. Just having the burden of his claim lifted is more than enough."

"I understand. But after I raised the possibility of the lawsuit, Pritchard contacted Cuthbert again. Afraid he might be sued and worse yet, that it might precipitate a criminal prosecution, Cuthbert offered to pay my legal fees, provided you agree not to sue. You might say we turned the tables on him. What do you think?"

What did I think? Walker had to be kidding. I said, "I'm getting a result that's even better than the best I could have imagined."

"Well, it serves Cuthbert right. After faking injuries, not to mention lying about your headlight, the cause of the accident, and his lost wages, he deserves to pick up the tab. Having wreaked needless havoc, it's the least he can do. And on that note, I'll let you enjoy your evening."

"Thanks to you, there's no doubt...I will."

***

One doesn't look a gift horse in the mouth. But what if the gift horse disappears? Is it time to panic? Or might a celebration be in order?

The following day, the Tuesday of the budget revote, the referendum occupied my mind. Admittedly, the foreboding that had prevailed on the day of the original vote had disappeared. Still, concern for endangered colleagues persisted.

As soon as I finished school, I stopped home and along with Mary, headed to the firehouse to cast our ballots. A line outside, about fifteen people, hinted at a high turnout. That was a double-edged sword. Perhaps folks who supported education but rarely voted on school budgets had been stirred to visit the polls. Alternatively, the anti-tax campaign of individuals like Babbitt may have motivated the misers. More likely, both factions were having their say. While Mary and I waited in line, several people wished me good luck with the vote. Presumably, they were unaware that a benefactor had already saved my job from the chopping block.

Following dinner, I read the local newspaper, did the crossword puzzle, and made lesson plans for the next day. At ten, Mary and I watched *Marcus Welby, M.D.* in our living room. When the show concluded, we awaited the eleven o'clock news. The broadcast began with an update on the never-ending Vietnam War; New York City's primary election results in which incumbent Mayor John Lindsay and former mayor Robert Wagner, Jr., were both defeated; and a report that Boris Spassky had become the new world chess champion. A pair of commercials followed, after which the anchor shifted to local news, headed by a rollover car accident on Route 29. Finally, she turned to the Grand Falls budgetary revote. She said, "The citizens of Grand Falls, who had previously rejected their school district's budget, approved it today. Turnout, fifty-percent higher than earlier, appears to have made the difference."

Mary looked my way. "Some teachers will sleep well tonight." She smiled.

I was certain her comment included me. I said, "Time we get to bed." I pressed the remote, turning off the television. A weight had been lifted from my shoulders. My anonymous donation had just vanished, but I had lost nothing. The taxpayers of Grand Falls had agreed to pay my salary and benefits. They were also willing to pay the same for colleagues of mine who otherwise would have been excessed. As I got up from the living-room couch, I glanced upward at and beyond the ceiling. I whispered, "Thanks."

Chapter XX

Contrary to the adage, witnesses testify that leopards can change their spots. But let us not get carried away. Rare exceptions offer no reason to discard the rule, one that provides valuable guidance. When encountering a leopard, expect it to retain its spots. And when it does, it's apt to wind up in a cage.

The Monday after the revote, I remained at school following the final bell. Unlike the preceding weeks when I had been staying late half the time to help students prepare for the American History Regents, I was alone in my classroom grading papers. It was the final week of what had been a unique spring. Angst-filled for months, it had concluded on a high note. Worries about my job had faded into the past, and as a bonus, my students were performing exceptionally well on their exams. An upcoming summer that once portended belt-tightening, stress, and a search for employment, had transmuted into an exciting vision. Over the weekend, while celebrating our good fortune, we had planned a 13-day trip in a rented RV to Philadelphia, Washington D.C., the Smokies, and other landmarks of the Eastern USA. Life was good…Indeed, it was better than that. Fresh from a visit to the canyon depths, I appreciated my lot even more. Life was great.

I checked my watch – 4:01. I gobbled down a snack pack of six peanut butter crackers as I hurried to the parking lot. Rather than walking to school in the morning, I had driven, allowing me to go directly to Nick Stoner's for our weekly golf match. I arrived ten minutes before our meeting time and headed to the first tee. Four-thirty arrived, but with only six of us there, we let a threesome, two men and a lady, proceed ahead of us.

"Last week Babbitt was AWOL," said Buster. "Now it's Babbitt and Coop. What the hell is happening?"

"Let's give them five more minutes." said Sam.

"What do we do then?" said Pete. "Have your foursome tee off? That'll leave Lefty and me as a twosome. Two against four, even in a scramble format, would be ridiculous."

"Total score, our two against your four," said Lefty, "oughta be perfect."

"Yeah, that works for me." Pete shrugged abashedly. "Okay, we need plan B."

I looked toward the parking lot. No sign of Babbitt or Cooper. The trio we had let precede us were well down the fairway. I said, "If they don't show by the time the group ahead approaches the green, suppose we play as two threesomes?"

"I could join Pete and Lefty," said Sam. "That should make for fair teams."

A couple minutes ticked away. Adopting Sam's suggestion, we teed off with our threesome going first. Buster and I played okay, while Speedy fired a thirty-nine, a rare sub-forty for him. Once done, Buster went into the clubhouse and ordered our pizza and beer. Speedy and I waited for the others behind the ninth green. In the meantime, I combined our individual scores, calculating our team score. "One twenty-three," I said. "The bad guys will be hard pressed to beat that."

Lefty, Pete, and Sam arrived at the last green. After Pete chipped close and tapped in, Lefty putted a twenty-footer to within three inches."

"It's good. Pick it up," yelled Speedy.

"Nah," said Lefty. "After the way I've putted, I need the thrill of rolling in a long one." He tapped the ball in, pumping his fist twice in a sarcastic celebration.

Sam lined up a twelve-footer, one with considerable right to left break. He stroked what looked like a good putt. On line, the question remained whether it had sufficient speed to reach the hole. An instant later, it died, hanging precariously on the high lip. Sam crumpled to his knees, emitting an excruciating wail. Strangling the ends of his putter, he rose and started toward his ball. The dimpled sphere, governed by the whim of gravity, perhaps aided by an auspicious breeze, tumbled into the hole. "Yeah!" Sam waved his putter high above his head. "Three schlockers and a downer...whipped cream on shit!" he shouted. "That's a par."

The trio departed the green. "How'd you guys do?" said Pete.

"One twenty-three," I said. "You boys wanna congratulate us now or after you total up your scores?"

"Well, just to make it official, I'll do the numbers first." Pete added up their card. "Son of a bitch," he grumbled once he combined the three scores.

"How many did we whip you by?" said Speedy.

"Zero," said Pete. "We got a tie, 123 apiece."

I shot Sam a look before shoving him gently. "Damn you, Doc!"

"What do you want from me?"

"All these many matches that we had you for a teammate, when did you make a clutch putt? We ship you off to the enemy, and first time out you hole a snake, pilfering our victory." I looked him in the eye. "Way to go. The golf gods couldn't shine on a nicer guy." I shook Sam's hand.

"You guys realize that we're gonna demand a rematch?" said Speedy.

"You're on," said Lefty. "Just one problem. When will we have another round with just the six of us?"

"After two no-shows and no response to my telephone message," said Sam, "I suspect Babbitt's sulking augurs a permanent farewell. Cooper, on the other hand, should return. Presumably his absence today has a good reason."

The five of us headed into the clubhouse. Buster greeted us near the door. "Who won?"

"Final tally was akin to a kiss from your nasty great aunt," said Speedy. "Match ended in a draw. Pizza about ready?"

"Yeah," said Buster, "but never mind that now. You gotta see what's happening on the evening news."

"I'm famished," said Sam. "Can't the news wait?"

"Not this." Buster hurried us all to the bar, behind which a television sat on a corner shelf.

On the screen, the sheriff was guiding a handcuffed Cooper from the courthouse. The reporter said, "We'll have more on this breaking story later. For now, this is Carlina Marks reporting from the Herkimer County Courthouse. Back to you, Alex."

"What the hell was that about?" said Lefty.

"Our playing partner and dear superintendent of schools was arrested and charged today after a sealed indictment was opened in County Court. His wife was charged as well. From what I could glean, for several years he's been stealing from the school district, paying personal bills with the district's credit card. He's charged with embezzlement and grand larceny."

A buzz, akin to that which pervaded the clubhouse, dominated our group.

I turned to Pete and said, "Looks like that concern you had a few weeks back has resolved itself. Can't imagine that you'll need to call Coop for cheating on the links. Seems that other folks with bigger fish to fry will deal with him."

Pete nodded slowly. "Once a cheater...always a cheater."

"Seems so," I said, "though I never thought of him as a cheetah. He struck me more the leopard type. And you know what they say about leopards: they don't change their spots."

***

Secrets are delicate. Curiosity is natural. Some confidences create legal or moral obligations. Ignorance can be bliss. It can also yield disaster. Until one knows the contents of a secret, choosing between ignorance and knowledge presents a vain conundrum. As Shakespeare might have put it had Alexander the Great sought advice from Hamlet: "To know or not to know, that is the Gordian Knot."

Wednesday is famously termed hump day. The Wednesday of the last week of school was my final hump before summer. I had graded all my students' exams. I had turned in their marks to the office. Like my students, I was primed for vacation. The last bell of the day had rung, and the students had streamed from my homeroom. I was packing my briefcase when Martha Raines, the senior member of the history department, poked her head into the doorway.

"You got a minute, Jim," said Raines.

"Sure...What's up?"

As she drew closer, she looked around the room. "No stragglers still here?"

I gestured at the otherwise empty space. "Just me."

Her voice low, she said, "Can you keep a secret?"

Years earlier I had learned that confidential information was a delicate commodity. Secrets were double-edged swords capable of gashing the recipient. Promising to keep a confidence could spawn peril. Legal or other strictures could mandate disclosure. I shrugged.

"It's information that I'm certain will interest you."

Piqued curiosity baited me to commit to silence. Judgment counseled otherwise. I said, "Much as I'd love to hear your tidbit, I can't promise. For all I know, it might create a legal duty of disclosure."

"I assure you. No risk of that."

I hemmed and hawed. "It might impose a moral obligation...might be something that one of my colleagues needs to know."

"Not that either." Raines gazed out the window and muttered under her breath, "What the hell." She turned back my way. "I'll take a chance and tell you. But do me a favor. Don't go out of your way to repeat it...you know, just for the sake of gossiping." She hesitated, seemingly weighing her decision to disclose. She said, "I'm retiring at the end of the next school year. Forty-two years in the classroom is enough."

The disclosure's impact on me was self-evident. Pushing it into the background, I said, "Congratulations." I understood why she wanted to keep the matter confidential. Plans can change. Creating expectations, both with administration and students, can generate pressures. Short timers lose sway. They confront lip service.

"I plan to wait until next January to make the announcement, not that I'm still debating. The decision is all but cast in stone. My husband and I signed on the dotted line last week for the purchase of a lot in this new community, Sun

City, that's being built in Arizona. The builder, Del Webb, will complete our house so we can move in on July 1st of next year. My son and his family – they currently rent – are buying our house here in Grand Falls…and might I add, at a very appealing price…Anyway, I figured the information would interest you. With just three history teachers in our department, my retirement means you'll move up from third to second in seniority. Impossible that our department, one of three or four bedrocks, will ever shrink below two. So, once I go, your job should be safe from the budget axe for the balance of your career."

In past years budgetary problems had me conducting the very analysis that Raines had recited. If either of the two history teachers with more seniority than I departed, whatever the reason, the threat that my position might be cut would vanish. I said, "I appreciate your telling me…And now that you have, you've got my word. Apart from telling Mary – and she never violates a confidence – it will not cross my lips."

"I thought I could count on you." Raines patted me on the back. "In case I don't see you, have a nice summer."

"You too," I said, as she started for the door.

I finished packing my briefcase. With my job safe for the balance of my career, the great plan that Mary and I had laid out for our lives was back on track, and all signs indicated clear sailing ahead.

***

A book is nice. A bookmark can be nicer yet, even better than a golden-brown toasted marshmallow.

Thanks to television's local news broadcasts, as well as the newspaper, I had learned additional details of Superintendent Cooper's arrest. According to the reports, he had enjoyed the use of a school district credit card for official expenses, including gas and service for his district-provided car. But Cooper had pushed the perk way beyond its limits. He had used the credit card to pay for personal expenses such as groceries, clothing, theater tickets, a television, and the installation of new gutters and windows at his home. He had even employed it to pay for alcohol, greens fees, and charges at a strip club while attending a conference in Las Vegas. His wife had employed the card for groceries, clothing, regular visits to a spa, and gas for her vehicle. An audit yielded an ever-growing mountain of evidence. Documents proving that the Coopers had stolen more than $13,000 over several years built a slam dunk case.

The final week of the 1968-69 school year reprised most last weeks. Students had no new work. On the final Thursday, the penultimate day of school, I had parties for my two senior classes. A half-day on Friday, an appetizer to summer, manifested a ravenous hunger for the extended hiatus. Though we teachers remained outwardly more restrained than the students, our anticipation of the break equaled theirs.

Throughout Grand Falls, particularly among the school faculty, Cooper's fall from grace dominated conversations. One of the community's own, a former student of its schools, had climbed to the peak of its educational mountain, only to freefall into a seemingly bottomless abyss. Lacking a golden parachute, accelerated by the gravity of a multi-count felony indictment, his fate, a hard landing, was inevitable.

For me the outcome bore unique irony. Cooper, my former classmate and longtime cohort in The Guys, a man who had displayed little interest when I had faced the loss of my job, had lost his. Rather than sympathy, members of the community were barraging him with shame. He had become a pariah. In place of an impressive oak-trimmed office, accoutered with a sumptuous executive desk, he would occupy a barren prison cell. In lieu of tailored, three-piece suits, he would don an orange jumpsuit. And instead of weekly rounds hitting dimpled spheres on the golf course, any balls and links he enjoyed would be forged of iron and shackled to his ankles.

Summer vacation, a two-month recess during which our family could relax and romp amidst the year's finest weather, always vivified me. But having just emerged from the consternation of potential job loss and financial catastrophe, I valued the vacation more than ever. Friday evening, Pete Longley had informed us that Laura was coming up from New

York City for the weekend. We invited them for a Saturday evening barbeque in our backyard, a celebration of Lisa's graduation. I grilled steaks on our outdoor fireplace. Mary prepared cheese-puff hors d'oeuvres, coleslaw, baked beans, French fries, and a sweet-potato casserole. Ice cream and watermelon capped the menu. On sticks that Lisa and Jerry had gathered, we toasted marshmallows, some of which we ate immediately, while others found their way into s'mores.

Laura said, "I've got a little something in the car for Lisa's graduation. There's also something for Jerry. I'll be right back." She circled around to the driveway, and returning a minute later, handed wrapped packages to the kids. "Go ahead, open them."

Lisa's revealed an edition of Antonia Frasier's *Mary Queen of Scots*. Jerry's contained Erich von Daniken's *Chariot of the Gods*. The kids each thanked Laura.

She said, "Oh, before I forget, each of your books contains a bookmark. You'll find them at page one hundred."

I watched, keeping one eye on the gift openings and the other on the marshmallow I was toasting.

"Oh, my God!" shrieked Lisa, the first to flip to page one hundred. She began to cry. She threw her arms, book and all, around Laura.

A second later, Jerry, who had been briefly distracted from his search for the designated page, screamed, "Holy..."

"What is going on?" said Mary.

Lisa raced to her mother with her book open.

Mouth agape, Mary's eyes were wide.

"What the...?" I said.

"Dad, look," said Jerry. He showed me his bookmark.

In disbelief, I eyed it, a check payable to me as trustee for Jerry in the sum of $9700. "What is this?"

"Just what it looks like." said Laura.

"You can't be serious." I read the document a second time. "How...Why?"

"All of you saved my dad and me back when I was in school. I would not be where I am today were it not for you. A couple months ago when I was in the area, my dad told me your job was in jeopardy. When I had dinner here, you (Laura

324

gestured my way) acted like issues with the school budget were no big deal. Suspecting that you didn't want to worry the kids, I dropped the issue, but I had my dad keep me apprised of the situation. Once he told me the budget had been voted down, I deposited the money to save your position, including your benefits. When the budget got thumbs up on the revote, the money was refunded to me. Having already given it away, I decided it could best be used to provide college educations for my little sister and brother. To me they're family. You all are."

The disclosure answered a question I had rehashed many times. I had learned the identity of my benefactor. But with my job restored, was it right to accept the gift? I glanced at Mary. Her shrug offered no help. I turned to Laura and said, "I...I can't take your money. It's not right, especially when I still have my job."

"It's not for you to decide," said Laura. "Or let me rephrase that. If necessary, it won't be your decision."

"What do you mean?" I said. "My name is on the check. Presumably the same is true for the other one."

"Yes, your name is on both checks," said Laura, "but only as trustee. If you refuse to accept the money and your fiduciary designation, I'll give the money to my dad, as trustee for Lisa and Jerry. He'll make sure the funds go for the kids' educations."

I looked at Pete.

His face lit with a devilish smile. He nodded repeatedly.

I turned back to Mary.

She said, "I think they've got you over a barrel...a sublime barrel."

Stick still in hand, I went over to Laura and gave her a hug. "Thank you so much."

"My pleasure...a great one."

I said, "Four years at a public college like my alma mater...well, its successor, the State University of New York at Albany, will run well below $9700."

"Fine," said Laura. "Perhaps Lisa and Jerry will choose private institutions."

I held up my stick. I gestured at the golden-brown marshmallow that occupied the tip. "It's not a pair of college educations."

"Fair point," said Laura, removing the marshmallow. About to put it into her mouth, she halted. "Tell you what. Make my next one a s'more. Then we'll call it even."

***

Clubs formed in childhood come and go. Now and then, one survives for over a quarter-century. Such lifelong harmony is momentously rare. But stir in sufficient respect, esprit de corps, and resolve, and the seeming impossible might be viable.

Monday found me catching up on chores around the exterior of our home. I mowed the lawn, and between a pair of arborvitaes adjoining the house's front façade, I planted annuals, a combination of impatiens, petunias, and marigolds. A forty-percent chance of afternoon thundershowers had me regularly checking the partly cloudy sky. At four o'clock, with dark clouds looming, I drove to Nick Stoner's to meet The Guys for our weekly round. I no sooner pulled into the parking lot than the Heavens let loose. Grabbing my golf umbrella, but leaving my clubs in the trunk, I raced into the clubhouse. Three of The Guys were already there, and the remainder, save Babbitt and Cooper, arrived within minutes.

Through the clubhouse's spacious, multi-paned windows, we stared out at the deluge. Thunder rumbled; my optimism crumbled; would-be golfers grumbled; a flash of lightning humbled; and I stumbled, nearly tumbled, jumping back, reacting to a booming clap.

"Maybe it'll let up in a few minutes," said Lefty. "These summer storms come and go."

A lack of concurring voices hinted that the five of us were less sanguine than Lefty.

"Any chance Babbitt or Cooper may show?" said Buster.

"Babbitt is done with us," said Speedy. "Yesterday, Walter Holzman stopped in the hardware store. He bumped into Babbitt a couple days earlier. Babbitt said he wanted nothing to do with us. Labeled us a bunch of two-faced bastards."

"He may have made the comment," said Pete, "but I doubt that's the real reason he failed to show."

"What does that mean?" said Lefty.

Displaying a sly smile, Pete stood mute.

"C'mon," said Buster. "You know something. Out with it."

"Well...it's like this. My neighbor is a clerk in Surrogate's Court. There's a proceeding involving the estate of Babbitt's great uncle. He died about a year ago. Didn't have a will or any direct heirs. Babbitt and his cousins from Pennsylvania are locked in a battle over the assets, not that there's a lot. The case required a look at the family tree. Turns out Babbitt's grandfather's mother was three-quarters white and one-quarter black. Babbitt is a fraction black. My neighbor says Babbitt went ballistic when he found out."

"I can only imagine." I glanced at Speedy. His stoic face was no surprise. Having faced prejudice from an early age, he was adept at silently absorbing the bigotry of racist ignoramuses. I said, "Babbitt is a dipstick. He's ashamed to face us. Talk about pathetic." I heaved a sigh. "Good riddance."

"Good riddance," echoed Sam.

"That still leaves Coop," said Lefty. "I understand he posted bail. Anyone think he'll be joining us?"

"Only if we start playing at the prison links up in Dannemora, assuming they add a course at the facility."

Buster's oblique assessment that Cooper was history drew non-verbal reactions. His reasoning bore too much merit to argue otherwise.

"Looks like The Guys are down to six," I said. "Less than half of the original thirteen from when we started in tenth grade."

"After a bit more than a quarter-century, that's not bad," said Lefty, "especially considering that four moved away after high school and one was killed in World War II."

"As for the recent losses…" Buster shrugged. "Leaves us with a great nucleus, not to mention that it's an even half-dozen, enough for two threesomes. And speaking of that, as soon as the rain stops, we're gonna have that rematch and whip your asses."

The reference to golf redirected our attention to the windows. Beyond the panes, the downpour continued, harder than before.

"It does not look good," said Sam.

I jabbed him in the side. "Wow, you figure that out all by yourself?"

"Genius like that made him class valedictorian," said Buster.

"Maybe it looks a little brighter in the opposite direction," said Lefty. "I'll check how it looks out the front doorway."

A minute later, Lefty returned. His glum expression hinted at that which wishful thinking had sought to deny.

"So, what's the verdict?" said Pete.

"If anything, it's darker yet out that way. And given the puddles in the parking lot, even after the rain stops, it'll be another hour before the greens will be puttable."

"So, what do we do?" said Sam. "Pack it in and call it a day?"

"No way," said Buster. "We can order our pizza and beer. Eat now. If it clears out…say by six or so, we can go out for…as many holes as we can squeeze in."

"We might even get nine in," said Speedy. "We've got the longest days of the year. Won't be dark till nine."

Speedy's last point was accurate, but given the state of the weather, inconsequential. That the course would be playable by seven was improbable. As for six, forget it. I said, "I'll get a pitcher and order the pizzas." I headed to the bar and placed our order.

When I returned to the table, pitcher in hand, Sam stared at me and shook his head.

"What's wrong?" I said.

Sam continued to shake his head. "Damn, you are one lucky guy, Ward. While you were gone, I suggested that now was the time to pare down the group to the good guys." Sam gestured at the five who were seated. "I recommended we give you your walking papers." He heaved a sigh. "Unfortunately, we need you, just to make up two threesomes, not to mention that touch football requires at least three on a side."

The affectionate razzing felt good. Aware of the stress occasioned by my job concerns, for months my buddies had refrained from mocking me. At last, I had reclaimed my rightful place as a trash-talk target. Years of experience had equipped me to deal with the teasing. I said, "Jeez...that wrecks my plans."

Sam went wide-eyed. "What plans?"

"Stan Hayner asked me to turn his threesome into a foursome. His offer made my day. But now, I'll have to turn him down. You've preyed on my conscience. Can't leave you guys in the lurch, not when you need me." I heaved a beleaguered sigh as I looked around the table. They were five, and I, one. I needed a shrewder approach, lest I come out on the short end of the repartee. I held out the pitcher of beer I had gotten at the bar. "Can I buy my way into this group?"

"That's more like it," said Buster.

I laid the pitcher onto the table and seated myself.

Buster put an arm over my shoulder. "Seriously, we're thankful things worked out for you at school."

"I appreciate that. You guys have meant a lot to me."

Sam gave me a look. "Okay, feed us the punchline. We asked for it."

"No, I mean it. These past few months when my job and livelihood were in jeopardy, you guys stepped up: medical care for my daughter; an interest-free deferment of my car loan; and at the risk of your businesses, publicly calling for approval of the school district's budget. And lest there be any confusion, your generosity is nothing new. Back in tenth grade, as a nerd, small for my age, I was ripe for the bullies. Thanks to you guys, I escaped that misery." I looked at Buster. "Your insistence that everyone be included made all the difference. You ensured that no one messed with Sam, and just because I was Sam's friend, I enjoyed the same security."

"Hey, it was the least I could do. But for Sam's father, my family would have been out on the street." Buster pointed my way. "And if it weren't for you, my life might have traveled a regrettable route."

Unable to grasp his reference, I furrowed my brow.

"Lest you've forgotten, let me refresh your memory," said Buster. "Junior year, when I ignited a smoke bomb in the supply room, Armstrong was chomping at the bit to expel me. Reform school, followed by prison, was a decent bet for my future. Rather than rat on me, you took the heat and saved my ass. Anything I've done to help you has been nothing more than repayment of a debt."

"Speaking of debts," said Pete, "count me in. Senior year, when I became a single father, I was embarrassed to show my face around campus. You, my buddies, made it clear that I was still one of The Guys. Even though I missed most of the fun, knowing I had friends meant everything. Sam's dad gave me a job with convenient hours, so I could provide for my family and still graduate. And when my mother passed and competing responsibilities threatened to turn my life upside down again, you (Pete gestured at me) came to my rescue. You provided a second home for Laura. As you well know, she deems you family."

"We feel the same about her," I said. "And just to set the record straight, the street ran both ways. Laura babysat and tutored our kids. They love her like a sister. And more recently, her generosity has reached bounds beyond..." Second thoughts, whether Laura preferred I not publicize her altruism, fettered my tongue.

Lefty chuckled.

"What's funny?" said Buster.

"Don't mind me. I was laughing at myself...And with everyone sharing, I might as well take a turn. Jim has already heard my tale." Lefty looked my way and winked. "Back in high school, I was a hotshot jock. Local newspapers splashed my photo on the sports' page. Major League scouts came to watch me. My ego, a balloon, inflated with hot air, expanded exponentially. I was full of myself. Throw in a propensity for skipping my share of a tab, and I merited certification as an inveterate pain in the ass! In the years since, I've lived in the past, bragging about my ancient exploits. Deep down I knew I was a loser...a failure, particularly as a father. My marriage...to a wonderful woman...went down the tubes. My irresponsibility and denial, buttressed by an excess of alcohol, wrecked our relationship. Fed up with my behavior, people made excuses to avoid me. But despite everything, you guys always put out the welcome mat." Lefty heaved a sigh. "I'm sorry for the way I've behaved. I'm trying to do better."

Lefty's confession drew a brief silence. Its contrition tabooed typical trash talk.

"Lefty has reconnected with his son," I said. "They've built a solid relationship. His son's a great student and an excellent tennis player."

"Pardon my boast, but he's a really good kid...a lot better than his old man," said Lefty. "I'm proud of him."

Buster turned to Speedy. "Apparently, we're a bunch of guys indebted to one another. No offense...perhaps a compliment, but unless I'm mistaken, you're the lone exception, indebted to no one."

"Exception?" said Speedy. "You gotta be kidding."

"What secrets obligate you?" said Buster.

"No secrets. Just that before my family relocated to Grand Falls, bigotry ruled my life. We were one of three African American families in a tiny Iowa town. I was one of three blacks in my school. The nicer kids ignored me. The meaner ones showered me with racial epithets. No one included me. On a good day, I was an outcast. On a bad one, I was a leper. The n-word populated my daily diet. During the second semester of seventh grade, when my family moved to Grand Falls, I anticipated more of the same. Not so. Next to Iowa, Grand Falls was a bouquet of roses. Of course, roses do have thorns. Most of the kids were neutral, neither abusive nor welcoming. A few treated me as *persona non grata*. But my first week here, Jim invited me to walk with him to school. So too, in the days that followed. It continued until we graduated high school. Every morning, my day began with acceptance, an inestimable blessing. If that weren't enough, Jim mentored me until I caught up to my classmates.

I felt a glow. Unwittingly, I had done good deeds. Those good deeds had been richly rewarded. I had gained a lifelong friend. I might have dwelled on the observation were Speedy not continuing.

"When we moved up to high school, tenth grade, I was happy to have two friends in my homeroom, Jim and Doc. Soon after, the group, the remains of which are seated here, was formed. I heard the talk. I expected to be excluded. I knew that Babbitt was trying to blackball me. I anticipated others would join his call." Speedy looked across the table at Buster. "You, the quarterback of the football team, one of the kings of the campus, demanded my inclusion. Thanks to you, I became one of The Guys. Rather than being ostracized, I belonged. If that weren't enough, you broadened my acceptance. You encouraged me to go out for the football team."

"Why not? You had a great pair of hands, and you were faster than any of our other flankers."

Speedy shook his head. "You can't fool me. More than that, altruism, concern for me, motivated you. Just like Jim and Doc, you made certain I got a fair shake. It was as if you had an emblem emblazoned on your shirt: 'Bullying Bigots, Beware of Buster.'"

A smile appeared on Buster's face. He looked around the table. Each of us returned the approving expression. He reached for his glass. "A toast to The Guys, the greatest group ever to walk the halls of Grand Falls High."

Glasses clinked and gulps ensued. Never one whose enthusiasm for beer was more than halfhearted, I had to admit the brew pleased my palette. I glanced out the window. The torrent persisted. Aspirations for a tour of the links had evaporated. No matter. Without ever having negotiated the path to the first tee, there in the clubhouse, we were savoring our quintessential day at Nick Stoner's. Good-natured trash talk may have been a delightful diversion, but heartfelt exchanges of mutual appreciation and friendship, far better. Moving my gaze over each of my pals, I quaffed my alcoholic beverage. The normally garrulous group sat silent, their lack of words, the hush, eloquent.

Youthful clubs come and go. Egos and spite turn relationships toxic. Life launches people in divergent directions. Contacts fade as former friends drift apart amidst meandering sands of time. Not so, with us. Our bonds, enduring, had stood the years. Smart money indicated that a quarter-century hence, The Guys, a close-knit nucleus of loyal friends, would remain tight.

From the distant reaches of my brain, my grandfather's words surged to the forefront. Cherish special moments. Inscribe their details into your memory. Archive them, that they may be summoned and relished in countless tomorrows' blissful nostalgia. And most of all, be grateful. I looked around the table again. Elsewhere plutocrats resided in magnificent mansions and castles; donned diamonds and gold; jetted around the planet; and sojourned in lavish yachts. They dined on white truffles and caviar and partook of the most venerable champagne. However wealthy they may have been, the bounty shared at our table transcended such material opulence. Friendship, camaraderie, and well-being could not be measured in dollars. The same could be said for memories and gratitude. Wisdom, what my grandfather had endeavored to convey, graced that category as well. I sipped more brew, imbibing my grandfather's wisdom. The more I aged, the wiser he grew. I eyed my buddies, indelibly stamping a wealth of wonderful sentiments into my memory bank. Mutual respect reigned...Gratitude gushed...And despite a raging storm on the links, calm and contentment prevailed.